The
MAN
Who Could Be
King

The
MAN
Who Could Be
King

—

A Novel

JOHN RIPIN MILLER

Little
a

Published by Little A, New York

www.apub.com

Amazon, the Amazon logo, and Little A are trademarks of Amazon.com, Inc., or its affiliates.

ISBN-13: 9781477820209 (hardcover)
ISBN-10: 1477820205 (hardcover)
ISBN-13: 9781477820193 (paperback)
ISBN-10: 1477820191 (paperback)

Cover design by Isaac Tobin

Printed in the United States of America

First edition

Contents

FOREWORD

In his wonderfully evocative *The Man Who Could Be King*, John Ripin Miller succeeds in telling two important stories simultaneously. An attempt near the close of the Revolutionary War by officers in the Continental Army to organize a military coup to seize power from the elected Congress is the story in the foreground. In the incident—known to history as the Newburgh Conspiracy because it occurred at the army's cantonment at that place in New York—General George Washington stymied the officers disgruntled over delinquent pay and a perceived lack of appreciation through a stunning theatrical display that highlighted his immense personal sacrifices for the cause of the nation's independence under a free government. The second story that Miller tells with admirable clarity and economy is how Washington persevered and prevailed over the course of seven years as commander in chief. Through vivid flashbacks, readers learn the essentials of Washington's triumphs at Boston, Trenton, Princeton, and Yorktown, and his composure during the struggles that characterized a series of defeats around New York City in 1776.

The people in Miller's work pop from the pages as three-dimensional figures. Some—like Alexander Hamilton, Thomas Jefferson, Marquis de Lafayette, Friedrich Wilhelm von Steuben, and Benedict Arnold—are famous or notorious in the annals of the war and United States history. Others—like John Armstrong Jr., John Laurens, Joseph Reed, Alexander

McDougall, Horatio Gates, and Benjamin Lincoln—exist on the periphery of memory but deserve to be better known. Miller makes discovering all these people a painless exercise.

Some readers may balk at Miller's deployment of a fictional military aide named Josiah as the narrator. No reason exists for worry or concern. Josiah is a faithful composite of the more than twenty-five men who served Washington as aides-de-camp or secretaries over the years of the Revolutionary War. Moreover, being an imaginary character, Josiah can speak unburdened by the contentions of actual historical relationships or the arguments among historians. In short, his voice is ideal for communicating impressions of General Washington's appearance, demeanor, and actions as well as probing the murkier world of his thoughts. Josiah casts a neutral eye on the world that is consistently plausible. While a bias emerges that is decidedly favorable toward Washington, it is a perspective that the great man earns through meritorious conduct.

Miller grounds his portrayals and words in authentic historical documents. He has researched extensively and impressively. These efforts make his story accurate as well as accessible. John Ripin Miller's *The Man Who Could Be King* is both good history and a good read for all interested in George Washington, the Revolutionary War, and how military subordination to civilian authority became an enduring principle in the United States.

William M. Ferraro
Research Associate Professor and Acting Editor-in-Chief (Managing Editor)
Washington Papers (Papers of George Washington)
University of Virginia

PROLOGUE

Notes for My Great-Grandchildren

Josiah Penn Stockbridge, 1843, Springfield, Illinois (edited and revised)

The dawn is overcast, the morning low'rs,
And heavily in clouds brings on the day,
The great, th' important day, big with the fate
Of Cato and of Rome.

—Portius, *Cato*, Act I, Scene 1

I often cannot recall recent events. And yet I do recall that week almost sixty years ago, and I remember it more vividly than any time in the eight years I served the General. You may wonder at my ability to write today in the early 1840s about events so long ago, but as I write now, I realize that outside of the important times recorded on the flyleaf of our family Bible, there is no period I remember better.

Of course I can't be sure of all the details of the nascent mutiny that almost changed our country forever. While I kept copies of much of the General's correspondence and many of my notes, perhaps I've got some of the names or the exact sequence of events wrong. I hope my great-grandchildren will excuse me for that, just as I also hope they will excuse me for recalling so many of my random thoughts that week. But February 22, the General's birthday, is a month from now; their school has already started its annual study of the General's life, and they want to come over and ask questions about him. It seems their schoolteacher believes the General had plenty of flaws. He did, but I probably know them better than anyone else, and I believe I can explain them better than any schoolteacher who wasn't there.

That brings me back to Monday, March 10, 1783, in Newburgh, New York, and the extraordinary events that followed over the next several days. I just don't understand why everyone writes about what was right and wrong about his generalship and presidency, and you never hear about that week. Maybe it's partly because of the way history is taught in our schools now. My great-grandchildren tell me the War for Independence ended with the surrender at Yorktown in 1781. No one teaches them that the Revolutionary War went on for almost two more years after Yorktown, albeit with very limited fighting, until a peace treaty was signed. We rarely talk about the conflicts during those two years and the consequences for our country, but the greatest conflict then, I believe, was within the heart and mind of our commanding general.

You are probably wondering how I happened to be there. I still puzzle about how I became chief aide to the General. We had met back in 1775 when the Second Continental Congress was meeting in Philadelphia. Joseph Reed, who the General retained after his appointment as commanding general, had introduced us. My qualifications, I thought, were slim. No military experience but a year at Princeton (despite my parents' misgivings), some experience apprenticed to an uncle in the family's Philadelphia merchant business, and a knowledge of French. He asked whether I liked to write and did I write well. I didn't realize at the time, but the General wanted an aide who was a good writer and could correct his own writing—he was very diffident about having had only one year of formal schooling. He also wanted an aide who could communicate with the French, already looking on them as potential allies.

The General didn't ask about my family, but he must have known that, unlike me, many of them were practicing Quakers who opposed the war for religious reasons, although I must admit their strong commercial links to Britain may have played a role. Back then almost every well-off family in Philadelphia had divided loyalties. Animosity increased during the war, leading to tarring, feathering, and worse atrocities that Americans now don't like to talk about, but back when the war started, at least in Philadelphia, nobody cared much if you had relatives on the side of the king. When we arrived later in Boston, the General retained Edmund Randolph as an aide. His father was a well-known loyalist, but this did not bother the General.

When the General offered me the position, I quickly said yes. Perhaps too quickly. I thought only of the glory and romance that would accompany my position and impress the women I was wooing, especially Prescilla, the woman I would later marry. I thought little, at least until that evening, of my fear of physical danger and the battlefield. I wish I could say it was noble Quaker conscientious objection to war that gave me second thoughts, but I don't think this fear had much to do with my religious upbringing; the more I analyzed my emotions, the more I realized I was just plain scared of being maimed or killed. All throughout the war, I would try to control and hide such fear. But I could never hide it from myself.

Back in 1775 most Americans thought there wouldn't be much of a war, or if there was, it would be over in less than a year. We believed the British would quickly grant us self-government, if not complete independence, and if they didn't, we would give them a prompt drubbing. When I said yes to the General, I not only assumed the war would be short but that all the challenges of recruiting and supplying an army from thirteen colonies would be easily surmounted. Washington would command, those commands would be obeyed, and thence everything would unfold in an orderly manner. I don't say that the General himself believed this—he didn't—but most of us did.

As it turned out, I was the only aide who spent the whole war with him. There were thirty-two in all but never more than five or six at one time. We were, as the General referred to us, his "official family." Patriotism, sense of duty, and the power of the General's personality were all motivating reasons for the aides' service. Still, there was much turnover in the group. Many of them, such as Alexander Hamilton and John Laurens, wanted military commands and action, a prospect that alarmed rather than enticed me. Some, such as Tench Tilghman, yearned to get back to their families. Others wanted to enter politics. James McHenry left to serve in the Maryland legislature. Colonel Robert Harrison left to serve as Maryland's chief justice. Hamilton served as an artillery and infantry commander and later as a member of Congress from New York—all that came before his service as our first secretary of the treasury and before his hotheadedness led him into that lamentable and fatal duel with Aaron Burr. One aide, George Baylor, just couldn't write well enough and was moved quickly to head a regiment. There was even an artist, one of the Trumbull brothers from Connecticut, who went to study painting in London with the American painter Benjamin West, but not before he produced some fine draw-ings of the British fortifications at Boston. And then there was Joseph Reed, who, after the defeats in New York, showed the intrigues that can plague a general's staff by going from the General's fawning admirer to his scheming detractor—but more about him later.

Most of his aides revered the General, but, as you will soon hear, I was far more skeptical. The reverence for the General should not be a surprise given the events that seemed to take place almost every day. For example, I remember when we arrived in Cambridge at the begin-ning of the war in 1775 and the General took command of the troops. The Virginia riflemen and the Massachusetts Marblehead Regiment, which included free blacks, got in a brawl over goodness knows what.

The General and his slave, Will Lee—the General always called him "my fellow"—were riding nearby. Someone else might have ignored the melee or called in the regimental commanding officers for a dressing-down later. Not the General. I saw the General and Will ride right into the middle of the brawl where the General dismounted, grabbed the two ringleaders, and lifted them in the air while cussing them out. The two men he grabbed were mean-looking six-footers and the General just lifted them up like they were dolls. Hundreds of surrounding men looked on for a moment in silence and then just fled. When I asked him back at headquarters what would have happened if he had failed, the General looked as if the thought had never occurred to him and just grunted, "Josiah, these state militia have to start fighting the British instead of each other."

Of course, the war aged the General. I'm not sure he could have lifted those men up in 1783, but back in 1775 he was six foot three, a lean 209 pounds, and could lift and throw iron bars or a ball farther than anyone I've ever seen. It's amazing to me that these days we just see portraits of the General in his last years with white hair and a paunch and hear the stories about his false teeth. What a specimen the General was when I met him. A slightly pockmarked face did not detract from but added to his rugged good looks. When Benjamin Rush said, "There is not a king in Europe that would not look like a *valet de chambre* by his side," this was no exaggeration.

The story of breaking up the brawl was like many stories that just grew and grew with retelling—later I heard the General had sent six men sprawling—until even I wasn't sure what I had really observed.

That I was a skeptic among a largely worshipful, emotional group of aides in retrospect should not be surprising. My fear of war may not have had anything to do with my Quaker upbringing, but my skepticism with respect to offices and titles had everything to do with my Quaker ancestors, who stood for the right to never doff their hats to anyone, including generals. So there I was, a twenty-year-old youth, brought up in the "plain," practical, and peace-loving world of the Society of Friends, suddenly adorned with the undeniably fancy and warlike title of lieutenant colonel. I had no military experience, no family farm to get back to, and my stake in my family business gave me the wherewithal to serve for thirty-three-dollars-a-month pay. The General finally prevailed on Congress to raise our pay to forty and then to sixty-six dollars a month, but whatever amount Congress specified was really meaningless, since many months no pay arrived at all.

At first Congress's broken pay promises irritated me, but when I thought how the General had volunteered to serve without any pay, it hardly seemed like I should complain. Indeed, many of my fellow officers had received far less pay than I had. It was just expected that officers should finance their service, including food and clothing.

Things were even worse for the troops. Yes, most had received bounties of twenty dollars or more to enlist and steady if depreciated pay, albeit a meager six and two-thirds dollars per month. But there were months when the promised leather jacket or pair of overalls or shoes did not arrive, and days when meals consisted of a slab of bread and a cup of beef broth mixed with burnt leaves.

Armies are always rife with rumors, all the more so when troops wait with no combat looming, as was the case at Newburgh in the winter of 1782 to 1783. It is especially true after seven years of broken congressional promises on pay, clothing, and food. And still more true after the broken promises and lack of action on petitions resulted in numerous small mutinies that the public knows nothing of, mutinies that had been suppressed but which we on the General's staff were all too well aware of. With the return from Philadelphia of General Alexander McDougall reporting no action by Congress on our petition, that week in Newburgh was as tense in its own way as any combat-filled week on the Delaware or at Yorktown, or week of suffering at Valley Forge or Morristown. I did not realize it at the beginning of the week, but the patriotic resolve of our troops, our officers, and our commanding General were about to be tested in ways that had never happened in the whole war.

Many times I have been asked what an aide-de-camp does. The French phrase means "camp assistant," and we were there, at all times, to help the General in whatever he needed. Our job was to take all the lesser matters off the General's hands that we could, so as to allow him to focus on the military decisions that needed all his attention.

In Newburgh we aides came to work every morning at Hasbrouck House, a farmhouse on a sloping hill above the Hudson River where the General and Lady Washington had lived, worked, and entertained since most of the army had moved north from Yorktown in the spring of 1782. The house had been acquired from a widow of a militia officer. It was chosen for its location north of West Point and close to the army depot at New Windsor. There were seven dark rooms plus a hallway used for sleeping and a separate kitchen linked to the house. The aides' office adjoined the General's study and office. The light came from one large window, candles that we burned throughout almost every day, and a huge fireplace through whose cavernous chimney you could see the sky. When it snowed, the flakes would melt on the fire. Our office, one of the three largest rooms, sometimes served as a waiting room for those wanting to see the General. Along with the two offices, there was also a bedroom for the Washingtons, an aides' bedroom, a room for clothing, a dining room, and a parlor room that was used by overnight visitors and also by Lady Washington.

We wrote and reviewed the General's letters, both public and private. The General insisted on answering every letter he received and he wanted to be sure when he sent out a letter that it conveyed his thoughts exactly and the spelling was correct. (The General, a notoriously bad speller, was particularly concerned about spelling.) Every morning after breakfast the General would gather several of us for a meeting and either dictate letters or, after giving his thoughts, tell us to write drafts.

Most of the letters were either pleas to Congress and the governors for money, clothing, and food, or responses to the letters that thanked, complimented, or extolled the General, often implicitly or explicitly suggesting in the most unseemly manner—at least in my opinion—that he should become king or a military dictator. Some present writers, out of republican sympathies, or because they want to enhance the General's reputation, dismiss such suggestions as beyond the General's consideration. As one who watched the General for almost eight years, I believe it was impossible for the General to not consider such suggestions, as you will soon find out.

The General, after making his inspection rounds, would gather us together and review what we had written. We knew the General's style, but he was a stickler, and no letter or order went out without his approval, sometimes not until late afternoon.

Then we had to write copies. Everything the General did was with an eye on history. He was very conscious of how he would look to future Americans, perhaps too conscious. We all felt it, even though he never said so. Why, that very week in the midst of the crises I shall soon describe, Colonel Richard Varick was coming across the Hudson from his office in Poughkeepsie and filing all the copies of the General's orders and letters so later Americans could read them. With our nation deciding between peace and continued war, I thought the General should spend less time on filing records and more on frustrating the plots against our country that week that I will soon tell you about. I have come to believe, however, that most of us, from the Founding Fathers to me, a lowly aide, were focused in those perilous times on what our descendants might think of us. I admit I rather enjoy the way my grandchildren and great-grandchildren look up to me and eagerly listen to my stories of the Revolution. Still, I never knew anyone like the General, who carefully calculated every daily action by how it would look decades later. Not that I suppose such action is sinful. It just struck me back then as odd and made me uncomfortable.

All the aides wrote letters concerning the General's orders and official correspondence. As the war proceeded, however, the General turned to me to write and edit his personal letters. These included his letters to Lady Washington when she was not with us as well as his letters to his plantation manager and his cousin Lund, and the numerous responses to charitable and personal loan requests. Whether it was caring for the children of his deceased brother, Samuel, giving bequests to the school for orphans in Alexandria, or loaning money to his neighbors (to the surprise of this son of a city merchant, it was apparently bad form for a Virginia planter to turn down a neighbor's request for a loan or to press too hard for repayment), the General increasingly sought my help in answering requests.

Another of our tasks was to be messengers and intermediaries. We carried his orders to the various generals, colonels, majors, and captains at all times of the day and night and often in the heat of battle. It gave us the feeling of importance, as if we were giving the orders ourselves. It was a duty about which I had mixed feelings. I never could overcome my fear of bullets. Fortunately, I rarely found myself in direct combat and never had to fire a weapon at the enemy. I always feared that the General suspected my timidity, but if he did so, he never let on.

The General also used us as hosts and entertainers. When the congressmen would visit—often they did so when we were in camp, although rarely in the danger of battle when the General was doing more important things—we hosted them and tried to answer their interminable questions until the General could return and see them.

My father chuckled when I told him one of my duties was to keep the General's expense accounts. My uncle considered me careless with money, and my family would not have trusted me back then with handling any accounts, let alone those of such importance. To say the General was careful about financial matters would be an understatement. The General told me he had been shocked and embarrassed when a friend and ally in the Virginia House of Burgesses, Speaker Robinson, had been found to have used public currency to guarantee personal loans. The General had never forgotten the shame attached to this conduct, and he made clear to us what he expected with our own handling of public monies.

I believe I told you the General didn't take a salary, but the arrangement with the Congress was that he would be reimbursed for expenses. The General footed many of the day-to-day bills, but when he entertained, which was often (Lady Washington was invariably present, and they would joke about how they rarely dined alone), he kept meticulous accounts. This was particularly true of the lunches he held for the congressmen, French officers, and numerous foreign visitors.

Another major accounting category was intelligence. The General never stinted when it came to paying spies or even friendly citizens who incurred risks to pass on information about British comings and goings.

I never saw a man so careful about his spending. I read after the war that the Congress had reviewed the bills the General had submitted, and they'd found an error: he had undercharged the Congress one dollar! Naturally I took some pride in that.

The General seemed quite content with being compensated for his expenses while taking no salary for his services. Early on, the General said to me, "Josiah, the approbation of my country is sufficient recompense for my services." That sounded quite noble to me until I realized what an insatiable desire the General had for approbation, and the fame and applause that went with it. I began to suspect that such a desire could become a dangerous drive. This made me apprehensive as the week at Newburgh wore on.

I've told you the official duties I had as an aide-de-camp. As the war went on, I sometimes thought my major, if unofficial, duty was just listening to the General. After the afternoon dinner with Lady Washington, various officers, and foreign and domestic visitors selected by Lady Washington—generally consisting of some fish, mashed potatoes, and soft vegetables since the General had started to have some trouble with his teeth—and after the meeting with aides to go over what we had written or rewritten during the day, the General would retire to his study with me for some Madeira and Brazil nuts. I suppose some of the aides resented this, but I was, after all, the senior aide in service for most of the war. The General had read widely and always had plenty of books on his desk, but one that was never absent was the *Rules of Civility* drafted by some French priest. I suppose you could call it a guide to conduct, but it contained the simplest rules you could imagine.

There were rules for speech, such as Rule 88: "Be not tedious in discourse; make not many digressions; nor repeat often the same manner of discourse."

There were rules for table manners, such as Rule 97: "Put not another bit into your mouth 'till the former be swallowed. Let not your morsels be too big for the jowls."

There were rules for personal conduct, such as Rule 82: "Undertake not what you cannot perform, but be careful to keep your promise."

And rules for relating to others, such as Rule 44: "When a man does all he can, though it succeed not well, blame not him that did it."

My favorite rule was Rule 4 (because, except when in the General's presence, I violated it all the time): "In the presence of others, sing not to yourself with a humming noise; nor drum with your fingers or feet."

The rules—all 110—were so obvious and simplistic that I wondered why the General spent so much time with them. I concluded that the General had received little training in the social graces as a child and was very concerned about embarrassing himself. I found it useful to memorize those rules because, especially with the rules for conduct, it helped me gauge how the General was going to react.

Many of those afternoons, the General and I sat in silence. Sometimes he mused aloud. I could never be sure he cared what my opinions were, but he would often ask for them. Many times he would ask for the latest information or rumors. I'm not suggesting I got close to the General. With the exception of Lady Washington—and perhaps his cousin Lund; his brother John Augustine; and his manservant and slave, Will Lee—no one was close to the General in the sense of being a close friend. But these were easy, pleasant meetings . . . until that week of March 9, 1783, in Newburgh.

When we aides weren't working, we spent plenty of time gossiping about the General and Lady Washington, generally about their wealth or sexual conduct. Most of us initially believed the General's wealth largely came from his marriage to Lady Washington. The General said nothing to discourage this assumption, but as I discovered in looking over his private correspondence, the General had substantial wealth before his marriage either via inheritance from his half brother, Lawrence, or from self-taught surveying, and this wealth was probably more assured than Lady Washington's when they married.

Most of the latter's wealth was tied up for decades in litigation, because her first husband, Daniel Parke Custis, had a grandfather, also named Daniel, who was a very wealthy man in the West Indies and had sowed illegitimate offspring far and wide. These children claimed to be the rightful heirs to his grandfather's vast Virginia and West Indian properties. It was apparently a close call as to whether Lady Washington would inherit much, if anything, of the lands she and Daniel Parke Custis had occupied. It took twenty years of litigation involving the top lawyers in Virginia and the Privy Council in London to give Lady Washington title to the properties, long after Daniel Parke Custis's death and Lady Washington's marriage to the General.

As for the gossip about sex, we aides were disappointed about the lack of grist for juicy speculation. There were plenty of rumors about the General being in love with a New York heiress and also a wealthy Virginia neighbor, but these stories all preceded his marriage to Lady Washington.

Most of the gossip about sex pertained to Lady Washington and the family of her first husband, Daniel Custis. It was rumored that her first husband's father, John Custis, had the same sexual proclivities as her grandfather-in-law and had produced a son, Mulatto Jack, to whom John, at least briefly, threatened to bequeath the family estate. Under Virginia's racial inheritance laws, this would have deprived Lady Washington and her first husband of their inheritance.

Another rumor was that Lady Washington's father, John Dandridge, had sired a Negro-Indian girl who was Martha's half sister.

Just a few years ago I heard a rumor that Lady Washington's grandson Wash had several affairs and children with slaves.

As for the General, we all knew that many Southern planters had hypocritical attitudes on slavery. It has been charged by newspapers hostile to Thomas Jefferson (I don't know if it is true or not) that our third president had relations and children with his slave Sally Hemings, which is surprising coming from a man who, I have read in his *Notes on the State of Virginia*, described Negroes as inferior and compared them to "oran-gutans." We never heard the General use such language, however, and he seemed so prim, proper, and concerned with his reputation that we doubted the General would engage in such sexual conduct. Maybe all the stories about interracial sex in Lady Washington's family explain why Lady Washington, while gracious to all and adored by the troops, seemed far more diffident than the General when it came to associating with free blacks and slaves.

We aides all agreed that theirs was a puzzling relationship. The British had tried to sow discord. Articles appeared in British-controlled New York newspapers claiming, on the basis of intercepted letters and eyewitness accounts, that the General often visited a mistress in New Jersey or had gone to this or that whorehouse. However, the British efforts were so clumsy—dates when the General was known by his troops to be elsewhere or in the company of Lady Washington—that they were more a source of amusement than of worry. We aides read the stories with much glee and thought them a great joke. The General told me he was used to false rumors; in the French and Indian War, it was widely believed he had been killed. I doubted, however, that Lady Washington was amused.

Sometimes we laughed over whether our proper leader even had relations with Lady Washington, let alone ran off hundreds of miles to visit a whorehouse. We concluded that their affection and love was so great they must have, although the lack of children—the children were all by Lady Washington's deceased first husband—caused some wonder. The General always wore a miniature picture of Lady Washington around his neck. He also made clear, in the many letters I reviewed, his desire that Martha stay with him as much as possible during the war, which she did. She was with the General for most of the war, enduring the cold winters and generally only returning to Mount Vernon during the summers to supervise the plantation. In late 1782 and early 1783, Lady Washington was with us every month, including that week in Newburgh. They appeared to dote on one another, and their private letters were full of affection, although I do not recall hearing any public expressions of that affection. I do know the General thought of Lady Washington often, particularly during her absences, and was very appreciative of her presence with us during the war. Often the General told me he would find more happiness in one month at home with Lady Washington than in all his service in the war.

I never did understand why Lady Washington burned all the correspondence between them after the General's death. There was nothing embarrassing in any of the letters I penned to her back at Mount Vernon, just expressions of affection, a yearning for her presence, and queries about the stepchildren and grandchildren. I think back to the letters we aides sent to our lady friends during the war, boasting of our positions with the General and setting up as many dalliances as possible during our leaves. (Of course, that was before my engagement to Prescilla.) Now, those are letters I wouldn't want published! I suppose Lady Washington burned their letters because, while the General and Lady Washington were public figures, they were very private people. I was told burning personal letters was a tradition in Lady Washington's family.

Keeping seventy-five hundred troops occupied at Newburgh and New Windsor and out of mischief, with most of the limited fighting taking place far to the south, was a challenge, and the General searched for projects to keep the men busy. This led to the Temple that will figure so prominently in the story I am about to tell you. Chaplain Israel Evans's proposal for a structure at nearby New Windsor for religious services and social gatherings quickly won the General's approval. It was a rough-hewn one-story log structure, but at 110 feet long and 30 feet wide, it was easily the most imposing edifice the army built during the entire war. It had a central hall and four side rooms for smaller meetings and office work. On the platform at the front of the hall, soldiers skilled in fine woodworking built a white columned balustrade with a dark railing. There, a chaplain could give a sermon, an officer could give a speech, or fiddlers could play a tune.

I'm often asked if we did anything for recreation in those encampments when there was little prospect of fighting. The troops threw the ball around, played cards, and drank their rations of rum. The General himself loved the theater and encouraged officers and troops to witness the shows he brought to Newburgh and New Windsor. Once, the Puritans in Congress passed a resolution that there should be no frivolous entertainment for troops such as plays. It is the only time I can remember the General saying a swear word directed at Congress. "Josiah," he said, "no damn congressman is going to deny me the pleasure of going to the theater."

And the General was true to his word. He must have seen Addison's *Cato*, his favorite play, ten times during the war, either in the camps or nearby cities. It was one of the few congressional orders that the General flouted. I do not believe a day went by when the General did not quote *Cato* at least once to me. On mornings of looming battles, the General would turn to me and, acting as if he had never quoted those opening lines before, say: "Josiah, the dawn is overcast, the morning low'rs, / And heavily in clouds brings on the day, / The great, th' important day, big with the fate / Of Cato and of Rome."

The General did not utter those words that week at Newburgh. No armed battle with the British loomed. And yet those words from *Cato* rang through my mind as we approached what I increasingly sensed was the most important conflict, if not armed battle, of the war.

Anyway, you now know why I was there in Newburgh and what we aides did in what I believe is the most eventful but least known week in our young country's history.

Chapter One

DAY ONE—MONDAY

The First Anonymous Letter

Meanwhile I'll hasten to my Roman soldiers,
Inflame the mutiny, and underhand
Blow up their discontents, till they breakfast
Unlook'd for, and discharge themselves on Cato.

—Sempronius, *Cato*, Act I, Scene 3

General Henry Knox delivered the letter. I remember the day—Monday, March 10, 1783—and Knox hauling his three hundred pounds across our threshold, approaching me with that pigeon-toed gait he had and thrusting his hand, minus his two lost fingers, toward me with several copies of the letter before our afternoon aides' meeting. I admired Knox because he always struck me as the epitome of the Continental soldier; he had been a New England bookseller, a self-taught student in the classics and military engineering, who became an artillery officer and worked himself up to be one of the General's most trusted and able commanders. Knox told me copies were circulating all over the camps. He asked me to show them to the General, who was out reviewing the troops.

When I read the letter, I knew why no one had dared to deliver it to the General on his daily rounds. It was brief, to the point, and anonymous.

Its full text read:

> A meeting of the Gen'l & Field Officers is requested, at the public building, on Tuesday next at 11 o'clock—
>
> A Commiss'd officer from each company is expected, and a delegate from the Medical Staff—
>
> The Object of this Convention, is to consider the Late Letter from our Representatives in Philadelphia; and what measures (if any) should be adopted, to obtain that redress of Grievances, which they seem to have solicited in vain.

A shock ran through me. "Tuesday next" was tomorrow. "The public building" was our recently completed Temple. The letter might sound innocuous sixty years later, but it wasn't to those who read it then. No one but the General circulated a letter calling for an officers' meeting, and here was a letter apparently calling an unauthorized meeting to redress the army's grievances. There had been grievances in the army throughout the war, and some had even led to mutinies—more than you might think. But those incidents had generally involved troops rather than officers. The first mutiny had come right during the siege of Boston in 1775. Thirty-two Pennsylvania Scotch-Irish mountain men had mutinied after agents of the Pennsylvania governor and legislature broke promises that the men would not do guard duty and would get certain clothing and pay.

I was stunned at this event so early in the war. Not so the General. He had apparently encountered similar episodes in the French and Indian War. After mounting overwhelming force to stop the mutiny from spreading, the General convened court-martials, which fined many of the mutineers twenty shillings from their next month's pay for the hospital fund and imprisoned the ringleader, Jonathan Leaman, for what I thought was an extremely lenient six-day sentence. The General then had me draft letters to the Pennsylvania authorities about failed promises leaving "the greater part of the army in a state not far from mutiny."

By 1783 the clothing and food situation had improved somewhat, due to French money, but the pay was delinquent as always. This was the eighth year of a war we had expected to end in a year, and over a year after the British surrender at Yorktown. And still the war and negotiations to end it dragged on. Rumors always plague an army, but given the circumstances, it was no wonder that rumors of mutiny and marching on Philadelphia to take over the government were rife at Newburgh.

Most of the troop mutinies that followed the early one in Boston were small, easily dispersed affairs. These uprisings were not because of lack of loyalty by our men to our cause. Our troops were honest farmers, tradesman, and fishermen, and they expected that promises made would be kept. When they weren't, there was trouble, and the Congress and the governors left the General to deal with the mess. Of course, the General could not allow the troops to just run off, no matter what the justification. But this letter delivered by General Knox that Monday was not about some Pennsylvania mountain men or even the 1781 mutiny of thousands, about which I will tell you later. This was a letter to hundreds of officers in the main army encampment. For months, rumors of a mutiny and a march on Philadelphia to seize control of the government had been circulating through the camps at Newburgh and New Windsor, New York, where our army had come after the victory at Yorktown. The soldiers had not been paid for months, and many officers had never been paid since the beginning of the war. Congress didn't want to levy taxes to support the war, and when it finally had to, the states didn't want to collect them. And then, when the states did collect taxes, they spent the money on their own needs.

It wasn't just the lack of pay. As General Nathanael Greene once told me, "Politicians think we can live on air as in heaven without eating or drinking." He could have added that the politicians didn't think we needed clothing either. Officers from friendly European nations were shocked to see troops often half naked or without shoes. The delegation of officers the General had sent to seek back pay and future pensions from Congress in Philadelphia had reported nothing but soothing words, all of which the anonymous letter writer and those who read the letter well knew.

I do believe that many Americans thought the war had been won with Cornwallis's surrender at Yorktown. But the General knew better. We were in Newburgh and New Windsor on the Hudson River because the British still held Savannah, Charleston, and, most importantly, New York City. General Guy Carleton commanded fourteen thousand British troops in New York City—far more than our forces of seventy-five hundred—and the General worried that Carleton would move upriver and try to split New England from the rest of the colonies. So there we were, a worn-out army with a headquarters, guardhouse, powder magazine, quarters for tailors, and other supporting buildings in Newburgh, along with a temple and hundreds of buildings for the troops in New Windsor. Fighting was at a lull, and peace negotiations had been going on in Paris for over a year, but these negotiations had produced no final agreement. King George III was reported to be incensed by Cornwallis's surrender and was threatening to send even more troops across the ocean, although the faction in Parliament led by Fox and Burke, which was against the war, seemed to be growing stronger. Benjamin Franklin had recently written the General and others that negotiations were taking a positive turn and the next month or two might bring peace and independence, but the General had heard this story before. Still, the General could have remained at Mount Vernon after Yorktown to not only enjoy home life but be closer to our other armies in the South. There were so many rumors of mutiny or a coup that I suspected the General's presence in Newburgh was not entirely motivated by military tactics.

And now came this anonymous letter. The author was obviously confident that the officers would attend the meeting. But then what? March on Philadelphia and take over the Congress? Or maybe the author had some other plan in mind. And who was the anonymous author? I remember thinking of so many possible answers to that question and not finding any convincing.

Was it General Horatio Gates or one of his aides? Gates was second-in-command at Newburgh. All of us on the General's staff knew he had resented the General's appointment and had yearned for the top command since the start of the war. Whenever I looked into Gates's face with its sagging eyes and Roman nose, I thought of a bloodhound, and he was indeed tenacious; nothing in his life had come without striving and capitalizing on his connections. No officer spent more time lobbying Congress to advance his career. A few years older than the General, Gates had served in the British army years ago in Germany and then had met Washington when they were both young officers fighting in the Braddock expedition during the French and Indian War. Unlike other officers, Gates and Washington, while outwardly cordial, apparently had never bonded.

Gates's desire for advancement and his resentment of the General had led to his involvement in the 1777 plot with the French-Irish adventurer Conway. The aim was to have the Congress remove the General and replace him with Gates. Referring to the Scriptures, we on the General's staff used to describe Gates as Old Leaven, like sourdough starter that had gone bad and had to be thrown out. As I reflected on the anonymous letter, it seemed quite plausible that a man who had plotted just a few years ago to usurp the General's role now saw a chance to seize control of the army and lead the mutiny.

Then again, there were other possible authors. Might it have been written by the British in the city to spread disunity? Or perhaps by some who wanted a meeting to threaten Congress into tax measures that favored creditors as well as the army? I knew there was a faction in Congress that was bitter about the weakness of the confederation and eager to strengthen the national government, as was Superintendent of Finance Robert Morris.

Still another possibility gnawed at me. Could the General himself have inspired the letter? I knew many were urging the General to take power. It had all started with a letter from the first chaplain of the First Continental Congress, Jacob Duché, in 1777 telling the General that the people no longer supported Congress, that the cause was hopeless with congressional leadership, and that if a peace could not be negotiated with the British, there should be a coup d'état with the General taking over the government.

The General had immediately dictated a response to the reverend disavowing this suggestion and had then made sure that copies of both letters were sent to Congress. I was not certain, however, if the General was assuring Congress of his loyalty or showing Congress that it must act more vigorously to help the army.

There were even calls from within Congress for the General to head up a military dictatorship, such as the call in 1781 from the Rhode Islander Ezekiel Cornell.

And then there was the statement of Congressman William Hooper of North Carolina, calling the General "the greatest man on earth" and leaving the conclusion to the imagination of the reader. Letters expressing such sentiments reached the General with rising frequency as the war proceeded, and I don't know how many people whispered such sentiments in the General's ear. Some of these sentiments weren't just whispered. Why, just a year and a half ago, I heard General Cornwallis at a dinner a day after his surrender at Yorktown say, "Well, General, it looks like the colonials will be exchanging one George for another." I didn't hear the General say anything in response; he had never indicated to me he approved such sentiments. And yet . . .

With these thoughts running through my mind, it was hard to concentrate on doing routine tasks while awaiting the General's return. I wrote an order asking for uniform haircuts (cut short or tied in a neat bow), a letter both thanking Robert Livingston for passing on information on peace negotiations and conveying Lady Washington's best wishes to Mrs. Livingston, a letter thanking General James Varnum for his oration extolling the General (there were always letters of this kind), and a letter thanking a society in Holland for sending a barrel of herring along with its best wishes to the General. It was all very usual correspondence, much of it responding to adulatory letters. Upon reflection, the letter to General Varnum didn't seem so routine when I recalled that he was another who not a year earlier had advocated monarchy with the General as king.

The General, as was his custom, returned in the early afternoon to prepare for dinner and accosted me with his usual question: "Josiah— dispatches?" I handed him the letter. There was no visible reaction. It was as if he had been expecting it. Of course, I couldn't read much into that. The General prided himself on controlling his emotions. The more momentous an issue, the less emotion the General showed. Oh, you've read about his tempestuous outbursts, and there were some, but I always believed most of them were calculated.

Motioning me to follow, the General marched into his study and poured two glasses of Madeira. That was unusual. Generally, the Madeira came out in the late afternoon after the three p.m. dinner and the meeting with aides to review the day's correspondence. I knew then how seriously the General had taken the letter.

"Well, Josiah, what do you think of this?"

I gave the General all the explanations that had run through my mind earlier that afternoon, except, of course, the one about the General inspiring the letter himself. Could the letter writer be someone in Philadelphia—perhaps a congressman or inspired by a congressman—frustrated by Congress's weakness and trying to force its hand? Or someone in New York—a British sower of discord—trying to split our army apart in a last desperate move to win the war? Or someone here in Newburgh seeking to overthrow the General—perhaps General Gates, who had earlier conspired to remove the General? I thought I detected the muscles in his mouth and chin tensing.

After a moment of silence, the General dismissed all my explanations except one. "This was written by one of General Carleton's"—the British general's—"aides. The British are getting more desperate. If they can break up our army, they can still win the war."

I didn't know how he could be so sure. Maybe the General did not want to suspect a fellow general or friends of the army in Congress. Perhaps he did not want to admit to me that he might have had a hand in the letter. But then, the General did not trust the British at all. Like many Americans, his views of the British were complex and constantly evolving. All his aides knew that, after being commissioned as a colonel in the Virginia forces in appreciation of his services during the French and Indian War, he had been turned down for a British army captain's commission. We knew how proud the General was and how much that must have hurt. The General once told me that being turned down for a commission wasn't as irritating as having to obey the orders of British junior officers he outranked who turned up, received far more pay, and knew nothing.

The General observed, "They just didn't believe we colonials were their equals. They treated us like conquered people, not British citizens." But the General held himself to a different standard, certainly treating the British with respect. Why, on the day back in the early 1770s when he convened a meeting in Williamsburg to ban British imports from Virginia, I heard he went riding with Earl Dunmore, the royal governor! And the General never took out his feelings on his British neighbors back in Virginia. He could separate causes from people. I reviewed letters he sent to the Fairfax family, neighbors who had fled back to England before the war. The letters were all full of fond reminiscences and hopes that they would return after the war. I always wondered whether the Fairfaxes received any of those letters. If they did, it was probably after the British had intercepted, read, and then resealed them.

Lots of Americans changed their views leading up to the war (including some of my Quaker friends), but I believe, after reading some of his old correspondence, that the General was one of the first to advocate separation. I came across a letter to George Mason in 1769 where the General wrote that, as a last resort, we should be prepared to take up arms in defense of our freedom. Oh, the stamp and other taxes without our consent bothered him, but what really incensed him was how the British forced all trade from the colonies to go through England. He couldn't sell tobacco, wheat, or anything else he grew, except to British agents called "factors," and he groaned about all the transportation and insurance costs he had to bear. The factors would send him back goods "of low quality and high price." The clothing, observed the General, "was always tight because these English tailors couldn't believe American colonials were so tall." Then the factors would resell the General's crops to other countries at huge profits, which of course they kept for themselves.

The General wasn't one for rhetorical flourishes, but I remember him saying with regard to the tea tax, "Josiah, Parliament hath no more right to put their hands into my pocket without my consent than I have to put my hands into yours without your consent." Not that the General approved of property destruction like the Boston Tea Party, but he more strongly disapproved of British countermeasures to close the port of Boston.

The General, I have heard, was one of the Virginia leaders in gaining the colony's adoption of a measure to ban imports of British goods and slaves. When Patrick Henry, Edmund Pendleton, and George Mason gathered at Mount Vernon before the First Continental Congress, Lady Washington took Henry aside and reportedly told him, "Be strong. I know George will."

The General's resentment of the British did not lead him, as it did some other leaders, to support reneging on debts owed to British merchants, including Wakelin Welch, the factor to whom the General was indebted. "That, Josiah, would show a complete lack of integrity. Imagine what our descendants would think of us."

I heard that, even after the war, the General offered to pay off his own debts to his factor, except for the interest accrued during the war. I had to admit that, while the General had financial interests and could be quite avaricious, he was certainly willing to sacrifice them to uphold principle—or create a picture of upholding principle for our successors, not that I suppose there's much difference.

Sometimes, the General's resentment of the British, mixed with his pride, produced a response that I, but not many others, knew all too well. I remember when, early in the war, the British sent envoys to explore peace. They offered to repeal all taxes not approved by the colonies and to consider—just consider—American membership in the Parliament. They sent a letter addressed "George Washington, Esquire." I saw the General when he read that letter—the squint of his eyes and pursing of his lips disrupted the impassive façade. He must have felt like he did back in colonial times when the British officers would not give him his due. Finally, the General commented, "They never change," and refused to send representatives to a meeting until the British sent a letter addressed to him as "General." When they finally complied, the General sent a team to parley, but he remarked, "They're three years too late."

Of course, the General's view may have been tempered by more than a British failure to address him by his proper title. They had not offered amnesty to American leaders, and the General knew full well what had happened to the military commanders of the Irish armed rebels just decades earlier—they had been disemboweled, then executed. He hardly could have relished such a fate. Often he joked with us that "my neck does not feel like it was made for a halter."

If the General sometimes restrained his emotions vis-à-vis the British, it was the opposite with the French, at least outwardly. The General would make a great show of affection for the French, but I sensed that underneath was a reservoir of caution, perhaps dating to what he regarded as their duplicity during the French and Indian War. The General knew how vital our alliance was and would make a point of publicly celebrating the French king's birthday and the birth of the Dauphin, ostentatiously feting the French officers. The French commanders, sensing the General's emergence as a world hero, were full of admiration for the General and would let him know it. But neither French compliments nor the General's reciprocation with friendly gestures seemed to affect the General's judgment. Despite French pressure, after the early misadventure in Quebec, the General avoided all enticements to claim that former French colony for our allies.

"Josiah," he pointed out to me, "we must think ahead. We do not want the French controlling Quebec, the country to the north of us, when they already, through the Indians, control the backcountry to the west of us and may soon take territories from Spain to the south of us. No nation, Josiah, is to be trusted further than it is bound by its present interests."

I responded that the French were our friends.

"Yes." The General sighed. "They are for now . . ."

This seemed a rather callous way to look at an ally, but then, the General, despite outward appearances, could be quite calculating in his judgments. He confided to me his suspicion that the French ambassador had members of Congress on the French payroll to help dictate negotiations at the end of the war. Still, the General wanted to preserve for all, especially the British, the picture of close French-American cooperation. When French sailors and American workers got into a brawl in Boston, the General showed no surprise but tried to prevent the news from spreading.

Sometimes it was hard to tell whether the General was more driven by his dislike of the British or by his ambition—nay, really an obsession—to win the war no matter what the costs, although I suppose it didn't make much of a difference. The General's obsession with winning the war led him to more considered and pragmatic actions, which his colleagues, although they did not challenge him, thought highly peculiar or, to say the least, unconventional. Nothing showed this more than the General's desire to use everyone, and I mean everyone—Negroes, Indians, and even women—to increase his forces against the British. I suspect congressmen, some of his neighbors down in Virginia, and many other Americans would have been shocked if they had known, but the General masked his actions very carefully.

Take the issue of Negro troops. When we arrived in Cambridge in 1775 to take command of the American forces, the Congress sent the General an order not to use Negro troops. Even John Adams, who was an abolitionist, sent him a letter with similar advice. This was awkward because Massachusetts, New Hampshire, Connecticut, and Rhode Island all had regiments with free black troops in their ranks. Naturally, being from an antislavery Quaker family, and the General being a slaveholder, I was interested in what the General would do.

"For the moment, Josiah, nothing," he said.

Then the General went out and inspected the New England regiments. When he came back, I asked him if I should draft a reply to the congressional order. "Well, Josiah, these units seem to be doing well." There followed an awkward pause, and then the General added, "Besides, we need everybody we can get to win this war."

With the General I had learned to never leave any doubts as to his directions, and this did not seem like a clear answer to my question. "General," I said, "do we just ignore this order?"

"Oh no, Josiah, we will just not enforce the order until I convince the Congress to rescind or acquiesce in my ignoring it." And so he did, although it took him many months while the order sat at the bottom of the pile on my desk. During that time, the General continued to probe the limits of congressional patience on this subject when General Varnum of Rhode Island proposed creating two battalions, not of freed blacks but of slaves. The General did not ask for Congress's approval but passed on the proposal to the Rhode Island governor implying, without stating, his own approval. The proposal was adopted and implemented as the General must have known it would be. When slaveholders demanded the return of their slaves from these units, the General never disagreed with their request; he just ignored it.

I was always intrigued by the fact that the blacks who fought with the British were predominantly Southern slaves who fled their masters, while the Negroes who fought with us were those who had already won their freedom or fled their masters in the North.

Then there was Colonel John Laurens's mission to South Carolina. The governor of South Carolina kept complaining about the lack of troops to defend Charleston. A major reason was that only three hundred militia, the smallest number in any state, answered the call to arms. Colonel Laurens, a fellow aide at the time—and an abolitionist—explained to the General that there was a simple way to remedy the troop shortage: South Carolina, which was the only state with more slaves than whites, should simply arm and train some slaves and, as an incentive to fight the British, pay them a bounty and offer them freedom after the war. I thought the scheme sounded a bit far-fetched, but Laurens was from an old South Carolina family, and his father was the president of the Continental Congress. Laurens was twenty-five years old and very idealistic, and he really believed he could convince the South Carolina legislature to go along. I remember he urged the General's approval of his mission on abolitionist grounds, but he was also careful to strongly appeal to the General's desire to use all means to win the war. "If this succeeds in South Carolina, we can try it in Georgia," he told the General. "Besides, if we don't do it, the British will, and their troop advantage will just increase."

Well, that was enough for the General. While the General never explicitly approved the proposal, Laurens headed for South Carolina, which I know he would not have done without the General's approval. The General had Alexander Hamilton, our fellow aide at the time and a close friend of Laurens, write a letter to the Congress urging support for the mission. Most of the letter Hamilton drafted sounded like the General at his most pragmatic: describing the shortage of American troops in the South to defend Charleston and harass the British and predicting that the British would arm the Negroes if we didn't. But some of the reasons sounded more like Hamilton, a devout abolitionist: all human beings were capable of being good soldiers with good leadership and such a move may help those among us who were unfortunate and may open the door to broader emancipation.

Congress didn't exactly approve, but it didn't disapprove of Laurens's mission either, providing that arming black regiments might proceed if the state of South Carolina agreed. The General had me write a letter, which he sent to Laurens, offering encouragement: "I know of nothing which can be opposed to them [the British] with such a prospect for success as the corps you have proposed should be levied in Carolina." Laurens tried hard and brought the issue to a vote of the South Carolina legislature, but he couldn't convince a majority. He had some support from the up country, but the areas controlled by the big rice-plantation owners just wouldn't go along. A year later the South Carolina governor made an offer to the British general besieging Charleston: the governor would lead South Carolina in breaking away from the Confederation if the British spared Charleston. They didn't, and Charleston still surrendered. It was the most ignominious defeat of the war, with fifty-five hundred prisoners of war falling without a fight into British hands.

Laurens wrote to the General that "prejudice, avarice, and pusillanimity" were the reasons for the defeat. The General wrote back to

Laurens lamenting that "the spirit of freedom" had been superseded by "selfish passion."

I believe the General was both displeased and angered that some South Carolina leaders were more concerned about preserving slavery than gaining independence. Still, at the time of the failure of Laurens's mission, I did not know if the General was really more angered by the South Carolina legislature's defense of slavery or the loss of potential troops for the war effort.

Given that the General owned a few hundred slaves and was known to have chased after slaves who fled his plantation, I was pretty sure his motivation was increasing our troop numbers, although with the General it was always hard to tell, and lately I have come to believe, for reasons I will tell you about later, that he may have been moved as much or more by idealism than pragmatism.

It was the same way with women in the army. Everyone knew there were women serving with and in the army. The General made it very clear he did not approve of camp followers; many of these women engaged in prostitution, but many were married to the soldiers. At first he tried to stop the practice, but the General, as I said, could be quite pragmatic, and one day he remarked, "Josiah, there may be some good in all this. Draft an order that when we are in camp, regiments should have the women wash and clean whatever clothes we have and prepare the food."

Dealing with camp followers was one thing; finding women who disguised themselves as men in order to serve in combat was another. This happened more than you might believe. I still remember General Knox coming up to the General to inform him that a Deborah Sampson had been discovered. She had used a male alias, Robert Shurtliff, cut her hair short, and bound up her breasts. Her fellow soldiers thought it odd when she didn't shave, but they figured the boy was just too young. Her secret would not have been discovered, except she fell ill at Yorktown, and a surgeon examined her.

"What do I do?" asked Knox, to which the General after a pause asked, "What kind of soldier has she been?" When told she had performed ably and been wounded twice, I knew the General was thinking, "I will have one less soldier." Finally his sense of practicality and convention prevailed and he told Knox, "Well, I suppose we shall have to discharge her. Just make sure she gets an honorable discharge and a letter of commendation."

"Yes, sir," said a bemused General Knox before he trotted off.

Then there were those women like Molly Ludwig who found themselves openly thrust into battle. Molly Pitcher, as she was known, had been delivering pitchers of water when her husband, manning an artillery piece, was shot and killed. Molly took over the piece and kept shooting. The next day General Greene presented her to the General, who got carried away and appointed her a sergeant, but I believe this was an honorary title. Lady Washington was not amused, especially when she heard about Molly's reputation for swearing. The General was always very mindful of Lady Washington. Soon after, Molly was eased out of the army, although with an honorable discharge and a letter of commendation I drafted.

People had the habit of seeing their own views reflected in the General's views, which the General encouraged with enigmatic comments. After the General's actions—or nonactions—on Negro and women troops, along with some ambiguous comments, I remember Abigail Adams congratulating the General on his support for abolition and women's rights. "My good madam," I heard the General reply, "you give me too much credit. I am only trying to win this war." Mrs. Adams left the meeting both convinced the General shared her views and impressed with his modesty.

Then there were the Indians. The General talked about treaties, preserving lands for the Indians, and all of us living together, but he certainly had no compunction about settlers moving west onto Indian lands. He dreamed of settling the Ohio country and bought land there. When it came to the war, however, the General saw things more pragmatically.

"Josiah," he said to me, "I learned in the last war that the best white men are not equal to Indians in the woods."

Despite what the General knew about the unease of settlers living on the frontier, he made great, albeit quiet, efforts to negotiate treaties with the Indian tribes, particularly the Iroquois nation, to enlist their support. First the General tried to raise Indian regiments, and then, when that proved impractical, he tried to raise Indian irregulars. The General was not a novice at negotiating with the Indians and had brokered many such arrangements during the last war. The Indians admired the General because, I was told, they believed he had supernatural powers. They had seen him in the French and Indian War shot at from close range hundreds of times but never go down. While most of the Indian tribes were sympathetic to the British, who offered to stop western settlement, the Oneidas and many Indian bands were supporters of the independence effort. The General could be ruthless, however, with those Indians who sided with the British. He sent General John Sullivan to destroy crops and villages when some of the Iroquois nation in New York joined the British.

The General's desire to use any possible means to pursue the war extended beyond troops. In New York in 1776, I remember how his disapproval of a mob tearing down a huge statue of King George III changed to acceptance when he calculated how many bullets could be made out of the fallen statue. Then there was the abortive effort to kidnap Prince William Henry during the prince's visit with the British navy in New York. Maybe this was a response to the British botched plot to assassinate the General by infiltrating his personal security guard, but I do believe he saw this as a way to bring the war to a speedy conclusion.

Anyway, you get the idea. The General was obsessed with only one thing, and that was defeating the British and gaining independence. And when one considers the plots and counterplots, I suppose I should have expected that the General would suspect the British of writing the anonymous letter. But I had no idea what the General's response would be.

"Josiah, draft an order saying that this letter calling for a meeting is outside the chain of command and highly irregular. State that by my order we shall hold such a meeting not tomorrow but at noon at the

Temple this Saturday to allow for mature deliberation of the subject raised in the letter."

At the General's dictation, I wrote: "After mature deliberation they [the officers] will devise what further measures ought to be adopted as most rational and best calculated to attain the just and important object in view." There followed a pause, and then the General added, "Josiah, state that the meeting will be presided over by the second-in-command."

I was perplexed, but not because the General had called the anonymous letter writer's call for a meeting "irregular." That sounded like the General, who wanted everyone to adhere to the chain of command and did not look kindly on anyone who tried to bypass him. Nor was I surprised by the call for "deliberation." That also sounded like the General, who sought to avoid impulsive judgments. But to call for such a meeting on the same subject four days later than the original meeting seemed to support the anonymous writer's purpose. And to state that the second-in-command should preside was mystifying. The General apparently did not want to attend the meeting, but why have General Gates preside? Surely the General knew that Gates and his circle had long tried to undermine him.

The General could sense my confusion and peremptorily cut me off before I could ask any clarifying questions. "Josiah, draft the order immediately during dinner for my review after the aides' meeting." I didn't question the General, much as I longed to. He could be quite open about requesting and taking advice, but once he issued an order, and gave what we aides called "the look," one did not tarry. So after I showed the order I had drafted to the General later that Monday afternoon (he added an announcement of a promotion, I assume to make the order seem more routine), the General directed me to make copies and see that they were circulated that night to make sure no one attended the anonymous author's Tuesday meeting.

Chapter Two

Day Two—Tuesday

The Second Anonymous Letter

A feeble army and an empty Senate,
Remnants of mighty battles fought in vain.

—Marcus, *Cato*, Act I, Scene 1

General Alexander McDougall was the one who delivered the second anonymous letter. Through one of our narrow windows I saw him ride up to headquarters amid the fluttering snowflakes and barge into headquarters. I always thought McDougall was a little full of himself, but he was certainly an able commander. When McDougall was in his cups, which was often, he loved to tell us of his migration from Scotland to America, his childhood on the streets of New York delivering milk, his sea years as a privateer, and what he regarded as the glorious time he served in jail as a leader of the New York Sons of Liberty. The stories were colorful, as were his vocabulary and his clothing.

That Tuesday morning, in his thick, stuttering Scotch brogue that never left him, he called out to me, "Josiah, it's another damn anonymous letter, and the men are reading and praising it like a Thomas Paine tract. Something is afoot. See that the General sees it at once." With that comment, he handed me the letter, strode out, mounted, and rode off.

I sat down to read the letter with mingled curiosity and fear. There were four pages of closely written text followed by a hurried anonymous end—"I am, &c"—where an honest man would have signed, but the writer did not. This letter was as long and eloquent as the first letter had been short and curt. By the time I reached the end, I may not have known who had written it, but I certainly had a sense of the forces we were up against. The letter had been written yesterday, probably for distribution at the meeting the General had abruptly postponed.

I had to admit that the writer understood the mood of the army. First he introduced himself and artfully bonded with his readers as a "fellow soldier" who had endured with them the "cold hand of poverty" and the "insolence of wealth," while having "mingled in your dangers." He wrote of how he had remained silent, hoping that his country would serve us with "justice" and "gratitude," but his patience was running out and that to continue his silence would be "cowardice." Thus inciting his readers, the anonymous author set out the case for action. They had fought for seven long years and were now on the brink of achieving independence for their country. What now was their country doing for them? Was it "a country willing to redress your wrongs, cherish your worth, and reward your services? Will you return to private life with tears of gratitude and smiles of admiration? Or is it rather a country that tramples upon your rights, disdains your cries, and insults your distresses? . . . And how have you been answered?"

To the soldiers, many of whom had not been paid, clothed, or fed for large parts of the war, and to the officers who had mostly served without pay and been given only vague promises of pensions after it, the answers to these questions were self-evident. I found myself agreeing with the author, my own indignation rising.

The writer recited what we all knew too well: we had meekly begged the Congress for justice to no avail. And this was while the war raged.

What hope had we if we gave up our swords? Our future, said the writer, would be to "grow old in poverty, wretchedness and contempt" and to become dependent and forgotten.

The writer then questioned the officers' courage and manhood: "To be tame and unprovoked while injuries press upon you is more than weakness. But to look up for kinder usage without one manly effort of your own—would fix your Character and show the world how richly you deserve the chains you broke."

Now, the writer delivered the challenge: Do you have the spirit to revolt? Do you have "spirit enough to oppose tyranny under whatever garb it may assume, whether it be the plain coat of republicanism, or the splendid robe of royalty?" He practically shouted through his pen: "Awake—attend to your Situation and redress yourselves. If the present moment be lost, every future Effort is in vain. Your threats then will be as empty as your entreaties now."

Having delivered the challenge, the writer pointedly advised what should not be done. There should be no more "milk and water" memorials to the Congress. He advised soldiers to "suspect the man who would advise to more moderation, and longer forbearance."

I was brought up short by what seemed like an attack on anyone, including the General, who might dare oppose the writer's views. And then came the writer's call for a "bold" and "last remonstrance . . . by men who can feel as well as write," which would make clear that Congress should not take the army for granted, and that "the Army has its alternative."

And what was the alternative? The writer offered two. The first alternative was, in the event of the anticipated peace, "that nothing shall separate you from your arms but death." What exactly could this mean? I asked myself.

The army was to stay armed and do what? Just sit in Newburgh and let British troops move back on the offensive? Or was the writer referring to the suggestion that had been talked about for weeks: that the army should march on Philadelphia and impose its will on the Congress? The writer apparently left this to the reader's imagination.

Then came the writer's second alternative. If the war should continue, "that courting the auspices, and inviting the direction of your illustrious leader, you will retire to some unsettled country, smile in your turn, and mock when their fear cometh on."

Presumably the army was to withdraw to the unsettled West, let the British crush the Congress and the state governors, and then occupy the whole Eastern Seaboard. The phrase "inviting the direction of your illustrious leader" seemed less like an attack on the General than an invitation, I read with relief, for him to join and lead the mutiny.

The writer allowed that if the Congress and presumably the states met the army's demands, the army would maintain its "allegiance," and when the war ended, the writer pictured for his readers a grand and heroic finish: "You would withdraw into the shade of private life—and give the world another subject of wonder and applause, an Army victorious over its enemies, victorious over itself."

I did not doubt for a moment the effect the letter would have on the army. I myself, normally a cautious person, was moved.

As the spell of the letter receded, I reflected more calmly on its nature and authorship. The letter was unerring in its aim at the emotions of the troops. It was so unerring that I immediately concluded it could not have been written by the British. No British military aide in New York could know so well the mood of the army. The letter in both its length and eloquence bespoke days of thought, and the quick distribution after the General's order and its invitation to the General as the "illustrious leader"—did this not show that the writer was right in our midst?

Equally clear, to me at least, was that no one could write such a letter without the backing of a significant number of officers. Every phrase bespoke the confidence of a man who already knew that a large number of officers and troops supported his entreaties.

As for my earlier suspicion of the General's role, I was relieved to admit that the conflicting counsels against the General's moderation and the invitation for him to lead the revolt showed that perhaps he had not authorized the letter, at least not directly.

And what of the choice posed in the letter: the call either for withdrawal to the West or keeping arms and possibly directing them against the Congress? As I tried to focus on my writing tasks for that day, I pondered the chances of success for the writer's entreaties at the coming Saturday meeting. Withdrawing to the West while the war continued seemed unlikely. That would mean many officers and troops leaving their families and farms behind. Certainly the writer knew this would not be an appealing prospect.

But what if a peace agreement was signed quickly? It might have already been signed with the news still coming by ship from Paris. No, the letter clearly assumed a peace agreement; the choice advocated was keeping arms, threatening the Congress, and, if necessary, marching on Philadelphia and overthrowing the Congress. This was a course of action that offered prospects of success. As I have said, there had been an increasing number of mutinies as the war progressed. After the early Pennsylvania mountain men mutiny, there was the Connecticut regiment mutiny, the Virginia officers refusing orders to join General Greene in the Carolinas, and the rebellious officers at Fort Pitt. Just two years ago came the most serious one yet: thousands of Pennsylvania militia had mutinied, killed some of their officers, and marched on the Congress.

I knew the details of the Pennsylvania 1781 mutiny because of my cousin Benjamin. He was a couple of years younger than I and somewhat of a ne'er-do-well. He enlisted in the Pennsylvania militia, the 11th Regiment with Colonel Stewart. We ran into each other later at Yorktown, and he told me the whole story. Many of the troops had enlisted for three years or the duration of the war. The Pennsylvania authorities wanted to hold them to the end of the war without the bounties that troops from other states were getting. The Pennsylvania troops began chafing at the perceived unfairness. Plus, fighting in ever more tattered clothing, the men lost patience with the repeated promises of shirts, caps, and pants that never came. Even after the mutiny started and the clothes were again promised, they were not delivered.

Benjamin said that if the General had used force, the mutiny would have spread, or at least continued. After all, twenty-five hundred troops was not a small number, and, as I well knew as the General's aide, the units from nearby states had little appetite for disciplining their Pennsylvania neighbors. At the time, I had wondered if the General's strategy was correct—he had ordered General Anthony Wayne to stay with the mutineers, even acting as a hostage through weeks of negotiations—but in the end the mutiny had ended with most of the troops reenlisting. (I never did know why General Wayne got the nickname Mad Anthony. His conduct during the mutiny was careful and cautious, and he scrupulously followed the General's orders to stay with and negotiate with the mutineers.) Benjamin told me that the mutineers were well aware of the General's sympathy with many of their requests.

The British probably thought the mutineers would join their forces, but the mutineers made clear from the beginning that their quarrel was not with their commanding officers but with Congress and the Pennsylvania Council. When the British sent emissaries, the mutineers turned them over to General Wayne, and they were shot. The British had encountered many mutinies but never one like that! The mutineers were not completely successful—some were hung but some got discharged, and some got a month's furlough, a month's pay, and some clothing before returning.

But these earlier mutinies were either privates led on occasion by corporals or sergeants or a small number of officers defying a single order. Here at Newburgh was a potential mutiny of the main army unit of seventy-five hundred led by and involving hundreds of the highest-ranking officers. Even those earlier smaller mutinies, particularly the last Pennsylvania one, might have spread but for the General's careful responses; now this week came a potential mutiny that invited the leadership of the General himself!

I realized that thinking back to those earlier mutinies offered little in the way of guidance. Still, the willingness of the authorities to negotiate according to the General's wishes back in 1781 showed that a mutiny today might intimidate the Congress into passing the necessary revenue measures. Those in Congress sympathetic to our plight already were proposing taxes on imports and exports. Collecting the revenue might prove more difficult but looked achievable. The governors and legislatures of nearby states could be intimidated, but even that might not be necessary. The revenues could be collected without the states' acquiescence just by continuing to occupy the ports of Philadelphia, Boston, and Charleston, and by moving into the port of New York— moves that would probably be uncontested by the British under any peace agreement bringing independence. Such a revenue-raising strategy might indeed succeed.

Success would probably need the cooperation of other army elements, particularly the officers and troops in the South who could move into Charleston. But if the main body in Newburgh raised the flag of insurrection, and if the General even just stood aside, other units would probably join. The Pennsylvania mutineers in 1781 had quickly been joined by New Jersey elements. If the General took the lead, I was sure almost all units would join.

If General McDougall was correct and the letter was already being read with enthusiastic approval, perhaps on Saturday the officers would make the decision to move with or without the General. With the writer's argument to resist the voices of "moderation," the letter seemed to make the argument to go ahead in either case. But the invitation to our "illustrious leader" showed that the movers behind the letter clearly preferred the General's support.

I went back to more mundane matters. I drafted a response to a confusing letter from Elijah Hunter in New Jersey, who begged the General to help recover Hunter's horses that had presumably been stolen by American militia. Then I drafted an order to William Shattuck to go into Vermont and track down two miscreants wanted by the Congress for treason. This assignment was made more difficult because the General did not want Shattuck to rile Vermonters led by Ethan Allen. (Allen was playing a double game—taking our side while at the same time negotiating for a union with Canada.) Then I drafted a plea to General Benjamin Lincoln, the secretary of war in Philadelphia, to urge on Superintendent of Finance Morris the rapid dispatch of needed clothing to the army. Oh, how many letters of this nature I had drafted.

The General arrived back shortly past noon, and before I could utter a word, he gave a list of orders he wanted sent to various units regarding the lack of discipline he had observed. Here the war might or might not be drawing to a close, a mutiny was in the offing, and the General was noticing the marching and formation habits of units and demanding that standards be upheld!

"General," I said, "we have another anonymous letter."

He grabbed it out of my hands, led me back into his study, and read the letter through not once but twice. He did not seem as calm as when reading the short letter the day before but perhaps that was my imagination. "Well, Josiah," he said, "this man has a good pen . . . he certainly appeals to the passions of the moment. And does not our army have grievances?"

With this comment, the General embarked on a speech I had heard many times, comparing the nobility of our troops with the corruption of some merchants and congressmen and the unwillingness of many of our citizens to pay taxes to support the war effort. "Chimney corner patriots" he called them—men orating from their cozy fireside seats while our underdressed, underfed, and underpaid army struggled on unassisted. The General lamented that the lust for private gain was increasingly replacing the desire to sacrifice for liberty. As the General's irritation increased, he went through the list of the worst offenders. There was Comfort Sands, that New York merchant who had promised and failed to deliver rations and then had finally delivered spoiled flour, rotten beef, and putrid whiskey. There was Congressman Samuel Chase of Maryland, who used his office to parlay knowledge of the arrival of the French fleet to buy wheat at low prices and sell at a huge profit. There were the citizens of Norwich, Connecticut, who rioted about paying taxes for the support of the army and then drank toasts to King George III. The General's anger reminded me of the sentiments oft expressed to me by my cousin Benjamin.

"Josiah," the General bellowed—all his coolness had disappeared, as this was one subject that could drive him into a rage—"if I had the power, I would impale these speculators on stakes five times higher and sharper than the one prepared by Haman for Mordecai." Then he caught himself as he saw my eyes widen at the phrase "if I had the power." He became quieter as he reflected on the contrast between the chimney corner patriots and the sacrifices of our army.

"It baffles the mind," the General said, "that these men would prey on their own country, their own army, like this. And such an army! Who has before seen such a disciplined army formed so quickly from such an inferior number of raw, untrained recruits? Who, that was not a witness, could imagine that the most violent local prejudices would cease so soon and that men who came from the different parts of the continent, strongly disposed by the habits of education to despise and quarrel with each other, would become"—in one of the General's favorite, albeit borrowed, phrases—"one band of brothers?"

The General's praise of the nobility of our army led me to recall that at first he had not reflected so kindly on the troops or officers under his command. Over the years he had changed his opinion. Perhaps this was because he recognized that, as the commander of an army from the thirteen colonies, he knew he had to win the allegiance of all, but

I do believe he came to appreciate the performance of all his troops, especially when he compared their tribulations with the easier life of the British and their Hessian allies. Now he spoke once again to me of how, years from now, posterity would not believe the miraculous behavior of our men.

"Josiah, historiographers will bestow on their labors the epithet and marks of fiction. It will not be believed that such a force as Great Britain has employed in this country could be baffled in their plan of subjugating it, by numbers infinitely less, composed of men oftentimes half starved, always in rags, often without pay, and experiencing, at times, every species of distress that human nature is capable of undergoing. Has any army suffered greater hardships than ours?"

The words had a familiar ring to me, and then I realized the General was expressing the same thoughts as he had in a letter a month ago to General Greene. The General had a habit of quoting himself—or me—without realizing it.

"Of course, Josiah," the General continued, "the composition of our troops has changed in the last eight years. There is more discipline and fewer desertions."

I listened dutifully as the General stated what I well knew.

"At the beginning, although fewer than twelve thousand troops stepped forward of the twenty-three thousand Congress asked for, they were all full of patriotic fervor. We had mainly New Englanders and Virginians. Many, however, left by the end of 1775 to return to their farms. Today we still have many farmers, but also more of the poor, landless, unemployed, indentured servants, and ex-slaves. What motivates men to fight, Josiah? Patriotism? Natural bravery? Present or future reward? Respect of peers? Patriotism is a great motivation, Josiah; an eighty-dollar bounty for reenlisting for the duration of the war and the chance to eat are apparently also great motivations. We have more troops now because there are greater prospects of both success and at least some financial reward. Yet despite the desertions and the turnover, the resilience has been remarkable, don't you think?"

He did not wait for me to answer the question. "Just think of the lack of food and clothing and, for most of the war, one-third having no shoes. Well, at least they are better fed and clothed now thanks to French money. They are few compared to the many who did not fight or profited by their endeavors, but they are indeed a band of brothers."

Ah, there was that phrase "band of brothers" again.

It was really remarkable how the General, who most perceived was by birth part of the Virginia aristocracy—which of course he wasn't—had come to love and repeat that phrase from the famous St. Crispin's Day speech in Shakespeare's *Henry V* when the king rallies his outnumbered army before the 1415 Battle of Agincourt:

> From this day to the ending of the world,
>
> But we in it shall be remembered,—
>
> We few, we happy few, we band of brothers;
>
> For he today that sheds his blood with me
>
> Shall be my brother . . .

I could see why the General loved this speech. It sounded to me very much like himself. And the officers and troops certainly responded to this phrase. The General was so aloof at times, but the troops, even more so the newer recruits, looked in awe at him.

I believe in part the troops respected the General because of his courage in battle. Someone showed me an old article from the French and Indian War where the General commented that he had "heard the bullets whistle" and there was "something charming in the sound."

To one who found whistling bullets more terrifying than charming, this was hard to fathom. I don't know whether the General still found being shot at "charming" or whether in his middle age he felt a need to act as if he did and an obligation to show courage to those he asked to follow him.

I have read that our military doctrine today follows the British model that suggests generals should always stay in the rear, the better to direct troop movements. The General would have deemed this preposterous. When a battle was developing, he would occasionally sit on a hill in the rear, but as soon as the battle was joined, the General would always move to the front.

Perhaps the respect of his troops was in part because they knew the General, while at times critical, appreciated them. The General instituted awards, ribbons, and what we now call purple hearts. A small matter, you may say, but, as far as I know, the General was the first commander in the world to show such recognition for enlisted men.

Or perhaps the respect stemmed from knowing that the General understood both his troops' potential and their limitations. The General had no illusions about human nature. "A common man can be a hero and a coward," he was fond of saying. "Discipline and leadership will go a long ways toward determining which it is." Such comments always made me feel uncomfortable, believing that I was more coward than hero. I often suspected the General knew this, but he never broached the subject and always acted as if I was a comrade in arms.

The General admired officers who were, as he put it, "educated gentlemen," unlike himself, but he expected more from them, and when they did not meet his standards, he demonstrated anger far exceeding what he showed toward enlisted men. I remember his curt words when he ordered the execution of an officer convicted of looting loyalist property; and I also remember how the General leaped off his horse, Old Nelson, and struck those officers fleeing British troops on Manhattan Island.

The General had mellowed on deserters, although not mutineers, as the war went on. The year before, several soldiers had returned six months after deserting, and the General gravely sentenced them to loss of pay for the time they were away! If that had happened during the early years, there would have been at least many lashes of the whip. Of course, those who did not return voluntarily and were caught still got the lashes. For soldiers who mutinied—and as I have said, there were more mutinies than those who now glorify the war admit—the General showed little mercy. The penalty recommended by officers at the court-martials of mutineers, at least for the leaders, was death. As the war drew on, the General less frequently issued pardons, particularly after the scare of the last Pennsylvania uprising. I understood the necessity of the executions, and I realized that the cause of almost every mutiny—the broken promises of food, clothing, and pay—could have been invoked, but wasn't, by all who served. Still I could not bring myself to witness those hangings.

At the beginning of the war, the General had been repeatedly frustrated by the lack of training and discipline among the men. This changed when, in the horrible winter we spent in Valley Forge, a middle-aged Prussian general named Friedrich Wilhelm von Steuben (at least he and Ben Franklin claimed he was a general) arrived in the camp. With his Italian greyhound Azor by his side, shouting in German at the men and often telling his translator to "swear at them for me," I first thought von Steuben seemed like a joke. But he did teach the men how to load and reload rifles and use bayonets. And, bless him, he did show us the use of latrines. I saw his impact when I looked at the neat rows of log cabins in New Windsor. After that winter in Valley Forge, von Steuben wrote the *Regulations for the Order and Discipline of the Troops of the United States*, a book carefully reviewed and approved by the General. I am told the army used the book for decades. Still, von Steuben was an easy target for regimental humor, and the General often laughed at von Steuben's complaint that, before anything would happen, he had to tell American troops not just to do something but *why* they must do something. (The General told me he himself had learned that lesson back in the French and Indian War and then had relearned it at the beginning of this war.)

The General looked down at the letter and read aloud the part about the hardships shared by the anonymous letter writer with the men. The General seemed annoyed and perhaps rightly so. Was this not a criticism of the General? With the letter in his hands, the General asked me, "Have I not taken the best care I could of my men? Yes, they have not been clothed or fed properly, but did I not write hundreds of letters to the Congress, governors, and the French pleading for money and supplies? Have I not, over and over, praised their ardor to Congress and have I not been their strongest advocate? Did I not institute sanitary practices to reduce disease? Did I not insist on mass inoculations against smallpox when many opposed it and did this not save many lives? Josiah, have I not shared the trials and tribulations of the army?"

I did not respond because I knew the questions were rhetorical. I just nodded. He had done all the things he said—I had written most of those letters. We lost twice as many men to disease as to battle. I know sixty years later, with the advances in treatment, that seems hard to believe. Still, that rate was probably lower than the British and the Hessians suffered, although that might have had less to do with the inoculations the General was so proud of and more to do with our being on the run and shifting campsites so often.

Then there was the matter of the General literally sharing his men's trials and tribulations. Perhaps the General claimed too much credit there. When we camped, the General always had the biggest tent or commandeered a farmhouse. The men did not begrudge this as they knew that the British generals by comparison lived in opulence and luxury. Perhaps I noticed because, despite coming from a wealthy family, as a Quaker I had been taught to live a life of simple frugality. Not that I ever complained about sharing his quarters and offices. And the

General at Valley Forge and here in Newburgh had not set up quarters for himself and his aides until tents or cabins had been built for all the men.

The General looked at the letter again and stared at the ceiling. "Josiah, this obviously came from within our camp, perhaps with the encouragement of some in Philadelphia." I was glad the General had dismissed the idea of a British plot.

Then he turned to the courses advocated. He at least partly echoed my own views. "The suggestion that we withdraw from our families to the West is hardly doable, although we could just stand down and stop firing at the British. The other course implied is that we march on Philadelphia . . ." Here the General's words trailed off. I noticed that he had used the word "we" in describing the choices put forth.

Then the General, perhaps realizing his use of words, asked me: "Josiah, do you think this diatribe against following the counsel of moderation is directed against me?"

"I don't think there's any question about that, sir. Who else are they afraid of successfully urging restraint upon the army?"

The General nodded and remained silent for a moment.

"Josiah, tomorrow morning I want you to go about the camps and try to gather information. Whom do the officers believe wrote the letter? How is it being received? What was the reaction to my postponing the meeting until Saturday? Report back to me before dinner tomorrow."

"Yes, General," I replied, realizing the meeting was at an end but expecting more instructions. The General waved me out of his study.

I stepped out of Hasbrouck House, realizing I badly needed a breath of the winter air blowing in from the Hudson. Was this all the General was going to do? Was he just playing for time before making a decision? That seemed likely, given the request for information and the General's propensity for delaying action until the last moment. Still, unless the mutineers abandoned their quest, which seemed highly unlikely, the General was going to have to make a decision. Was he planning on leading the mutiny? Or planning on opposing it? Or just standing aside? I couldn't tell which way he was leaning.

I started thinking about some of those letters we had received urging the General to seize power before the young country destroyed itself. I've told you about the letter from Reverend Duché. Just last May the General had received a letter from Colonel Lewis Nicola. The colonel, age sixty-five, had been born in Dublin and served all over Ireland in the British army before moving to Philadelphia and joining the revolutionary cause. Nicola was a man greatly admired by the General and the officer corps. He had conceived and executed the idea of taking partially disabled men and forming them into an Invalid Corps to guard powder magazines, ports, hospitals, and bridges and take on other light duties. The Invalid Corps struggled with the same problems as the rest of the army, and Nicola in his letter to the General railed against the lack of pay, awful food, and bad clothing, and blamed this all on the Congress.

In a premonition of the anonymous letters, Colonel Nicola feared "the settling & satisfying [of the army's] just demands will be little attended to, when our services are no longer wanted." Nicola saw a dire future: "the recompense of all our toils, hardships, expense of private fortune, during several of the best years of our lives, will be . . . beggary." Writing in a tone similar to that of the anonymous letter writer, he stated, "We who have borne the heat & labor of the day will be forgot and neglected by such as reap the benefits without suffering any of the hardships . . ."

Like the anonymous writer, Nicola predicted the army would after peace not give up their arms unless Congress fulfilled its promises, which he doubted: "From several conversations I have had with officers, & some I have overheard among soldiers, I believe it is generally intended not to separate after the peace 'till all grievances are redressed, engagements & promises fulfilled . . . [but] neither officers nor soldiers can have any confidence in [congressional] promises."

To Colonel Nicola, the blame for the army's plight rested completely with the congressional form of government under which the states existed: "large bodies" of "wise and moderate" representatives could not lead with the "energy" of a king. "A monarch may often be governed by wise & moderate counsels, but it is hardly possible for larger bodies to plan or execute vigorous ones." Looking into history of "modern republics," he noted that they were few in number and "their luster has been of short duration, and, as it were, only a blaze." Nicola pointed to the Dutch Republic—which while "mistress of nearly half the commerce of the earth"—didn't have a strong enough government to protect itself and was forced to rely on neighboring monarchies.

Nicola feared that such would be the fate of the fledgling United States without a king: "Has it not evidently appeared that during the course of this war we have never been able to draw forth all the internal resources we are possessed of, and oppose or attack the enemy with our real vigor? . . . This war must have shown to all, but to military men in particular, the weakness of republics."

Colonel Nicola proceeded to explain to the General his plan in which all those who had served in the army would be compensated with land in the West. It was clear to him what form of government the veterans should have: "I have little doubt, when the benefits of a mixed government"—a limited, constitutional monarchy—"are pointed out and duly considered, . . . such will be readily adopted."

A monarch, of course, meant naming a king, and Nicola, without naming the General, left no doubt who that king should be: "in this case it will, I believe, be uncontroverted that the same abilities which have led us, through difficulties apparently insurmountable by human power, to victory and glory . . . would be most likely to conduct and direct us in the smoother paths of peace," particularly since the abilities of this unnamed person "have merited and obtained the universal esteem and veneration of an army." Nicola delicately allowed that since "some people have so connected the ideas of tyranny and monarchy as to find it very difficult to separate them, it may therefore be requisite to give the head of such a constitution as I propose, some title apparently more moderate" than king, although he argued there was a "strong argument" and "material advantages" for the "title of king."

The General's response to the colonel's letter was blunt and forceful. Dictating to my fellow aide, David Humphreys, the General was at pains to make clear that "no man possesses a more sincere wish to see ample justice done to the army than I do." Still, he expressed "surprise and astonishment" at Nicola's proposal. The General stated his strong disagreement and that he would be the last person to consider such a scheme, which he viewed with abhorrence; further, he thought "such ideas existing in the army" was "painful" to him. The General urged Nicola to "banish these thoughts from your mind." The General's response was certainly direct, and Colonel Nicola, intimidated and perhaps fearing for his command, apologized three times to the General. And yet I don't believe the correspondence, unlike with Reverend Duché's letter, was rushed to the Congress. Nicola's letter struck a chord with the General's aides, and I know some copied the letter and showed it to others.

My thoughts returned to the second anonymous letter. I wanted to believe that the General was not the author. After writing thousands of letters under the General's dictation, I was pretty sure the General had not dictated this letter. It was too flowery—definitely not the General's style and probably beyond his abilities. But had he ordered it? And if he had not, was he going to seize the leadership of the mutiny? Maybe the diatribe against "moderation" was meant to convince others it was not the General's doing.

The General's orders to gather information seemed such an inadequate response if he wanted to stop a mutiny. Why not call in officers for questioning and threaten court-martials? Then again, the General was obsessed with gathering information and intelligence before making any decision. Some said this obsession was a fault that had led to opportunities being lost throughout the war. But then again, in this way, big mistakes had been avoided. The General was known for being tempestuous and brave. He was that, but I also knew him to be a very cautious man—some said too cautious—when it came to throwing his troops into battle.

"Josiah," he was fond of saying, "delay in gathering information may lead to loss of a tactical victory here and there. That may prolong the war. But failure to gather information may lead to the destruction or capture of our small army. As long as we persevere, the British and the Parliament will eventually grow weary of the struggle."

He did not have to say that the capture of the army meant the capture of himself. I knew from reading the intercepted British letters that many of the king's officers believed that the bagging of the "gray fox," as the General was called, would mean the Crown's triumph in the war.

Chapter Three

DAY THREE—WEDNESDAY

The Third Anonymous Letter

All, all is ready.
The factious leaders are our friends, that spread
Murmurs and discontents among the soldiers.
They count their toilsome marchers, long fatigues,
Unusual fastings, and will bear no more
This medley of philosophy and war,
Within an hour they'll storm the Senate-house.

—Sempronius, *Cato*, Act II

It was too early on a frosty Wednesday morning to head for the Red Tavern, where the junior officers congregated, but the task of gathering the information the General had requested couldn't wait. I rode through the camps in New Windsor where the troops were housed and some officers were already on duty, making my way from state to state, trying to be as unobtrusive as possible. I did not have to ask many questions. Where officers gathered around campfires or lolled in headquarters' tents, the conversation seemed to not touch any subject other than the letters. "It's about time" and "I don't care who he is, he speaks for us" were commonly held views, not only among the officers but also the soldiers.

I started in the Virginia camp. The attitude toward the General seemed full of wistfulness and hopefulness. A captain in the Virginia regiment came right out and said, "We and the General have been patient long enough. It's about time the General led us to the right city . . . and I don't mean New York." His comment was echoed by other officers, who said it had become far more important for the General to lead the army to Philadelphia, where the Congress resided. In the New York camp, some said if the General wouldn't lead, someone else would, and it was clear they were referring to the second-in-command, General Gates, although his name was not mentioned, perhaps because some knew I was on the General's staff.

Once I ventured to ask about the practicality of settling in the West or holding on to our arms. A junior officer responded, "Any course is better than the present." A lieutenant said, "We know what the letter writer really wants and that is what we all want: to march on Philadelphia. We need to finish the job that the Pennsylvania mutineers started two years ago."

There was some, but not much, mystery about who wrote the letter. At the Massachusetts camp, one officer, Captain Noah Allen, thought it might be a British plot, but he was one of few. Most of the rumors focused on General Gates's aides, Majors John Armstrong Jr. and Christopher Richmond.

In the New York regiment, I ran into Colonel Courtland, whom I respected greatly. When I asked how the letter was being received, he said, "with glee and approbation, Josiah." When I asked if he had any ideas who wrote the letter, Courtland confidently named Gates's aides: "The writing on the copies is Richmond's, but I have heard the author is his friend Armstrong." Colonel Courtland's aide claimed others had seen Major William Barber, another aide to General Gates, deliver the letter to the adjutant's office, which distributed orders and letters by high-ranking officers to all units.

Other officers, such as Colonel Swift and Major Webb in the Connecticut regiment, shared Colonel Courtland's view. I knew Armstrong to be ambitious, headstrong, eloquent, and devoted to General Gates. If he was the author, he would not have written the letter without General Gates's authorization.

Still, many of the officers I questioned didn't know and didn't care who wrote the letter. "Whoever wrote that letter, Colonel, sure knows how to write" was a common refrain.

While I was making my rounds, I saw the General stop at the campgrounds of the New York regiment to review the troops. As usual, there were huzzahs for the General. It may have been my imagination, but I thought the cheers sounded more dutiful and less enthusiastic than usual. But then, when he appeared before the Pennsylvania troops, the huzzahs seemed louder. Jumpy as I was, I imagined that might be because the troops anticipated that the General would agree to lead the mutiny.

I sought out, discreetly, my cousin Benjamin. He told me the Pennsylvania troops would happily march on Congress again but that it might take leadership from the officers. Benjamin raised his eyebrows. "Many resisted last time, but if the senior officers led the way . . ."

Benjamin's regimental commander, Walter Stewart, had returned from Philadelphia and was known to have visited many units throughout the army, spreading word of the dismal reception given our latest petition to Congress. Stewart, as I well knew, was a close friend of General Gates.

I had reached the encampment of the New Hampshire regiment and was starting to sound out some of the officers gathered around a fire when Colonel Joseph Reed, whom I knew, handed me still another anonymous letter that was circulating. "Here, Colonel, have you seen this?"

The letter was neither as short as the one requesting a meeting nor as long as the one prodding the army to revolt. It had obviously been written upon receipt of the General's order shifting the meeting to Saturday. The writer artfully acknowledged that his earlier letters might have alarmed those who had never heard such sentiments so openly expressed. "Ye well knew that it spoke a language, which till now had been heard only in whispers, and that it contained some sentiments which confidence itself would have breathed with distrust."

Fearful that the General's order might be interpreted as disapproval of the call for a meeting, the anonymous writer cleverly argued that the General, by calling the Saturday meeting, was displaying his approval of the writer's intentions.

> Till now, the Commander in Chief has regarded the steps you have taken for redress, with good wishes alone, though ostensible silence has authorized your meetings and his private opinion has sanctified your claims. Had he disliked the object in view would not the same sense of duty which forbad you from meeting on the third day of this week [Tuesday], have forbidden you from meeting on the seventh [Saturday]?

The writer then went on to voice approval of the General's delay of the meeting until Saturday, making it seem as if the General's opinion was the same as the writer's.

"Is not the same subject held up for your discussion, and has it not passed the seal of office, and taken all the solemnity of an order—this will give system to your proceedings, and stability to your resolves, will ripen speculation into fact, and while it adds to the unanimity, it cannot possibly lessen the independency of your sentiments."

The writer then explained the anonymity of his three letters, saying his name was not necessary since his views reflected the feeling of the entire army. However, he closed with a threat to reveal his identity if it would be "necessary . . . to hold up any individual among you as an object of the resentment or contempt of the rest."

This, I thought, was clearly an attempt to intimidate any officers who might dare to speak against his call for action at the Saturday meeting. Was this a message to the General to join the mutiny or be denounced in front of his officers? I thanked the New Hampshire colonel, put the letter in my pocket to show the General that afternoon, and, covering up my consternation as best as I could, tried to continue my rounds.

Back at headquarters before the afternoon dinner, I showed the latest letter to the General. He grunted and, after reading it, put it on his desk with the others. Otherwise he showed no emotion. After motioning to me to sit opposite him in my usual perch, the wooden straight-backed chair, the General asked what I had learned on my morning visits. I told him that Major Armstrong was the probable author and that there seemed to be a yearning among many of the troops that the General lead the mutiny. He showed no surprise and simply thanked me.

"Well done, Josiah." Then, after a pause, he muttered, "Well, the Old Leaven"—our nickname for General Gates—"is again beginning to work under a mask of the most perfect dissimulation and apparent cordiality."

I was relieved that the General had finally accepted that General Gates and officers inside the camp were pushing the insurrection. Still, if the General believed this and disapproved, why did he not order General Gates and Major Armstrong to our headquarters and ask for an explanation, or even arrest them for sedition? Of course, such arrests would portray the army as divided to the outside world and the Congress, which I knew went against the General's desire to portray the army as having one voice.

I waited for any further orders, expecting that he would at least ask me to summon General Gates or Major Armstrong. Instead he simply stated, "I want a letter drafted to Congressman Jones."

Joseph Jones was a Virginia congressman whom the General had learned to trust and who the General knew would pass on his thoughts to many of his congressional colleagues. The General asked me to include copies of the three anonymous letters and his order postponing the meeting. Then he dictated the letter to me, a lengthy one.

I remember writing—and have confirmed from looking at my notes—how the "temper of the Army" was "very irritable on account of their long protracted sufferings." I then conveyed the General's suspicions about the propagation of schemes in Philadelphia linked to "dangerous combinations . . . forming in the Army" and that since the return of a certain gentleman from Philadelphia, sentiments had been circulating in the camp that "the Army would not disband until they had obtained justice." The General was referring to Colonel Stewart, cousin Benjamin's commander. The General, however, as I well knew, had an aversion to making direct accusations. Perhaps he was just following Rule 89 in his *Rules of Civility*: "Speak not evil of those who are absent for it is unjust."

The General then referred succinctly to his order delaying the meeting, stating that "I did this on the principle that it is easier to divert from a wrong to a right path, than it is to recall the hasty and fatal steps which have already been taken."

I remember thinking that the General may not have been a writer on a par with some of his compatriots, but he had no trouble expressing himself with deft phases.

Toward the end of the letter the General seemed to be portraying himself as all that stood between the Congress and mutiny. "It is commonly supposed, if the Officers had met agreeably to the anonymous summons, resolutions might have been formed, the consequences of which may be more easily conceived than expressed. Now they will have leisure to view the matter more calmly and seriously. It is hoped they will be induced to adopt more rational measures, and wait a while longer for the settlement of their accounts."

Then the General returned to the justness of the army's cause and his displeasure with Congress. "There is no man . . . who will not acknowledge that Congress have the means of paying . . . Are we to be disbanded and sent home without this?" The General went on to lay out the army's fear that Congress would continue to stall until peace and the disbanding of the army had occurred and then do nothing. The General asked that I close the letter with what could be considered a warning or a threat:

> Let me entreat you therefore, my good Sir, to push this matter to an issue—and if there are delegates among you, who are really opposed to doing justice to the Army, scruple not to tell them—if matters do come to extremity—that they must be answerable for all the ineffable horrors which may be occasioned thereby. With great truth and sincerity I am—Dear Sir Your Most Obedient and affectionate servant,
>
> George Washington

What was the General intending? He was clearly informing Congress of the threat of mutiny. He was conveying suspicion of congressional involvement and implicitly warning Congress not to meddle with the army. He was asserting the justice of the army's demands. He was portraying himself as loyal to the Congress and trying to avoid the mutiny. Finally, he was warning that Congress better act if it did not want to suffer terrible consequences and perhaps dropping just the slightest hint that he, George Washington, would not protect the Congress from those consequences.

There were many themes indeed, and I could not puzzle them all out. But no sooner had I finished taking his dictation of the letter to

Congressman Jones than the General was dictating a letter to Congressman Alexander Hamilton. "Include copies of all three anonymous letters and my order postponing the meeting with this letter too, Josiah." He said to tell Hamilton that "it is firmly believed by some that the scheme was not only planned but also digested and matured in Philadelphia."

The General paused, smiled, and said to me, "Josiah, add that 'of course I will suspend my opinion until I have better grounds to found one on.'" The General continued, "Also add some language about the justness of the army's cause and my earnest desire that its demands should in a lawful manner be addressed."

The letter was for the most part similar to the letter to Congressman Jones, but I detected a suspicion on the part of the General that Congressmen Hamilton and Madison might have encouraged the events of the last three days.

Did the General really believe the plot originated with congressmen instead of General Gates? Did he fear some combination of the three? The evidence I had gathered seemed to point to Gates. Maybe the General wished to just make sure that certain congressmen like Hamilton and Madison did not support Gates. It was always hard to tell with the General. But I was sure of one thing—no one of the congressmen or politicians who the General dealt with was more astute in the art of politics than the General. To say that "some" said the plot had been hatched in Philadelphia but he was "suspending" his own judgment was a fine touch.

The General, I knew, held Hamilton in high regard. He had earlier been an aide to the General, but Hamilton's zeal for military glory had driven him to ask for a combat assignment and led his fellow aides, behind his back, to call him the Little Lion when we weren't calling him Hammy. Perhaps my dislike for Hamilton was based on the way he strutted around exulting in his eagerness for battle. Did people like Hamilton really have no fear? I had fear. I did not want to admit some others had no fear. Maybe they just covered up their fears better than I did.

As an aide, Hamilton had quarreled with the General several years before. Some silly business about Hamilton asserting the General had not shown him sufficient courtesy. The General apparently had summoned Hamilton and then waited at the top of the stairs for Hamilton, who was slow to appear. When the General expressed irritation, Hamilton exploded and announced his departure. We all tried, without success, to convince Hamilton to calm down and stay. The General tried to make amends with Hamilton and ignored his huffy resignation letter, but the latter would have none of it.

I always wondered if Hamilton had used the incident to get transferred to his own command. Anyway, things had been patched up. Hamilton had performed ably, even gloriously, at Yorktown, leading the charge against the outer British redoubts. All was forgiven. The General recognized military merit, and Hamilton was a great admirer of the General, although I always thought Hamilton, an ambitious man, must have realized, at least belatedly, that he could not rise far in any postwar government without the General's patronage. In any event, the General knew how hotheaded Hamilton was and just weeks ago had written him a veiled warning that "the Army was a dangerous instrument to play with," as if he feared Hamilton would encourage what was happening that week.

Looking back, I am now fascinated by how the General reacted to Hamilton and others we now in the 1840s call our Founding Fathers and how they reacted to him. The General was certainly aware of how others referred to Hamilton as "that West Indian bastard" and admired him for his humble upbringing as well as his bravery and intellect. Hamilton's ambition—once Abigail Adams, visiting the General, compared Hamilton to both Julius Caesar and Cassius in the same sentence— did not bother the General, who thought Hamilton's openness about his ambition was rather charming. At times, I thought the General looked upon Hamilton as a wayward son, but a most promising one.

With Thomas Jefferson there was no closeness, although they both came from Virginia. The General thought him very talented but impractical. Traveling all over the colonies, the General saw the future of the country in manufacturing, while Jefferson thought everyone should stay a farmer and that anything commercial was demeaning.

The General and Jefferson also had different views of the opposite sex. I understand Jefferson changed later, but back then he did not like men mixing with women in public meetings—something about such mixed contacts leading to the degradation of morals. The General had no such qualms. He loved the ladies and engaged with them as equals in conversations.

The General and Jefferson came to have different views on slavery. I recently read Jefferson's *Notes on the State of Virginia*, and I cannot comprehend how a man who had earlier written about the iniquities of slavery could now write of Negroes as "inferior." We knew back then that Jefferson was a hard taskmaster determined to make a profit on every slave, and that, unlike the General, Jefferson continued to buy and sell slaves, even breaking up families. Later, I learned that Jefferson had turned down a gift of thousands of dollars from the Polish nobleman Tadeusz Kosciuszko to help free and support his slaves. But, as I will soon relate, I discovered during the war that the General intended to take a different course.

For a man who prided himself on his love of science, Jefferson had some peculiar views. I read later that he was opposed to medical research in hospitals, goodness knows why. The General prided himself on being practical. He was always asking the doctors what they were learning about wounds and diseases.

Still, the General appreciated Jefferson's advice and talents. "Thomas has a fine pen," he said after having the Declaration of Independence read to the troops in the summer of 1776. Only later did I realize that Jefferson had lifted most of the opening line of the Declaration from what the General's neighbor, George Mason, a man the General greatly admired, had written in the 1776 Virginia Declaration of Rights.

The General's aides, but not the General, mocked Jefferson when, as Virginia's governor, he ignored warnings from the General and others, did nothing to call out the militia to defend Richmond, and then fled the advancing British army. The Virginia legislature conducted a full-scale inquiry of Jefferson's alleged cowardice—he was rumored to have fled in his pajamas and hidden in a tobacco barn. I was more sympathetic. If the British sent a brigade to hunt and kill me, I wondered if I would not have run and hid in a barn. Upon hearing about Jefferson's travails, my fellow aide David Humphreys remarked to the General, "That will be the end of Jefferson's career," but the General said Humphreys should not be so harsh. "Not every man is born to be a fighter," said the General. "Thomas is a thinker and a writer. And a mighty fine writer for whom we should be grateful." As one who was constantly in fear of being exposed as a coward, I was relieved to hear the General's defense of Jefferson. The General certainly went out of his way to seek Jefferson's opinion on political matters during the war.

Jefferson had recovered from his earlier disgrace and, after being cleared by the legislature, was now over in France with Franklin and Adams. The General was not sure Jefferson was fit for this role. "He understands and admires the French. Whether he really understands Americans who live outside his own Virginia circles is another question."

John Adams described how Jefferson seemed "to appear meek with his stooped, lounging manner, but he is as ambitious as Oliver Cromwell." In the General's mind, ambition was a good thing, but he could not understand why Jefferson would hide his ambition behind apparent meekness. Of course, as I well knew, the General hid his own ambition behind not meekness but the appearance of patriotic disinterestedness.

When the General became president later, I am told that Jefferson would criticize the General behind his back. When he talked openly with the General during the latter's presidency, however, I'm sure he was very deferential and careful, such as when he reportedly urged the General to run for a second term, telling him, "The states will hang together as long as they have you to hang on."

I do think Jefferson, like so many others, was jealous of the General. I cannot understand why he wouldn't participate in any of the public memorials after the General's death, but maybe he was busy plotting his own presidential campaign. By the 1800s, sensing the overwhelming public sentiment, Jefferson had resumed calling the General a "great man."

Of Benjamin Franklin, the General had no doubts. "There is a man who understands America and the French too." The General's respect for Franklin dated back to the French and Indian War. He told me that Franklin had come through with horses and supplies in western Pennsylvania when all others had failed him and said he was not surprised at Franklin's ability to outfit privateers such as John Paul Jones to raid the English coast from France. "That man has extraordinary abilities."

I suspected that the General, who had come from what we now call the middle class and had made himself into a surveyor—the wealth from his wife, as I've noted, came much later—admired the way Franklin had come from middling origins and had started out by teaching himself the trade of printing and then gone on from there.

The General's praise of Franklin may have had something to do with Franklin keeping the General well informed on what he was doing in Paris. He flattered the General by putting a bust of him in his Paris office and letting the General know he had done so. Then again, Franklin probably thought this was good politics with the French. I learned after the war that the French idolized Washington as much as they admired Franklin and that Franklin obtained the last French loan by promising the proceeds would go to the General rather than the Congress. Some of Franklin's letters on military strategy amused us, as, when hearing of the shortages of arms and powder, he recommended the use of pikes, bows, and arrows.

While the General would have denied it, I always thought he was as susceptible to effusive praise as any man. And Franklin, either genuinely or not, was quick to supply such praise. He reported to the General that the French considered him "one of the greatest captains of the age," and, after Yorktown, a letter arrived from Franklin telling the General that our triumph there would "brighten the glory that surrounds your name and that must accompany it to our latest posterity." With such letters from a man as celebrated as Franklin, that week I could not help but wonder if the celebration of the General's deeds might tempt him to take power.

John Adams puzzled the General. Adams had nominated the General to be commander of the American army, but according to the General, he constantly talked about the General having too much power and fought giving him the power to appoint his own subordinates. "Josiah, he seems to want to command the army from the halls of Congress." During that week in Newburgh, more than once I began to suspect that Adams might be right about the General wanting too much power.

In many ways they were opposites. The General was tall, muscular, and athletic; Adams was short, rotund, and ungraceful. It must have been hard for Adams, a scion of austere New England Puritans, to be easy friends with one whom he perceived to be the descendant of an opulent Virginia planting family. The General respected Adams's learning but was made uneasy by the way he tried to show it. While Adams spoke of the General as "the exemplification of the American character," when word got back to the General that Adams regarded the General as "unread and unlearned," the General was not surprised.

Perhaps because Adams was concerned with his reputation almost as much as the General was with his, the General was suspicious of Adams—after all, it is easy to cast as a flaw in others a trait you yourself possess. But the General must have felt empathy over the one infirmity they both faced: trouble with their teeth.

Sometimes the General's virtue, or show of virtue, offended Adams. Adams resented the General's not taking a salary during the war, fearing the General was putting the country in his debt as a way to gather more power. I believe that, while the General cared about Adams's opinion, he cared more about the opinion of his countrymen. The General calculated every action, including the refusal of salary, in terms of what his countrymen might think. Since the war and the General's death, I have heard that Adams bemoaned the pain of seeing someone "wear the laurels I [Adams] have sown," and I have also heard that Adams privately denounced the celebration of the General's birthday as "idolatry."

Adams, like the General, cared about his place in history. My friend Benjamin Rush told me that Adams wrote him that "the history of our Revolution will be . . . that Dr. Franklin's electric rod smote the earth and out sprang General Washington . . . and thence forward these two conducted all the policy, negotiations, . . . and war." Maybe this feeling of jealousy is understandable. The General eclipsed everyone—after all, before the war was even over, towns, colleges, counties, and mountains were being named after the General, coins were being minted with his image, and his birthday was being celebrated. Of one thing I am certain, however: while the General expected his due—why, he resigned as an officer in the French and Indian War because he felt the British were not showing him proper deference—jealousy of others was not one of his flaws. Maybe that was because he overshadowed all those around him and never needed to feel jealous.

I felt then and feel now that one of Adams's criticisms of the General might be partially justified. Adams is reported to have derided the General as a "great actor." Even to me, who saw the General up close, it was hard to tell how much of him was real and how much was a carefully constructed persona. Did the legend create him or did he create the legend? Then again, does it really make a difference if one acts virtuously, cultivates virtuousness, or is really virtuous? Does it matter if a general acts with courage and discipline in battle or if he is really disciplined and courageous? And if the outcome is the same, what is the difference?

Abigail Adams was another matter. The General charmed her, as he did all the ladies, and was in turn charmed. "Josiah," said the General, "John Adams thinks he knows more about military matters than anybody in the army, but he knows far less of such matters than his wife." He repeated the line to others, leading me to believe that he wanted his opinion to get back to both Mr. and Mrs. Adams.

Then again, it got back to the General that Abigail had written a friend that the General "has a dignity which forbids familiarity: an easy affability which creates love and reverence. He is a temple built by hands divine." I don't doubt she wrote that. Mrs. Adams came out of one meeting with the General, turned to me, and said, "The General is a singular example of modesty and diffidence whose dignity and majesty surpasses any European king." The General could do that to people.

Even Mrs. Adams's admiration, however, was mixed with trepidation. Once she told me that "if he was really not one of the best intentioned men in the world, he might be a very dangerous one." Those words floated through my mind that week in Newburgh.

The General's views on Patrick Henry were surprising. Most seem to think that the General was put off by Henry's radicalism. But this was not the case. Of course, perhaps we should not consider Henry a Founding Father since he opposed the Constitution under which we have prospered, but then so did James Monroe and many other heroes of the Revolution. (Still others, like Jefferson, had trouble making up their minds.) The General admired Henry's courage, not only for speaking out so early against British rule but for his willingness in the House of Burgesses to argue for expulsion of a previously respected member accused of taking a bribe.

The General also admired Henry for what he did afterward as governor of Virginia. "Josiah, to oppose repudiation of the debt and back levying taxes to support the war—that took courage." The General appreciated that Henry, a great orator, backed the war with more than words. He had led a campaign in 1776 to raise funds for blankets that kept large parts of the army from freezing to death.

The General and Henry were actually a mutual admiration society. Perhaps that was because their skills complemented each other. The General was in awe of Henry's oratorical abilities. I am sure the General was not the first one to say of Henry, "Josiah, he speaks like Homer writes." After all, the General, while he occasionally uttered fine phrases, on big occasions often stammered. Henry, who realized the General's lack of formal literary training, went out of his way to praise the General's other attributes. He has "the charisma of competence," Henry said. Henry was quite ready to praise the oratory skills of his colleagues at the Continental Congress, but he was quick to say, "If you speak of solid information and sound judgment, Colonel Washington is the greatest man on the floor."

We all knew that these two Virginia governors, Henry and Jefferson, hated each other during the war. The General thought it had something to do with Henry's more outward manifestation of his religious views, but he stayed out of that feud despite entreaties from friends. The General was very careful to husband his resources for the struggle against the British.

Another nonsupporter of the Constitution whom Washington admired was Thomas Paine. During the bleak fall of 1776, when all seemed lost as the army stumbled in retreat across New Jersey and thousands pledged loyalty to the king, Paine had published *Common Sense*. It was indeed a "time that tried men's souls." When some of our fair-weather friends in Congress and the military were sniping at the General, Paine remained a stalwart supporter. The General bought up hundreds of copies of *Common Sense* and distributed them among the troops.

The General and Paine shared an interest in science. One aide told me they had boated down a New Jersey river at night studying the emission of gases. Later, to the General's pleasant surprise, Paine had helped draft petitions by officers to the Congress for back pay. I understand that after 1789, when the General became president, Paine turned on him. Paine got himself thrown in jail over in Paris during the French Revolution, and the General—at least in Paine's opinion—did too little to help secure his freedom.

The two men the General most admired were his neighbor George Mason and the Marquis de Lafayette. I got the impression that Mason, several years older than the General, was a mentor—certainly the General made clear his opinion that Mason had the greatest political mind in the colonies. They did not correspond much, but an aide from Virginia told me that, before the war, the General did not make a speech or advance a motion in the House of Burgesses without Mason's guidance. (The General's deference to Mason came through in a rather paradoxical way to me. The General, with some pride, told me more than once that he had designed the expansion of Mount Vernon himself while his great neighbor had hired an architect.) The General was always interested in hearing news of what Mason was saying and thinking. After the war was a different story. Mason also opposed the Constitution and, while such opposition did not hinder the General's relations with others, this apparently cooled their friendship, perhaps because of their previous intimate political association.

As for Lafayette, the General believed he should be considered a Founding Father of our nation despite the fact that Lafayette was not an American. I believe that the reception given the marquis by the Congress and the whole country in 1826 was fully deserved, and if the General was still alive, I am sure he would have heartily approved. The marquis was unlike many foreign officers who came with great pretensions, little military talent, and a desire for high salaries, and who had won their rank because Congress bequeathed it on them. He charmed and disarmed the General immediately. At their first meeting, when the General apologized for the condition of our troops compared to what Lafayette must have been used to with French troops, the marquis dismissed the comment and replied, "I have come here to learn, *mon général*, not to teach." There may have been some self-interested flattery in that remark, but noble sentiments were ingrained in Lafayette's everyday discourse. Once he told me, "I would have gladly stripped Versailles of its furnishings to have clothed our troops," and I do believe he meant it.

Lafayette soon won the General's confidence not only with his ability to lead troops in battle—he became one of the army's top generals—but with his ability to persuade his French peers of the desirability of joining and helping to finance our struggle. Unlike most other foreign officers (including his compatriot comte de Broglie, who envisioned himself with a rank exceeding the General's), Lafayette wanted no salary or high titles, and he quickly endeared himself to the Americans put under his command. "Our marquis," as we called him, didn't hurt himself with the General by his loyalty back in 1778 at the time of the Conway Cabal—when General Gates, the French-Irish adventurer General Conway, and some congressmen were trying to either remove or rein in the General's authority. Given the General's pride, neither did the General's opinion of the marquis lessen when the marquis named his son "George Washington Lafayette," and the General became the son's godfather.

What I found most extraordinary about the marquis was his incredible idealism and his willingness to express his sentiments, even if they were sometimes grandiose. "Josiah, our country," he said, referring to America, "fights for liberty for all countries and all generations."

This idealism extended to other issues, and while he was in awe of the General, he was not afraid to challenge him. The abolition of slavery was one such issue. Many of the General's aides, including Hamilton and me, could see the contradiction between constantly calling for freedom from British slavery while maintaining the slavery of the Negroes. We knew from the General's correspondence back to his cousin Lund at Mount Vernon that the General, unlike other Southern planters, had ordered Lund not to buy or sell human beings, so as to keep families together. We also knew that he had ignored Congress's order banning Negro soldiers, established free black regiments, and implicitly approved the unsuccessful efforts of Colonel John Laurens to convince the South Carolina legislature to free slaves to fight the British. Still, as I said earlier, we attributed some of these actions to his pragmatism about winning the war. We knew the General was still a slaveholder and that, while the General had stopped buying and selling slaves, he had still tracked down some of his slaves who had sought freedom. All this made us reluctant to raise the subject with him. Possibly this was because of what we imagined Lady Washington's view on slavery to be. Well, not exactly imagined—Lady Washington often commented on how "bad" and "lazy" the Negroes were.

In Cambridge, the free Negro poet Phillis Wheatley sent the General a poem extolling the General's virtues and urging he be given a throne and crown. The General ignored the invitation to power but graciously invited Miss Wheatley, "a person so favored by the muses," for a visit. We noticed, however, that the visit took place when Lady Washington was away at a party for the wives of officers. Some of the Southerners may have thought the meeting of the General, a slaveholder, and the Negro poet Miss Wheatley odd, but if so, they did not dare challenge the General.

Anyway, when Lafayette embraced a cause—and abolition was one—nothing would deter him from pursuing it with anyone at any time or place. I still remember back in 1779 when he announced to me that he was going into the General's study to urge the General's support of abolition. The meeting went on for almost an hour, and when Lafayette emerged, he was ebullient. I asked him what had happened.

"What a magnificent man is the General," he responded. When I asked for a more detailed account of the meeting, he was more than willing to respond. "Well, Josiah, I started by espousing the view that if we wanted freedom from the British we could not deny it to American

Negroes. I expected the General to object, but he readily agreed. 'Slavery is debilitating not only to the enslaved but to those who enslave them. I can see that just looking at my Virginia neighbors. I wish with all my soul, my dear marquis, to see the development of a plan by which slavery in this country may be abolished by slow, sure, and imperceptible degrees involving education of the slaves. Otherwise, our country will see much mischief.' I asked him, 'Why not abolition at once?' and he told me that the slaves he knew had been denied the right to learn to read, and education was needed if abolition was to succeed."

I tensed up. This was a subject that all of us aides had never dared broach with the General, particularly knowing Lady Washington's views. Finally, I said, "That may be all well and good, Marquis, but what is the General willing to do about it?"

"That," replied the marquis, "was what was so extraordinary. I suggested he write an essay telling the American people why slavery ultimately must be abolished."

"And what did the General respond?" I asked, already guessing the General's response.

Lafayette continued, "The General grumbled about writing an essay, said it was beyond him and that he was more suited to deeds."

When I heard this, I was not surprised. I could not help think of Thomas Jefferson, who had already written great essays on the iniquity of slavery but had also become known for his harsh treatment of his slaves. The General, with so little confidence in his own education, certainly abhorred writing essays. Whether it was the war, religious freedom, the union, or in this case slavery, he always shied away from putting his views on paper in favor of setting a personal example. Still . . .

Lafayette anticipated my next question and said, "So, Josiah, I asked him, 'What deeds do you have in mind, General?' and he replied, 'I intend upon the death of Martha and myself to free all my slaves and provide for their welfare and education.'"

While the marquis was jubilant, saying "what a great man" the General was, I was less so, thinking that, while this would be a great act, why not take the action now? But the reference to Martha was telling. We on the General's staff all knew that Martha had decided views on the rightness of slavery and held title—what a terrible word—to the majority of slaves at Mount Vernon. And we also knew that the General did not cross Lady Washington.

The marquis continued, "I then asked the General if he would subscribe to a colony of free slaves I wanted to establish in the Caribbean, and he said he would."

This didn't seem like a very practical idea to me, but the marquis was not one to be stopped by practicalities.

Well, here we are in the 1840s, and we are still talking about colonization. Our representative, Abe Lincoln, keeps touting the idea, and I suppose it is better than President John Tyler's suggestion that we lessen slavery by annexing Texas and "diffusing" slavery westward. Still, I have come to believe there can be no ultimate solution but the one the General suggested: abolition preceded by and coupled with education.

While I was skeptical, the General did free his slaves and provide for their education and welfare under his last will and testament. I wish the General had acted sooner, but he was ahead of his time. Some Founding Fathers were abolitionists, but they were not born into slaveholding families. And I don't know of any Southern planters in 1799 who freed their slaves, let alone dipped into their own pockets to provide for their slaves' education and welfare. I suppose that's why next week our local abolition group here in Illinois will hold its annual meeting on the same day it celebrates the General's birthday.

But back to the Marquis de Lafayette. Given his propensity for grandiose sentiments, I truly believe he looked upon himself as a romantic hero from medieval times and upon the General as the greatest dragon slayer of them all. While Lafayette could stand up to the General on issues such as abolition, he was blind to any flaws in the

General's character. "Josiah," he told me, "when I first met the General, I beheld a man so tall and noble and majestic. Our great advantage over the British is our General. He is a man formed for this revolution and is worthy of the adoration of his country."

As one who had shared the General's quarters for years, I thought at the time this was a great exaggeration born of Lafayette's desire to see himself as a knight-errant giving devoted allegiance as his lord pursued the grail of our revolutionary struggle.

Why did so many swoon over the General? Was I the only one to see, along with his good deeds, his temper, vanity, and posturing?

The General was quite calculating in how he appeared to men like Lafayette or women like Abigail Adams. Every step, every word, every pose was, I thought, designed to impress whoever was in his company. My Quaker upbringing had taught me that one should present oneself in a simple and forthright manner without artifice (although I admit that on occasion I liked that Prescilla looked on me as a shining knight).

The General was certainly simple when it came to his uniforms—probably because he was following Rule 52 in those infernal *Rules of Civility*: "In your apparel, be modest and endeavor to accommodate nature rather than to procure admiration." He never wore the medals that states and foreign governments bestowed upon him. However, even before a battle, he spent minutes having Will make sure every hair and thread was in place—just another example of how the General calculated his every military and political move.

That week at Newburgh, and the years since, have, in some ways but not all, altered my opinion of this part of the General's character.

In any event, none of these figures whom we look back on today as Founding Fathers, except for the General, was present that week in Newburgh. How the drama played out rested with the mutineers, the army, and the General.

As the mutiny loomed, I remember retiring on Wednesday evening confused, nervous, and excited about what would follow on Thursday.

Chapter Four

Day Four—Thursday

Councils of War
Reflections on Generalship

How does the lustre of our father's actions,
Through the dark cloud of ills that cover him,
Break out, and burn with more triumphant
    brightness!
His suff'rings shine, and spread a glory round him;
Greatly unfortunate, he fights the cause
Of honour, virtue, liberty, and Rome.

—Portius, *Cato*, Act I, Scene 1

On Thursday the General did not make his usual morning rounds. I was sent to fetch numerous officers to meetings with him, and they came and went all day. Generals Knox, Rufus Putnam, McDougall, and Hand; Colonels Brooks, Glover, and Ogden; Majors Shaw and Davis; and Captains Howard and McReynolds were just some of the officers who met with the General. I do not remember their names, but there were six or eight others. Many returned for second meetings.

The General did not even pause for the usual three p.m. dinner, much to the annoyance of Lady Washington and Mrs. Hamilton, the Washingtons' housekeeper.

The meetings themselves did not seem unusual, although the fact that the General was meeting with officers individually or in groups of two or three did. It was the General's habit to seek advice at meetings attended by many of his commanders, sometimes calling in junior officers and even privates on occasion. That was something that both pleased and irritated his commanders. It was not something generals did back then, although I am told that the practice is now encouraged at West Point. Certainly his British counterparts did not do this. The notion that Generals Gage, Howe, Clinton, or Cornwallis would hold a council before acting on any crucial matter was laughable. I thought it was one of the General's virtues and a practice you would not guess from his sometimes imperious manner. Of course, the meetings I'd attended over the past seven years had left me wondering if the General was really seeking advice or if he was guiding the meeting to a view he already held, the better to solicit the enthusiastic support of his commanders, who then believed they had been part of the decision.

There was one other thing that was highly unusual about Thursday's meetings. None of the General's aides, including me, were included. This, I admit, annoyed me. I was present at most of the General's meetings and afterward was frequently directed to draft a letter or an order, but not on that day. I had never seen the General so secretive. I had no doubt the meetings concerned the coming Saturday meeting and the circulating letters, but beyond that I was left to speculate. Despite my curiosity, I did not ask the General to let me attend. I almost never addressed the General unless asked and neither did the other aides at Newburgh.

Benjamin Walker, David Humphreys, and I were left sitting at the big table in that dark main room wondering what the officers were planning behind the study door. I couldn't help wondering what questions were now being discussed. How to derail the gathering forces of mutiny at or before the Saturday meeting? Perhaps, but since the General had indicated in his Tuesday order that he would not attend, how was this to be accomplished? Or was the discussion over how to channel the Saturday meeting toward the General assuming leadership of the mutiny and a coming march on Philadelphia? That the officers summoned were those most loyal to the General seemed beyond question. With the possible exception of Nathanael Greene, who was down in the Carolinas; Hamilton, who, now a member of the Congress, was in Philadelphia; and Lafayette, who was back in France, those meeting with the General had most loyally followed him and backed him from the early days of the war.

Loyalty to the General did not characterize the attitude of all the commanders. You had to understand that Congress appointed many of Washington's top commanders based on politics or what the Congress conceived to be its military expertise. And often officers used their congressional backers to lobby for their promotions.

In some cases, these military climbers were generals with their eyes on General Washington's place. There was Charles Lee, the former British officer who aspired to the top commander's role and was a favorite of congressmen early in the war. I respected Lee's military judgment, but it was hard to take seriously a general who liked dogs more than people—Lee always had a pack of dogs on a leash following him. Anyway, the Lee movement disintegrated when he was captured by the British in flagrante delicto with a madam in a tavern. The British exchanged him in a prisoner swap, which fueled the rumors that Lee had advised his captors on military strategy against our forces. How else to explain the swap for junior officers? I couldn't imagine the British swapping Lafayette or Greene. Anyway, the General could be very forgiving—or perhaps he was assuaging potential congressional allies. He welcomed Lee back, at least until Lee refused to lead the charge at the Battle of Monmouth, and the General dismissed him right there on the field and replaced him with Lafayette. That old fool Lee thought he could count on his congressional influence and demanded a court-martial to clear his name. He was convicted of refusing to follow orders, resigned in disgrace, and went off to his estate in the Shenandoah Valley to breed dogs and horses.

To my embarrassment, the man who had introduced me to the General, Joseph Reed, sent a letter to Lee implying support for his bid to replace Washington as commanding general. Lee's response arrived while Reed was away, and the General, thinking it was a message from one of his commanders, mistakenly opened the letter and discovered Reed's disloyalty. The General, in a deft touch, had me write a letter to Reed in which the General apologized for opening the letter. When he received the General's letter, poor Reed, realizing the General knew all, profusely apologized for his disloyalty and sent his resignation to Congress.

Military and personal embarrassments always seemed to befall potential rivals of the General, particularly when some in Congress were lobbying to replace him. Take General Horatio Gates—the Old Leaven to the General and Old Granny to his troops—who, I was convinced, was behind the Armstrong letter. I'll give Gates his due: the victory over General John Burgoyne at Saratoga in 1777 had brought the French into the war. Still, the officers I spoke to gave most of the credit there to Benedict Arnold for both the strategy and combat leadership. (Two years later, Arnold tried to hand over West Point to the British and lost credit for even his good deeds.) I admit I never respected Gates after I saw him refuse to accept a major command from the General before Trenton so that he could go off to Philadelphia to lobby his congressional friends for a promotion.

Gates had powerful supporters. An effort was instigated after Saratoga by that congressional appointee, the French-Irish General Thomas Conway, to get Congress to replace the General with Gates. Conway and a former aide to the General, Quartermaster General

Thomas Mifflin, tried to use the Board of War to achieve their purposes. (Enemies of the General came from all sides: Conway was one of those congressional appointees, but Mifflin, like me, was an ex-Quaker from Philadelphia and a former aide of the General's.) Lafayette and Laurens put a stop to the maneuvering, the former by threatening to resign and go back to France and the latter by writing his father, who was president of the Continental Congress.

Reed and Mifflin, mind you, were the exceptions. In my experience, almost all the General's aides were loyal, maybe too loyal. They were always challenging the General's detractors to duels, which was ironic, given how the General disapproved of dueling. I am told in his youth he went to great lengths to avoid duels, even apologizing to one potential opponent. Anyway, both the Conway and Lee affairs got the General's aides' dueling pistols out. (Not mine, mind you, although I offered encouragement.) Laurens challenged Lee to a duel, which ended with Lee writing the General a letter of apology, and one of the General's former aides, John Cadwalader, challenged Conway to a duel and wounded him. Cadwalader would have killed him in another duel, but Conway wrote a letter apologizing to the General and then resigned and returned to France.

The Conway Cabal crushed, the General, as was his fashion, forgave Gates, the intended beneficiary of the "Cabal," who still had strong support in the Congress. But Gates could not escape one of those events that always seemed to thwart the General's rivals. At Congress's insistence, Gates was promoted and given command of the Southern Army. In August 1780, he led his army into a disastrous defeat at the Battle of Camden and then disgracefully fled the field. Congress set up a special inquiry to investigate charges of cowardice, and Gates was suspended from command.

After the suspension was lifted, the General welcomed Gates back. He probably thought Gates would be grateful and follow the General's orders. Given this week's letter by Gates's aide Armstrong, I thought the General had made a big mistake, unless, of course, the letter was at the General's bidding.

With all the rivalries—which the citizenry knew little about—it did make one reflect on the abilities of the various generals and the ability of General Washington himself. Was he a great general, as some of my fellow aides believed, or was he overrated, as the teacher told my great-grandchildren? That week at Newburgh I reflected on that question as I have many times since.

The General's role as commander in chief all started with his appointment by Congress in 1775, which probably mystified the many who aspired to that command. The General always said that he did not seek out or campaign for the appointment. "Josiah, I did not solicit command but accepted it after much entreaty. I did not seek this burden."

Knowing the General and the conflict between his ambitions and his modesty—or at least his attempt at projecting modesty—I suppose there may be some truth to this, but I also had my doubts. The General, unlike other delegates, wore his red-and-blue French and Indian War military uniform to the 1775 Congress. Along the way from Mount Vernon to Philadelphia he went out of his way to review the militia regiments that had been assembled. To what purpose, you may ask, if not to call attention to his military experience? The General once implied to me that he did this to show Virginia's willingness to fight, but I was not completely convinced.

During the previous Congress, the General got himself appointed to all the committees that dealt with a military solution to our quarrel with Britain. He was on the committee to organize supplies, the committee to procure weapons and manufacture gunpowder, and the committee to explore financing of the war. I was told that during these meetings the General spoke rarely and briefly, although, since he was the only member with military experience from the French and Indian War, his words were heard respectfully.

Charles Willson Peale, the artist, told me that the General's brevity was a great asset because most of the delegates indulged in long speeches, wearying of the lengthy orations of others but enjoying their own. When someone spoke without eloquence or adornment, the delegates were subconsciously impressed. "That Washington makes sense" was a common refrain. According to Wilson, the General never boasted of his past military exploits, which further impressed the delegates, who were all trying to impress one another.

Stories of the General's exploits certainly affected the congressmen. From all I could tell, however, while his experiences in the French and Indian War may have been legendary, they said more about the General's bravery than they said about his generalship. Yes, he had defeated a small force of less than fifty French soldiers, but there were rumors that the French commander was on a diplomatic mission. The General had been forced to surrender Fort Necessity, and I have heard secondhand stories that he picked a poor location to defend that fort.

The General's military reputation at the time of his appointment really rested on one of the worst defeats in British military history. In the summer of 1755, a few hundred French and Indians ambushed and routed thirteen hundred well-armed troops commanded by the British general Braddock. Braddock was on his way to capture the French Fort Duquesne, the site of the present village of Pittsburgh. Braddock had recruited a twenty-three-year-old colonial aide, George Washington, one of the few soldiers with experience in the region. While the battle was a debacle, Washington emerged a hero. Captain Brown, who claims to have been there, told me the General, while ill from dysentery, rallied the troops during the ambush, took four bullets through his coat, and had two horses shot out from under him. After he was reported killed, the news of the General's survival, when most British and colonial troops had perished, added to his reputation. It was widely believed that General Braddock had ignored the General's advice about the impending ambush and that Braddock, realizing his error, had, while dying, bequeathed his manservant and horse to the General. That story I first heard from a soldier who had heard it from his father, but then I also heard it from others.

I once asked the General his opinion of General Braddock. "He was a brave and good officer, Josiah. He tried to rally his troops in the most adverse circumstances, but while our colonials fought well, his British troops fought poorly." When I pursued the matter and asked if General Braddock had ignored his advice, the General would only say that Braddock's experience had been on the battlegrounds of Europe, but he would go no further. This may have been due to General Braddock expressing a high opinion of the General, who was always loath to criticize others, especially those who spoke well of him.

Then there was the story that the Indians had stopped shooting at the General during Braddock's defeat because they were convinced the Great Spirit looked over the General. Nobody ever confirmed that story for me.

Going back to the French and Indian War, I was left wondering whether the stories were factual, fictitious, or just embellished. But the Congress and now his troops did not wonder. All the General would tell me about his experiences in the last war was that spending hours in the freezing Allegheny River Valley of the Pennsylvania backcountry made Valley Forge seem almost idyllic. That the General rarely boasted to me or others of his feats just made people believe them and admire him all the more.

I remember thinking that, even if most of these stories were true, and Congress believed every one of them, how did this qualify the General to command an army of thousands of men? Still, no one else could claim the distinction of having been a colonel who had led hundreds of Americans in battle. In the end, who else could the delegates have chosen? The commander of New England's troops, Artemus Ward, had acquitted himself well at Bunker Hill, but he was an elderly and obese shopkeeper. Lee had experience but was British-born and considered eccentric. Gates, who had not served as a delegate or in colonial legislative bodies as the General had, did not inspire confidence or trust.

In the end, I think, along with his military experience and the incredible stories of derring-do, what made the Congress select the General as the supreme commander was that it knew him as a fellow delegate who had served for years in a colonial legislative body. The General confessed to me that he spent more time listening to delegates at dinners and nodding than he spent preparing for the Congress's work. I believe the congressmen wanted one of their own whom they could trust to show the Congress deference.

I was told that, as president of the Congress, John Hancock expected his fellow New Englander, John Adams, to nominate him as commanding general. So Hancock was shocked when Adams nominated the General and Adams's cousin Samuel seconded the nomination. Hancock must have been deluded to believe the Congress would appoint a merchant just because he was president of the Congress, when his only military experience was marching a silk-stocking company on the Boston Common.

Naturally, the General played his reluctance to take command to the hilt. In commenting on an aide's aspirations to run for Congress, the General once told me that the lesson he learned from his first unsuccessful effort to run for the Virginia House of Burgesses was that a reluctance to put oneself forth was both modest and effective in getting others to campaign for you. I am not so sure this is as true now in the 1840s as it was back then—or if it was just true for General Washington. In any event, others such as Lee, Gates, and Hancock lobbied for the commanding general position, but the General not only didn't lobby but I am told he made a show of not doing so. The day before the Congress's decision, the General told me he had asked Edmund Pendleton, a fellow Virginian, to talk him out of accepting the appointment. Then I heard he fled the room when he was nominated, to show his modesty. Patrick Henry reported that, after the General's unanimous selection, the General told him, "Remember, Mr. Henry, what I now tell you. From the day I enter upon the command of the American armies, I date my fall, and the ruin of my reputation." I know Henry repeated this statement to one and all, which just increased Congress's opinion of the General's modesty and patriotism. When he addressed the Congress after his appointment, he told that body he was not worthy and not equal to the task, which was probably wise, given their high expectations and what was to follow.

Today everyone believes that after Congress appointed the General, and certainly after the early battles around Boston, we were in an all-out war with Great Britain. This was not true. Many congressmen hoped that the General's appointment, his dispatch to Boston, and a show of strength would bring the British to their senses and avert or stop the war. The General himself was ambivalent. He told me he did not want war and reflected that "a Brother's sword sheathed in a Brother's breast and that the once happy and peaceful plains of America drenched with blood" was not a desirable outcome. But, with the alternative of becoming slaves and losing our rights as Englishmen, how "can a virtuous man hesitate in his choice?"

The British, as it turned out, made the choice quite easy. By the following year, after many battles and several fruitless petitions by the Congress to the king, all hope of peace had vanished.

After the General's appointment, there were the letters to Lady Washington, his stepson, Jacky, and his mother. I have read those and many others, and they are certainly full of affection—although perhaps not the General's letter to his mother. (She was rumored to be a Tory and kept complaining to all that her most illustrious son was treating her shabbily, although from what I knew about the house in Fredericksburg the General had bought her and the money I kept sending her, this was hard for me to believe.) Every one of the General's letters explained that he really did not want the assignment but that he feared that refusing would dishonor him and irreparably damage his reputation. Perhaps the General really believed this or perhaps this was a pose. I wasn't sure back then. Maybe it was a little of both. The General certainly did care about his reputation.

After the General's appointment came the long trip north to Boston. The General told me that he did not like ceremonies, but he stopped at every town to review troops and receive the assembled people's blessings. Why, he even stopped for a whole afternoon in New Haven to review three companies of Yale students. His speeches to the New York and Massachusetts legislatures, which I helped draft, struck just the right note. There was the appeal to patriotism and his becoming modesty in assuring the people who had suffered under British generals that he was no military tyrant. "When we assumed the soldier, we did not lay aside the citizen" was one of my better phrases, and the legislators practically swooned. Whatever doubts they had about this new commander from Virginia vanished.

And the General did need to woo state legislatures, who tended to appoint militia commanders for their political connections. Even the General's political skills did not stop the legislators from initially appointing eight major generals to please their constituents, along with the Congress foisting foreign officers on him with high ranks and little military experience but whom the congressmen found amiable. Fortunately, the General still had the powers of promotion, and he quickly moved up those officers who showed merit. Throughout the war, the General had to protect his forces from political interference, and you can well understand there were many hurt feelings as a result.

Fortunately, the junior officers and enlisted men shared the General's views that appointments should be based on merit—even the Massachusetts militia, which initially elected their own officers, came around to this view—and their opinions filtered back to the congressmen and state legislators. The General occasionally moaned to me about the politically appointed officers, but he always kept his calm and showed great deference when dealing with the Congress.

As we stood on the Dutch stoop in the back of the headquarters, the General told me that he had learned in the French and Indian War to hold his temper on such matters. As Congress had done in this war, the royal Virginia governor Robert Dinwiddie had then appointed the General's senior commanders and upbraided him for his protests, for his strategy, and for aggressively demanding pay for his men. The General (then a state militia colonel) had resigned in protest. When he told me about this, he looked down to the Hudson and then said, "Josiah, I learned to hold my temper on appointments in the last conflict. I will not let my feelings now betray this cause." Congress, the governors, and the state legislators never stopped trying to influence the General's strategies or appointments, and every one of the General's decisions was scrutinized, but the General held his temper.

So was he a great general? The answer, I felt then and still feel now, over a half century later, depends on which campaigns you look at. Is it the successful siege of Boston, the disaster in New York, the bold triumphs after crossing the Delaware, the long series of defensive battles after Valley Forge, or the final victory at Yorktown?

Then again, maybe it was not the battles at all but his relationship with our ragtag army that made him a great general—a relationship that would play such a great role at Newburgh that week.

I. SUCCESS AT BOSTON

The first great challenge was at Boston. With all the earthworks filling in the bay to enlarge the city these days, it is easy to forget that Boston was then a peninsula, only connected to the mainland by a thin gated neck. The Massachusetts militia was guarding this point to keep the British bottled up within the city.

We arrived in Cambridge on July 2, 1775, and moved into the home of the Harvard president, whom we stuck in a bedroom. That only seemed appropriate for the president of a university with so many loyalist faculty. There was much pressure to immediately attack General Gage's forces in the city. Congress had decreed that there be twenty-three thousand troops, but when you counted those who actually were sent by the states—generally for one-year terms instead of the whole war as the General had requested—minus those who deserted or were too sick to fight, the number was not even twelve thousand. Still, this number was perhaps equal to the better-trained and -armed British troops in Boston and was as close as we would come to numerical parity until Yorktown.

Many in the New England militia were eager to fight. The General took a different view after seeing our undisciplined companies shooting at each other's sentries; the lack of food and sanitation; and, most importantly, the shortage of powder—there were only three cartridges for every soldier. While the General may not have been impressed with the unruly troops, he merely commented that "their spirit exceeds their strength," leaving me with the impression that he had encountered similar challenges twenty years earlier. He did remark to me, "This supply situation is lamentable but no worse than in the last war." He closed his eyes, then said in a quieter voice, "Though we didn't have to buy the flintlocks of departing soldiers then just to stay armed."

After watching the New England troops in several skirmishes, the General opined hopefully (in a letter I sent to his cousin Lund) that they could be dirty and nasty but fought well when led by good officers. The newly arrived Virginian riflemen—carrying rifles, not muskets—were more skilled and proud of their marksmanship, claiming that they could hit a point on a target at three hundred yards. When I passed on this claim, the General chuckled in disbelief but said, "It won't hurt if the British hear such boasts and believe them."

The General set out to establish more sanitary camps and institute training. The stench was overwhelming, and simple bathing and waste disposal practices had to be started. Overall, the men and officers responded well to the General's efforts to create discipline. The General used court-martials and punishment to enforce discipline over both enlisted men and officers, but I noticed that he blended punishment with persuasion. When Lady Washington arrived in early December of 1775, she arranged dinners for scores of officers so the General could inculcate the new standards of discipline and the officers, in turn, could set the example among their men.

In response to his requests, Massachusetts, New York, and Rhode Island sent more troops, and New Jersey sent a secret arms shipment—secret because of fears that the local citizenry along the way would steal the powder. Governor Trumbull of Connecticut sent both troops and 1,391 barrels of flour. Along with the flour was a note saying, "May the God of the Armies of Israel shower down the blessings of his Divine Providence on you as He did on Moses and Joshua."

It was the first of many missives I opened comparing Americans to the ancient Israelites, King George to Pharaoh, the newly formed states to Egypt, and the General to Moses. It occurred to me then and later that Moses was not just a general but the ruler of his people. The General sent a note thanking the governor for the flour, but he did not mention Moses. Nor did he directly respond when others made the comparison. I always thought, however, that these constant comparisons must have had some effect on the General, and especially so during that week in Newburgh when he must have contemplated becoming our new country's ruler.

Meanwhile, although we surrounded Boston, the British navy controlled the seas. Several Massachusetts and Maine coastal towns appealed to the General to divide his forces and give them protection against British raids. The General's replies, which I drafted, said no in the most diplomatic way possible and encouraged the towns to raise militia for their own defense. Pressure grew as the British ships that October burned Falmouth to the ground.

I suppose the British felt that such violence and terror would break the will of Americans—they even had a German name for this approach, *Schrecklichkeit*—but it had the opposite effect. The General made clear to me that he was not going to divide and weaken his forces, so as to let the British break the siege of Boston.

Why the British, with their superior firepower and training, did not try to break out of the siege is puzzling. Perhaps this was because the General had letters sent to patriots in Boston exaggerating our strength. I did not know at the time why he did this, but now I believe he knew the letters would be intercepted by the British and would deter them from trying to break through our surrounding forces.

With pressure building for us to attack, the General convened councils of war with his commanders. Here I first encountered a routine I would see again and again throughout the war: the General advocating the launching of a major offensive and his officers talking him into waiting and preparing further (which I believed was his intention all along).

The congressional committees—I can't remember how many—came and visited. Their main message was one of impatience for action. Being from other states, they seemed little concerned about the destruction of Boston and the killing of its inhabitants that would ensue. Not so the General. But I wondered what he would do. Yes, the health and training and even the supply of powder had increased. The General's exaggerations of our strength may have discouraged the British from breaking the siege, but it also encouraged the congressmen to believe that victory was imminent—if only the General would stop being so cautious and attack. Congress was of two minds: wait and see if the British would yield to petitions, and move to attack at once.

Meanwhile, the rough numerical parity of our forces was threatening to disappear. Most of these men had short-term enlistments. The

Connecticut and Rhode Island troops' enlistments expired in December of 1775; the New Hampshire and Massachusetts troops' enlistments expired in January. As some men departed, others arrived from these states. The numbers dipped to eight thousand, then rose back up to twelve thousand. This didn't exactly help training. It seemed like every day in December the General was out addressing another regiment, urging the men to continue until the end of the Boston siege. Nothing irritated the General more than the states' unwillingness to enlist men for long periods.

That December, as we sat by the fire in his Cambridge headquarters looking out at the freezing Charles River, his frustration at the states erupted. "Josiah, they are so enraged at the British troops that have been quartered here that they will not support a standing army. Do they realize the average British private has served and trained for years? And they expect me to drive these troops out of Boston without powder while disbanding one army and recruiting and training another, all within musket shot of twenty British regiments. If I had the power"—there was an uncomfortable pause as there always was when the General talked about what he would do if he had the power—"we would establish a national standing army."

"If I had the power . . ." The General used that phrase hundreds of times, and I kept thinking of those words during that week in Newburgh.

The General's irritation at the huge turnover would continue throughout the war, but with the help of cash bounty and land grant offers, and improving prospects, we were able to enlist men for longer terms, some for the duration of the war.

General Gage, the first British commander in Boston, was the only British commander who personally irritated the General. The cause of the irritation was General Gage's insistence on treating American prisoners of war as common criminals and putting them in jail. This treatment was extended to American officers because Gage would not recognize any rank not given by the king. To the General, this violated not only the rules of war but the treatment expected by those of English descent. The General did not respond in kind to the British prisoners we held, despite the urging of many subordinates and congressmen. "We will not, Josiah, sink so low. Our struggle must be based on the principles that Englishmen have adhered to for centuries."

It was in the early months of 1776 that there occurred a series of events that the General's admirers attributed to his skill, his critics attributed to either luck or British incompetence, and the General attributed to Providence.

First General Knox was able to drag almost sixty captured mortars and howitzers from Fort Ticonderoga in New York all the way to the outskirts of Boston. This was an outstanding feat, but Knox's movement of artillery was helped when the roads, usually muddy in the spring, mysteriously froze.

Then the General ordered our troops, under cover of darkness, to seize the surprisingly unoccupied Dorchester Heights that loomed above Boston. With the help of covered wagon wheels and salvos from our troops elsewhere, the British neither saw nor heard the operation— a fog enshrouded the lower parts of the Heights—and were unable to stop us. With no fog at the top of the Heights, in one night thousands of our troops dug fortifications and entrenched our newly arrived cannon. I heard the General exhorting the New Englanders, "Remember, it is the fifth of March [the anniversary of the Boston Massacre]. Avenge the deaths of your brethren." I watched those nearby pass the General's words to the men out of earshot and imagined the message spreading throughout the troops.

The next morning, with the weather fine, the General and I climbed the Heights again to see what the troops had accomplished. It was exhilarating to see Boston and the British troops spread out beneath the Ticonderoga cannon and the General standing among our dirty, triumphant men.

I later heard from a captured British officer that General Howe, who had replaced General Gage, looked through his telescope in the morning and remarked, "The rebels have done more in one night than my whole army could do in months." The British told the citizens of Boston that a force of ten thousand had dug such fortifications in one night. Actually, it was less than two thousand, but with the General's words of urging and praise ringing in their ears, they may have dug like ten thousand.

With the guns looking down on them, the British started sending troops by boat across the Charles River to mount an assault on the Heights. Again, however, another of those providential events occurred. The fine day suddenly turned stormy; wind and fog wrecked many boats and drove others back. As night fell, so did snow and sleet. At that point, the British realized they faced a devastating bombardment from above, to which they could not respond, and started negotiations. Their message essentially was: "Give us safe passage by ship out of Boston; in return, we will not harm any inhabitants or buildings in Boston."

The General readily agreed. "Josiah, we not only save the city from destruction and give assurance to other seaboard cities the enemy may occupy, but this withdrawal will be regarded by the public both here and across the seas as a great victory."

He was right. The British people looked on the withdrawal as a huge defeat—Blundering Tom was the label they applied to poor General Gage—but the colonists marveled at how Boston had been reclaimed with so little loss of life.

As I've mentioned several times, the General would probably have denied it, but I don't think he made a decision without considering what today we are starting to call public opinion.

In the intervening years, I've read that every commander in our army who attended the council of war claimed credit for the Dorchester Heights strategy. It is true that the General first advanced the idea of a frontal assault and then was gradually persuaded to mount the move on the Heights. I remember the General at the time commending his commanders for their wisdom, but did they really convince him? Or did the General just allow them to bring him to the decision he favored all along? With the General, I never could be sure.

Yet I don't think it was just that the General used smart military tactics at Boston. It was how he knitted the forces from many states together. I told you how he broke up the brawl between the Massachusetts and Virginia regiments. I vividly remember another incident that showed the General's political rather than military touch. When the British evacuated, and the General had sent a letter congratulating the Congress, the General let Massachusetts' General Ward lead his regiments into Boston while the General and other troops trailed behind. Massachusetts' troops exulted, but the citizens of Boston knew to whom they owed their rescue and newfound freedom, and influential citizens like Abigail Adams, whose house in nearby Braintree had shaken with the cannon blasts, marveled and spread exaggerated tales of the General's modesty. I can assure you the General was not modest. I never saw a man more vain about his public appearance and public perception. He just appreciated that the citizens would view him more favorably if he appeared modest.

The General retained this humble demeanor—and his sense of humor—when Harvard, no longer a hotbed of loyalist professors, gave him an honorary degree. Since I believe it was the first degree Harvard ever gave to a military officer, it just further enhanced the General's reputation for modesty. After the entry to Boston, we attended a church service where we heard a sermon on Exodus by the Reverend Abiel Leonard comparing us to the ancient Israelites and implying again that the General was Moses. The General sat quietly in his square pew, surrounded by the joy and admiration of men and minister.

II. DISASTER IN NEW YORK

The unfortunate aftermath of the victory at Boston was that it raised expectations—many congressmen and their constituents expected quick, bloodless victories that would end the war. They were soon to be disillusioned by the campaign in New York. By the end of that campaign, the British appeared to be on the verge of winning the war, and the General's reputation appeared to be in tatters.

When the British sailed out of Boston for Halifax, most everyone expected that after refitting, the British navy would return to New York with troop reinforcements. It was understood that the Continental Army would move down to New York to meet them. The General was dubious about defending New York City. In a complete reversal of the situation in Boston, the British would not be bottled up; they would have the ability to strike whenever and wherever they wanted. Not only would the British have a large numerical advantage but they would have us surrounded rather than vice versa.

"Josiah," the General muttered to me one afternoon after all the British troops had departed Boston, "certainly we don't want the British to move from New York up the Hudson and cut off New England from the rest of our states, but the city itself means very little. Besides, it is probably the most Tory-infested city in America. I would prefer to draw the British army out of the city into the interior and fight them with Indian tactics to maximize our own advantages. Eventually, the Parliament will tire of the war, and we will prevail."

Yet the Congress was still dictating military strategy and believed it was important to morale that every major city should be defended.

Later, the General confessed to me that he should have resisted Congress. "Goodness knows, Josiah, that in the last war I carried out foolish plans by Governor Dinwiddie and always paid a price." I assumed he was referring to his decision to move ahead to Fort Necessity back in the 1750s without a full complement of troops, thus leading to that embarrassing surrender. "Josiah, we shall not let governors or Congress do this to us again."

What the Congress and the General did not know was that the British soon would appear off New York City, reinforced from London with hundreds more ships than left Boston and almost twenty thousand additional troops, including thousands of hired Hessian soldiers, who were among the finest professional fighting men in Europe.

General Charles Lee had been dispatched by the General to New York to draw up a defensive plan. The problem was that when you defend everything, you defend nothing, something the General should have realized. The British ships soon appeared and dominated the waters around the city. Much time in endless councils was spent trying to decide where the British would strike. A large number of our out-numbered and little-trained troops were concentrated in Long Island, but many troops were stationed in Manhattan and New Jersey. The General remained in Manhattan. The British landed in Long Island, made short work of American defenses, and easily drove our troops back with huge casualties.

When the General and I crossed the East River to Long Island and moved inland, we were met by thousands of fleeing troops. It was a scene I was to see frequently during the war: American troops fleeing their better-armed, better-trained, and more numerous adversaries and the General riding full bore ahead on Old Nelson trying to rally his officers and men.

A semblance of order was restored, and night fell with thousands of American troops backed up against the East River awaiting annihilation in the morning. What then took place was that combination of providential intervention, American inventiveness, and generalship in the face of adversity that characterized the turning of routs into marginal defeats during the war.

The General quickly decided that to leave his battered troops until morning would invite obliteration. "Defense where there is no prospect of victory and no place to retreat to, Josiah, is doomed to failure," the General said to me on many occasions, and while I do not recall, that might have been the first time. In the midst of a pelting rain, the General called on the mariners and fishermen from Massachusetts to commandeer all the barges and small boats possible and move five thousand of our troops across the East River in the middle of the night and early morning.

Unfortunately, it became clear that not all the men would cross safely before the sun rose. No matter . . . a dense fog suddenly descended upon the East River so that the British could see nothing when the morning came. Every last man was evacuated. The General took the last boat, and the British, by now understanding what was happening, fired through the fog, their bullets whizzing by the General and our boat. I tried to follow the General's example and remain standing in the boat, but I was frightened and relieved when we reached the center of the river and I could sit down without appearing too cowardly. Colonel Benjamin Tallmadge told me it was one of the General's most brilliant decisions of the war; the General's critics said it was pure luck.

As our barge approached the shores of Manhattan through the remaining wisps of fog, I pondered for the first time a question that haunted me the whole war. What would the General do if he were captured? This increasingly became the British aim, as they rightly believed the General's capture would stomp out the rebellion. The General often spoke admiringly of his hero, the Roman counsel Cato, for committing suicide to vindicate liberty rather than accept a life under tyranny. Still, the General loved his family and life so much that it was hard to imagine such an outcome. Would he ask me to write melodramatic letters to Martha and his stepchildren about honor and duty? We all took the idea of British plots to capture the General much more seriously after the summer of 1776. First an anonymous letter exposed the General's housekeeper, Mary Smith, as a British spy, and she fled to England; then, another letter attributed a poison plot to the British governor in New York, William Tryon; and finally, several of the General's own private guards confessed to a plot to spirit the General away. These incidents rattled headquarters, but the General told his aides to keep the information secret, as he was afraid public disclosure might encourage violence by citizens against loyalists and distract from the war effort. The General, as I said, was never one to be distracted from the greater task at hand.

I reflected on the possibility of my own capture and recognized that, while I thought little of this at the beginning of the war, my views had started to evolve. Slowly wasting away from untreated illness or lack of food and water on one of those ships off New York where the British had started to keep prisoners seemed a most unromantic way to die. Forsaking the return to the family merchant house to work with a father who believed me unfit was one thing; forsaking a recent fiancée who would not bear my children was another. As the war wore on, I found myself thinking less of heroic death from combat or imprisonment and more of Prescilla.

What followed our escape across the East River was the saddest part of the war and raised great doubts about the General's ability. Even I, his aide, who had admired his generalship in Boston, was ready to join the critical chorus, although I never said so to the General. We again did not know where the British would strike next, and so the General kept his forces concentrated to the north on Manhattan Island.

On September 15, when the British and their Hessian allies landed smartly near what is now Thirty-Fourth Street on the East River, our limited forces—there is no other way to put this—ran for their lives. The General rode down from Harlem to see his officers and men fleeing. I have said the General was a calculating man, but in that moment calculation gave way to spontaneous anger. He struck several officers in an unavailing effort to stem the flight. I thought for a moment he was going to charge right into the British lines. I was a hundred yards to the rear and saw several officers grab his reins and persuade him to withdraw.

The British could have pursued our troops up Manhattan, but for some reason—perhaps because they wanted to await the landing of more troops—General Howe chose not to. I have read that this was just another example of how bad British generalship made the General look good. In any event, many of the General's advisors advocated setting fire to the city that night. The General, believing the recapture of the city was impossible given British control of the waters surrounding it, and also believing New York to be infested with loyalists, was reluctantly inclined to agree. An order from Congress solved the General's dilemma, arriving with explicit instructions not to destroy New York. Fires started in the city soon afterward, probably set by rebels angry at the British and their loyalist friends, and most of lower Manhattan burned anyway.

As the British troops finally moved northward, our troops performed with more discipline, firing and retreating before overwhelming numbers in an orderly manner. There then took place one of those strange events that always left one wondering whether the General had behaved irrationally or with strategic genius. As the British advanced, their bugles blew as if they were chasing foxes. This was, to say the least, insulting to our men, and the General, who had stationed some of his best Virginia, Connecticut, and Maryland troops in a brush-covered ravine, ordered an attack as the British started across an open field. Our men fired from behind trees, stone walls, and fences, the bugles stopped blowing, and the British beat a hasty retreat, leaving many of their dead behind. The victory was small, but after the previous days of disorganization, the news spread quickly and lifted morale.

Morale was further reinforced when the British tried to land behind the General at the north end of Manhattan. They could have captured the General and destroyed the main American army, but again, for reasons known only to the Almighty, they chose to land at the marsh at Throgs Neck. While they labored across the marsh, Pennsylvanian riflemen decimated their ranks, forcing a withdrawal. The General then withdrew our forces across the Harlem River to the Bronx while another fortuitous change in the weather brought storms that delayed a further British attack.

When the next attack came, a few miles away at Pell's Point, a Massachusetts brigade under Colonel John Glover retreated in good order, inflicting heavy losses. The brigade, one of our best outfits, was made up of New England fishermen, Negroes, and Indians. As superior British forces advanced, our first line of defense would rise and fire into the British ranks. As the British drew their feared bayonets for a charge, our first line swiftly retreated behind a second line. The next line then rose with the British approach and fired before retreating, while reloading, behind a third line. In this manner, an orderly retreat was maintained while inflicting heavy losses on the enemy. While these tactics were later widely used by our forces and attributed to the General (although he never claimed authorship), I know they were initiated that day by Colonel Glover at Pell's Point. The General embraced and used these tactics for the rest of the war against more numerous advancing enemy forces, although I suppose he deserves some credit for knowing how to adapt.

The General moved his forces across the Hudson to retreat through New Jersey, but not before we watched the saddest defeat and biggest indictment of the General's leadership in the whole war. Fort Washington on the northern tip of the island was still manned by over a thousand Americans. The General decided to withdraw those troops to join the main force in New Jersey, but at a council of his generals, he allowed General Greene, who was later to distinguish himself as one of our ablest generals, to convince him to leave the fort occupied. The argument was that the fort was impregnable and was tying up large numbers of British and Hessian troops. The General acceded, and I do believe that, although he called many councils of war in the future, he never again allowed such a council to override one of his strong instincts. Loyalists, of whom there were many in New York, showed the British how to attack the fort, and our forces, outnumbered by over four to one, after fighting valiantly, surrendered. Surrender did not save many of our survivors, who were then bayoneted by the Hessians, outraged by their losses in the previous days. All of this the General saw by telescope from the Jersey shore. It was the only time I saw tears come to his eyes. The General refrained from blaming others and cursed himself for making a horrendous mistake, which it certainly was. He also took full responsibility, which was great fodder for his critics.

Some of the General's critics, especially General Charles Lee, started spreading the word that the General was "indecisive" and implied he should be replaced, presumably by Lee. But the critics were not among the ranks. The soldiers adored the General for his willingness to take the same risks they did in facing enemy fire. Perhaps they also realized that five of the hundreds of British frigates in New York waters had more firepower than all the American guns on shore and that their British and Hessian opponents were better fed, better clothed, and better trained, and outnumbered our men by over three to one. I have since learned that the average British private had fifteen years' service, while our men had, in many cases, only served months.

Nonetheless, the General's reputation, which had been so strong after Boston, had now sunk to where his critics in Congress and elsewhere were emboldened. The General, as always sensitive to public opinion, was well aware of all this. I drafted a letter to his cousin Lund at Mount Vernon saying that he was never so unhappy and that he was tempted to resign but that many were telling him that "if I leave the service, all will be lost."

The General mused to me that the challenge was to match our strategy to the strength of our troops, and he believed that New York had provided the necessary lessons. Never again would he defend major cities where the British controlled surrounding waters. And never again would he ask his men to defend points, no matter how well fortified, when the odds were long. "Josiah," he said wryly, "the honor of making a brave defense does not seem to be a sufficient stimulus when the success is very doubtful and falling into the enemy's hands probable." Rather, the General intended, no matter what the advice of Congress or other generals, to adopt a strategy of retreating before the superior British and Hessian forces, exacting a cost where possible, and launching surprise attacks where circumstances showed the probability of a favorable outcome. While he called frequent councils of war on tactics, I never saw the General deviate from that strategy.

As we retreated across New Jersey that chilly November, the critics' voices grew louder. The British crossed the Hudson after us, capturing supplies and weapons. Congressmen, openly, and Generals Lee and Gates, behind his back, asked why the General did not stand and fight. But the General followed his strategy, and while I had my doubts at the time, it proved to be correct. How did these critics expect the General, with two thousand men—there were many desertions—to stop the ten thousand British and Hessians occupying New Jersey towns? Of course, if you counted all the Americans under arms, including the armies commanded by generals appointed by Congress such as Heath, Lee, and Gates, as well as the militia in twelve states, the British numerical superiority largely disappeared. But the other generals kept their forces in New York, New England, and the uncontested part of New Jersey and, counting on the loyalty of friendly congressmen, refused to join our forces. And what good did a thousand militia in North Carolina or any other state do to help us in New Jersey?

We retreated across New Jersey with the British and Hessian troops in pursuit. Our numbers grew smaller—the desertions and expiring enlistments vastly outnumbered new recruits. It was amazing to me how the spirit of freedom seemed to ebb as the prospects for victory diminished. At the same time, however, with smaller numbers, our professionalism was rising. General William Howe's strategy seemed to be to deliberately occupy New Jersey as he had New York City, while his brother, Admiral Richard Howe, occupied Newport and the surrounding parts of Rhode Island.

I found our retreat and the British occupation of New Jersey in the fall of 1776 the most demoralizing time in the war. At least three thousand (and some said as many as ten thousand) citizens in New Jersey pledged allegiance to the king. Why, even one of the signers of the Declaration of Independence, Richard Stockton, did so. In many towns, the British were welcomed and dined. General Howe thought that, if the British occupied another key state, the resistance would be broken, and the majority of Americans, who he believed loyal to the crown, would rise up and take control of their towns. While the citizens defecting were many, in our largely middle-class country, it seemed to me the defectors were mostly rich or poor.

I know that, while maintaining his outward calm to troops and congressmen, the General despaired during the war. I, too, despaired, at least to myself, for our whole effort. Over a glass of Madeira, the General had me put down his musings again about resigning in a letter to his cousin Lund. As ever concerned about his reputation, the General said that if he did not resign, he would lose what was left of his reputation, but if he did resign, ruin would follow. Then, as if taken aback by his own words, he quickly said, "Josiah, don't tell anyone." I didn't, but felt the war was on the verge of being lost. I didn't realize—and perhaps the General didn't either—that we were entering the third major campaign that was to change the course of the war and restore, perhaps forever, the General's reputation.

As I look back, many positive things came out of our retreat through New Jersey and across the Delaware River. First, one of the General's chief rivals, Charles Lee, was captured by the British after he left his troops for a sexual escapade with a woman engaged in prostitution. Second, while our forces were much smaller than in Boston or New York, they had become far more professional. Third, as the British approached the Delaware River and Philadelphia, the congressmen panicked, and, with only the General standing between them and the British, in early December issued directives giving the General full powers over the army. No longer would Congress be meddling in military strategy. General Gates, seeing the change, started moving his troops southward to join us. Finally, those who welcomed the British and Hessians soon had cause for regrets as, despite General Howe's orders against it, farms and homes were pillaged. I remember hearing the stories of rapes committed by British and Hessian soldiers, stories that even now I cannot comfortably repeat.

If General Howe could do things over again, I am sure he would have sent everything he had at our weakened army and destroyed or captured us and the General. I believe there is a good chance that he could have succeeded. Instead, after spreading his forces across New Jersey, he followed the European custom of suspending operations for the winter.

Nonetheless, I have never seen the General so depressed. He knew that the British had us on the run and that, not only in New Jersey but throughout the colonies, the feeling was growing that the war would soon be over. "Josiah, we must somehow find a way to achieve a victory or else the play will be over," the General told me. I don't believe the General was thinking of some major triumph on the battlefield but some event that would rally public support and restore morale. The General read newspapers avidly, and, while I thought it odd, sometimes he seemed more concerned with the public's opinion of events than the map of the battlefield. But I now realize he also read the newspapers to gauge how Americans felt about the independence effort. Their feelings in late 1776 were, to say the least, quite pessimistic. In retrospect, this is not surprising, given the huge number of Americans who were either loyalist or neutral.

Despite writing letters of despair to Superintendent of Finance Robert Morris about the probability of a congressional evacuation of Philadelphia, the General saw some hopeful signs. With the enemy in winter quarters, with our forces starting to rise with reinforcements from Southern states, with our ships running the blockade from the West Indies bringing blankets and clothing, and with our foundries producing more arms and powder, the General mused that perhaps the winter was the time to implement the second part of his strategy—to attack where surprise and numbers created an advantage.

III. TRIUMPH—THE FIRST CROSSING OF THE DELAWARE

Many officers and aides claimed credit for the idea for crossing the Delaware and attacking the Hessians at Trenton. All I can say is that many may have had the idea, but the General had talked to me already in mid-December about recrossing the Delaware to surprise the Hessians at Trenton or the British at Princeton. He knew that, by concentrating our forces on a New Jersey Hessian outpost, for the first time we would have a rare numerical advantage. Trenton was a village where the Hessians were camped for the winter, just south of the lower falls of the Delaware River that separated Pennsylvania from New Jersey. If we could get our artillery across the Delaware, we would have a huge advantage in guns. Just as important, the General knew that, while our forces had risen to near 2,400 with arrivals from the South, we were again about to be decimated at the end of the year as enlistments expired.

The decision was made in one of those councils the General loved to call to pick apart a proposal. By the end of the meeting, he had gathered unanimous support. Some of the generals who might have counseled caution were not there. Gates, after finally heeding the General's order to come down from the North, refused a command. Pleading illness, he went on to Philadelphia to criticize the emerging plan to his friends in Congress and, I was told, to lobby for the General's removal in favor of himself. Then also, Charles Lee, the General's other major rival and critic, was still held a prisoner by the British.

My, it was cold that Christmas evening! The trail to the river was filled with the bloody footprints of shoeless soldiers. The troops lined up beside the dark, icy river, not knowing if they were marching back to Philadelphia or across the Delaware. (The General had grown very wary about leaking plans to enemy spies.)

The raid involved four parties, and two of the smaller parties never made it through the ice across the river, while a third party crossed the river and created a diversion in southern New Jersey. Fortunately, the General was with the main and far most numerous party. The Pennsylvania boatmen and the Marblehead mariners had lined up all the boats within sixty miles on the river. The larger Durham boats, almost eight feet wide and forty feet long, were used to ship the artillery across, which was no easy task.

As we started across the river, I remember thinking the whole operation should be called off. It seemed preposterous. The nickname the General chose for the operation, Victory or Death, seemed melodramatic to me, but the last word seemed more appropriate as I envisioned the destruction of our remaining army, the capture of the General, the inevitable fall of Philadelphia, and, last but not least, my own demise. If these events happened, they would so destroy the spirit for independence that the pledging of allegiance to the king, which had swept through New Jersey, would sweep through the rest of the colonies and end the war. We'd fail to gain independence just as the Scottish had thirty years earlier.

I don't know how the men did it, but it was so cold I believe they preferred moving to standing still in that weather. The men passed the General as they moved onto the boats, and his commanding presence inspired confidence. Our force had shrunk to mostly battle-tested and resolute veterans, many of whom had been with the General for the whole war. We bumped into and off blocks of ice, and the waves crested over the sides of our boats, drenching every inch of our ragged clothing. Some were standing and paddling, and others were holding oars to ward off the ice. On a normal, more placid crossing, those of us in the middle would have sat down, but not on that night—no one wanted to sit in the icy water that had already submerged our shoes and the bottoms of our leggings. It took so long for our main party to cross the river that, even if everything went well thereafter, I thought we would never reach Trenton before morning and surprise the Hessians.

The most amazing incident took place after the crossing when we came to Jacobs Creek. Under the light of a few swinging lanterns, it was hard enough for the men to climb up the icy bank but far more difficult for the horses. As the General tried to bring Old Nelson up the embankment, the white chestnut-faced horse slipped and started sliding down into the creek. The General grabbed his mane and, with one swift movement, righted the horse. I was not much of a horseman, but I was left marveling at how strong and skilled the General was. Those who described him as the finest horseman in the colonies did not exaggerate by much.

The General divided his force into two parts, with one marching straight toward Trenton where the Hessians were encamped and the other sweeping around to the side and rear. Then one of those peculiar things happened that the General's critics again attributed to luck and he to Divine Providence. While we were indeed running late and the sun had started to rise, snow began falling so that none of the Hessian sentries could see our approaching forces.

You may have read that the Hessians were drunk with Christmas revelry. Don't believe it. The Hessians were on alert—we learned on our way to Trenton that they had skirmished that evening with a small group of American militia—and when we attacked the outlying guard posts, they turned out smartly with their weapons and showed great discipline. But our force was overwhelming, and our artillery fired with devastating effect down the main streets of the town. Then the General shouted, "March on, my brave fellows, after me," and our troops did just that, their spirits rising as more and more Hessians either fell in our hail of bullets or surrendered.

My goodness, it was a bloody scene. I had never seen such carnage, and I desperately tried to control my increasingly upset stomach. When I commented to the General on the bloody corpses and crying wounded, the General would only say, "Josiah, it was just as bad at the massacre with Braddock. The groans of the wounded pierced my heart then. Believe me, Josiah, it is much better to see the corpses of the enemy rather than your own men." I thought General Knox, who like me had not fought in the previous war, described the scene quite well when he reminisced to me later: "The hurry, fright and confusion of the enemy was [not] unlike that which will be when the last trumpet shall sound."

Our losses were small, and I do believe the Hessians lost almost a thousand men to death, wounds, or capture. I saw no signs of drinking, except when some of our men broke into the Hessians' rum supply and celebrated, much to the General's annoyance. But this breach of discipline did not stop the General from turning to me and saying, "Josiah, this is a glorious day for our country."

What we learned later was that the victory set off all sorts of recriminations between the British and the Hessians and a frenzy of debate in Britain about the morality of hiring mercenaries to fight Britain's wars, particularly against British subjects.

We withdrew back across the Delaware. The General, always alert to popular opinion, dictated numerous letters to governors and congressmen, north and south, relaying the news of our Trenton success. I think the letters also had another purpose: allaying fears of the General. Some said the added powers the Congress had given the General made him a dictator, although I think it finally just made him, in truth, the commanding general. If he was a dictator, at that time he certainly continued to show deference to the Congress. Whether he would do so that week in Newburgh was another matter.

IV. Triumph Again—The Second Crossing of the Delaware

The first battle of Trenton had ended, but what many do not know is that the second battle of Trenton was far more crucial to our success. The idea of recrossing the Delaware for another surprise attack on enemy outposts may have come from Colonel John Cadwalader, who had led the other crossing party into New Jersey and reported the panic among the British and Hessians after the first battle of Trenton. There then came another one of those endless councils the General called, this one at the widow Harris's house on the Pennsylvania side of the Delaware. The General presented the recrossing as Cadwalader's idea, whether it was or not. The General, as I've said, never seemed to present any idea as his own. I always assumed this was to make sure there was free discussion. It was amazing how the General, with his questions, guided that meeting from almost outright opposition to unanimous support. After all, here was the proposal that our army, after two days' rest, still exhausted and bedraggled, should move to attack again.

I believe the deciding factor, besides the chance to sow more panic among the enemy, was that many enlistments were to expire at the end of the year. While our forces were growing—it was amazing how news of one victory could lead to new enlistments even in two or three days—hundreds were unfit to march, and at the end of the year our forces might fall dramatically with the loss of the Delaware regiment, Glover's Marblehead Regiment, and many other individual troops.

The General knew that the undermanned outposts in southern New Jersey offered tempting targets, but the supply obstacles were greater than before the first crossing. Merchants in Pennsylvania had joined merchants in New Jersey in refusing to sell food and clothing for the increasingly worthless Continental currency. The army's commissary in Pennsylvania, Carpenter Wharton, was incompetent, corrupt, or both, and the General had to go over his head to Superintendent of Finance Robert Morris in Philadelphia to bring supplies from Virginia and New England. Worse, the Delaware was now completely frozen, which, while enabling the men to cross on foot, would make it more difficult for horses, artillery, wagons, and tents, which moved more safely across water in boats. Most important was that the end of the year was upon us; if the General could not convince many of the troops to reenlist, there would not be the numbers or time for one more surprise attack.

I saw the General himself address most of our troops. I am told that today the terms of service are longer and, besides, the money offered is greater. But then it was a close thing. I remember the General's first appeal, even with a ten-dollar reenlistment bounty, moving few. The General had told me, quoting his favorite play, *Cato*, "I'll animate the soldiers' drooping courage, with love of freedom, and contempt of life. I'll thunder in their ears their country's cause, and try to rouse up all that's Roman in them." But it was not easy.

They had signed up for a year or six months, and they wanted to return home. But the General would not be denied. I remember his words, "My brave fellows, you have done all I asked you to do, and more than could reasonably be expected; but your country is at stake, your wives, your houses, and all that you hold dear."

This appeal resonated because the men had heard many tales of British and Hessian rape and plundering as their armies pursued us across New Jersey. The General went on, "You have worn yourselves out with the fatigues and hardships, but we know not how to spare you. If you will consent to stay one month longer, you will render that service to the cause of liberty, and to your country, which you can probably never do under any other circumstances."

A pause followed with much murmuring in the ranks, such as "I'll stay if you will." A few men stepped forward, and then more and more. Those men, and what they were to do in the next two weeks, would turn the tide of the war. They deserve the utmost credit. But I doubt it would have happened without a general who was willing to plead with his troops. I remember thinking at the time that British generals did not have to make such appeals. The thought of them appealing to rather than commanding their men was ludicrous.

Lately I have read that the General was both distant and imperious, as my great-grandchildren say their teacher has told them, but he was not that day. The men responded because they respected and admired a general who shared their privation. The General faced a problem: he didn't have the twenty-dollar bounty money he was now offering. An urgent appeal to Robert Morris produced enough funds, thanks, I am proud to say, to the contributions of some of my fellow Quakers— Philadelphia merchants who objected to fighting but less so to aiding those who did fight for independence. What the General would have done if that money had not arrived, I am not sure. Perhaps he would have made another appeal to the troops or perhaps he would have paid at least part of the bounties out of his own pocket. In any event, with the reenlistments and new enlistments inspired by our first Trenton victory and the news of enemy atrocities, our force had grown to thirty-three hundred men, the largest force we'd had in months. The militias operating in New Jersey were also starting to grow.

The General again moved the bulk of our forces across the Delaware to attack, but his plans soon had to change. General Howe in New York, alarmed by the reports from Trenton, stopped General Cornwallis from a leave trip to England and ordered him with reinforcements to Princeton. Upon his arrival, learning of our recrossing of the Delaware into Trenton, Cornwallis moved a column of over ten thousand British troops from Princeton for a direct attack on our forces.

The General seemed unconcerned. "Josiah, the British like to move in columns along roads. They may be ten thousand strong, but there can only be a few hundred at the head of the column. We will harass them from the woods along the road and then withdraw. It will be sunset before they reach Trenton. They will then attack as they always do, but they will have to cross the Assunpink Creek bridge. I noticed in our success a few days ago that the bridge can be covered well by both artillery and rifle fire. The lead elements of their column will not be able to cross the bridge. By that time it will be nightfall, and I can tell you from my experience in the French and Indian War that the British do not like to fight in the dark."

All of this came to pass. Over a thousand of our men held up the advancing column, exacting a heavy toll. Then the men fell back in an orderly manner across the bridge, where the General had stationed himself to offer thanks and encouragement. He saw that all men were instructed to fire low as the British and Hessians approached. Our troops tended to waste bullets firing over the heads of the British, but as the General pointed out to me, there was another reason for his instruction: a wound in the leg is better than a wound in the arm, because two other troops will have to drop their weapons in order to help the wounded soldier to the rear.

When the British tried to move their columns and guns across the bridge at Assunpink at sunset, they met such fire that the bridge was soon covered with red-coated bodies spouting blood. This was not just the Hessians but His Majesty's finest. I knew the Parliament would hear about this defeat.

Not all Americans managed the retreat across the bridge. With the General, I watched from the hill behind the creek as an American chaplain was forced to strip naked and kneel while he was bayoneted over and over by the Hessians as surrounding British soldiers cheered. Later,

I learned from the captured Hessians that their overall commander, Colonel Rall, outraged at the defeat at the first battle of Trenton, had urged his troops to take no prisoners. I thought of all the Hessian prisoners we held and the effect the preacher's murder would have on the hundreds of our troops who had witnessed it. Even though I was raised a Quaker, I found myself lusting for revenge. The General must have sensed what I was thinking because after grimacing, he turned and said, "Josiah, write an order that all Hessian prisoners are to be treated well and see that every commander receives the order and reads it to his troops. Include an explanation that we fight for a greater cause and that with good treatment we will convince the Hessians to change sides."

I don't know whether the General acted out of Christian principle or whether he was just pragmatically focused on how best to win the war. One could never tell with the General. I am told that no Hessian prisoners of war tried to escape, even when they had the opportunity, and that over a third decided to settle in America after the war.

As the General predicted, the British did not attack at night, but they brought up further reinforcements. This brought another council, which I assumed would end with us withdrawing across the Delaware. The other obvious choice was to stand and fight in the morning, not a tempting strategy given that Cornwallis would probably try to cross the creek at other places during the coming day and hit us from the sides and the rear.

In the end, we made a third, unexpected choice: to make an end run around enemy forces and strike the main British post, now more lightly defended, at Princeton. The idea came from General Arthur St. Clair, or else the General put him up to it. At first the idea was met with derision. Most of the men had not slept for almost forty-eight hours. But as the meeting, directed by the General with his usual skill, continued, opinions started to change. The General called in local citizens who reported that Cornwallis was marching still thousands more troops from Princeton to Trenton in anticipation of what, I later learned, the British general believed would be "the final battle of the war." A captured British officer later told me that Cornwallis had told his commanders, "We've got the Old Fox surrounded now. We'll go over and bag him in the morning."

The Old Fox, however, was not to be there in the morning.

The troops built fires, left them burning, and then started noisy pick and shovel work. The purpose was to convince the British and Hessians that either another early-morning attack like the first battle of Trenton was imminent or we were digging in to stop another assault on the bridge in the morning. Meanwhile, the troops wrapped the wagon and artillery wheels with cloth to muffle the noise as they moved out. Again no one was told where they were going. Local guides directed us to trails that would bypass Cornwallis's forces.

There then took place a very curious change in the weather. The day before, when Cornwallis had advanced from Princeton, rising temperatures had turned the roads and trails to mud, slowing progress. Now the temperature quickly fell below freezing again, leaving the roads and trails hard enough for our rapid movement. The skies were darkened with clouds covering all stars and obscuring roads. Providence, I decided, was at work again.

Still, not everything went as planned. A few militia units, panicked in the dark and mistaking our own troops for the enemy, fled toward Burlington, New Jersey. The General, however, had shrewdly placed our regular units between militia units to minimize such panics. Our movement was so rapid that Horace Walpole in Britain after the war compared the General on that evening to the Roman general Fabius, and European military experts marveled at how a body of troops could move so fast, especially in the dark. What they didn't know was that our sleep-deprived soldiers were frequently stumbling and held upright by friends.

The morning brought a beautiful day, and we quickly advanced more than half the way to Princeton across Stony Brook and along the

Quaker bridge road. But then occurred a piece of damnable ill luck. We were spotted from the main Princeton–Trenton road by the last British column moving to support Cornwallis at Trenton. Actually we spotted each other about the same time. The General had an excellent view and immediately dispatched me to ride to General Hugh Mercer and order him to move up his Pennsylvania militia brigade from a ravine and defend against what British officers always do—attack.

Our initial defense was successful, but the main British column commanded by Colonel Mawhood kept attacking, shot most of General Mercer's officers out of their saddles, drew bayonets, and charged into our breaking lines. I rode as fast as possible, fearing as I never had during the whole war that I would be caught and bayoneted. General Mercer, after trying to rally his men, followed. I looked behind me from a nearby ridge and saw General Mercer fall from his horse. He was quickly surrounded by redcoats, who from their cries thought they had chanced upon General Washington. They yelled at Mercer, demanding, "Damn you, rebel, give quarter." I heard him shout, "I am no rebel," and he drew his sword to lunge at his tormentors. They bayoneted him several times, thinking they had killed the General. I just sat on my horse, looking back, shaking with terror and exhaustion, ashamed that I had left General Mercer behind. I was not proud of my actions that day, but I could not think of anything but my own safety.

As I rode back toward our main forces, I encountered the General, who did not seem at all dismayed by Mercer's retreating brigade. "Josiah, we have them. This is one of those rare times when by chance we have them outnumbered." Shouting at me to stay in place and await further orders, he led an array of Delaware, Connecticut, and Maryland regiments, rallied the retreating Pennsylvania militia, and rode toward the enemy, shouting, "Parade with us, my brave fellows! There is but a handful of the enemy, and we shall have them directly."

It was truly amazing. Following the General's example, our troops poured forward. I looked down from a nearby hill. The General was out front on Old Nelson, and the British troops were firing at him from no more than thirty paces. And yet they did not hit him. It reminded me of those old Indian tales about the General having supernatural protection and the story of how he found the sound of bullets "exhilarating." It all struck me, who had never lost my fear whenever I was near the front lines, as unbelievable. But watching the General that day from one hundred yards to the rear, both the tales and story seemed so true. The thought occurred to me that maybe the General wanted a glorious death. It would have enhanced his reputation, something he surely desired. But it did seem that Providence was indeed watching out for the General that day.

Later, I heard soldiers speak of that day with wonder. As our troops led by the General surged ahead, the British troops broke, just as we had so many times. Seizing his chance, the General urged his troops in pursuit: "It is a fine fox chase, my boys." Our riflemen were relentless, and I saw the bodies of hundreds of British soldiers shot in the back while fleeing. I had never seen British soldiers flee like this, nor had any of our troops. I did not tell my Quaker relatives, but I must admit it was an exhilarating experience.

The General reorganized our troops, and we moved quickly on to Princeton, where we forced the surrender of the few British defenders and helped ourselves to supplies. Only the total exhaustion of our troops kept the General from moving on and attacking the major British supply depot in Brunswick.

The day had been a glorious one. The General immediately sent out messengers to various militia units throughout the state ordering attacks on British installations. The General seemed to have forgotten his disdain for volunteer units now that his regulars had whipped the British. Cornwallis ordered his troops back from Trenton not to seek us out—although they still greatly outnumbered us—but, amid the confusion, to abandon their posts and retreat to the safety of New York. The British troops and their Hessian allies had seemed so disciplined and organized just a week before. Now they were in total disarray as our regular and irregular forces harassed them all the way back to the Hudson River. "General Washington is coming," the British troops screamed as they fled across New Jersey. Of course, the General could not be in so many places; it just seemed that way to the now-disorganized British and Hessian troops.

In the days that followed, thousands of citizens were burning their certificates of allegiance to the king signed just weeks before, and thousands more across the land rushed to enlist. The General was acting as New Jersey's chief executive. Upon the General's instructions, I wrote orders allowing loyalist families safe passage to British-held New York. The General worried that, after all the pillaging by the British, Hessians, and loyalists, the latter might now face massacres.

I delighted in reading the intercepted letters of British junior officers. One wrote, "We have been outgeneraled." Another complained to his relatives at home that "our men fight well, but our generals are no match for Washington."

Just a month ago I had written those letters for the General to his cousin Lund back at Mount Vernon, despairing of his reputation. Now the congratulations were pouring in. I do believe our people thought Divine Providence was at work. One letter to the General that I opened said, "The Lord has smote the enemy and you are our Moses." The General wrote courteous responses but made little comment to me on these extravagant comparisons, which led to my later concerns. Still, I could tell how relieved he was as we settled into quarters at Morristown, New Jersey. His reputation had been not ruined but resurrected.

Later, we received congratulations from Frederick the Great: "The achievements of Washington and his little band of compatriots between the 25th of December and the 4th of January, a space of ten days, were the most brilliant of any recorded in the annals of military achievements." For a general concerned about what others thought of him, those were sweet words, coming as they did from one of the greatest military strategists of all time.

The General did not gloat, but, always concerned about his place in history, he said to me, "Josiah, this has been a glorious time. Will our descendants remember us?"

I did not realize it at the time, but during that month, the War for Independence was won. I believe the British and Hessian troops, including the officers, knew after the two battles at Trenton and the one on the road to Princeton that they could not prevail.

It was hard to see that truth as the war continued for seven more years. The British moved still more troops to America. There was the ordeal at Valley Forge where over 20 percent of our soldiers died from lack of nourishment and exposure, and the even worse ordeal two winters later at Morristown. There were more battles, most in Pennsylvania and most ending inconclusively, increasing Congress's frustration with the General's largely defensive strategy against our more numerous opponents. There was some brutal fighting in the South as the British organized thousands of loyalists there, but since I was not present as Generals Greene and Lafayette commanded our troops there, I do not have firsthand knowledge.

Just as with the victory at Boston, expectations were unjustly raised; soon, memories of the triumphs on the Delaware started to fade from the minds of some of the congressional and military critics. Still, the accolades from European observers like Frederick and the British press, the devotion of the troops and the General's staff, and the cheers from the citizenry, many of whom had relatives among the troops, intimidated the General's would-be rivals and critics. Those closest to and furthest from the action held the highest opinion of Washington's generalship.

The Congress was highly upset when the General evacuated Philadelphia. So was I as I thought of Prescilla and what fate would befall her when British forces occupied the city. The stories of rape from New Jersey left me imagining the ravishing of Prescilla by British or Hessian soldiers or the plundering of my family. But no importuning by Congress or me could convince the General to repeat the mistake of New York.

When Philadelphia, almost as much a loyalist stronghold as New York, fell in the fall of 1777, the Tory sympathizers welcomed the British with huzzahs, dinners, and luxurious balls where Philadelphia's ladies flirted and puffed themselves up like pigeons for the British officers. I pictured Prescilla with her narrow waist, modest bodice, flowing black curls cascading down her neck, and soft brown eyes at those balls, and soon, I admit, I feared her seduction by a British colonel in a handsome uniform. Looking back, I am ashamed of my fears. Prescilla sent me a message that she never attended one ball and stayed home as much as possible to avoid British troops on the streets. I suspect my family did not behave as admirably, breaking the boycott of trade with Britain and financing "humanitarian" supplies for British forces.

The true importance of the victories in late 1776 and early 1777 was made clear to me when the General and I dined with General Cornwallis almost five years later on Chesapeake Bay the day after the surrender at Yorktown. I was sitting next to Cornwallis when he leaned over and said, "Your general may not have been a great general at the beginning of the war, but he certainly became a great general." Then he rose, offered a toast, and said, "When the illustrious part that your Excellency has borne in this long and arduous contest becomes a matter of history, fame will gather your brightest laurels rather from the banks of the Delaware than those of the Chesapeake."

Of course, while foreign leaders and most of our own people had come to admire the General's military skills, generals like Gates and the soon-to-be-released Lee still pleaded their cases to and conspired with the Congress. General Arnold defected and wreaked havoc down into Virginia, and men like John Adams continued to opine that they knew more about military affairs than the General.

I fear all these happenings have colored scholars' opinions of the General's leadership and will continue to. Still, after Trenton and

Princeton, the General's position was secure with the people and especially with the troops. Both the General and the Congress knew that if Congress replaced him, the hearty men who had fought at Trenton and Princeton and the citizenry would indeed rise up.

That's what made the week at Newburgh so tense and dramatic for a person such as me who believed in republican principles. All the troops needed was a signal from the General, the signal that never came in earlier mutinies. Of course, if the commanding officer led the way, could it really be called a mutiny? I suspected that if the General led, the troops would follow, and the congressmen, instead of debating the terms of peace with Britain, would find themselves racing to their homes for safety—that is, if they escaped the gallows.

During the years between Princeton and Yorktown, I saw even less emotion from the General than before. The one exception occurred in 1781 when the British sailed up the Potomac and raided Mount Vernon. It was not the raid that incensed the General but his cousin Lund's response. I took the personal dictation of the General's letter berating his cousin for saving Mount Vernon by providing supplies and slaves to the raiders. "It would be better that Mount Vernon had burned to the ground," the General advised his cousin. The words took me aback, knowing how the improvements at Mount Vernon had been the General's solace throughout the whole war. Still, I believed the emotion expressed by the General was genuine. Given the General's concern with his reputation, he probably feared his troops and the citizenry would think less of him because his cousin's collaboration, understandable as it was, had spared Mount Vernon.

V. Victory at Yorktown

Yorktown was the General's final test, and again it showed how views of his leadership changed from campaign to campaign. For years, through all the defensive battles after Trenton and Princeton, the General had been talking with the French generals about trapping a large British force on the coast where the General would concentrate our combined forces unexpectedly and, with the help of the French fleet, force a British surrender. The General's first choice was New York. I think he still smoldered from the thrashings the British had given us there and looked on a victory at New York as the ultimate vindication. Actually, the General would have been happy if the French fleet attacked the British forces in Charleston. I remember traveling hundreds of miles and enduring interminable formal dinners with the French generals and admirals at Newport, Rhode Island, and Wethersfield, Connecticut. The General shrugged and said to me, "We should remember the French are a people old in war and very strict in military etiquette." The French were opposed to any joint land and sea operation directed at New York. Perhaps they feared that the British fleet there was too powerful. Perhaps they were just reluctant to commit their troops. With the French troops camped in Newport, this had been a problem for years.

Anyway, when General Rochambeau sent the General word that the French fleet under the comte de Grasse would be sailing from the Caribbean to the Chesapeake, and Rochambeau's troops would be willing to join our forces, the General quickly abandoned New York for the new opportunity. Under Cornwallis, the British army fought many battles in the South, but harassed by Lafayette, they had withdrawn to Yorktown on the Virginia coast. I have read criticism of Cornwallis's decision, but at the time it seemed quite logical. He was looking for a place to rest his troops, await reinforcements for a campaign through Virginia, and have access to and from General Clinton and the main British garrison in New York.

He probably took into account the possibility of a French fleet cruising up from the Caribbean. He may have even envisioned the General moving his forces down from New York—after all, if that happened, General Clinton would certainly find out and send troops and supplies by sea that would be more than enough to both hold off and defeat our forces.

What Cornwallis underestimated was the General's ability to move both our fifty-eight hundred men and the French force of forty-eight hundred south so rapidly without arousing Clinton's suspicions. It was almost a repeat of what happened after the second battle of Trenton. The men lit campfires close to New York City, and small detachments harassed the British forces on the perimeter of the city. The General had me pen letters to citizens in New York and New Jersey—some of which he knew would be intercepted by the British—hinting at a coming American-French siege of New York. The wagon wheels again were covered with cloth so the departure would be as quiet as possible. The General moved his forces to the Yorktown peninsula while Clinton and Cornwallis still thought the General was quartered up the Hudson. The General's critics said Cornwallis, like all the British generals, was stupid and that this was just another example. But Cornwallis had a long and illustrious career that extended well after Yorktown, serving the British in Ireland and later in India. I have read he won many battles and was one of the king's most decorated generals. We considered Cornwallis by far the ablest of the British generals.

It was amazing to me how deferential the French commanders were to the General. They yielded command of their troops on the long march to Virginia and refused to accept Cornwallis's surrender, insisting upon Lafayette's urging that the British surrender directly to the General. Perhaps the French were being diplomatic, but based on their own observations and the reports from their superiors in Paris, I believe they had concluded that the General was one of the world's great commanders. I have in my files a copy of a letter from the French general Rochambeau pleading with the General to review the French troops: "If your Excellency does not find a moment to come and see this part of your army, I am afraid the whole of it will desert, so great is their desire to see their General." I suspect letters such as these must have boosted the General's spirits during all the internecine struggles with Congress, governors, and jealous fellow American generals. I did notice, however, that the opinion held by Congress of the General rose as opinion abroad of the General soared.

Despite his now rising reputation, the General was always open to suggestions. The General recognized that the French knew far more than he did about laying siege to enemy strongholds. He happily followed the suggested French strategy for the digging of trenches in a V-shaped pattern closer and closer to the Yorktown fortifications to enable our artillery to pound the British positions. This made it possible for us to overrun the British outposts, necessitating Cornwallis's surrender.

Over the years, many have asked me why Cornwallis did not try to have his outnumbered six thousand men escape when the French fleet arrived off Yorktown, especially when General Clinton, learning too late of our march to Virginia, failed to send him reinforcements. The answer is that he did try, sending his troops across the York River to prepare for an escape by his main forces. But again the Divine Ruler seemed to intervene. Ferocious winds arose, wrecking some of the British boats while driving the others back to the peninsula.

At Yorktown, the General once again was right at the front with the troops. I do believe he wanted to personally lead the charges on outlying British positions, but the General was always willing to give recognition to talent—especially if that talent supported him. He happily let Hamilton, Lafayette, and Laurens lead the last charges that made clear to Cornwallis the hopelessness of his position. I heard the speech he gave to Hamilton's men, including the free black soldiers from Rhode Island. No one could inspire troops like the General.

I remember a cannonball landing near us. I jumped, hoping the General had not noticed. Our chaplain, Israel Evans, urged the General to move back. The General coolly replied, "Mr. Evans, you had better carry that home and show it to your wife and children."

I'll never forget the dejected looks of the British and Hessians as they surrendered while the British band, unaware of the irony, played "The World Turned Upside Down." That most of our troops were dressed in rags while the French and British wore fancy uniforms did not diminish the glee that everyone in our ranks felt. The General's commanders were understandably exultant after the surrender, but the General, who was less downcast in defeat, was more restrained in victory, probably because he did not believe the king would back off. Or maybe it was because of Rule 22 in those *Rules of Civility* he always kept on his desk, which stated: "Show not yourself glad at the misfortune of another, though he were your enemy." Whatever the reason, I heard him warn against celebration. "Let history huzzah for us," he told us. But Lafayette would have none of that. "The play, General, is over," he said.

So was he a fine general?

My great-grandchildren's schoolteacher may believe Washington was overrated as a general. This also seems to be the view of some modern writers I have read. I can tell you the French did not believe this, and neither did the British and Hessians after Trenton and Princeton, nor did Frederick the Great or leaders of the British Parliament. No doubt future historians will point to his New York defeats or credit his successes to poor British generalship. But as Benjamin Franklin pointed out in a letter to a British friend, a copy of which he sent to the General, "An American planter was chosen by us to command our troops and continued during the whole war. This man sent home to you, one after another, five of your best generals, baffled, their heads bare of laurels, disgraced even in the opinion of their employers." He could have added that those five generals commanded troops that were more numerous and better trained, armed, and clothed than the General's.

After the war, I learned that the British had sent half of their army and two-thirds of their navy to our shores—at a time when Britain was at war with France and Spain. Overall, His Majesty sent forty-three thousand British troops to America. On top of this, they enlisted twenty-nine thousand Hessian mercenaries and twenty-one thousand American loyalists, primarily from the South. And that didn't include the hundreds of British ships and upward of twenty thousand sailors. I suppose if you counted our various armies and all the dispersed part-time state militias, you could come up with a large number that partly closed the gap. But the British forces were under centralized command. The General never had more than twelve thousand fit men under his direction.

The General had his failings. He let the Congress push him into defending New York, where we got whipped, and he himself pushed the overcomplicated and disastrous forays to emancipate Canada. He had the misguided view that the threatened loss of Canada would lead to a quick end to the British war on our states. He once confessed to me this was his greatest mistake in the war. "Josiah, how could I have been so stupid as to send those men on such an absurd and fruitless expedition?"

But as I said, the General learned from his mistakes. As the war progressed, he relied less on complex battle strategies in favor of simpler ones. He overcame initial congressional meddling and his own inherited preference for gentlemen officers to make appointments based on merit rather than the British process of combining birth, connections, and merit in their appointments. I saw his attitude toward discipline change. He started out by hanging mutineers and severely whipping those he caught deserting. He never wavered regarding the first group, but midway through the war, he started pardoning returning deserters. His attitude on disciplining officers evolved. He always was in favor of court-martialing and punishing officers who did not perform, but his definition of performance changed. The value the General placed on criticism and advice, always great, even when opposed to his own or fellow generals' plans, increased.

The General's appreciation of dissent and free speech was brought home to me earlier at Newburgh by the court-martial of General McDougall, the crusty Son of Liberty with the Scottish brogue whom the General trusted and respected. McDougall was accused of slandering General Heath in front of subordinates. The panel of officers convicted General McDougall and recommended a severe and public reprimand. Yet the General hesitated for weeks. When I asked him why, he would only say, "This matter potentially has implications that go far beyond whether General McDougall is reprimanded." I could not see what he was talking about. McDougall was a fine general, certainly more able than the politically appointed General Heath, but along with criticizing Heath's generalship, General MacDougall had called Heath "a knave" in front of junior officers and troops. How could you maintain a command structure when one officer was openly criticizing another? Maybe, I thought, the General's reluctance was due to his personal fondness for General McDougall. There the matter rested, until weeks later when the General called me in and dictated a brisk order upholding the court-martial verdict. The General attached a footnote to the order, however, that free speech was very important if an army was to function effectively, and criticism such as that leveled by General McDougall should be encouraged, albeit not this kind of personally disparaging criticism.

The General knew when to withdraw, when to defend, and when to attack. He generally concentrated rather than divided his forces, a lesson he first learned from General Braddock's mistakes and then again from his own in New York. He could be bold without being suicidal. He knew there were times to be cautious, as he was for most of the war, but also times to be daring, as he was at Trenton and Princeton. Perhaps the British generals were slow to follow up on their successes and really pursue our forces, but the General took advantage of their slowness. I do not recall the General ever criticizing individual British generals, although once he wryly observed that, as a group, they were better generals during battles than between battles. But then the General rarely criticized anyone outside his command. I suspect he knew that criticizing British generalship would diminish his own reputation for both generalship and modesty.

Above all, the General held together our army at its darkest hours when no one else could have. As Lafayette remarked after the Battle of Brandywine, "With his stately appearance and dignified courage, no one else could provoke such waves of enthusiasm among our troops." But would these qualities enable the General to overcome the challenge on Saturday?

Chapter Five

Day Five—Friday

Final Preparations

And let me perish, but in Cato's judgment,
A day, an hour, of virtuous liberty
Is worth a whole eternity in bondage.

—Cato, *Cato,* Act II

It is not now a time to talk of aught
But chains or conquest, liberty or death.

—Cato, *Cato,* Act II

There were twenty-four hours until the Saturday meeting, and I could feel the tension rising throughout the camp. When I rode out across the various bivouacs, officers and men avoided my glances, and their conversation focused on whether it would rain that day, a subject that rarely received so much attention. No one asked how the General was doing, no one asked about the status of treaty negotiations, and no one mentioned the meeting the following morning.

I observed the General make his usual morning round of the troops, and there was no doubt this time—the huzzahs were muffled. This did not seem to deter the General, who calmly made his observations to commanders on the men's appearance and what drills were planned for the day.

The General retired to his study around noon. I remember opening the door to pose a question about some inconsequential order regarding the furnishing of regimental colors to the regiments that did not possess them. The General was at his desk reading *Cato*.

What did this portend? Cato had said, "Would Lucius have me live to swell the number of Caesar's slaves, or by a base submission give up the cause of Rome?" Cato had then committed suicide rather than abandon his republican beliefs in Ancient Rome.

Again, I concluded it was unlikely that the General would avoid tomorrow's meeting by committing suicide. After all, Cato faced capture by Caesar's allies, and the General did not face capture by the British or by Gates's allies, at least not yet. But did the reading of *Cato* foreshadow opposition to the mutiny so as to preserve our own nascent republic? Perhaps, but it might be too much to imply from the General's fascination with Addison's play. After all, standing on the General's desk were two other favorites, biographies of Caesar and Alexander, and these men, while possessing noble traits, were military dictators whose example might lead the General in the opposite direction. The only other books in evidence were the usual *Rules of Civility*, Philip Miller's *The Gardeners Dictionary*, Arthur Young's *A Course of Experimental Agriculture*, and Humphrey Bland's *Treatise of Military Discipline*. (The General had earlier commended Bland's *Treatise* to his officers but had come to believe that Bland—commander in chief of the British army in Scotland after the Battle of Culloden—was too attuned to the mores of European armies fighting pitched battles, something the General had learned to avoid.)

Of one thing I was sure—the General had a tremendous ability to blot out extraneous, even significant, matters when faced with a truly important political or military decision. Before the war, his seventeen-year-old stepdaughter Patsy had died from epilepsy. I was told Martha had worn mourning clothes for months. While the General had been moved—I once thought I saw him with tears in his eyes when Patsy was mentioned—and had gone out of his way to comfort Lady Washington, he never spoke to me of Patsy during the war.

At Yorktown, the General's twenty-six-year-old stepson, Jacky, had joined him. I am sure this pleased the General, as Jacky had never volunteered for duty during the war. Jacky served as an aide—a rather undistinguished one, in my opinion—but while at Yorktown, he contracted a camp disease that led to his death at his uncle's nearby estate a few weeks later. The General had joined his wife for several days of grieving at Mount Vernon and planning for the raising of Jacky's and his wife Eleanor's four children, with the General and Martha adopting the two youngest, Wash and Nellie. The General, however, was soon back with the troops at Newburgh. The deaths of Lady Washington's children, just as the failure to have their own, were subjects that Lady Washington and the General avoided while going about their respective duties. Lady Washington doted on her family and, with the death of her two remaining children, focused her attentions on her grandchildren. The General did as well, but never to the detriment of civic or military duty. I always felt that Lady Washington, even when she was tending to the needs of the troops, did so because she felt that was what the General wanted.

I wondered if the General talked with Lady Washington about the pending meeting. I never heard them discuss it, but I assumed they did, based on what seemed like an amiable, respectful relationship where confidences were shared, albeit out of the sight or hearing of others.

The General never revealed much of his emotions, but when I told him I was contemplating marriage, he expressed enthusiastic approval.

"It is a wonderful state, marriage, and all should enjoy it." That he enjoyed marriage, I have no doubt, but he seemed reluctant to express any intimate details of his own enjoyment of that institution, just as he seemed reluctant to express his feelings to me on the Saturday meeting. I had no idea what advice Lady Washington would have given the General, as she had never given advice on a subject of this nature to him in my presence or, so far as I knew, in anyone else's.

Once in a while, if she did not approve of what the General was doing, Lady Washington would reach up and grab him by the lapels—she was at least a foot shorter than he was—and address him as "General." But these infrequent occurrences generally referred to matters of the household, servants, or supplies. They rarely involved military matters, except when Lady Washington had arrived outside Boston. There she'd told the General that from then on she was going to direct and oversee the repair of socks and leggings through organizing ladies' groups and was henceforth to supervise the distribution of clothing and blankets and monitor their quality. The General had smiled and quickly acquiesced, which was a smart move on his part.

Everywhere the army went, Lady Washington organized local ladies into sewing and knitting groups—small brigades fighting the relentless wear and tear of the war. Our army suffered from shortages of clothing throughout the war, but the holes in what clothing the men wore were promptly attended to by Lady Washington and her female volunteers. Needless to say, Lady Washington was exceedingly popular with the troops. One regiment even called itself "Lady Washington's Dragoons."

I always marveled at how and why Lady Washington stayed with the General for most of the war. Unlike the General, I don't believe she had ever traveled beyond Virginia and Maryland before. She certainly could not have enjoyed staying in our camps during the freezing winters, but I never heard her complain, not even when she suffered from jaundice in 1781 and the Washingtons returned a gift of fruit sent under a flag of truce by the widow of a British paymaster. I would not have dreamed of asking my Prescilla to join me during those times. I sometimes wondered if Lady Washington even enjoyed those interminable dinners she hosted for our officers and visiting dignitaries. You would never know from the way she guided the conversation, generally with the purpose of creating bonds between junior officers and spouses from different regions. She was more articulate than the General at such affairs. He would occasionally stammer, which led some visiting foreigners to believe that Lady Washington was the brighter of the two. I can't imagine she enjoyed camp life, but I was told that she enjoyed listening to military music. She seemed to turn up whenever the fifers played. Having learned chess from my fellow aide, Benjamin Walker, she enjoyed playing the game.

Often I wanted to ask Lady Washington her reaction to camp life. But I never could. It might have seemed impertinent, and besides, I always thought there was a big gulf between us, much more so than the gulf between the General and me. I looked on her as a Virginia plantation mistress, and I knew that her upbringing and attitudes on everything from women to food to manners to slavery were far different than mine. She was no Abigail Adams when it came to publicly expressing opinions on the events of the day. Yet, like the General, she had an instinct for the democratic gesture, as when she invited the workmen fixing their quarters in the winter of 1777 to have lunch with her. Sometimes I thought her personality was more inscrutable than the General's; she seemed to play a role set out for her by either the General, herself, or both. I have heard the spouses of presidents lately referred to as "First Ladies." Lady Washington acted as First Lady years before we had presidents.

A little later, when I opened the door to ask the General about honoring Virginia's Governor Harrison's request to ship some hard French currency (the General being the American leader entrusted by the French to handle the proceeds of their loan), I found the General staring out the window at the snowy slope leading down to the Hudson River.

Perhaps he was praying for guidance, but while praying, meditation, and Bible reading were much favored by Lady Washington, the General never seemed to join her. I have read that the General was a Deist, but if that means someone who believes in a God who leaves the world alone, that does not describe the General. He was always talking about Providence, the Almighty, the Great Disposer of Events, and the Divine Ruler who intervened in the affairs of man and whom he believed had intervened many times during the War for Independence. From the fog that had shrouded the movement up Dorchester Heights outside Boston, to all the British bullets at close range that had missed the General, to the winds that had foiled Cornwallis's escape at Yorktown, the General believed that thanks was due the Ruler of the Universe.

I believe he saw himself acting as the servant of Providence, although he certainly believed in individual responsibility. Often he would recite the line from Cato, "'Tis not in mortals to command success, but we'll do more . . . we'll deserve it."

This is not to say that the General was a Christian in the sense that Patrick Henry or Samuel Adams was, or I am. Unlike Lady Washington, who prayed daily, the General never prayed outside a church to my knowledge. Nor did I ever see a letter of his that invoked the name of Jesus. But then again, the General did not write essays to disprove the divinity of Our Savior the way Jefferson did. He did serve on the vestries of two Anglican churches near his home in Virginia, but this was as much a civic as a religious duty. Back in those days of established state churches, serving on a church vestry meant directing the building of roads, ferries, and bridges.

With religion as with so many other endeavors, it was hard to separate the General's private life from his public one. We aides used to joke among ourselves as to which church service the General was going to attend any given Sunday. One time it was Roman Catholic, another it was Dutch Reformed, another it was Baptist. I have Jewish friends in Philadelphia who tell me the General wrote letters to many different Hebrew congregations, so I wouldn't be surprised if the General attended Hebrew services too.

I suspect, however, that the General's wide-ranging church attendance was due less to a thirst for religion and more to a desire as the nation's leader to draw Americans of different faiths together. In Massachusetts, I saw the General stop our troops from burning an effigy of the Pope on Guy Fawkes Day.

The General certainly believed in religion as a force for good in public life. The hall where the meeting was to be held on Saturday was built primarily as a chapel because the General wanted to encourage religious devotion. He fulminated against alcoholism, gambling, and swearing among the troops, but since he partook of both liquor and gambling, I suspect his tirades were more directed at excesses that would undermine the army than based on religious principle.

Once, he issued an edict against swearing, but he soon realized the hopelessness of enforcing such an edict. Despite what Parson Weems has written in his glorified account of the General's life, I can assure you that the General did swear, albeit on very rare occasions such as when he saw his officers fleeing the British in New York and strove to stop their flight.

After dealing with Governor Harrison's request, I stood there looking at the General and wondering what he was thinking. He turned from the window, sat down at his desk, picked up a pen, and began scratching away on a piece of paper. I hesitantly asked if he needed my help. He was not in a good mood, for he did not answer my question but grimaced and waved me away with a brusque swing of the hand. Generally, he would stand when I entered the room. After all, Rule 28 of his *Rules of Civility* instructed him, "If anyone comes to speak to you while you are sitting, stand up although he be your inferior." Not today.

I awkwardly withdrew, my mind full of questions. Was he writing a letter to the troops to be presented at the meeting he apparently was not going to attend? If so—the question uppermost in my mind—was he intending to welcome and lead the insurrection or oppose it? Or was he just writing still another letter to Congress pleading for payments to the men?

As I sat down at my table to get back to work, I tried to list the countervailing forces tugging at the General. On the one side was the General's vision of a republic, which he had pledged to uphold many times to Congress and various state legislatures. Often I had heard the General speak with contempt of Cromwell's overthrowing of the English king and installing himself as a dictator. Just as often I had heard him speak with admiration of the Swiss cantons that had formed themselves into a republic. He himself had served for years in and, I believe, had some fond memories of his service in the House of Burgesses and the Continental Congress.

And yet . . . there were all those letters and pleas he received to assume control of the government and to become dictator, if not king. It was not just the mutterings of the troops or the villagers in the towns we passed through, although there was plenty of that. In many of the states, outstanding citizens had voiced the same sentiments. Merchants and farmers hailed the General because he restrained our troops from seizing goods and crops. I have told you about the Duché letter and then the Nicola letter in May of 1782. I earlier mentioned the letter on monarchy from Major General James Varnum of the Rhode Island militia. That came two months after Nicola's letter, and the writer, Varnum, was a man of far higher reputation than either Reverend Duché or Colonel Nicola.

Varnum—a big, vigorous, college-educated lawyer who never held back from telling the General his thoughts—had earlier in the war successfully proposed the idea of raising black troops from slaves. Greatly respected by the General and Varnum's fellow Rhode Islander General Greene, he had left the Rhode Island militia to be his state's delegate to Congress and was not pleased with what he found there. He expressed outrage at the lack of respect shown the army by Congress.

Varnum found our then system of government too weak (a sentiment shared by most of us), described the Articles of Confederation as "that baseless fabric," and did not think our countrymen up for the challenge of democracy. "The Citizens at large are totally destitute of that Love of Equality which is absolutely requisite to support a democratic Republick: Avarice, Jealousy & Luxury control their feelings," he wrote the General.

General Varnum's solution to the people's failings was simple: "absolute Monarchy, or a military State, can alone rescue them from all the Horrors of Subjugation." Varnum, like many, did not fault the British system of government so much as that the system was imposed from three thousand miles away by an incompetent monarch without our consent.

When the letter arrived, I remember thinking, *If these are the sentiments of a leading citizen of a state such as Rhode Island where republican suspicions of the military run strong, imagine what the feelings must be elsewhere.* I could not think of many men with both military and legislative experience (it was later that he became the chief justice of the Northwest Territory) more respected than General Varnum, and I knew that respect was shared by the General.

The General replied to Varnum that he could not "consent" to Varnum's view, but unlike in his reply to Nicola, he did not specifically disavow Varnum's proposal. Again, as with Colonel Nicola's letter, and unlike with Reverend Duché's letter, no copies of Varnum's letter were passed on to the Congress.

The General once said with a laugh, "Josiah, no one will fear me as a monarch because I have no natural children to whom I can pass the throne." I could not figure out whether this was really a joke or a realization of how easy it would be to become king of our new country. I did not know how many times in letters or private conversations officers or civilians had made proposals similar to Duché's, Nicola's, or

Varnum's. I was sure there were many such pleas, not to mention all those comparisons to Moses.

Was the General starting to change? I noticed that the tone of his letters to General Benjamin Lincoln had changed. As always he complained of the troops getting meager rations and being released with "not a farthing of money to carry them home," but to this was added the criticism that the congressmen and other civilian officials were still regularly getting all the salaries of their offices. "It is vain," Washington wrote, "to suppose that Military men will acquiesce contentedly with bare rations, when those in the Civil walk of life (unacquainted with half the hardships they endure) are regularly paid the Emoluments of office." It was the first time I had noticed the General not just pleading for his men but showing irritation at the conduct of the civilians who had appointed him. Had he reached the point where, although being the last person to "consider" installing himself as king or dictator (as he had responded to Colonel Nicola), he was now considering just that? The General had always sympathized with his unpaid troops from the days of the French and Indian War, but now he added the criticisms of, and implicit threats to, civilian-elected officials.

Just months earlier, the General and I had passed a tavern in a small New York town on our way to Newburgh. Its old sign—a picture of King George—lay on the ground against the tavern wall. Swinging above us was a new sign featuring a picture of a different George. I commented on how he had replaced the king in the eyes of our people, but the General merely grunted and said nothing. I knew, and the General must have known, that across the states, the toast of "God save the king" had been replaced by "God save great Washington."

Reflecting on what the General would do tomorrow inevitably led me to reflect on what would happen after the General's decision. If he refused to lead or bless the rebellion, would it still take place and succeed? It seemed possible, given the mood of the men, but not probable. Who, other than the General, could lead such a rebellion and win public support? General Gates was the obvious choice. His aides adored Old Granny, as they called him, but his ignominious defeat at Camden had dimmed his support among the troops, the political leaders, and the people. Still, he was an ambitious man eager to claim fame and glory, and the frustration of the officers and men would give him a potent force to lead on Philadelphia. I knew from the earlier mutinies that, if Gates's units followed him, other units might quickly join. The New Jersey unit had joined the Pennsylvania units a year before, and I knew how worried we were in headquarters about commanding the loyalty of other units that might be called upon to put down that mutiny. And that was a mutiny without any officer leadership, let alone a top-ranking general like Gates.

But what if General Washington joined and led the rebellion? Or what if he stood aside but gave it his blessing? I did not like the idea, but I had to admit the chances for success were great. The army at Newburgh would follow him gladly, and I was pretty sure other units, which had the same grievances, would follow also. I thought again of all those mutinies during the war. There was the expectation they would fail because of deft and strong actions by the General to quell them. Still, the politicians had fled Philadelphia for Princeton while the General had worked his magic. With the General in the lead, I suspected many politicians in the states, and many congressmen too, would join what they perceived to be the future ruling government.

And what of the people? Many still harbored hostility toward the military dating back to the conduct of British troops in colonial days. And Americans' repeated noble support for the war was marred by a strange reluctance, particularly in New England, to pay the taxes to fund a standing army. Many surely still believed in republican principles despite the frustrations and deprivations the long war had brought. And yet my cousin Benjamin told me that the Pennsylvania mutineers a year ago had met with a more friendly than hostile reception from the public. The people knew from their relatives in service how ill served our troops had been. More important was the relationship of the people to the General. He could not go anywhere without people applauding and bowing. To many, he embodied the Revolution. He had become the cause. Why else had the British focused so much energy on either assassinating or capturing him?

The war had been just as much to throw off British rule as to establish some little-thought-out republican government. The replacement of a distant parliament and king with a popular American ruler such as the General, instead of with an ineffective and despised Congress, would seem natural and appropriate. And the loyalist population, which was still numerous in the South, New York, and other places, would feel more comfortable with a king, albeit not the one with whom they started the war. Who could better bring the warring citizens together than the General? While success was not a certainty, I was forced to conclude that an insurrection led or blessed by the General would probably succeed.

Suddenly I started thinking about what I had dreaded the whole week. What would I do if the General led the insurrection? I respected the General and thought he would be a wise ruler. Still, I was a republican, and my Quaker upbringing influenced my outlook. No one led our meetings, no one stood between us and the Lord, and this naturally led us to be suspicious of divine or less divine rulers. Still, even among my brethren, there would be sympathy for an insurrection led by the General. Why, even my Prescilla had raised the subject with me one time when she got angry about my failure to receive pay. What if the General expected me to accompany him on the march to Philadelphia? Would I have the courage to say no? Did I really want to say no?

It was in the early evening on Friday, after the midday dinner but before supper, that I was gratefully diverted from worrying about these questions when the General opened his door and waved for me to come in. I practically jumped from my chair and bounded toward his study, certain that the General would have me draft something relating to tomorrow's meeting or at least divulge his plans. It was not to be. After offering me the usual glass of Madeira, the General seemed determined to talk about every subject but the impending mutiny.

"Josiah," he said, "what do you think of my writing a book about farming? Would you help?"

"Sir, of course, but, as you know, I have lived my whole life in a city and know little about farming."

"Well, Josiah, my neighbors talked to me on the way back from Yorktown and suggested I write such a book."

That the General was obsessed with farming I well knew from his detailed letters I sent almost every week to Mount Vernon's manager, his cousin Lund, as well as the agricultural treatises from England that often adorned his desk. Still, it seemed incredible to me that he could really be thinking of such things at a time like this.

"Well, sir, why do your neighbors believe you should write such a book?" I asked.

"Oh, because of this new plough I have invented and my idea for a mechanical seed spreader. The crop rotation I have implemented to get away from tobacco. You can't feed our nation on tobacco. How to diversify the activities on a plantation. You see, Josiah, tobacco is finished as a cash crop in Virginia. I was among the first in my neighborhood to shift land to wheat and corn. Then I was the first to develop a major herring fishery on the Potomac. We've caught hundreds of thousands of herring and shipped them to the West Indies. Then we built mills to weave clothing out of flax and hemp. And there is the whiskey distillery."

The General then paused and chuckled. "Of course, I was also the first to try to mine iron ore in Virginia. That was a complete failure . . . as was my effort to plant wine vineyards."

Still, it all sounded quite impressive to a city merchant's son. The General started talking about manures and moving mud from the Potomac and mixing it with animal droppings. "Well, I don't know much about farming, sir, but if I can help put things together, I will do so," I said to the General before I started to nod off, thinking of his troubles with punctuation and spelling.

"No," the General exclaimed abruptly, "it's not a good idea. People will think I'm immodest."

I couldn't see what was immodest about writing a book on a subject you knew something about, but I didn't argue. The General was always thinking of how he would look to Americans in the future. Maybe he thought later Americans would think he was focusing on his farm instead of winning the war or setting up a government.

"Josiah," the General said, shifting the subject, "what do you think this country will look like in thirty years?" I mumbled something about a growing population and migration west of the Appalachians. "True," replied the General, "but will the new Western states stick with us or go with Spain?"

That possibility had never occurred to me. "Why should they go with Spain, sir?" I asked.

"Because right now most of the produce of the whole Ohio Valley goes through the Port of New Orleans. Their cultural and political ties are with us, but their economic interests are with Spain, France, England, or whoever controls New Orleans."

The General was just warming up. He went on about how religious conflict and slavery boded ill for our new nation. From all the different religious services I had seen the General go to, and my conversation with Lafayette about the General's views on slavery, these comments did not surprise me. But the General continued on and said that the division between the East and the West was just as threatening, which in retrospect, given our recent North-South arguments, seems surprising. The General went into a rambling monologue on how crucial it was to connect the East and West with canals and roads so that the trade of the Ohio Valley and points westward would flow eastward. Of course, from his correspondence, I knew that the General's interest in national development was interwoven with his personal financial interests. He had bought land in the Ohio Valley and western Pennsylvania. The General had always been a supporter of the Potomac Canal project to link Virginia with the Ohio Valley and his own lands. I had heard rumors that during the French and Indian War he had pushed General Braddock to march to Fort Duquesne in western Pennsylvania through northern Virginia. Some said the General urged such a course for military reasons, but others said he was trying to increase the value of his own lands along the route. In any event, General Braddock chose the Pennsylvania route, although I don't know if that decision had anything to do with his crushing defeat. Similarly, the General's plans for a Potomac canal never came to fruition. Instead, a couple of decades ago, New York established the link westward with the Erie Canal. While I know the General would have preferred a canal starting in Virginia, I am sure he would have been pleased with the Erie Canal and the roads that have been built.

I knew to steer away from questions about how canals and roads would affect the General's finances. The General was incredibly sensitive about any questions regarding public decisions affecting his own financial interests. I have already told you how he turned down a salary for his wartime efforts to show his decisions were uncolored by personal considerations. Lately, with victory possible, he had received letters from several state legislatures suggesting land grants to the General in appreciation of his efforts. Knowing of his insatiable desire for land, I had been surprised at how the General delayed his responses to solicit the advice of many leaders.

Jefferson wrote back that, while accepting the grants was justified, refusing them would "enhance your reputation," and I knew what the General's response would be. The issue now was not only ethics but reputation, and reputation trumped all with the General. Nonetheless, I suppose it doesn't matter why one does the right thing—as the General invariably did—if the right thing is done.

The General poured himself a second glass of Madeira. He was truly in an expansive mood. "You are of course right, Josiah, about the growing population over the coming years. But that will depend on whether we continue to stay the home for the poor, oppressed, and persecuted of the world." Once the General got on the subject of America as the refuge of the persecuted, especially those facing religious persecution, there was no stopping him, and I knew better than to interfere.

My own upbringing as a Quaker, and living in a city such as Philadelphia, which swarmed with refugees, made me an advocate for America playing this role. But I sometimes wondered how this Virginian planter could possibly have become so enthusiastic about America as a beacon to refugees. Perhaps it was a concern for refugees; perhaps it was a desire to fill our lands. As was his wont, however, the General swerved from his idealistic goals to how to pragmatically achieve such goals. "The challenge, Josiah, is how we encourage refugees to come here without so offending their European rulers that they take actions against either the refugees or ourselves. This will involve diplomacy worthy of Franklin."

This led the General into a discussion of what education the immigrants—or, for that matter, those already here—should receive. Nothing could make the General wax more enthusiastic than the subject of a national university. The General had received no university education—nor, as I have said, much formal education of any kind—but he still considered himself an expert on the subject. He had taken great care with his stepson Jacky's education at King's College in New York (I believe it is now called Columbia), although from what I heard, Jacky played more than he studied. The General envisioned most Americans going to a university, but his support for an American national university seemed based on his desire to bring students from the different states together, as well as on his fear that Americans, like some he knew, would go off to Europe for their higher education. The

General was suspicious of education abroad and the European manners and habits it might encourage.

Then the General turned to what he really wanted to talk about: what he would do to improve Mount Vernon. It had always amazed me how detailed his letters were to his cousin Lund. He wrote those letters himself and just asked me to check for punctuation. It was good that he thus limited my contribution. While I understood the General when he wrote about the architecture of the house, I had little knowledge of the trees and plants that the General wrote about. Today he did not talk about the added wings, story, and colonnaded porch of which he was so proud. Instead he was thinking about Mount Vernon's future gardens. Gardens in America, the General had decided, were too much under the influence of the English. He intended to surround Mount Vernon with the first truly American landscaping.

"Josiah, at Mount Vernon there will be no more geometric patterns and English yews and hollies clipped into balls. No, that is what too many of our countrymen think is fashionable. Instead, there will be a vast green surrounded by American trees such as white pines and hemlock from the Northeast and ash and oak trees from the South. There will be pink groves of crab apple. I will get magnolias from South Carolina."

Lest I found this list too romantic, the General returned to the pragmatic: "All these English gardens have trails that end with statues. We will be practical. My trails will wander off and end among scented flowers with toilets painted white with a red roof. Our own honeysuckle will climb the walls and scent the air."

The General was surprisingly anti-British when he talked about farming or gardening, but of course most of the books he read on these subjects came from England. Later, I learned that after the war he had hired a farm manager from England. I am sure he used the man's skills while pursuing what he considered his own American ideas about farming and landscaping.

The General did not confine his gardening desires to his own plantation. He ordered his troops at Newburgh to plant vegetable gardens. Some of his officers looked askance, but the General thought the gardening would be good for the men's souls and the vegetables and fruits good for their bodies (most importantly, for preventing scurvy).

After talking about his gardens, the General paused. Covered with snow in early March, the Hudson Valley was a dispiriting place for a Virginia planter longing for his land. Finally, he said, "Josiah, I would rather be at Mount Vernon than emperor of the world."

I think he meant it, but I knew the choice that week was not between Mount Vernon and emperor of the world but between Mount Vernon and assuming power over the states.

The General then lowered his eyelids and drifted off into barely coherent melodramatic mumblings taken from letters to his friends. "At Mount Vernon . . . that, Josiah, is where I wish most devoutly to glide silently through the remainder of my life. The days of my youth have long since fled to return no more. I am now descending the hill I have spent fifty-one years climbing, but I will not repine; I have had my day. What I want, Josiah, is to return to Mount Vernon and just move gently down the stream of life until I sleep with my fathers." Using his favorite biblical metaphor, the General talked of "just living under my own vine and fig tree."

The General had lately taken to speaking, writing, and rambling with barely coherent sentiment about his advancing age, although he was only fifty-one. Still, the war had aged him. His hair had grayed, a slight paunch had emerged, his hearing had waned, and he talked incessantly about becoming a private citizen pursuing a private life. He talked as if he were at the end of his career, which may come as a surprise, given his later roles in convening the Constitutional Convention and serving as president.

Considering what was going on at Newburgh that week, when I heard these musings about his death and yearning for the quiet of

Mount Vernon, I couldn't help reflect on whether such wishes meant that he would try to stop the mutiny and then return to Mount Vernon or whether he was just so weary he would let the rebellious officers go ahead while he returned to his estate.

Still, I kept thinking that the General, so vain about his place in history, must be weighing what posterity would think of him. Would he be looked on as the savior of his country for taking over the government or would he be looked on as the savior for stopping the rebellion? While the General tried to avoid looking like he cared about fame or his place in history, sometimes he would slip in my presence. This was the man who had once said to me when dozing off, "To obtain the applause of my compatriots and their descendants would be a heartfelt satisfaction. To merit such applause is my highest wish."

Sometimes he would explicitly acknowledge his focus on fame by saying, "Josiah, I am growing weary of the pursuit of fame."

That the General was an incredibly able man I had no doubt. But with my Quaker upbringing, I was uneasy about his constant, albeit somewhat hidden, seeking after applause. Should not human beings seek to do good deeds for their own and the Lord's sake rather than the approbation of others? Then again, I had never known the General to do bad deeds, so maybe my concern about the General's mixed motivations was ungenerous.

While my mind raced, the General had been thinking his own thoughts. Soon, fully awake, he dismissed me from his study, leaving me to ponder whether seeking fame was interwoven with, or could be separated from, seeking power.

Chapter Six

Day Six—Saturday

The Showdown

This sun, perhaps, this morning sun's the last
That e'er shall rise on Roman Liberty.

—Sempronius, *Cato*, Act I, Scene 2

I'll animate the soldiers' drooping courage,
With love of freedom, and contempt of life.
I'll thunder in their ears their country's cause,
And try to raise up all that's Roman in them.

—Portius, *Cato*, Act I, Scene 2

The General spent the early morning in his bedroom attended by his aide, Will Lee, as was his custom. To say the General was fastidious would be an understatement. His deep-blue coat was always freshly brushed. His faded-yellow buff waistcoat and breeches always perfectly matched. His shirt was always of the finest linen. The yellow buttons on the lapels and the buckles on his breeches were all as highly polished as his boots. His graying, reddish-brown hair was combed smoothly back in a small queue. Except for the three silver stars on his epaulettes, you would not know his rank. The General's appearance was elegant but simple. As I have said, he refused to wear the medals that had been given him, declaring to me that this would be immodest. For the same reason he abandoned the blue sash he had initially worn across his breast. The French officers, who loved ribbons and medals, found this peculiar. And this, as I said earlier, from the man who had introduced the wearing of medals by his own enlisted men.

Will Lee was almost as well dressed as the General, who ordered his aide's clothes from either the General's indentured tailor at Mount Vernon or, where possible, the same Philadelphia tailor favored by the General. Will may have been the General's slave as well as aide, but we joked in headquarters that he looked more smartly dressed than many of the generals in the army.

Thus, resplendently dressed as always, the General convened our usual staff meeting on Saturday morning without any reference to the climactic meeting approaching later that morning. David Humphreys, Benjamin Walker, and I sat at the big rough-hewn table in that central room, our office, of seven doors and one window. The General faced us. The meeting opened with discussion of what could only be described as a smelly situation. Most of the recently arrived beef at the Contractors' Issuing Store was so spoiled as to be inedible. Perhaps the weight of the coming meeting was affecting the General as he eschewed his usual diatribes about corrupt contractors taking advantage of our troops. He merely directed, and Walker transcribed, a message to the quartermaster to cut off all dealings with the offending supplier and threaten that gentleman (if he could be called such) with unspecified retribution if the deception was not rectified.

There followed a discussion of a proper response to the French ambassador, who had written the General a lengthy letter about the difficulty of negotiating a final treaty with Great Britain despite agreement on conditional terms. The ambassador held out hope for a resolution soon but also acknowledged that the war might continue for another year. He linked such a possibility with the recent six-million-livre loan, which the ambassador noted, with disappointment, had largely been consumed by Superintendent of Finance Morris on past debts, rather than helping the General in the field where it could do some good in putting an end to the war. The letter included a not-so-subtle plea for the General to continue the pressure on the British in New York so that the British might not put more pressure on the French West Indies. The General asked Humphreys to draft a letter that was sympathetic to the ambassador's position but reversed the call for pressure by asking that the French fleet look to coordinate with the Continental Army in an assault on New York, thus replicating the triumph at Yorktown.

Last on the list was an easily accomplished thank-you note to an artist in Dublin—a request that the General accept an admiring seal showing him trampling upon what the Irishman obviously believed to be a common enemy. A day did not go by without someone extolling the General with a letter or sending a seal or drawing showing homage to the General.

The General then dismissed us without a word about the noon meeting. Humphreys, Walker, and I looked at each other. How could this be? We all intended to go to the meeting. We knew the General had signaled his intent earlier in the week not to attend the meeting, but not to even mention it seemed a little much. Was it possible the General did not care about what happened at noon? Maybe there was some plan afoot that he was keeping to himself.

Just a few minutes later, however, the General opened his study door, waved me in, and sat down in his chair. "Josiah, go up to the Temple, take detailed notes, and bring them back here. It will be good to have a record of everything that transpires." I looked at him for further orders, but the General had returned to writing what appeared to be a letter, although in very large script. I hesitated. Did I have the courage to ask him what he expected to come of the meeting? The

General finally looked up and gave me that stare with which all his aides were familiar. It was a stare that conveyed impatience, the feeling that you were imposing on his time, and the question of why you weren't following orders.

"Yes, General," I said and then retired.

I stumbled back to my desk. My first thought was that the General obviously did not plan on attending the meeting. Did this mean he was just going to stand aside and let Gates's aides take over the leadership of the mutiny and propel it forward? My fellow aides did not believe this possible—maybe the General had supporters who would speak against such an outcome. Then another thought occurred to me. Perhaps the General had lined up supporters who would lead the meeting, endorse the anonymous letters, and ask him to command the army's march on Philadelphia to take over the government? I remembered the General had absented himself from the meeting of the Continental Congress when he had been chosen commanding general so that no one would claim he had influenced the proceedings. Was he pursuing the same tactic now? He could explain to any later critics of the government take-over that he was not present and did not influence the army's decision, that only reluctantly had he accepted the army's desire that he should lead it to enforce its just claims.

We aides started walking toward the Temple a little after ten a.m. It was almost a two-hour walk, and earlier in the war we might have ridden, but now we were trying to save forage for the horses. Looking at Humphreys's and Walker's faces, I believed they shared my anticipation and dread about what was going to take place. One of us mentioned how it was March 15, the ides of March, but none of us speculated, at least out loud, on the connection to the date when Brutus killed Caesar and tried to overthrow the Roman government. Was Gates playing the role of Brutus and stabbing the General? Was the General playing the role of Cato and defending the republic against Caesar? Or was the General playing the role of Brutus, and if so, stabbing whom?

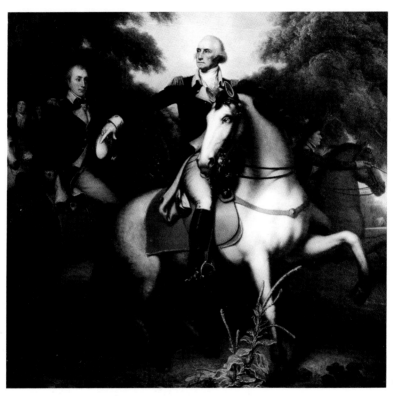

General George Washington at Trenton

General George Washington before Yorktown

*David Humphreys,
aide to General
Washington, later
ambassador to Spain*

*Alexander Hamilton,
aide to General
Washington, later
secretary of the treasury*

John Laurens, aide to General Washington, unsuccessfully sought approval of South Carolina legislature to arm slaves

Major General Horatio Gates, alleged chief conspirator in nascent Newburgh mutiny

Major General James Varnum, writer of letter to General Washington urging absolute monarchy or military dictatorship

Phillis Wheatley, free black poet, wrote ode to General Washington and later met with him

*Marquis de Lafayette, outstanding general, admirer and
supporter of General Washington*

*Martha Washington, wife of General Washington and
chief organizer of clothing repairs for army*

With my head spinning, I decided that such historical analogies, while interesting, led me nowhere.

I admit I was as nervous as before any battle, perhaps more so. Soon I could see the streams of officers ascending the hill to the long, one-story, dark-wood Temple. The coterie of General Gates's aides was just ahead of me. Majors John Armstrong Jr., Christopher Richmond, and William Barber; Colonels Moore and Stewart; and Lieutenant Colonel James Hughes were in a group. I did not see General Gates, but I was surprised to see that surgeon William Eustis and Quartermaster General Timothy Pickering were with them. Pickering had earlier served briefly as an aide to the General. Their circle was wider than I had thought. While most of the officers walking up the hill seemed rather sober and grim, I thought, perhaps mistakenly, that the Gates group seemed rather jaunty and assured, as if they knew what was about to take place.

Looking up at the Temple, I recalled once again how the construction and operation of that project had not always run smoothly. Much lumber had been stolen by troops to sell at a profit to locals. In the end, however, every unit had contributed—wood, nails, labor, etc.—to the building's construction under the chaplain's supervision. The General said the purpose was to create a space that would provide not only administrative offices but worship services for a whole regiment—thus the name "Temple." But the purpose was also to serve as a gathering place where troops from all states could mingle for social occasions—thus, along with the side rooms (for supplies, administration, the quartermaster's office, and meetings), there was an orchestra pit at the front for musical ensembles.

The General was a believer in both the usefulness of the troops seeking divine guidance—he encouraged Chaplain Evans to hold services there for adoration of the Supreme Being—and the importance of tying the bonds between the troops from east and west, north and south. The General often stated that the army was the only large group with a national spirit, and the Temple was constructed to foster that spirit, both in worship and festivity. As it happened, in the short time the Temple had been available, socialization rarely occurred and for the most part was between members of the same units. The New England troops had different tastes in alcohol than the Southern troops, and the latter were not keen on fraternizing with New England units filled with blacks. Some visitors were puzzled that this building should be the site for both religious observances and parties with alcohol consumption, but this did not seem to puzzle the General.

I doubt, however, he had anticipated its proposed use that week in March of 1783 by officers who were preaching rebellion.

We passed the hitching rail and entered the Temple. It must have been ten minutes prior to noon, but most of the benches were already filled. Still, Humphreys, Walker, and I found seats in the second row. (I wondered if officers were nervous about what might happen and did not want to be seen too close to the front.) We contributed to the general hum of conversation, but I do not remember what we said to each other, except that we were all reluctant to speak about the business at hand.

Precisely at noon, General Gates walked from the back through the murmuring crowd, mounted the podium at the front of the orchestra pit, and banged a gavel. I have never heard hundreds of men become quiet so quickly. There were a few coughs and the shuffling of feet but otherwise not a sound.

General Gates called the meeting to order and asked for the doors to be closed. He announced that the first order of business was to consider the "despairing" news from General McDougall, Colonel Ogden, and the officers who had returned from negotiations with Congress in Philadelphia. Since everyone knew of the documents that had been distributed the past several weeks and reported "no progress" in our efforts to gain back pay or pensions, General Gates opined that there was no need to read these out loud. Instead, he said the floor would be open to anyone who wished to rise and offer suggestions on what the army's course should be. I assumed one of his aides was about to declaim on the fruitlessness of our efforts with Congress and make a proposal for action in accord with the suggestions of the anonymous letters.

Suddenly, however, cries came forth from the front of the Temple as a door opened and General Washington entered. The General strode to the front of the room, turned to General Gates, and asked for leave to address the meeting. I say "asked," but the General's decisive tone showed it was more a command than a request.

General Gates looked a little flustered, but there was not much he could do but heed the General's request, especially since several officers from each section of the floor almost at the same time yelled out "Let's hear the General" and "So moved." The cries from the floor happened so quickly that I almost thought it was all prearranged.

The General took several pages from his waistcoat pocket, which, from the second row, I could see had been written in large letters by the General himself. It was probably the manuscript I had observed the General writing that morning. The General replaced General Gates in the front of the room, waving for him to take a seat. No one I have ever met had such a commanding presence as the General, and the officers now looked attentively forward with upraised faces. The General apologized for his presence, which was "by no means my intention when I published the order directing you to assemble." So important was this moment for the future of the country that the General said he "had committed my thoughts to writing" and asked "the indulgence of my brother officers" to grant him liberty to read from what he had written. The General then took out his papers and began.

I know there are many accounts of what the General said that day, and in what order, but I copied the General's manuscript later and have reread it hundreds of times in the sixty years since. The quotations that follow reflect exactly what he wrote except for one sentence the General seemed to ad lib, which has been quoted by many and which you will hear about shortly.

The General did not waste any time in addressing what he knew was the subject of every officer's attention: the anonymous letters. "By an anonymous summons, an attempt has been made to convene you together—how inconsistent with the rules of propriety! How unmilitary! And how subversive of all order and discipline—let the good sense of the Army decide."

There was no surprise here. The General had indicated as much in his order moving the meeting to Saturday. The officers might agree that improper procedures had been followed, but what about the substance of the second anonymous letter? Where did the General stand?

The General continued speaking in an even voice. First he tried to identify with the feelings of his audience, which the General sensed approved the letter. He gave credit to the author for "the goodness of his pen" but did not give "credit for the rectitude of his heart." He observed that the letter appealed more to "passion" than "to the reason and judgment of the Army." Otherwise, he asked, why would the letter writer remain secret and attack a "man who should recommend moderation"—in other words, someone who thought differently than he thought? The General was obviously sensitive about what he perceived as an attack on himself, but I did not think that point would carry much weight with the frustrated officers.

The General then acknowledged that the army's grievances deserved a hearing, although not the hasty and irregular one called for by the writer, and went on to emphasize his own history of identification with the army's grievances. He recalled that "as I was among the first who embarked in the cause of our common country . . . as I have never left your side one moment . . . as I have been the constant companion and witness of your distresses . . . as my heart has ever expanded with joy, when I have heard [the army's] praises, and my indignation has arisen, when the mouth of detraction has been opened against it—it can scarcely be supposed, at this late stage of the War, that I am indifferent to its interests."

I could see heads nodding, for everyone in the room knew how the General had shared their hardships and fought for their interests. But then the General asked how these interests were to be promoted. He quickly demolished the second alternative promoted by "the anonymous addresser": to move west to unsettled country and leave the country we have left behind to defend itself. The General pointed out that would mean leaving wives and children behind or, if taken with us, leaving behind the farms that fed us.

Again the officers nodded.

Then the General addressed the writer's other, and what everyone knew was the writer's preferred, alternative: "If peace takes place, never sheath your Sword, says he until you have obtained full and ample Justice." The General stated that this meant turning the army against our country and its government, "which is the apparent object unless Congress can be compelled into an instant compliance," something we all doubted would happen.

At his moment I still was not positive as to which direction the General was going. Was he going to endorse moving on Philadelphia? The General immediately gave his answer. "This dreadful alternative . . . has something so shocking in it that humanity revolts at the idea," said the General forcefully. I finally had my answer, and I found myself exhaling with relief. The General would not lead the mutiny, and I would not have to face the dreadful choice of following my General or my own republican beliefs.

The General said such an idea could not emanate from a "friend to this country," that only an "insidious Foe" such as "Some Emissary, perhaps from [the British in] New York," could sow "the seeds of discord and separation between the civil and military powers." Still I did not for a moment believe, nor did I believe the General believed, that this was a British plot. I could understand, however, why the General wanted to make the officers believe that the proposal came from the British rather than from among his own officer corps. The General went on to call both alternatives "impracticable," but I sensed most of the audience disagreed, at least as to the alternative of retaining our arms.

It was here that the General started to lose his audience. He tried to convince us that Congress would act on the army's just grievances. He went on and on about that "honorable body," which he asserted "entertains exalted sentiments of the Services of the Army; and from a full conviction of its Merits & sufferings, will do it compleat Justice; that their endeavors to discover & establish funds for this purpose have been unwearied, and will not cease till they have succeeded, I have not a doubt."

The trouble was that the audience had considerable doubts, which I am sure the General shared. We remembered all the broken congressional promises about pay and clothing. We remembered the broken 1780 promise of pensions for the officers. We remembered that our recent delegation to Philadelphia had met with soothing words but no action.

I could hear occasional mumblings, asides, and shifting on the benches. I knew by this time that the General was not going to accept the writer's invitation to lead the coup and was firmly against it. But I had my doubts as to whether the officers would follow his lead, especially since I was sure that some had been primed to control the meeting and rouse the officers with tirades against congressional inaction.

When the General stated that the deliberations of Congress, a large body, with many interests to reconcile, were of necessity slow, and asked rhetorically, "Why then should we distrust them," the mutterings rose. I expected at any moment that officers were going to stand up and shout, "You know why we should distrust them!" I heard an officer behind me mumble, "We have waited long enough." Tensions held down for months and years seemed about to erupt. At any second, I feared someone would yell out for our officers to leave their leader and start a new revolution. What would the General do? What would I do?

The General looked up and seemed to sense he was losing his audience. He departed from his text, paused, reached into his pocket, and slowly pulled out a letter. I was pretty sure it was a letter from Congressman Jones, who had written the General, holding out hope for favorable action on our petition. The General obviously wanted to read the letter in an effort to convince us that Congress would act. After unfolding the letter in his hands, however, and looking at the first paragraph, the General mumbled barely a few incoherent words and then lapsed into silence. He seemed distracted, even agitated. Still the silence went on. As the seconds went by, I became embarrassed. Had the General suffered some kind of stroke or seizure? He seemed paralyzed. Not a word left his lips. The grumbling that had been rising while the General defended Congress started to subside. We had never seen our commander in such a state, so much in apparent need of sympathy. Soon there was complete silence. I now felt not only embarrassed but sorry for the man who had so often intimidated me.

It was at this moment the General reached into another waistcoat pocket and pulled out a pair of spectacles. I knew he had received these from Dr. Rittenhouse in Philadelphia only a month before, and I knew that he needed them to read small handwriting such as the script of Congressman Jones. But up until now, the General had only used the spectacles in his study. His officers, excepting me, had never seen the General wear his spectacles. The General, as I have said, was vain and proud about his appearance and reluctant to show any infirmity in public, and certainly not before hundreds of officers.

A long "ah" rose from the benches as the officers, for the first time, saw the General's spectacles in his hands.

As the General started, with trembling hands, to put his spectacles on, he looked up, paused, and then declared in a halting voice, but one that now could be heard in the back row of the quieted assembly, "Gentlemen . . . you will forgive me . . . and permit me to put on these spectacles . . . for I have not only grown gray . . . but almost blind in the service of our country."

There was total silence. While I am sure it was only seconds, it seemed like minutes while the General tried to adjust his spectacles in order to read from the letter. I heard sobbing from around the Temple. Finally, calls came forth softly and then more loudly: "We're with you, General." The calls slowly turned into shouts. Then "Tell us what to do" cries emerged, followed by "Tell us and we will follow you." The outpouring continued to come forth. I realized a loyalty built over seven long years would not be broken asunder by a few schemers. I was stunned. The General appeared stunned too.

Then he slowly put his spectacles aside and, with occasional glances at his own prepared speech, he proceeded to do just what his officers were asking: tell us what to do. First, in an increasingly firm voice, he pledged "to exert whatever ability I am possessed of, in your favor." But in return he asked his officers "not to . . . sully the glory you have hitherto maintained," to "rely on the plighted faith of your country," to "value your own sacred honor," and "to express your utmost horror and detestation of the man [the anonymous writer] who wishes, under any specious pretences, to overturn the liberties of our country, and who wickedly attempts to open the flood gates of civil discord and deluge our rising empire in blood."

After pausing and gazing into many of our faces, the General looked down at the speech he had written and ended his remarks with words that I can still vividly recall today. "By thus determining and thus acting, you will pursue the plain and direct road to the attainment of your wishes. You will defeat the insidious designs of our enemies, who are compelled to resort from open force to secret artifice. You will give one more distinguished proof of unexampled patriotism and patient virtue, rising superior to the pressure of the most complicated sufferings; and you will, by the dignity of your conduct, afford occasion for posterity to say, when speaking of the glorious example you have exhibited to mankind, [that] 'had this day been wanting, the world had never seen the last stage of perfection to which human nature is capable of attaining.'"

Nobody moved a muscle. I thought the General was looking me in the eye, but others have since told me they thought he was looking them in the eye. Then the General put his spectacles and his remarks, along with the unread letter, back in his waistcoat pockets, turned, and strode out the door that he had entered just a few minutes before.

Years later, Major Samuel Shaw, who had attended the meeting and was also one of the officers who had visited with the General on Thursday, wrote me that "there was something so natural, so unaffected in his appeal as rendered it superior to the most studied oratory. It forced its way to the heart, and you might see sensibility moisten every eye."

Like me, Shaw knew the challenges the General faced at the meeting. "On other occasions," Shaw wrote, "he had been supported by the exertions of an Army and the countenance of his friends; but in this he stood single and alone. There was no saying where the passions of an Army, which were not a little inflamed, might lead; but it was generally allowed that longer forbearance was dangerous, and moderation had ceased to be a virtue. Under these circumstances he appeared, not at the head of his troops, but—as it were—in opposition to them; and for a dreadful moment the interests of the Army and its General seemed to be in competition. He spoke—every doubt was dispelled, and the tide of patriotism rolled again in its wonted course."

No sooner was the General out the door than General Knox, in his booming voice, moved, with a second by General Rufus Putnam, that the officers reciprocate with affection the General's sentiments and express their unanimous thanks. This motion was met with thunderous "ayes."

Back in the chair on the podium, General Gates looked bewildered. The contrast with General Washington was remarkable, even if unfair. No one had the presence of Washington. All of Gates's features looked more pronounced than usual, and not to his advantage: his ruddy cheeks seemed more ruddy, his stooped shoulders more stooped, his aquiline nose more pointed, and his thin, graying hair more stringy. Unable in his role as chairman to speak, Gates peered around as if looking for a colleague to help him out.

Instead, General Putnam rose and, without waiting for recognition, moved, with a second by General Hand, that one general, one field officer, and one captain be appointed to a committee (the motion then named General Knox, Colonel Brooks, and Captain Howard, three of the officers most loyal to the General) to draft a resolution embodying the General's sentiments and report back within half an hour with the resolution for our approval. Again a thunderous round of "ayes" greeted the motion, and off marched General Knox, Colonel Brooks, and Captain Howard to one of the side rooms, leaving all of us chattering with our neighbors, before an increasingly discomfited General Gates. We all felt we were present at a dramatic and seemingly spontaneous moment, and then I recalled that Generals Knox, Putnam, and Hand and Colonel Brooks and Captain Howard had been among the scores of officers who had bustled in and out of our headquarters that Thursday.

We did not have to wait thirty minutes. It seemed less than five minutes before the committee marched back into the auditorium with a resolution. Maybe I was the only one who felt that it seemed an uncommonly short time to draft what appeared to be a two- or three-page resolution. I was beginning to suspect that the rapid motions thanking the General and appointing a committee, along with the resolution from the committee, had all been planned in those Thursday meetings.

As General Knox read the resolution aloud in his authoritative voice, the message could not have been clearer. The resolution affirmed the army's service to its country out of the "purest love and attachment to . . . rights and liberties" and that "no circumstances of distress or danger shall induce a conduct that may tend to sully the reputation and glory of which they have acquired at the price of their blood"; resolved that "the Army continue to have unshaken confidence in the justice of Congress" to arrange adequate funding for a sum equal to half pay for the officers' retirement years; requested the commander in chief to write the president of the Congress "entreating . . . a most speedy decision"; expressed the army's "abhorrence" and "disdain" and rejection of the "infamous propositions contained in a late anonymous address to the officers of the Army"; and finally praised General McDougall and the other interlocutors with Congress for their "prudence" and asked that they continue their "solicitations at Congress."

I was struck by how many of the phrases in the resolution echoed the phrases of the General's address. Perhaps this was just a coincidence or maybe the committee members had good memories.

The officers roared their approval as the presiding General Gates looked around the room, apparently searching for one of his colleagues to speak. He finally called on Quartermaster General Pickering, who I thought showed great courage in arguing against the resolution. He pointed out the army's hypocrisy in damning with infamy letters that only days before they had read "with rapture." I had to admit Pickering was right. He reminded the assembly that nothing had changed in the intervening time. But things had changed—the General had spoken and completely swayed the officers' feelings. General Pickering was shouted down. General Gates, sensing the situation was beyond his control, called for a vote, and the motion was adopted unanimously with not even General Pickering voting no. With that, the meeting ended upon a motion for adjournment.

As I left the Temple, I could sense the warm feelings of those around me. It was as if we had realized that we had averted danger and had followed the idealistic, but right, course. I walked back to Hasbrouck House with David Humphreys and Benjamin Walker, and we talked about how remarkable it was that the General, who most, including us, regarded as an unremarkable speaker and writer, had changed the direction of the meeting so abruptly. As I reflect back, I have come to believe that the General was a more remarkable speaker and writer than we gave him credit for. It is often written that, during his presidency, the General was not a politician. Of course, he was a great politician in large part because he was not perceived as a politician. It was the same with his writing and speaking. The other Founding Fathers orated and wrote with embellishments, including frequent Greek and Latin allusions. Everything they wrote was a distinguished essay, every speech a great oration. And I notice these essays and speeches are quoted often and inserted in school textbooks. The General, by contrast, wrote for his audience, albeit, because of his lack of formal schooling, his writing included many misspellings. He spoke to his audiences as he had that day at Newburgh. And, unlike on other less important occasions, he did not stammer.

Many times I saw the General move audiences. I told you how he had done so prior to the second battle of Trenton with his plea for the troops to reenlist. Just months after Newburgh and the reoccupation of New York City, the General took leave of his closest officers—those who stood with him that week at Newburgh—at Fraunces Tavern near the Battery on Manhattan Island. He had not prepared any speech to my knowledge and had declined my offer to help. All he gave was a simple toast, but all of us who were there were moved to tears.

"With a heart filled with love and gratitude I now take leave of you. I most devoutly wish that your latter days may be as prosperous and happy as your former ones have been glorious and honorable."

The same emotions were evident that fall when he resigned his commission to the Congress, then housed in Annapolis in the hope that a more attractive city might attract more delegates. But only twenty representatives even bothered to show up to honor the man who had probably saved their positions and perhaps their lives. That was a speech I edited, although most of the words and thoughts were the General's. After referring to the army, forged into a "band of brothers," he went on, haltingly, "Having now finished the work assigned me, I retire from the great theatre of action; and bidding an affectionate farewell to this august body under whose orders I have so long acted, I here offer my commission and take leave of all employments of public life."

The congressmen there, all of whom thought of themselves as more accomplished speakers than the General, wept, including the presiding officer, Congressman Mifflin, who had been part of the Conway Cabal plot to replace the General.

And yet on the way out, I heard one congressman remark, "He is a great man; if only he was a great speaker."

Humphreys, Walker, and I returned from the Temple to Hasbrouck House that Saturday afternoon. We stood outside the General's study, eager to deliver the great news.

Finally, as the General's chief aide, who the General had commissioned as the reporting scribe on the meeting, I tentatively knocked, and the General bid us enter. I opened the door to the study, where we found the General sitting at his desk calmly reading Henry Hume's *The Gentleman Farmer*.

"Well, Josiah," said the General rising, "you took notes on the meeting?"

"Yes, sir," I replied. "Would you like to see them?"

"Yes, Josiah," he said, reaching out his hand.

I turned over the notes, but I could no longer restrain myself. "Sir, the meeting ended most satisfactorily with the officers unanimously approving a resolution endorsing your sentiments. I wrote the text of the resolution for you to see," I said, pointing to the notes.

The General sat back down in his chair. As he read the resolution and my other notes, he handed me a draft of a letter to the president of the Congress to be sent the following day. After I corrected some misspellings and grammatical errors, it read as follows:

I have the honor to inform your Excellency, for the satisfaction of the Congress, that the meeting of the Officers, which was mentioned in my last, has been held Yesterday;

and that it has terminated in a manner, which I had reason to expect, from a knowledge of that good Sense and steady Patriotism of the Gentlemen of the Army, which, on frequent occasions, I have discovered. The report of the meeting, with the other papers, which will accompany it, I do myself the honor to transmit to Congress, as soon as they can possibly be prepared. With the highest respect, I have the honor to be your Excellency's most obedient servant,

George Washington

That was it. It was as if nothing had happened, that the meeting I had just witnessed had been perfunctory. There was no mention of the General's role or his amazing speech. Just the emphasis on the patriotism of the army. For a man I knew to be as concerned about his reputation as anyone, the letter read as if he had not even been present. Then I remembered the General had forwarded the mutinous letters to Congress earlier in the week. The Congress would know or would soon find out from the stories of others what had happened and give the General the credit he was due. For those looking at his note, the General's reputation for modesty would reach new highs. "What a great man and so modest," many would exclaim.

But I knew that the General was as proud and as concerned with getting his due as Achilles. The General, I realized, capitalized on his reputation for being greater than he appeared. As I think back, I realize the General had mastered the art of masking his talents so as to seem less threatening and therefore more admirable. Even when it came to diplomacy, where he always opined to me that "I am no diplomat," his finesse in handling the French generals and admirals would have made Franklin proud.

Seeing my bewilderment, the General said, "Josiah, after reading your notes, we shall send a longer and more carefully drafted letter tomorrow or the next day with all the appropriate documents and make the case why the events of today should move Congress to action." With that comment, he waved us away.

We walked—or in my case, bounded—out of the General's study when suddenly the question that had nagged at me since the meeting brought me up short: I thought to myself, *Was the whole incident with the spectacles spontaneous or had it been planned?*

I was probably the only officer at the meeting who was even asking such a question. It had, I am sure, occurred to no one else in that room swirling with emotions, but then no one else had observed the General as actor the way I had during the last seven years.

I was filled with sudden resolve. *I must ask him,* I thought. I turned, leaving my fellow aides behind, knocked again, and opened the door to his study.

"Yes, Josiah. What is it?" he said, looking up and fixing me with a stare that indicated his impatience.

I froze and suddenly I had trouble speaking. "Oh, nothing, sir," I said, turned, and stumbled out the door.

Two days later, the General, with my help, drafted a lengthy letter to Congress that flattered that body; extolled the army's suffering, patriotism, and virtues; pointed to the army's unanimous rejection of mutiny; and closed by asking for speedy action on the army's petition. The letter not so subtly tried to shame the Congress, stating that the General could not believe Congress would refuse the army's petition and leave unpaid Congress's debt of gratitude. He borrowed from the anonymous letter, asking if "they [the army] are to grow old in poverty, wretchedness and contempt."

The General had emphasized that the recent meeting showed "the last glorious proof of patriotism which could have been given by men who aspired to the distinction of a patriot Army; and will not only confirm their claims to justice, but increase their title to the gratitude of their country."

The General again did not mention his own role in the Newburgh threat but alluded to his disinterestedness by reminding Congress that he, the General, who could afford it, had not taken any pay, implying that Congress could not ask such a sacrifice of the less well endowed. In case Congress could not understand his message, he directed me to include the copies of the army's resolution and the anonymous letters imperiling Congress that he had sent earlier that week, as well as copies of many of his earlier pleas to Congress that it honor its promises to the army.

As I think back, I recognize the General was using the same strategy on Congress he had used with the officers: conveying the assumption that, with such a glorious cause, the Congress would of course rise to the occasion and do the right thing.

My other major letter that week was to Alexander Hamilton. I think the General harbored suspicions that Hamilton and Madison were trying to link the claims of the public creditors with the claims of the army. The General had no objections to the claims of public creditors, but he thought those claims should be second to those of the army. He did not like the financiers wrapping themselves in the protective popular cloak of the army.

The General renewed his plea to Hamilton for action on the army's petition but asked me to insert that "the Army was not something to be trifled with." Did the General mean that Hamilton should not use the army to push the claims of creditors? Or was he threatening what might happen if the Congress did not act on the army's claims?

Perhaps the General—not so simple a man as people thought—chose his words so that Hamilton and his friends could reach both conclusions.

I later heard that I was not the only one who doubted whether the General would confront the mutineers. John Adams and James Madison had their doubts too, but after the General's stand, knowing they would retain their congressional powers, they rushed to extol the General's virtue.

Lastly, the General dictated a short letter to me for circulation to the whole army. He spoke of "the pleasing feelings which have been excited in his breast by the affectionate sentiments expressed toward him" at the Saturday meeting.

The General did not come across to many as a feeling or affectionate man, but I do believe he meant those words, and I remember thinking at the time that for a British general to have expressed such feelings for and to his troops would have been considered unseemly and would never have happened. But then, no British general would have commanded such devotion from his troops as to be able to do what the General did at the Temple.

Epilogue

'Tis not in mortals to command success,
But we'll do more, Sempronius; we'll deserve it.

—Portius, *Cato*, Act I, Scene 2

We were reminded often in the succeeding weeks of how high the stakes were during that pivotal week in Newburgh. News of a peace treaty, albeit a preliminary one, soon reached us. Still another mutiny of the Pennsylvania militia erupted in June over Congress's stinginess about pay. They were just a few hundred militia, many new recruits, but they drove the Congress out of Philadelphia all the way to Princeton. The General sent fifteen hundred troops, who easily dispersed them. Safe under the protection of the General, the Congress resumed its duties (the Congress still later moved on to Annapolis), and the General again minimized his role. In his letter to Congress, he dismissed the militia mutineers as "recruits and soldiers of a day," in contrast to the glorious army that had suffered through the entire war. The Congress was oblivious, but I kept thinking what might have happened if those several hundred raw Pennsylvania militia had been seven thousand five hundred regulars led by hundreds of officers. And what if that force had been augmented and led by the General?

Every day I kept thinking what might have happened if the week of March 9 had taken a different turn. I might have been in Philadelphia with Prescilla, helping the General govern the country. Or we might have been in a civil war, tempting the British to scuttle the preliminary treaty and reenter the fray.

Even today in the 1840s I ponder where our country would be if the General had led a successful insurrection or even if the General had stood aside and been succeeded by a general less virtuous and noble. I read about these South American countries that gained independence from Spain in the 1820s. Now most of them are ruled by military juntas or generals, and I do not know if they have more liberties or fewer than under Spanish rule.

The General's strategy with Congress worked, up to a point. I drafted letter after letter to governors and congressmen, in which the General used the events at Newburgh to extol the glorious patriotism of the army and shame those officials into doing what was right. In April Congress fell short of the nine states needed to grant a decent benefits package—it was rejected by the New Englanders, who had urged other states to send troops to their aid back in 1775 and 1776. Incomprehensible!

Finally, my recollection is that the General did get the Congress to give eighty dollars plus three or four months' extra pay to enlisted men, five dollars per month to invalids for life, and a lump-sum payment of one-half of five years' pay to the officers, with the latter payment delayed until the following January. That was something, although not all that the officers and troops had hoped for. The compensation was in Continental currency worth far less than its stated value and in notes that later might or might not be honored. The General urged the troops and officers as they left the army that spring to hold on to those notes, but most sold them way below value to speculators who, years later after the establishment of our government, profited handsomely. The

General had hoped for more, but I suspect he doubted his own words that day in March about placing faith in the Congress.

The General certainly knew by the fall of 1783 what was happening.

"Josiah, we have a Congress and states who will do just enough to escape the odium of the public's wrath. Then we have those leeches who have sucked blood from our great band of brothers the whole war."

Still, despite the General's and my disappointment at the inadequate congressional action, we are certainly better off than if we had gone through a civil war and a military dictatorship such as our neighbors to the south. The army received something, we do have an independent union, and it is a republic not run by caudillos or a Bonaparte.

And what of the other officers so active in the army at Newburgh that winter in 1783? Laurens died in some useless skirmish down in Carolina well after the war had been decided. What a great loss. Hamilton became secretary of the treasury and later was killed in that lamentable duel with Aaron Burr. My fellow aide, Humphreys, became a diplomat for our new government, minister to Spain. My other fellow aide at Newburgh, Walker, became a congressman. Varick, the General's record keeper, became mayor of New York City. Colonel Brooks, who helped draft the resolution, became governor of Massachusetts.

And what of those who laid the groundwork for the potential insurrection? Gates ended up in the New York State legislature. I read that the General, as president, gave Armstrong a minor position in the New York port, which he parlayed later into a lengthy career in government ending as secretary of war under President Madison. I found this hard to understand. The General pretended as if nothing untoward had happened. He never evinced to me any resentment against the potential mutineers. Perhaps it was to make sure the public had no doubts about the honor of the army. Perhaps the General was following the strategy he had followed with General Lee and Continental Congress President Mifflin (who went from being a member of the Conway Cabal to president of the Continental Congress): he hoped to make those who opposed him turn into supporters because he ignored their transgressions. Ignored, but I doubt the General forgot. Any human being in that situation must have remembered and harbored resentments. I believe that the General held numerous grudges—he just believed that a leader should appear above such petty human emotions. And he was, as usual, successful in conveying the appearance he wished to make. I suppose this is another example of the General as actor. Then again, if you will yourself to overcome petty emotions, does this make you an actor? Or does it just make you someone who molds your personality so as to accent positive rather than negative traits?

I returned to Philadelphia, married Prescilla, and went into the family merchant banking business, where I stayed until we moved to Illinois several years ago to be with our children and grandchildren. I was one of the few aides who did not go into politics. Three—Hamilton, Randolph, and McHenry—served in the Constitutional Convention. The General wrote several times to me after my service and was always gracious. He thanked me for sharing his troubles, giving wise counsel, and guiding his "official family," the term he used to describe his aides.

I remember the letter the General sent me in early 1784. He did not seem to show any regrets about his decision a year before at Newburgh. He told me, as he did others, "I am become a private citizen on the banks of the Potomac and under the shadow of my own vine and fig tree." Then, referring to our past conversations, he said, "I am no longer a soldier pursuing fame." The letter made me chuckle. Thousands of Americans wished they were famous like the General, and he just wanted to live under his fig tree.

I read the books and articles that come out on the General now. There seems to be a dichotomy between what some of these learned men think and what the majority of our people think. While most biographies of the General are flattering, some perhaps too flattering, the views of the General that my great-grandchildren are getting from their teacher—that his generalship was overrated; that he was intellectually inferior to Adams, Jefferson, and the other founders; that he supported slavery because until the end of his life the General was a slaveholder; etc.—seem to be the start of an emerging trend, and we shall probably see more such assessments in the future.

As my pen nears my final pages, I hope I have set the record straight on some of these matters, as I will try to do for my great-grandchildren next week.

While you read pros and cons about the General, you never read about Newburgh and how we have a democratic government because of what the General didn't do that week. There are plenty of books and articles about what he did, but none about what he didn't do: seize power.

After years I have come to realize that the General certainly was ambitious, but ambitious for the applause of his countrymen—not for power over his countrymen. Yes, the General cared about his public image and sought fame. Gouverneur Morris said the General's greatest moral weakness was his "inordinate" love of fame. But so what? The General sought fame but not power. I will try to tell my great-grandchildren that there is a huge difference, and because of that difference, unlike our neighbors to the south, today we rule ourselves. Why, the whole balance between the executive and the legislative branches is due to the General. I read how Madison and Hamilton drafted the Constitution. But there never would have been a president included in that noble document if the delegates had not been looking at the General sitting right in front of them. They never would have allowed a chief executive if they had not known it would be the General.

Of course, there are some doubts about our presidential-congressional system these days. The last presidential election would have mortified the General, decided by slogans like "Tippecanoe and Tyler too" and drawings of Harrison living in a log cabin when he really lived in a mansion. Still, almost 80 percent of us voted, which I'm told is the highest turnout ever. Now we have a president and Congress that can't agree on anything. I don't know how many votes Congress has taken on whether to have a national bank. The other day, a crowd burned President Tyler in effigy, threw rocks at the White House, and cried out for his impeachment. Still, all these European visitors come over here and tell us what a great system of government we have, and I suppose it's better than any other.

I am pleased that our people are not unduly influenced by the press or academics. That's why we will be celebrating the General's birthday tomorrow with as much spirit as the Fourth of July. The people realize, as Congressman Fisher Ames wrote, that the General may have made errors in judgment, but there were no blemishes on his virtue. Of course, the politicians know where the people stand, and they constantly invoke the General's name. Why, on the General's last birthday, I read in our local newspaper how one of our state legislators, Abraham Lincoln, who is no fool, compared the General to the sun: "Washington is the mightiest name on earth—long since mightiest in the cause of civil liberty, still mightiest in moral reformation. On that name no eulogy is expected. It cannot be. To add brightness to the sun, or glory to the name of Washington is alike impossible. Let none attempt it. In solemn awe we pronounce the name, and in its naked deathless splendor leave it shining on."

Tomorrow Lincoln will probably show off his ring, which he claims contains a piece of the General's hair. It's amazing how many politicians wear rings they say contain a piece of his coffin or a lock of the General's hair. I don't blame them. It's almost as many as the homes and hotels that claim "George Washington slept here."

I don't blame these politicians. They, like the people, sense the General was a great man. They know he resigned his General's commission and declined to run for a third term as president, but I doubt many have ever heard of Newburgh and how the General refused power there. They do not know what temptations he must have faced. The General not only exercised power but turned away from power. Looking at some of our recent presidents, and what I expect will be the case with presidents to come, I think that is the rarest of qualities.

I believe the American people sense the greatness of someone who can seek fame and still turn away from power, but it is ironic that foreigners seem better able to voice their admiration for this supreme trait of the General. Perhaps this is because of their experience with absolute monarchs. On the way from Newburgh to the General's resignation before Congress, we met with a Dutch businessman, Gerald Vogels, in Philadelphia. "Josiah," he said, "I will write my wife that I just saw the greatest man who has appeared on the surface of this earth." At the time I thought this a gross exaggeration, but with the exception of our Lord and Savior, I am not sure now that this was an exaggeration at all.

I don't know if it is true, but I read that King George III asked the American painter Benjamin West what the General was going to do after resigning his commission, and West told him the General, instead of becoming king, only wanted to return to his farm. The king reportedly responded, "If Washington does that, he will be the greatest man in the world."

And of course there's that story of how Napoleon, who knew something about seeking both fame and power, said despairingly when imprisoned on St. Helena: "The people expected me to be another Washington."

No wonder the English poet Lord Byron turned his "Ode to Napoleon Buonaparte" into an ode to the General.

> the first—the last—the best—
> The Cincinnatus of the West,
> Whom Envy dared not hate.
> Bequeath'd the name of Washington,
> To make man blush there was but one!

What these powerful Europeans knew and what many Americans sense is that the General did not seek power or riches. Instead, I have come to realize, all the General sought was the praise of his countrymen. He received that, and he deserves it.

While I was so proud of what the General did that day, I have reflected on whether I was wrong to doubt the General's intentions that week. Many now assume in retrospect that the General, because he refused power, never was tempted. I don't think so. I suspect the General himself had doubts as to what course he should or would follow. But if he had doubts, if he had temptations, does that not make him all the greater? I keep thinking of one of the General's favorite lines from Cato: "'Tis not in mortals to command success, but we'll do more . . . we'll deserve it."

His countrymen may not be aware of what the General did at Newburgh that week, but they know about his turning back his sword to Congress and refusing to run for a third term as president. The poet Philip Freneau, although critical of some of the General's policies as president during his second term, conveyed that feeling when he wrote:

> O Washington!—thrice glorious name,
> What due rewards can man decree—
> Empires are far below thine aim,
> And sceptres have no charm for thee;
> Virtue alone has your regard,
> And she must be your great reward.

I look forward to meeting with my great-grandchildren soon. I will answer their questions about what I did during the war, of course omitting my fear and avoidance of combat in close quarters. My great-grandchildren will ask me all sorts of questions about the General. I will try to answer them, but I also will tell them the story of Newburgh. I will focus on the General's rather than my own role.

Yes, I will tell them that the General had flaws. Maybe our country will someday see a better general. Maybe someone else will bring delegates together to draft a new constitution. Maybe someday we will see a greater president. But after telling them the story of Newburgh, I will try to convey to my great-grandchildren that the General's true greatness lay not so much in what he did but what he didn't do. Then I will dig out and show them this 1791 news clipping from the *Hartford Courant* dug up and sent me by my old Connecticut colleague David Humphreys after the General's death.

> Many a private man might make a great President; but will there ever be a President who will make so great a man as WASHINGTON?

AFTERWORD

This is a novel about George Washington and power, or rather, the greatest temptation to assume absolute power ever faced by any American leader. It is also a book about one of the least known but most momentous episodes in American history. As the reader has discovered, our first army—poorly fed and clothed, often unpaid, and with little hope of promised retirement benefits—while camped on the Hudson River in New York during a week in the last months of the Revolutionary War, faced a long-put-off decision: whether to gain what the army believed was its just due by marching on Philadelphia and taking over the civilian government. That decision would establish whether our country was to have civilian supremacy over the military or go the route followed by most revolutions toward a military dictatorship.

Any reader of an historical novel will find himself wondering what is fact and what is fiction—or speculation. What you have read here of that week in early 1783 in Newburgh and New Windsor, New York, is overwhelmingly factual, and the more surprising the information, the more likely it is to be factual. Where I suspect the reader will be surprised that something included in the novel is factual or may want more information, I have provided short background essays in Appendix A, which the reader may pursue at leisure.

I have also provided in Appendix B the full text of some of the key documents from that period, e.g., speeches, letters, resolutions, etc., that convey the tensions and suspicions of that fateful week.

Looking into the supporting material in Appendixes A and B, the reader will see that even much of what is fiction is closely tied to fact. Josiah, the General's aide, who narrates the story, and who I have come to know as well as any of my ancestors, is, alas, fictional. However, his duties and activities as an aide-de-camp of General Washington are based on those of the thirty-two men who served in that position during the war. The conversations are also imagined, but they are almost always based, sometimes in total, on letters, sometimes either of the characters quoted, or of others describing the characters. In all cases the views I have attributed to the characters, including Washington, are the views held by those characters during the late eighteenth century, although not necessarily on the precise date. I have limited myself to selected essays and documentation in the appendixes, because to cite every letter and source would take more pages than the novel itself.

The speculation in this novel centers on four questions: who was behind the incipient revolt; whether the revolt could have succeeded; whether Washington ever considered leading it; and if so, how he wrestled with the temptation of taking leadership of the revolt and setting up an American monarchy or military dictatorship.

Historians have espoused many views on who was behind the potential mutiny. Most point to officers at Newburgh led by General Horatio Gates, some point to members of Congress, and some point to both. There is little doubt, however, that Gates's aide, Major John Armstrong Jr., wrote the letters that sparked the crises, and I do not believe Armstrong would have written such letters without General Gates's approval.

On the question of whether the revolt might have succeeded, there are opposing views. Some historians say the revolt would have failed. Some see the revolt as partially successful with a passive mutiny leading the army to stop fighting the British and weakening civil authority. Still others believe that the revolt, particularly with General Washington's leadership, would have overthrown the government, resulting in a coup d'état and a military government or monarchy.

The most speculative and pivotal parts of the book—and really the major reason for writing it as a novel—is how George Washington considered and was tempted to lead the revolt and set up an American monarchy or dictatorship. Most historians have ignored these questions, largely, I believe, because they assume that since Washington was a man of great character who did not take leadership of the revolt, he must not have been tempted. To the contrary, I believe that it would have been impossible for any person in that situation not to have considered such a course, as shown by the barrage of written and oral pleas to become king or dictator that Washington received, which we know to be factual, and which form an important part of this novel. Washington certainly knew that he alone had the ability to lead a new government in the perilous transition to peace. I believe his temptation and his triumph over that temptation, rather than diminishing Washington, enhance his greatness.

For those seeking to read more about our country's first leader, there have been hundreds of biographies, too many to read or list. Just about all focus on his early life, his generalship, his bringing about of the Constitutional Convention, and his role as our first president. There are few that devote more than several pages to the week at Newburgh in 1783. I believe one of the most underrated and unread biographies of Washington is the first one written, *The Life of Washington* by Supreme Court Chief Justice John Marshall, published soon after Washington's death. Marshall's five-volume (and later one-volume) biography has the disadvantage of being both overly long and written so soon after Washington's life that it does not benefit from years of research and perspective. It has the advantage, however, of being written when memories were fresh by one who knew Washington. The latest biography, by Ron Chernow, *Washington,* is easier to digest, as are biographies by John Ferling, James Flexner, and Richard Norton Smith. To grasp Washington's character and his incredible hold on the American people in the eighteenth and nineteenth centuries, the best books are Barry Schwartz's pathbreaking *George Washington: The Making of an American Symbol,* Joseph J. Ellis's penetrating *His Excellency* (where Ellis writes of the General's "Last Temptation"), and Richard Brookhiser's thoughtful *Founding Father,* as well as Gary Wills's *Cincinnatus: George Washington and the Enlightenment: Images of Power in Early America* and Edward G. Lengel's *Inventing George Washington.* I found the best histories of Washington's generalship during the Revolutionary War to be David Hackett Fischer's *Washington's Crossing* and John Ferling's *Almost a Miracle.* Very little has been written about the critical period after Yorktown and before the signing of the peace treaty—the period when the week at Newburgh takes place—but two books have remedied this: Thomas Fleming's *The Perils of Peace: America's Struggle for Survival after Yorktown, 1781–1783* and William M. Fowler Jr.'s *American Crisis: George Washington and the Dangerous Two Years After Yorktown, 1781–1783.*

For those interested in pursuing Martha Washington's life and twisted family background, *Martha Washington, First Lady of Liberty* by Helen Bryan contains much information. For books about the founders' attitudes about slavery, there are Henry Wiencek's books on George Washington and Thomas Jefferson as well as his exploration of the subject in the October 2012 issue of *Smithsonian* magazine. There have been many books on Washington's colleagues during the Revolution, but for sheer reading pleasure few rival Harlow Giles Unger's *Lafayette.*

To all the authors listed above and many others, I am indebted. Without their historical research, I would not have been able to construct this novel.

I wish to thank William Ferraro and his colleagues at the Washington Papers of the University of Virginia, who are compiling the foremost collection of Washington's papers and provided me with copies of those written during the eventful week at Newburgh, as well as many excellent suggestions. Editor-in-Chief Ferraro was also invaluable in checking for historical inaccuracies. Also of inestimable help were Kathleen Mitchell, Aaron Robinson, and Lynette Scherer at Washington's Headquarters State Historic Site, Chad Johnson at the New Windsor Cantonment State Historical Site, and Joan Stahl at the Mount Vernon estate and gardens, as well as the Library of Congress and the Massachusetts Historical Society. I have benefited from the help of Nick Robinson, librarian at the University of California at Berkeley's Institute for Governmental Studies, where, as a visiting scholar, I wrote and researched much of this book. Without Nick's help, this techno-peasant would not have been able to navigate through computers to many crucial sources. Linda Bennett of the Marin Public Library also helped track down sources, and Joseph Escalle provided almost weekly help with computer challenges.

To B. Gerald Johnson, a friend and colleague in an earlier political life, I am indebted for suggesting that the story be told through the eyes of the aide, Josiah. Debra Saunders and Wesley Smith gave great encouragement and ideas about structuring, which have been gratefully adopted.

To the late William Safire, author of the historical novel *Freedom* about Abraham Lincoln's role in the Civil War, I owe the idea of explaining in the notes in Appendix A much of what is real and what little is fictional.

There is a time in the writing of every book when someone steps forward and stimulates the author's lagging spirits. That person was Louisa Gilder, who for almost two years patiently edited and improved this book, asking questions that needed to be answered and suggesting scores of improvements in the style and language.

Later, Carmen Johnson, David Blum, and Jeff Belle of my publisher, Amazon, all stepped in to provide much help.

For proofreading I owe thanks to many for spotting grammatical, spelling, duplication, and just plain mistakes: Editor-in-Chief William Ferraro, the late Paul Kraabel, Stuart Wagner, June Miller, Stephanie Brown, and Sidney Saltz.

A special thanks is due to the anonymous elderly lady who sat next to me when, as a congressman back in the 1980s, I attended a Daughters of the American Revolution observance of Washington's birthday alongside the statue of the General on the University of Washington campus. Following a long speech about Washington's deeds in winning the Revolutionary War, organizing the Constitutional Convention, and serving as our first president, she leaned over and said, "Congressman, they always talk about what he did and never about what he didn't do." When I asked what she meant, she responded, "He didn't seize power when the troops wanted to revolt in 1783 at Newburgh." Being totally unaware of the events of that week, I was interested by her remark, which resulted in decades of off-and-on research and the writing of this book.

Lastly, I thank my partner and friend, Stephanie Brown, who has encouraged, supported, and tolerated this effort for almost six years.

The author takes responsibility for all errors, as well as the opinions expressed on how General Washington surmounted the challenges that fateful 1783 week in Newburgh. I further take responsibility for the moral convictions expressed justifying the *Hartford (Connecticut) Courant*'s words in the 1790s quoted at the end of this novel as to why, no matter what has happened in the past or may happen in the future, George Washington may be esteemed the greatest figure in American history.

APPENDIX A: NOTES

Prologue

Josiah Recalling Events Sixty Years Ago for His Great-Grandchildren, pages 3-4

It is difficult for us to imagine the hold that the Revolutionary War had on Americans in the first half of the nineteenth century. World War II would be analogous today, but even World War II only arguably saved our democracy, while the Revolutionary War both created and saved it.

In the nineteenth century, veterans who had served in the Revolutionary War were idolized, and in an age when books were scarcer and electronic media did not exist, children and grandchildren gathered around the hearth to hear their parents and grandparents tell their stories.

Nonetheless, the period after Yorktown and before the peace treaty, 1781 to 1783, was not much better known in the 1800s than today. Already schools had started to simplify the story so that the surrender at Yorktown in 1781 then, as today, was portrayed as the end of the Revolutionary War. The process of forgetting or perhaps deliberately ignoring the period between 1781 and 1783 had already started. Why dwell on events like the subject of this novel, the nascent insurrection, which might have besmirched the narrative of the unceasing and heroic struggle to found our country? Such a focus, while actually deepening the appreciation of what our founders did, might have, albeit briefly, detracted from the imposing narrative of Josiah and his comrades. (For those wishing to learn more about this period between 1781 and 1783, there are two excellent books, *The Perils of Peace: America's Struggle for Survival after Yorktown 1781–1783* by Thomas Fleming and *American Crisis: George Washington and the Dangerous Two Years After Yorktown, 1781–1783* by William M. Fowler, Jr.)

Washington's Schooling and His Letters, page 4

Washington's early education, as Josiah's comments and just about every early biography of Washington have noted, was skimpy. The General had very little formal schooling, probably the equivalent of one year in fourth grade from a private tutor.

Washington was, however, like many in that era, a prodigious letter writer. Volumes of his letters and orders have survived, except for most of the letters to Martha, which, to the regret of historians, she burned. There are detailed editions of Washington's writings, such as John C. Fitzpatrick's *The Writings of George Washington*, but I have found the most readable, albeit selected, edition of Washington's writings to be contained in *Writings*, edited by John Rhodehamel. I have therefore quoted that edition whenever possible. Many letters are quoted in this novel, and sometimes the quotations are contained in the conversations or views attributed to Washington.

Divided Family Loyalties in the Revolutionary War, page 5

Divided loyalties of families such as Josiah's were commonplace in the Revolutionary War, although by the 1840s when Josiah tells us his story, some families were already hiding their earlier fidelity to King George III. In *Tories*, Thomas B. Allen explains just how numerous

Tory Americans were. Allen dismisses John Adams's much-cited estimate that a third of the population had loyalist sympathies. Instead, he cites historians Henry S. Commager and Richard B. Morris for the estimate that if you added those who were either loyal to the crown or neutral, you probably had well over a third of the population (Thomas B. Allen, *Tories*, xiv–xxii). While no surveys were taken, it is generally recognized that percentages differed from area to area, e.g., New York City had a higher proportion of loyalists than Boston.

Breaking Up Fight between Soldiers from Virginia and Massachusetts, page 7

The confrontation between General Washington and the Virginia and Massachusetts troops sounds like fiction, but it isn't. There are numerous accounts, and the most vivid is by Massachusetts soldier Israel Trask:

> Together the general and William Lee rode straight into the middle of the riot. Trask watched Washington with awe as "with the spring of a deer he leaped from his saddle, threw the reins of his bridle into the hands of his servant, and rushed into the thickest of the melees, with an iron grip seized two tall, brawny, athletic, savage-looking riflemen by the throat, keeping them at arm's length, alternately shaking and talking to them." Talking was probably not the right word. The rioters stopped fighting, turned in amazement to watch Washington in action, then fled at "the top of their speed in all directions." (See David Hackett Fischer, *Washington's Crossing*, 25)

This confrontation understandably enhanced General Washington's reputation for physical prowess among the troops and left them in awe of their General.

Current Erroneous Image of Washington as a Gray-Haired, Paunchy Old Man, 7

The image we have today of Washington reflects Washington in later years, when he was painted by Gilbert Stuart years after the Revolutionary War. That image was already gaining currency at the time of Josiah's old age. In contrast, Benjamin Rush's view that "there is not a King in Europe that would not look like a *valet de chambre* by his [Washington's] side" was widely shared by Washington's contemporaries and is reflected by the new sculptures of Washington in all his youth and vigor now found at Mount Vernon. These sculptures are based on modern forensic science and give us an accurate picture of how General Washington, a handsome six-foot-three inch, 209-pound physical specimen, really looked to others during the Revolutionary War.

General Washington's Aides, pages 4-5, 6, 9-12, 16-18

The aides mentioned here, except for Josiah, all existed, and their backgrounds and duties were as described. They were part of an evolving coterie of thirty-two who served the General during the Revolutionary War. (Those wishing to pursue the history of General Washington's aides may want to read *Washington and His Aides-de-camp* by Emily Stone Whitely or the biography of one of Washington's aides, *Tench Tilghman, The Life and Times of Washington's Aide-de-camp* by L. G. Shreve.)

General Washington's Headquarters, page 9

General Washington's headquarters and living quarters were in Hasbrouck House, which still stands in Newburgh, New York, and has been restored. Newburgh was a city of fifteen hundred people during the war, and the General, Lady Washington, and several of his aides lived and worked in Hasbrouck House, a seven-room stone house acquired from Catherine Hasbrouck, widow of a militia colonel who had died in 1780. Mrs. Hasbrouck went to live with relatives in nearby New Paltz. The rear of Hasbrouck House (which still exists today) looks down across a grassy hillside at the Hudson River. The most attractive room was Lady Washington's parlor. For those interested in seeing the headquarters, you can visit Washington's Headquarters State Historic Site in Newburgh year-round. It was the first publicly owned historic site in our country (acquired in 1850), and events commemorating Washington and the Revolution are held regularly.

GENERAL WASHINGTON'S ACCOUNTING, 11-12

The General's handling of accounts was super careful to the point of being ridiculed. The congressional finding, which Josiah recounts, about Washington undercharging the taxpayers by one dollar for his expenses during the war, did take place. (See E. James Ferguson, *The Power of the Purse: A History of American Public Finance, 1776–1790*.)

GENERAL WASHINGTON'S GUIDE TO CONDUCT, 13

The *Rules of Civility & Decent Behavior in Company and Conversation* was, as Josiah noted, a constant guide and companion of the General's. The full version has been translated by John T. Phillips II, who also provides a history of this guide to etiquette in the *Compleat George Washington Series*. *Rules of Civility* can also be found in many sources, including at the beginning of *The Writings of George Washington* cited above.

Some of the rules may seem antiquated to modern eyes and seemed so even to Josiah reflecting back in the 1840s. The General took them seriously, however, and I have therefore quoted them exactly on many occasions in these pages.

Martha Washington's Wealth, pages 14-15

I assumed, like many, that Martha was the wealthy partner in the Washington marriage. This is true but with the caveat mentioned by Josiah: her wealth was largely inherited, and the inheritance was tied up for decades due to litigation by the heirs, many illegitimate, fathered by Martha's first husband's father. The lengthy litigation gave great business on both sides of the dispute to many of Virginia's finest lawyers. While this litigation went on, the family's main wealth derived from George.

Martha Washington's Interracial Relatives, pages 14-15

Regarding Josiah's reference to Lady Washington's mixed-race relatives, according to Helen Bryan's *Martha Washington, First Lady of Liberty*, Martha's half sister, Ann, was fathered by Martha's father, John Dandridge, with an Indian-Negro woman. Similarly, Martha's first husband, Daniel Custis, had a black half brother, fathered by Daniel's father, John Custis.

The financial, sexual, and interracial background of Martha's family has been explored by Bryan, and so has Washington's by Bryan, Henry Wiencek in *An Imperfect God*, and others. There were numerous rumors spread by the British about George Washington's sexual activities outside his marriage to Martha, but there is little supporting evidence, particularly of interracial sex. What there is rests on a family legend about a slave at Mount Vernon, Wes Ford; speculation on a visit by Washington to his brother John Augustine's plantation ninety-five miles from Mount Vernon (where the alleged slave mother resided); and a visit by his brother's family and slave to Mount Vernon. If there was an interracial relationship, the evidence, weak as it is, points to John Augustine. While Josiah notes the contemporary discussion of Jefferson's sexual relations with his slave Sally Hemings—it was then known that Jefferson lived in Paris for years with Hemings, and there is now DNA evidence supporting the relationship—there is no such evidence for such a relationship involving Washington. As Edward G. Lengel, editor of the Washington Papers Project at the University of Virginia, acknowledges, while you can never absolutely prove a negative, by this standard, "one might as well assume that half the population of the United States may be descended from Pocahontas." (See Edward G. Lengel, *Inventing George Washington*, p. 191.) According to Lengel, and I agree, Washington was not only a prude but also too concerned with his public reputation to engage in what society then would have regarded as improper conduct.

CHAPTER ONE: DAY ONE, MONDAY—THE FIRST ANONYMOUS LETTER

THE FIRST ANONYMOUS LETTER, 20 (QUOTED IN FULL IN APPENDIX B, PAGE 272)

MUTINIES DURING THE REVOLUTIONARY WAR, PAGES 20-21

Mutinies took place throughout the Revolutionary War, far more on the American side than on the British side. These had very little to do with the devotion of the sides to their respective causes. As described earlier, in the 1781 Pennsylvania mutiny, American troops were devoted to the cause of independence, but the devotion of the state authorities and Congress to paying, feeding, and clothing the troops was much less. The causes of the very first mutiny in 1775 described here were typical of the causes of all the American mutinies: lack of pay, food, and clothing. "Taxation without representation" may have inspired the Revolution, but sometimes the troops who fought the battles may have wondered if the Revolution was against all forms of taxation, as state legislatures and the Congress were far more diligent in raising troops than in raising the taxes to care for them. Committees and riots against taxation were common during the war. (See John Ferling, *Almost a Miracle*, 350, 351.)

The corruption and incompetence of the authorities in buying and dispensing supplies compounded the deprivations suffered. These failures by Congress and the state legislatures were a constant concern to General Washington. One could almost compose a volume just of the letters Washington wrote to Congress and the governors pleading for relief. Later in this book, some of these letters are quoted, including allusions to the threat of mutiny. (For an overview of mutinies during the Revolutionary War, see John A. Nagy, *Rebellion in the Ranks*.)

Travails of American Common Soldier, pages 20-22

The quotation from General Greene's letter to a South Carolina militia general that politicians think the army "can live on air and water" expressed the view typical of higher officers toward the Congress and the states. These officers saw months without pay, weeks without clothing, and days without food as the norm.

There are very few firsthand accounts of the difficult lives led by enlisted men during the war. The best and most readable is *A Narrative of a Revolutionary Soldier: Some Adventures, Dangers, and Sufferings of Joseph Plumb Martin* by Joseph Plumb Martin. By contrast, British and Hessian troops were equipped, fed, and trained as well as any troops in the world. An average enlistment of a year for the American soldiers compared with fifteen years' service and training for the average British private.

Reverend Duché's Appeal to Washington to Lead a Coup D'état, 24 (quoted in Appendix B, 257-262)

Jacob Duché was a Philadelphia clergyman whose prayer at the First Continental Congress helped sparked the revolutionary cause. Duché, however, had become a "defeatist" who believed the American cause under congressional leadership had grown hopeless. Duché wrote to Washington that "'tis you Sir, and you only, that support the present Congress." The American people, according to Duché, supported General Washington rather than the Congress and "the whole world knows that its [the army's] very existence depends upon you, that your death or captivity disperses it in a moment." If Congress could not negotiate an end to the war, argued Duché, Washington should lead a coup d'état.

In his reply, Washington is reported to have rejected the suggestion as "ridiculous" and immediately sent on copies of Duché's letter the next day to Congress. This action, as we will see, enhanced Washington's standing with Congress. (See Barry Schwartz, *George Washington: The Making of an American Symbol*, 133.)

Appeals to Washington by Congressmen Cornell and Hooper, page 24

The calls by Congressmen Cornell and Hooper for Washington to expand his leadership went beyond Reverend Duché's appeal, as the congressmen represented Americans who still believed the war could be won. (See John Ferling, *Almost a Miracle*, 471; Barry Schwartz, *George Washington: The Making of an American Symbol*, 21.)

I have found no response by Washington to either Cornell or Hooper's appeals. These appeals were typical of those Washington received throughout the war up to and through the week at Newburgh.

General Washington's Attitude toward the British before the Revolutionary War, pages 26-30

Washington's antagonism toward the British did indeed, as Josiah surmises, go back to their treatment of him during the French and Indian War. Washington and other colonial soldiers believed, with good cause, that the British military held them in contempt. While this contempt was reflected in the British disregard for colonial (including Indian) knowledge of tactics and terrain, nothing highlighted their contempt more than the British practice of having British officers of inferior rank serve over more senior and experienced colonial officers of higher rank. That this practice specifically affected Washington's rank and commands, as well as the British refusal to commission Washington to a high rank, has been documented by many of Washington's biographers. (See Ron Chernow, *Washington*, 39, 40.)

Nothing better sums up Washington's antagonism toward British policies prior to the Revolutionary War—earlier than many American leaders—than his letter to neighbor George Mason in 1769 where he stated, "Our lordly masters in Great Britain will be satisfied with nothing less than the deprivation of American freedom," and "that no man shou'd scruple, or hesitate a moment to use arms in defence of so valuable a blessing" (*The Writings of George Washington*, 129–32).

"HANDS IN MY POCKET," PAGE 27

Washington's "hands in my pocket" quote objecting to British taxation without representation appears in many sources, suggesting he stated this view many times, but the most complete version I have found is in a 1774 letter to a loyalist neighbor, Bryan Fairfax: "I think the Parliament of Great Britain hath no more Right to put their hands into my Pocket, without my consent, than I have to put my hands into yours for money" (*The Writings of George Washington*, 155, 156).

Washington's Support of Recruiting Black Rhode Island Troops and Arming South Carolina Blacks, pages 30-33

Washington discreetly supported General Varnum's proposal to have Rhode Island raise black troops. (See John Ferling's *Almost a Miracle*, 342.) Some historians, including John Ferling, are dubious of Washington's support of Laurens's proposal to arm South Carolina's slaves because there are no public statements by Washington stating his support. Other historians, such as Thomas Fleming, believe Washington supported Laurens's proposal as evidenced by his writing to Laurens, "I know of nothing which can be opposed to them [British reinforcements going to Charleston] with such a prospect of success as the corps you have proposed should be levied in Carolina . . ."

While Washington may have had mixed feelings, I find it hard to believe that Alexander Hamilton, Washington's trusted aide, would have written to John Jay as president of the Congress endorsing Laurens's proposal to arm South Carolina blacks without Washington's approval. Hamilton wrote in part:

> The contempt we have been taught to entertain for the blacks makes us fancy many things that are founded neither in reason nor experience; and an unwillingness to part with property of so valuable a kind will furnish a thousand arguments to show the impracticability or pernicious tendency of a scheme which requires such a sacrifice. But it should be considered that if we do not make use of them in this way, the enemy probably will and that the best way to counteract the temptations they will hold out will be to offer them ourselves. An essential part of the plan is to give them their freedom with their muskets. This will secure their fidelity, animate their courage, and I believe will have

a good influence upon those who remain by opening a door to their emancipation. (See Ron Chernow, *Alexander Hamilton*, 122)

Similarly, if Washington had not been supportive of the proposal, I find it difficult to believe that he would have written a letter to Laurens commiserating over South Carolina's rejection of the proposal. Washington wrote in part:

The spirit of freedom which at the commencement of this contest would have gladly sacrificed everything to the attainment of its object has long since subsided, and every selfish passion has taken its place. It is not the public but the private interest which influences the generality of mankind nor can the Americans any longer boast of an exception. (See Thomas Fleming, *The Perils of Peace*, 127)

Washington's Attitude toward Women Soldiers in the Revolutionary War, pages 33-34

There are many stories of women in combat with the American army, including those described by Josiah here. The one of Deborah Sampson, whose alias was Robert Shurtliff, seems well founded. That Washington only discharged her after a surgeon, examining her wounds, discovered she was a woman indicates that Washington spent little time determining whether a recruit was a man or a woman. With regard to woman soldiers, there seems to have been a Revolutionary War version of "don't ask, don't tell." The story of Mary Ludwig, a.k.a. Molly Pitcher, is less certain, although the story had great currency at the time and Congress gave Mary Ludwig a pension for her alleged service. (See Walter Hart Blumenthal, *Women Camp Followers of the American Revolution*, 69, 70; Holly Mayer, *Belonging to the Army*, 20, 21, and 144.)

Washington's Attitude toward Indians in the Revolutionary War, pages 34-35

Washington frequently acknowledged to others, as he acknowledged to Josiah, the superior ability of Indians when it came to fighting in the woods. (See Ron Chernow, *Washington*, 88.) Washington understood the Indians' suffering at the hands of the settlers but was not able to implement his dream of integrating the Indians into American civilization. (See Chernow, *Washington*, 666.) At no time did Washington's feelings toward the Indians lead him to advocate restricting settlement of the colonists. To ban settlement anywhere in the promised land would have been as far-fetched to Washington as banning the Israelites from settling any part of the Holy Land.

Washington's Order Calling the Saturday Meeting, pages 35-36 (quoted in Full in Appendix B, pages 272-273)

Chapter Two: Day Two, Tuesday—The Second Anonymous Letter

THE SECOND ANONYMOUS LETTER, pages 37-40 (quoted in Appendix B, pages 273-278)

The quotes here are all taken verbatim from the letter. The author is a masterful writer who understands the grievances of the army and plays on the insecurities of his readers, who feared with much justification that the American people did not appreciate their service and would not reward their efforts after the war ended. The writer cleverly makes the case that the army's leverage will disappear if it doesn't act while it is still armed before the peace treaty is signed.

Pennsylvania 1781 Mutiny, pages 41-43

While John Nagy's previously cited *Rebellion in the Ranks* covers the 1781 Pennsylvania mutiny, as well as other mutinies, two books focus exclusively on the 1781 mutiny that Josiah learns about from his cousin. *Mutiny in January* by Carl Van Doren is a judicious and well-researched account of the largest mutiny of American troops to actually take place during the Revolutionary War. *The Proud and the Free*, a fast-paced novel by Howard Fast, tries to create a Marxist framework by picturing the 1781 mutiny as a working-class revolt by troops against a bourgeois and planter officer class. There were undoubtedly resentments against officers, but as Van Doren makes clear, what distinguishes the Pennsylvania mutiny was the troops' focus on grievances against the Congress and state governments, not against their officers. The mutinous troops' apparent respect for many officers, including Washington and General Anthony Wayne; the willingness of these troops to undertake actions against the British under the command of American officers; and their rejection of British overtures, going so far as to arrest and turn over British emissaries to American officers, are not the actions one would expect from the usual mutineers angry at their officers.

Josiah Calculates the Chances of a Revolt Succeeding, 43

As I mentioned in the Afterword, given Washington's character and the fact that he did not lead the mutiny, historians have assumed he never considered that course. Similarly, since the mutiny did not take place in the end, historians have spent little time assessing whether it would have succeeded. To the extent such consideration has been given, there have been varying opinions about the chances of success. Thomas Fleming sees the army marching on Philadelphia and, without predicting whether the revolt would have succeeded, sees the possibility of a civil war, the British "irresistibly tempted to get back in the game," and the potential collapse of the Confederation (*The Perils of Peace*, 273).

Barry Schwartz believes that "Washington could have taken over the government by military coup . . ." (*George Washington: Making of an American Symbol*, 44).

Those expressing skepticism about the success of a revolt point to the innate reservations of Americans about the military based on years of British quartering of troops and the ties of soldiers and officers to their families.

Yet, as Josiah calculates, it is hard to dismiss the chances of success, which I believe were quite good. By the end of 1782, all the major cities and seaports were occupied by the American armies except for New York, where London had sent General Carleton, whose mission was the withdrawal of the fourteen thousand troops there. The Congress might have fled Philadelphia, which it did during the short-lived Pennsylvania mutiny put down with Washington's help in 1781. But even if it found a town willing to host the Congress, where would it have found the revenue to carry out any governmental functions?

Control of seaports meant that a revolting army would have immediately controlled the vast majority of revenues coming to the government set up in 1776 since those revenues were derived from imposts on trade. The revenues raised by the states through taxation were meager, and the states showed no inclination to turn over the revenues they did raise to the national government.

A revolt, especially one led by Washington, would have quickly established the only national government with both revenues and a military arm. The states would have been given a stark choice: join the new government (which already controlled several states through the army's occupation of the major cities) or resist and try to go it alone. The latter alternative would not have seemed very attractive. Either the states would have fallen victim to a military filled with its own sons or, more likely, the revolting army with Washington leading the new government would just have waited for the holdouts to join the new government, feeling the same pressures not to go it alone that they felt in 1776 and were to feel during the Constitution ratification process in 1789.

The pressure to join the new government would have increased; a government with Washington at its head promised all the benefits of the previous one plus benefits for the soldiers, without the Congress's reputation for incompetence. Foreign nations would have augmented the pressure. Given that nations like France had premised their loans on their respect for Washington and not the Congress, it is easy to see to which government foreign states would have given their backing. After all, the loans from France and Holland and the moral support of others were not based on the Declaration of Independence but on a desire to lessen British influence. This had been accomplished, and both repayments of loans and the continued lessening of British influence would seem more likely under a respected military leader like Washington.

As for the British, a majority had finally come to power in Parliament, which favored an immediate withdrawal of British troops and independence for America under whatever government was set up. As Washington had predicted, if the states continued the war long enough, the British would eventually tire of the struggle. All in all, I believe, while nothing was certain, the prospects for a revolt were good.

LETTER TO ELIJAH HUNTER AND ORDER TO WILLIAM SHATTUCK, PAGE 44

The orders and letters that Washington issued at Newburgh are contained in part in the various biographies previously cited. There are many full compendiums, such as the Washington Papers at the University of Virginia made available to the author by Editor-in-Chief William Ferraro, as well as *The General Orders of Geo. Washington, Commander-in-Chief of the Army of the Revolution, Issued at Newburgh on The Hudson, 1782–1783* at the Harvard University Library and *The Itinerary of General Washington*, edited by William S. Baker and published by J. B. Lippincott & Co. in 1892. Every reference to an order or letter at Newburgh, such as this letter to Elijah Hunter on Hunter's stolen horses and the order to William Shattuck sending him to Vermont to track down criminals, is based on actual orders and letters.

Corruption and Profiteering, pages 44-45

Profiteering takes place during every war, and the Revolutionary War was no exception. Chase and Sands, cited here, are two notable examples of corruption among many hindering the American war effort. (See Thomas Fleming, *The Perils of Peace*, 187.) The victims of those who profited were the half-naked and distressed soldiers. This precipitated the eruption of Washington's volcanic temper about the triumph of private greed over public spirit. Washington said, "Chimney corner patriots abound: venality, corruption, prostitution of office for selfish ends, abuse of trust, perversion of funds from a national to a private use, and speculations upon the necessities of the times pervade all interests" (Gore Vidal, *Inventing a Nation*, 48).

The General, as was usually the case, did not let his anger escape into print. That he left to his aide Alexander Hamilton, who wrote scathing letters under the pseudonym Publius attacking Chase, a signer of the Declaration of Independence, for sullying the American cause by trying to corner the wheat market in advance of the arrival of the French fleet. (See *Alexander Hamilton, American* by Richard Brookhiser, 40.)

American Soldiers Overcoming Incredible Odds, 46

The theme of the American soldier overcoming incredible odds in prevailing over the more numerous, better trained, and better equipped troops of the British Empire was expressed many times by Washington, although never more eloquently than in the letter to General Greene:

"If Historiographers should be hardy enough to fill the page of History with the advantages that have been gained with unequal numbers (on the part of America) in the course of this contest, and attempt to relate the distressing circumstances under which they have been obtained, it is more than probable that Posterity will bestow on their labors the epithet and marks of fiction; for it will not be believed that such a force as Great Britain has employed for eight years in this Country could be baffled in their plan of Subjugating it by numbers infinitely less, composed of Men oftentimes half starved; always in Rags, without pay, and experiencing, at times, every species of distress which human nature is capable of undergoing." ("Letter to Nathanael Greene," *The Writings of George Washington*, 484.)

In overcoming the improbable odds, Washington is careful to never refer to his generalship but instead always refers to the valor of the American army.

BAND OF BROTHERS, 47

The phrase "band of brothers" was probably first uttered by King Henry V in his St. Crispin's Day speech in Shakespeare's *King Henry V*. It has recently been the title of Stephen E. Ambrose's book on a US army airborne company in World War II and the title of an album by Willie Nelson, and has been attributed to Lord Admiral Horatio Nelson in describing his captains in 1798. But years before Lord Nelson, George Washington was using the phrase to praise those who came together from thirteen states to fight under his leadership. His most notable use was in his farewell address to the armies of the United States on November 2, 1783, when Washington, after again pleading for just treatment for his troops, marvels at how troops from such diverse backgrounds had come together to overcome the might of the British Empire (again modestly overlooking his own role):

> Who, that was not a witness, could imagine that the most violent local prejudices would cease so soon, and that Men who came from the different parts of the Continent, strongly disposed, by the habits of education, to despise and quarrel with each other, would instantly become one patriotic *band of brothers*, or who, that was not on the spot, can trace the steps by which such a wonderful revolution has been effected, and such a glorious period put to all our warlike toils? (See *The Writings of George Washington*, 543)

In another reference, Washington in a later letter writes to General Knox, "My first wish would be that my Military family, and the whole Army, should consider themselves as a *band of brothers*, willing and ready, to die for each other." (John Frederick Schroeder, *Maxims of George Washington*, 95; Joseph J. Ellis in *His Excellency* cites Washington's use of the phrase in his farewell at Newburgh, 146.)

WASHINGTON'S FIRST COMBAT EXPERIENCE, 47-48

While Washington was restrained in describing his French and Indian War experiences to Josiah, Washington describes his first combat with French and Indian forces in a letter to his brother John Augustine in May of 1754. After laying out the results of the victory and assuring his brother that he was not wounded, Washington closes by stating, "I can with truth assure you, I heard bullets whistle and believe me there was something charming in the sound" (*The Writings of George Washington*, 48). The words found their way into a London periodical, and King George III reportedly commented, "He would not say so if he had been used to hear many" (Ron Chernow, *Washington*, 44).

Washington's Valor Compared with That of Other Generals, 48

When compared to other generals of that period (American and particularly British), Washington's desire to rush to the fore was notable not just to Josiah and made him beloved by his troops. "March on, my brave fellows, after me" and "Parade with us, my brave fellows" were words of Washington quoted by observers at many battles. (See, for example, David Hackett Fischer, *Washington's Crossing*, 241, 249, 334.) While almost every book about Washington has numerous reports of his great leadership when his men went into combat, I have found no accounts of British generals, such as Gage, Howe, Cornwallis, or Clinton, demonstrating similar leadership.

Medals for Enlisted Men, page 48

While at Newburgh, Washington introduced awards for service by enlisted men. This may not sound like much, but no army, as far as it is known, had previously given awards to other than officers. To Washington, this was a way to boost morale and recognize that the American army was different than the armies of kings. First came a white stripe for three years' service with "bravery, fidelity and good conduct," and then two white stripes for six years of such service. Beyond that, Washington created a badge of merit, which later became the Purple Heart, an award for military merit for both officers and enlisted men with a figure of a heart in purple cloth or silk edged with narrow lace or binding to be worn over the left breast. Wearers could pass guards without challenge like officers, and names were recorded in a book of merit, even if the wearer had been previously punished. While the chevrons were awarded to many, and the purple hearts, at least then, were awarded to few, the idea for decorating enlisted men was clear to Washington: "the road to glory in a patriot army and a free country is thus open to all" (William M. Fowler Jr., *American Crisis: George Washington and the Dangerous Two Years After Yorktown, 1781–1783*, 103).

COLONEL NICOLA'S APPEAL TO WASHINGTON, PAGES 52-55 (QUOTED IN APPENDIX B, PAGES 262-270)

Colonel Lewis Nicola, the author of the appeal to Washington cited by Josiah, was born in Ireland, served twenty years in the British army, and then migrated to Philadelphia, where he established a dry-goods store, founded a library, and was a curator with the American Philosophical Society. At age sixty, he volunteered for the American army. An able recruiter and administrator, Nicola conceived the idea, which Congress approved, of recruiting thousands of wounded veterans, unable to serve in combat, into an invalid corps performing light duties such as guarding supply depots and hospitals and protecting local property. The heart of Nicola's letter to Washington lays out the thesis that a republic (he cites Holland as an example) would not remain independently strong over centuries, let alone fulfill the promises to its military that Congress made, and that a monarchy, albeit with some improvements over the English form, offered the best chance for America surviving and the army receiving justice. He contrasts the weak performance of the American Congress with the "noble" performance of the army under Washington and draws the conclusion as to who should lead the future American government.

> This war must have shown to all, but to military men in particular the weakness of republics, and the exertions the army has been able to make by being under a proper

head, therefore . . . in this case it will, I believe, be uncontroverted that the same abilities which have led, through difficulties insurmountable by human power, to victory and glory, those qualities that have merited and obtained universal esteem and veneration of an army, would be most likely to conduct and direct us in the smoother paths of peace. (See Thomas Fleming, *The Perils of Peace*, 196, 197; Barry Schwartz, *Washington: The Making of an American Symbol*, 134; Ron Chernow, *Washington*, 428.)

Nicola suggests that Washington's title, at least temporarily, should be a more "moderate" one than king. His letter to Washington is a lengthy one, too long to quote here in full, because in addition to laying out the case for a monarchy over a republic, he lays out the woes of the army, elaborates a lengthy scheme for paying veterans involving western lands, and warns (similarly to the anonymous letter) that the army should not lay down its arms if it wants justice for itself.

WASHINGTON'S REPLY TO NICOLA, PAGE 54

Washington's reply rejecting Nicola's proposal is as brief as Nicola's is verbose. (See *The Writings of George Washington*, 468, 469.)

Washington expresses surprise at Nicola's proposal, says he is pained by and disagrees with the proposal, and pledges to keep Nicola's letter secret. He goes on to state his support for the justice of the army's grievances and urges Nicola to forget his proposal:

Sir: With a mixture of great surprise and astonishment I have read with attention the sentiments you have submitted to my perusal. Be assured Sir, no occurrence in the course of the War, has given me more painful sensations than your information of there being such ideas existing in the Army as you have expressed, and I must view with abhorrence, and reprehend with severity. For the present, the communication of them will rest in my own bosom, unless some further agitation of the matter, shall make a disclosure necessary.

I am much at a loss to conceive what part of my conduct could have given encouragement to an address which to me seems big with the greatest mischiefs that can befall my Country. If I am not deceived in the knowledge of myself, you could not have found a person to whom your schemes are more disagreeable; at the same time in justice to my own feelings I must add, that no man possesses a more sincere wish to see ample justice done to the Army than I do, and as far as my powers and influence, in a constitutional way extend, they shall be employed to the utmost of my abilities to effect it, should there be any occasion. Let me conjure you then, if you have any regard for your Country, concern for yourself or posterity, or respect for me, to banish these thoughts from your mind, and never communicate, as from yourself, or anyone else, a sentiment of the like nature. With esteem I am . . . (See *The Writings of George Washington*, 468.)

While the sentiments ring true, it is doubtful, given previous entreaties, that Washington was truly surprised by Nicola's letter. Feelings similar to Nicola's sentiments of May 1782 were to reach Washington with more regularity as the week in Newburgh in March 1783 approached.

The Old Fox, page 55

"The old fox" and "the old gray fox" were phrases Josiah rightly ascribes to the British during the war to describe Washington. Over the years, it became a term of respect as "bagging the old fox" became the all-consuming goal of British military strategy. The British increasingly became convinced that capturing cities and destroying armies, while helpful, was not as decisive a step toward victory as capturing the American commanding general. They may have underestimated the staying power of American forces in seeking shortcuts to victory, but the focus on Washington reflected their own, as well as Americans' opinion of Washington's central role in the conflict.

CHAPTER THREE: DAY THREE, WEDNESDAY—THE THIRD ANONYMOUS LETTER

JOSIAH DISCOVERS GATES'S AIDE, MAJOR JOHN ARMSTRONG JR., AS THE ANONYMOUS LETTER WRITER, PAGES 58-59, 61

Although there was some uncertainly early on, there is not much controversy today among historians on who wrote the anonymous letters. While they may disagree on other issues concerning the Newburgh affair, such as General Horatio Gates's and others' roles, all seem to agree with Josiah that Major John Armstrong Jr., an aide to Gates, was the writer of all the anonymous letters. (For more on Armstrong's role, see Thomas Fleming, *The Perils of Peace*, 268, 269; Richard H. Kohn, *The Inside History of the Newburgh Conspiracy*; *The William and Mary Quarterly*, April 1970, 206.) Armstrong, twenty-four years old, was already known to be ambitious and an eloquent writer. After the Revolutionary War, his authorship then less well known and the Newburgh affair having receded into the background, Armstrong had a distinguished career, rising to become President Madison's secretary of war during the War of 1812.

The Third Anonymous Letter, pages 60-61 (quoted in full in Appendix B, pages 278-280)

Fearing that the officers would take General Washington's order for a Saturday meeting as a rejection of the anonymous letter writer's purpose, Major Armstrong cleverly argued that General Washington fully supported the mutineers' goals espoused in Armstrong's second letter or he would not have called a meeting at all.

Washington's Letters to Jones and Hamilton, pages 62-63

Washington's letters to Jones and Hamilton are, along with several others, almost identical in purpose: pleading the army's cause, warning of the danger of mutiny, and urging action by Congress to satisfy the army's claims. But beyond these themes was Washington's unconfirmed suspicion that Gates and Armstrong may not have been acting alone and that they had allies in the Congress.

Historians have differed on this. Some believe that Congress's role was minimal and that Gates and Armstrong acted largely on their own initiative. Some believe that a few congressmen were involved because they wished to strengthen the national government and pay off creditors. Others believe that, while a few congressmen may have been involved, they were bluffing. Still others believe that congressmen, seeking a strong national government that would pay its debts to creditors as well as the army, thought the threat of a mutiny would strengthen their hand with their colleagues either with or without a mutiny. (All these various theories were laid out in the 1970s in *The William and Mary Quarterly*, in articles by Richard H. Kohn, 1970, 187–220; Paul David Nelson, 1972, 143–58; and C. Edward Skeen and Richard H. Kohn, 1974, 273–98.) I incline to Kohn's belief that Gates and Armstrong played the major role, and, regardless of the role of some congressmen, there is no doubt in my mind that Gates's actions were real and the threat was real. None of the historians cited above speculate, as this novel and Josiah do, on the impact that all the pleas to Washington to lead a new government as a king or dictator must have had on the General.

Alexander Hamilton, pages 64-65

While the Founding Fathers (and mothers) were plentiful in their praise and sparing in their criticism of Washington, whom they looked on as a father figure, the reverse was true when commenting on their fraternal colleagues. In a letter to Abigail Adams, John Adams described Alexander Hamilton as "a proud Spirited, conceited, aspiring Mortal always pretending to Morality, with as debauched Morals as old Franklin who is more his Model than any one I know."

In later letters to her husband, Abigail described Hamilton "as ambitious as Julius Caesar . . . his thirst for fame is insatiable." She stated further: "Beware of the spare Cassius [Hamilton], has always occurred to me when I have seen that cock sparrow" (Gore Vidal, *Inventing a Nation*, 133). While this correspondence took place later than Newburgh, such feelings by Hamilton's military and political colleagues were commonplace, although they were definitely not shared by Washington, who always had a high opinion of Hamilton.

While the founders were sparing in their criticism of Washington, on occasion feelings of jealousy toward the man who dominated the revolutionary cause did emerge. Perhaps because Washington, for the most part, stood above the jealousy of others, he was immune from exhibiting jealousy in return. It does not seem to have been part of his nature. As this novel brings out, Washington seemed more concerned with what the public and history thought of him than what his colleagues thought of him. His admiration for Hamilton was so well known that he was referred to as Hamilton's surrogate father and even ridiculously rumored to be Hamilton's real father, sired on a teenage trip by Washington to the West Indies. Because modern science has proved Jefferson's siring of children with his slave, Sally Hemings, it is tempting these days to believe every juicy sexual rumor. Unfortunately for the prurient, Washington's visit to the West Indies took place years before Hamilton's known birth, thus showing this rumor, like many rumors about Washington's sex life, to be implausible. What is likely is that Washington, despite their different circumstances of birth, saw a similarity in their backgrounds: they both lacked formal schooling as youths (Hamilton attended King's College, now Columbia) and, while both depended on more fortunate elders for early advancement, they both were largely self-made men (Hamilton in law and Washington in surveying), with both considering themselves, perhaps surprisingly, outsiders. (For more on this intriguing connection, see Ron Chernow, *Alexander Hamilton*, 86, 87.)

Although fulsome in his praise, Hamilton, while more immune from feelings of jealousy toward Washington than most of the Founding Fathers, did occasionally slip. In a letter to his father-in-law, Hamilton stated "all the world is offering incense" to Washington. (See Chernow, *Alexander Hamilton*, 152.)

THOMAS JEFFERSON, PAGES 65-68

For a man of known broad tastes, Jefferson had some decidedly narrow views on certain subjects, which drew Josiah's attention. According to Jefferson, permitting women to "mix promiscuously in the public meetings of men" could lead to a "depravation of morals" (Gordon S. Wood, *Empire of Liberty*, 506). Women should not hold any government positions, including those they had already held, such as postmaster (see Rosemarie Zagarri, *Revolutionary Backlash: Women and Politics in the Early American Republic*, 159). One should suspect that "blacks . . . are inferior to the whites in endowments both of body and mind"

(Wood, 539). Sane people do not turn voluntarily from farming to manufacturing (Wood, 627). Treatment of patients was all right in hospitals; medical research was not (Wood, 723). Chemists should ignore deep discoveries and concentrate on producing better bread and butter (Wood, 724). It is natural that someone of Josiah's Quaker background would have found Jefferson's above views peculiar and offensive, even in those times.

Washington (or rather Josiah) was correct that the furor over Jefferson's alleged cowardice as governor during the war would dissipate despite an attempt at censure by the Virginia Assembly. (For a sympathetic treatment of Jefferson's woes as a wartime governor, which omits the alleged hiding by Jefferson in a tobacco barn, see Jefferson's biography by Dumas Malone, *Jefferson the Virginian*, 357–68. For a more critical but balanced appraisal of Jefferson's conduct, see John Ferling, *Almost a Miracle*, 478, 479.)

Regarding the authorship of the Declaration of Independence, whose opening lines Josiah attributes to George Mason, Jefferson is not the only great writer in America in that period to be indebted to the prose of others. In the Virginia Declaration of Rights, George Mason writes "that all men . . . have certain inherent rights . . . namely the enjoyment of life and liberty, with the means of acquiring and possessing property, and pursuing and obtaining happiness and safety." Others in state declarations of human rights used some of Mason's prose, just as Jefferson did, and Mason in turn was indebted to the Bill of Rights in 1689. Besides, one can argue that Jefferson's version was more pithy and eloquent than Mason's: "that all men . . . are endowed by their Creator with certain unalienable Rights, that among these are Life, Liberty and the pursuit of Happiness."

Many of Jefferson's colleagues, while suppressing their criticism and for the most part their jealousy of Washington, were, as with Hamilton, more open about their ill feelings toward Jefferson. Along with praise, Adams said that "Jefferson thinks . . . to get a reputation as a humble, modest, meek man, wholly without ambition or vanity. He may even have deceived himself in this belief, but if the prospect opens, the world will see and he will feel that he is as ambitious as Oliver Cromwell" (Edward J. Larson, *A Magnificent Catastrophe*, 29).

Jefferson replied in kind about his rival, Adams, comparing him to "poisonous weeds" and describing him as "vain, irritable, stubborn" and "endowed with excessive self-love" (David McCullough, *John Adams*, 318, 489).

With Washington, Jefferson was unstinting in his praise through most of Jefferson's career, especially when addressing Washington. "The moderation and virtue of a single character has probably prevented this revolution from being closed, as most others have been, by a subversion of that liberty it was intended to establish," Jefferson wrote in 1784 (Richard Kohn, *William and Mary Quarterly*, 1970, 220). But as Jefferson tried to prepare for his own presidential accession in 1796, he started to let slip criticisms of Washington, among them that he believed Washington was lucky and overrated. He also ridiculously lumped Washington in with Jefferson's opponents as a pro-English "apostate." (Jefferson's allies reprinted fake British letters accusing Washington of being a British sympathizer.) Jefferson, as Josiah notes, publicly avoided the ceremonies surrounding Washington's funeral. (See Edward J. Larson, *A Magnificent Catastrophe*, 39, 55.) But after Washington's death, Jefferson, influenced either by public opinion or his own more objective second thoughts, was saying that Washington "was a wise, a good, and a great man." Jefferson visited Lady Washington at Mount Vernon to make amends; he also hung a painting of Washington and displayed a bust of the General at Monticello. (See Ron Chernow, *Washington*, 600.)

Benjamin Franklin, pages 68-69

Benjamin Franklin, he whose electric rod transformed the earth; Patrick Henry, he who spoke "as Homer wrote"; and George Washington were probably the three most famous Americans at the time of the Revolution. As such, the first two seemed immune to any feelings of jealousy toward Washington, although Henry bore ill feelings toward Jefferson, which were reciprocated. (For two descriptions of this conflict, see Richard Beeman, *Patrick Henry*, 131 et seq., and Dumas Malone, *Jefferson, The Virginian*, 382.) One can attribute Franklin's oft-expressed admiration of Washington to his diplomatic skills, but Franklin was quite capable of rendering balanced, critical judgments of many with whom he served. His portrayals of Adams were devastating. Franklin wrote to Washington after his Yorktown triumph that it will "brighten the glory that surrounds your name and that must accompany it to our latest posterity. No news could possibly make me more happy" (Thomas Fleming, *Perils of Peace*, 162).

Franklin had become wary of representing a Congress that was held in low esteem by the French. While French generals considered Washington one of the "greatest captains" of the age, French ministers were contemptuous of a Congress that defaulted on its financial obligations and spent French loans not to secure military victory but to pay off domestic debts. Franklin realized that, with the possible exception of himself, Washington was the only American whose reputation was immune from attack by Americans or the French. Washington's reputation, wrote Franklin, was "free from those little shades that the jealousy and envy of a man's countrymen and contemporaries are ever endeavoring to cast over living merit" (Walter Isaacson, *Benjamin Franklin*, 391).

JOHN AND ABIGAIL ADAMS, PAGES 69-71

John Adams, like George Washington, was much concerned about his reputation, perhaps even more so, and certainly more openly. This is a man who early in life said, "Reputation ought to be the perpetual subject of my thoughts, and the aim of my behavior" and "How shall I gain a reputation . . . shall I look out for a cause to speak to, and exert all the soul and body I own to cut a flash? In short shall I walk a lingering, heavy pace or shall I take one bold determined leap?" (See Edward J. Larson, *A Magnificent Catastrophe*, 11, 13.)

Unlike Washington, Adams, as Josiah observes, saw himself threatened by, and was jealous of, the reputation of others. Adams bemoaned the pain of seeing another "wear the laurels which I have sown" (Barry Schwartz, *Washington: Making of an American Symbol*, 22). Benjamin Franklin and George Washington, being the most famous Americans of the time, were natural wearers of the laurels and targets of Adams's jealousy. Benjamin Rush's words summed up Adams's feelings:

> [T]he history of our Revolution will be one continued lie from one end to another. The essence of the whole will be that Dr. Franklin's electrical rod smote the earth and out sprang General Washington. That Franklin electrified him with his rod—and thence forward these two conducted all the policy, negotiations, legislatures and war. (See Barry Schwartz, *George Washington, The Making of an American Symbol*, 87)

While Adams often praised Washington's attributes, the praise was often mixed with apprehension of Washington's potential power. Thus, Adams gloried "in the character of Washington because I know him to be the exemplification of the American character" yet belittled that character as "a character of convention" (Barry Schwartz, *The Making of an American Symbol*, 5, 179).

Along with Jefferson, Adams disparaged the celebration of Washington's birthday and what he believed was the idolizing of Washington. "Among the national sins of our country [is] the idolatrous worship paid to the name of George Washington . . . ascribed in scripture only to God and Jesus Christ" (Schwartz, 194).

Adams attributed his own feelings of envy and fear toward Washington to sizable elements of the American people who he claimed joined him in wishing Washington would retire for fear he would otherwise be set up as king. Adams took very seriously the threat posed in this novel, and later wrote:

> It was a general sentiment in America that Washington must retire. Why? What is implied in this necessity? . . . Does not this idea of the necessity of his retiring, imply an opinion of danger to the public, from his continuing in public, a jealousy that he might become ambitious? And does it not imply . . . a jealousy in the people of one another, a jealousy of one part of the people, that another part had grown too fond of him, and acquired habitually too much confidence in him, and that there would be a danger of setting him up for a king? Undoubtedly it does, and undoubtedly there were such suspicions; and grounds for them too. (See *Works of John Adams*, vol. 9, 541.)

Abigail shared John's praise of Washington but did not, at least openly, share his jealousy. While John and Abigail agreed on their evaluations of most of John's contemporaries, with regard to Washington one detects a disagreement. John's praise of Washington was at times qualified and stinting. Abigail's praise, starting with her initial description of Washington in a letter to her husband, was unqualified. "You had prepared me to entertain a favorable opinion of George Washington, but I thought the half was not told me. Dignity with ease and complacency, the gentleman and soldier, look agreeably blended in him." Her later descriptions were equally unstinting: "A temple built by hands divine," "the most amiable of men," "a singular example of modesty and diffidence," whose dignity and majesty far surpassed King George III, were all descriptions offered by Abigail of the General (Gore Vidal, *Inventing a Nation*, 72). Finally, upon Washington's death, Abigail wrote in a private letter to her sister, "No man ever lived, more deservedly beloved and Respected . . . If we look through the whole tenor of his Life, History will not produce to us a Parallel" (Michael and Jana Novak, *Washington's God*, 4, 5).

Adams's recognition of his own envy, and Washington's lack of it, showed through in his remarks at Washington's funeral. "Malice could never blast his honor, and Envy made him a singular exception to her universal rule" (Barry Schwartz, *George Washington: The Making of an American Symbol*, 92).

Josiah shared Adams's appreciation and envy of Washington's acting ability. Adams attributed the General's hold on public audiences to "Shakespearean and Garrickal Excellence in Dramatic Exhibitions" and later described Washington as the "best actor of Presidency we have ever had."

PATRICK HENRY, PAGES 71-72

Patrick Henry praised the oratory at the 1774 Continental Congress, but "if you speak of solid information, and sound judgment, Colonel Washington is by far the greatest man on the floor" (Richard Norton Smith, *Patriarch*, 12). Henry, the archenemy of executive tyranny, made one exception: he supported appointing Washington as a "near dictator" during the war (Beeman, 115). Washington remained a supporter of Henry until the end of their lives (Ellis, *His Excellency*, 267).

Josiah states that Henry and several Founding Fathers opposed the adoption of the Constitution. The Constitution has become so revered over the years that we assume all our Founding Fathers supported its adoption. Not so. Some opposed it outright. Others opposed it without amendments. (Supporters had already pledged a bill of rights by amendment if it was adopted.) Others opposed it in favor of extending the Articles of Confederation. Henry, Mason, Governor George Clinton of New York, and John Hancock all at one time or another opposed its adoption. And Thomas Jefferson was a late and lukewarm supporter.

When a few of Jefferson's republican allies in the news media and elsewhere criticized Washington during his second presidential term, Henry rose to Washington's defense with phrases about such criticism inhibiting those seeking public service that have echoed down through the years: "If they slander General Washington, what must we expect when lesser men serve" and "If he whose character as our leader during the whole war . . . is so roughly handled in his old age, what may be expected of men of the common standard?" (Ron Chernow, *Washington*, 752).

THE MARQUIS DE LAFAYETTE, PAGES 73-78

Lafayette's admiration for Washington was so great that we cannot read his words today without believing Lafayette was a rock star "groupie" instead of one of the ablest and most distinguished soldiers and diplomats of his time, and one who, we will see, challenged Washington on issues such as slavery.

To others, Lafayette spewed comments about the General such as: "Our general is a man formed, in truth, for this revolution which could not have been accomplished without him. I see him more intimately than any other man, and I see that he is worthy of the adoration of his country," and "Every day, I learn to admire more his magnificent character and soul . . ."

It is fortunate that Lafayette evinced such opinions because he spent millions in today's currency of his own money on the Revolution, became one of the Continental Army's ablest commanders, more than anyone convinced the French government to support the rebels, and further changed Washington's views on slavery.

Lafayette's written comments on Washington to Washington were, if possible, even more glowing than his comments on the General to others:

> Everything that is great, and everything that is good were not hitherto visited in one man. Never did a man live whom the soldier, statesman, patriot, and philosopher could equally admire, and never was a revolution brought about, that in its motives, its conduct, and its consequences could so well immortalize its glorious chief. I am so proud of you, my dear general, your glory makes me feel as if it were my own—and while the world is gaping at you, I am pleased to think, and to tell, the qualities of your heart do render you still more valuable than anything you have done.

While the words today may seem grandiloquent, Lafayette lived the life of a medieval knight whose cause was the American Revolution and whose hero was George Washington. He genuinely believed, as did thousands of others, that America's advantage over Britain lay in "the superiority of George Washington."

Not surprisingly, Lafayette named his son after the General.

Those interested in reading the above and other interactions of Lafayette and Washington may wish to consult *Lafayette* by Harlow Giles Unger. This delightful biography describes how Lafayette, living the life of a romantic fourteenth-century knight, changed the shape of America and France in the eighteenth and nineteenth centuries.

Slavery, Lafayette, the Black Poet, and Washington's Last Will, pages 74–77

Lafayette may have been an avid admirer of the General, but he was not timid about advancing his views to Washington on many issues, including slavery.

The conversation with Washington reported by Lafayette to Josiah is imagined but does reflect the known views of each on slavery at that time. For example, in 1783, the same year as the eventful week at Newburgh, Lafayette sent a letter to Washington proposing that Washington join him in an effort to start removing the moral stain of slavery by buying an estate in the West Indies on which "we may try the experiment to free the Negroes." Washington wrote in response that to "encourage the emancipation of the black people," he would be "happy to join you in so laudable a work." Lafayette, who admitted that it may be a "wild scheme," apparently did not pursue the matter.

How we evaluate Washington (or any other historical figure) on the slavery issue depends on whether we evaluate him against the standards of his time or ours. Abraham Lincoln, when he was inaugurated as president in 1861, denied that he was an abolitionist. (We recognize the political pressures Lincoln was under and honor him for what he did a few years later.) Washington, seventy years before Lincoln's inaugural speech, was already stating his support for the gradual abolition of slavery, including in his own state of Virginia.

In a 1786 letter to John Frances Mercer, Washington writes, "It being among my first wishes to see some plan adopted, by the legislature by which slavery may be abolished by slow, sure & imperceptible degrees."

The evolution of Washington's position on slavery is fascinating. He was born into a slaveholding family, inherited slaves, and in his early years and even later bought, sold, and recovered slaves. Something happened in his middle years, however, that distinguished him from his planter neighbors. Aside from realizing the economic inefficiency of slavery, he came to be repelled by the buying and selling of human beings, which he decided not to engage in, despite having an excess of slaves that for economic reasons he should have sold. Washington wrote of his refusal to buy or sell slaves "because I am principled against this kind of trafficking in the human species."

The experiences during the war undoubtedly hastened Washington's evolution on the slavery issue, exhibited by his implicit support of Laurens's proposal to arm South Carolina blacks as well as his observations of the performance of free black troops from New England. While some of the northern units were all black, others, with Washington's approval, remained mixed or integrated. I was surprised to find that the first integrated US army units came into being not after President Truman's order in 1946, nor after President Eisenhower's implementation of that order in 1953, but under General Washington during the Revolutionary War.

Washington's actions, while not trumpeted around the land, were certainly known, particularly to the blacks affected. The best-known black intellectual and writer of the time, Phillis Wheatley, was a free Negro poet who had been published in London. Prior to her meeting with Washington described by Josiah in this chapter, a meeting which did indeed take place, Wheatley lauded America as "the land of freedom's heaven-defended race!" and sent the General the following ode:

> Proceed, great chief, with virtue on thy side,
> Thy ev'ry action let the goddess guide.
> A crown, a mansion, and a throne that shine,
> With gold unfading, Washington! Be thine.

After receiving the ode in 1775 outside of Boston, Washington apologized for his delay in responding and stated, "I thank you most sincerely for your polite notice of me in the Elegant lines you enclosed. And however undeserving I may be of Such encomium and panegyric, the style and manner exhibit a striking proof of your great poetical talents . . . If you should ever come to Cambridge or near headquarters, I shall be happy to see a person so favoured by the Muses and to whom nature has been so liberal and beneficent in her dispensations. I am with great respect your obedient humble servant."

This is hardly the response that either a slave or a free black would expect from a Southern slaveholder in the eighteenth century, and it shows Washington's evolution on the slavery issue. (See Ron Chernow, *Washington*, 220.)

That Martha Washington did not attend Washington's meeting with Wheatley is conjecture on my part but quite likely. Lady Washington's views on slavery were probably askew from her husband's and undoubtedly affected the General's last will so it only applied to his and not her slaves. (See Ellis, *His Excellency*, 260.) In a letter upon hearing of the death of a slave child, she wrote, "Black children are liable to so many accidents and complaints that one is hardly sure of keeping them. I hope you will not find him much loss. The Blacks are so bad in their nature that they have not the least gratitude for the kindness that may be shewed to them" (Helen Bryan, *Martha Washington*, 335). Based on Washington's letters, orders, and transcripts by others of his conversations, we can say with confidence that these are words that would never have come out of the General's mouth.

Washington has been criticized for not being consistent or public enough on the slavery issue. He did not, for example, fight to keep slaves from being returned from British control to their owners after the war. He did not make public declarations on the issue, at least until his will. While as president in 1794 he introduced into the Senate a Quaker petition from New England calling for the immediate abolition of American participation in the international slave trade, Washington, like some other Founding Fathers, seemed to rely on the 1789 constitutional provision calling for the abolition of the slave trade in 1808 to bring about the end of slavery.

Washington and Lafayette's conversation about the former providing for the freedom and welfare of his slaves after his death is imagined, like the conversation on Lafayette's proposed estate for free slaves, but again it is also perfectly plausible and consistent with Washington's recorded views and his later actions prior to his death. Washington's last will and testament is an extraordinary document. Not only did he provide the opportunity for freedom for his slaves, but, consistent with his belief that effective abolition must include education, he provided money—money not easily available to him—for his slaves' education, training, and welfare if they chose freedom. And this at a time when Virginia law banned the education of blacks.

Some modern historians think that if Washington really believed in freeing his slaves, he would have done so sooner. Again, we are confronted with the question of what standard you use to judge a historical figure, the standard of his own times or ours. Yes, Washington only freed his slaves after his death, but I am not aware of any other Virginia planter who freed his slaves in his will in 1799.

Other Founding Fathers, such as Franklin and Hamilton, were abolitionists, but they were not born into slaveholding families with large numbers of slaves. Other Founding Fathers, such as Thomas Jefferson, were born in similar slaveholding circumstances as Washington but refused to free their slaves. Henry Wiencek's article "Master of Monticello" brings out the differences in how these two Founding Fathers treated their slaves, including how Jefferson turned down a gift in 1817 from the Polish noblemen Tadeusz Kosciuszko (the equivalent of $280,000 in today's dollars) to free his slaves. Wiencek shows how Washington, in his last will and testament, rebuked his era and showed "that if you claim to have principles, you must live by them" (*Smithsonian* magazine, October 2012). To the complaint of those historians who wish Washington had been more public in his opposition to slavery, Washington's last will and testament certainly attracted public notice. Abolitionist groups held their annual meetings in the early 1800s on Washington's birthday. They, like the black poet Phillis Wheatley, and many others, had no doubt where Washington stood.

Why Washington evolved from slaveholder to abolitionist is not totally clear. Josiah would probably say that, while moral and economic factors played a role, Washington, as usual, had his eye on history and what later Americans would think of him. But as Josiah would also likely observe, if one does the right thing, what difference do the reasons make?

Chapter Four: Day Four, Thursday—Councils of War, Reflections on Generalship

Conspiracies against Washington, pages 81-84

Looking back, it is hard for us to imagine that other generals and political leaders wanted to replace Washington. We must remember that Congress appointed many of the top generals so that almost every major general had the support of a congressional faction. Further, the war stretched on for over seven years, and in such a lengthy struggle there were ups and downs. One of the most depressing periods was after the defeat in New York and during the retreat across New Jersey. With thousands pledging allegiance to the king at that time, as Josiah notes, it was only natural that many should seek new leadership. Josiah comments on Generals Lee and Gates wanting to replace Washington, and there were probably others who harbored similar ambitions.

The so-called Conway Cabal was the best known of these conspiracies. It reached fruition in 1777 during the encampment at Valley Forge. There were three leading characters: General Thomas Conway, an Irish-born French general seeking fortune and promotion in the French army, who received his appointment from Congress and was the organizer of the effort; General Thomas Mifflin, the quartermaster general under fire for corruption and incompetence; and General Horatio Gates, the victor at the Battle of Saratoga, whose role was more ambiguous. The creation of an independent Board of War, which was chaired by Gates and had Mifflin as a member, and the appointment of Conway as the army's inspector general were the tools for replacing Washington with Gates or Mifflin, but a trail of letters and comments exalting Gates and demeaning Washington undermined the plotters' efforts. A letter from Conway to Gates fell into Washington's hands with incriminating language, and it soon circulated: "Heaven has been determined to save your [Gates's] country, or a weak General [Washington] and bad counsellors would have ruined it" (Douglas Freeman, *George Washington*, vol. 4, 593).

Impatient members of Congress, particularly the newer delegates, were receptive to criticism of Washington for not ending the war quickly. Eventually, however, Washington's supporters rallied to his defense. His practice of appointing officers on the basis of merit served him well as scores of officers from many states petitioned Congress against appointing Conway, a French major general, over American officers with greater experience and qualifications. Lafayette implicitly threatened Congress to cut off French aid and wrote Washington that "stupid men . . . without knowing a single word about war, undertake to judge you, to make ridiculous comparisons; they are infatuated with Gates" (Ron Chernow, *George Washington*, 316).

A committee of the Congress visited Valley Forge and gained appreciation for Washington's strategy for outlasting the British. The president of the Congress, Henry Laurens (who just happened to be the father of Washington's aide John Laurens), and luminaries like Patrick Henry stepped forth. Finally, the troops made their wishes known. As one observer noted, their views were clear: "The toast among the soldiers, Washington or no Army" (Douglas S. Freeman, *George Washington*, vol. 4, 606).

Ultimately, Conway overplayed his hand, threatening to resign so many times that Congress eventually took him up on his offer. Mifflin also resigned while Gates hastened to disavow his role. Washington, meanwhile, remained calm and dignified, letting others wage the fight.

Eventually Conway ended up in a duel with one of Washington's aides, John Cadwalader. After being severely wounded, and before returning to France, a beaten and humiliated Conway wrote an apology to Washington:

> I find myself just able to hold the pen during a few minutes, and take this opportunity of expressing my sincere grief for having done, written, or said anything disagreeable to your Excellency. My career will soon be over. Therefore justice and truth prompt me to declare my last sentiments. You are, in my eyes, the great and the good man. May you long enjoy the love, veneration, and esteem of these states whose liberties you have asserted by your virtues. (See Ron Chernow, *George Washington*, 322.)

No one in the ranks or in Congress ever challenged Washington's authority again. In Henry Laurens's words, this saved the revolutionary effort from "ruin." It also left Washington so triumphant that many wondered what he would decide coming out of that week in Newburgh five years later.

(For those interested in reading more about the Conway Cabal, see Douglas S. Freeman, *George Washington*, vol. 4, pages 586–612; Ron Chernow, *George Washington*, pages 316–22; and James Flexner, *Washington, The Indispensable Man*, pages 111–16.)

WASHINGTON AND DUELING, PAGE 83

Washington's aides—Laurens, Cadwalader, and others—challenging the General's detractors to duels was indeed, as Josiah observes, ironic, given Washington's disapproval of duels, which were then a common practice. While his disapproval was based on sound moral principles, that disapproval, surprising coming from this battle-tested general, produced huzzahs. I suspect it was a position Washington took after considerable thought. And if he had been a slight, craven-looking figure, I don't doubt Washington would have participated in duels. But Washington was a strapping physical specimen known to have faced great tests in battle and to have taken lessons in dueling. Since no one could doubt his courage or his skill, what was to be gained? By refusing to duel, as in many aspects of Washington's life, Washington won accolades by doing the unexpected.

In 1755, Washington got into a political argument with a man of small physical stature, William Payne. Payne knocked Washington down with a stick. Washington was restrained by friends from assaulting Payne, but a challenge to a duel under the customs of the day was soon expected. Instead, Washington retired, thought the matter over, and invited Payne to a meeting the next day where he apologized for being in the wrong. Where a duel was expected with Washington victorious, none took place, leaving Payne and others astonished and impressed with Washington's display of character. (See Douglas S. Freeman, *George Washington*, vol. 2, 146.)

Washington considered his actions carefully and often did the unexpected with surprisingly good results. Speak little, and when you speak, people will listen more. Decline to discuss your genuine exploits, and people will consider them even greater. Apologize to someone rather than challenge them to a duel that you are expected to win, and people will admire you all the more. The pattern is quite clear, and the behavior, foreign to politicians of our century, was admired in Washington's day.

1. Success at Boston

Comparison of Washington to Moses, pages 92, 97, 120, 140

Governor Trumbull's note with the flour comparing Washington to Moses, a note Trumbull really wrote, was not an isolated comparison. The war abounded with biblical references, particularly on the American side, and Josiah's description of the constant comparisons of the colonists to the ancient Israelites, of King George to the Pharaoh, and of Washington to Moses was, if anything, understated. We have never had an American leader compared to a biblical figure the way Washington in his time was compared to Moses. Many colonists saw themselves as the heirs to the promised land and Washington as the "reincarnation of the faithful Hebrew deliverer" (Barry Schwartz, *Washington: The Making of an American Symbol*, 176). Hundreds of sermons after Washington's death compared him to Moses. Reverend Timothy Dwight noted, "Comparison with him [Moses] is become almost proverbial."

When Washington wasn't being compared to Moses, he was being compared to the saints. Clergymen wanted to insert Washington's farewell address into the Bible as an epilogue. (See Ron Chernow, *Washington*, 813.) No wonder Josiah was worried about the comparisons to Moses affecting Washington's judgment about taking power that week at Newburgh.

II. Disaster in New York

Public Opinion Turns against the Revolution, pages 103-107

Earlier we learned that those who were neutral or loyal to the king made up a sizable portion of the American population. After the massive defeat in New York in 1776 and the retreat across New Jersey to the Delaware River, one can imagine the impact on American public opinion. The British were not oblivious to this development. Relying on intelligence from General James Robertson and others (in military parlance today, we would call these men "old American hands"), the

British believed that the Revolution was the work of a few "hot-headed designing men" and that two-thirds of Americans were loyal to the king. (See David Hackett Fischer, *Washington's Crossing*, 160.) Their strategy, therefore, was to pacify, restore order, and encourage a loyalist government in occupied New Jersey. Toward that end, the British offered amnesty, guarantees of life and property, and a chance for advancement to those who took a loyalty oath and pledged allegiance to the king.

The British belief in majority loyalist numbers was naive, but not naive was their claim that thousands of New Jersey residents took the loyalty oath to the king. As one Continental soldier observed, those taking the oath "consisted of the very rich and very poor, while the middling class held their constancy" (David Hackett Fischer, *Washington's Crossing*, 162). One of New Jersey's richest men and a signer of the Declaration of Independence, Richard Stockton, signed the oath to the king after harsh treatment and imprisonment. (He later renounced the oath, took a new oath to the Congress, and retained his home and property, which today is the official residence of New Jersey governors.)

Unfortunately for the British, the pacification policy went awry. Foraging became compulsory foraging, which turned into plundering, which turned into widespread rape upon the part of the British and especially their Hessian allies. Gang rapes by both British soldiers and officers were documented in diaries of British officers and American investigations. As American civilians responded by taking up arms, the British invoked the European laws of war that a man fighting out of uniform was a bandit or assassin who could be executed at once. To the Americans who believed civilians had the natural right to defend their liberties, such conduct quickly turned friends of the British into fierce foes. With the failure of the British pacification policy, the victories at Trenton and Princeton described by Josiah sparked a wholesale rejection by New Jersey residents of loyalty oaths to the king, the taking of new ones to the Congress, and widespread attacks on British forces. (For those wanting to read more about the war for public opinion in New

Jersey in 1776 and 1777, see the chapter "Americans Under Foreign Rule" in David Hackett Fischer's *Washington's Crossing*, 160–81.)

III. Triumph—the First Crossing of the Delaware

The Impact of the Battle of Trenton, page 108-12

No battle in the Revolutionary War receives more attention in our high school history textbooks than the Battle of Trenton. But, if anything, the importance is understated. There were just two American combat deaths (more died of exposure to cold) compared to the enemy's twenty-two killed, eighty-four wounded, and almost nine hundred Hessian prisoners! It was the first American victory following a string of defeats. Josiah was right in exulting over the triumph. The British historian George Trevelyan wrote: "It may be doubted whether so small a number of men ever employed so short a space of time with greater and more lasting effects upon the history of the world" (Ron Chernow, *Washington*, 276).

IV. Triumph—the Second Crossing of the Delaware

Washington's Plea to His Troops, pages 113–14

A sergeant present at the plea by Washington to his troops to reenlist before the second crossing of the Delaware recalled the speech in 1832:

> My brave fellows, you have done all I asked you to do, and more than could [be] reasonably expected; but your country is at stake, your wives, your houses, and all that you hold dear. You have worn yourselves out with the fatigues

and hardships, but we know not how to spare you. If you will consent to stay one month longer, you will render that service to the cause of liberty, and to your country, which you probably can never do under any other circumstances. (See David Hackett Fischer, *Washington's Crossing*, 272–73.)

Josiah marvels, as can we, that a general would make such an appeal to his troops. Not only was this beyond what a British general at that time would do but, according to Fischer, beyond what any general in the world would have done then.

"An officer asked the general if the men should be enrolled. 'No,' said Washington, 'men who will volunteer in such a case as this, need no enrollment to keep them to their duty'" (David Hackett Fischer, *Washington's Crossing*, 273). In 1776, from the General on down officers in the American army were, to the astonishment of Europeans, addressing privates as gentlemen. Washington made his appeal based not just on rank but on principles of honor and "human dignity and decency."

That this appeal came from a general who expected and received deference from his troops made the appeal all the more remarkable.

FOREIGNERS' ESTEEM FOR WASHINGTON'S GENERALSHIP, PAGES 120, 122

While Washington outmaneuvered the plotters in the Conway Cabal, what really solidified both congressional and public opinion behind him was the exalted opinion of Washington's generalship held by European and British officers and leaders. Congressmen, who, as Lafayette observed, knew nothing about war, may have had occasional doubts about Washington's generalship, but there were no doubts among either America's enemies or allies.

In terms of the war, the most crucial opinions came from British officers who came to believe that the war could not be won because Washington was superior to any British general. Josiah refers to the intercepted letters of British officers. Lieutenant Colonel Allan MacLean wrote: "Poor devils as the rebel generals are, they have outgeneraled us more than once, even since I have been here, which is only six weeks . . . Lord Cornwallis is, I believe, a brave man. But he allowed himself to be fairly outgeneraled by Washington, the 4th of January last at Trenton, and missed a glorious opportunity when he let Washington slip away in the night" (David Hackett Fischer, *Washington's Crossing*, 344).

Even British general Clinton recognized Washington's outgeneraling of Cornwallis: "His Lordship, thinking that Washington would wait for him till the next day, deceived by his fires . . . into this belief, neglects to patrole to Allentown—over which Washington's whole army and the last hope of America escaped" (David Hackett Fischer, *Washington's Crossing*, 344). The same was true of the Hessian officers who convened a court-martial to find out why they had inferior leadership.

The British government in London tried to suppress the news of the American victories at Trenton and Princeton, which of course just made that news all the more devastating when it came out. Realizing that the British had huge advantages over the Americans in numbers, training, experience, and arms, British writers drew what to them was the obvious conclusion: the only way the Americans could be winning was that Washington was a superior general and that generals such as Clinton just could not match Washington when it came to the "abilities to plan [and] . . . to execute" (John Ferling, *Almost a Miracle*, 358).

While the British and Hessians may have criticized themselves and each other as well as crediting Washington, other Europeans just hailed Washington's generalship. Josiah accurately quotes the French general Rochambeau as well as Frederick the Great, who, after the victories at Trenton and Princeton, extolled Washington:

The achievements of Washington and his little band of compatriots between the 25th of December and the 4th of January, a space of ten days, were the most brilliant of any recorded in the annals of military achievements. (See Ron Chernow, *George Washington*, 283.)

Similarly, Horace Walpole compared Washington's exploits to those of the Roman general Fabius. (See David Hackett Fischer, *Washington's Crossing*, 324.)

Cornwallis himself, who most Americans recognized as Britain's finest general in the war (and whose talents were later recognized by British kings over decades and many continents), acknowledged the emergence of Washington's superior generalship not just at Yorktown but earlier, in the Delaware campaigns. Cornwallis did so at a dinner with Washington after he surrendered to Washington at Yorktown in 1781. That generals would gather right after a decisive battle for a drink and dinner may seem quaint today. We can't imagine Eisenhower exchanging toasts with a German general. Yet that is what happened after Yorktown, when Josiah accurately quotes Cornwallis's toast to Washington:

> When the illustrious part that your Excellency has borne in this long and arduous contest becomes a matter of history, fame will gather your brightest laurels rather from the banks of the Delaware than from those of the Chesapeake. (See David Hackett Fischer, *Washington's Crossing*, 362.)

v. Victory at Yorktown

Foreigners' Esteem for Washington's Generalship (cont.), pages 125, 127

As happens so often, a hero is recognized sooner by those more distant than by those closer to home. In this case, those at home quickly fell in line with the opinions of those abroad. Benjamin Franklin was surrounded and influenced by French, Dutch, Russian, and Prussian generals. Franklin conveyed their sentiments to the Congress back home. Thus, while some in Congress or a few rival generals may have carped, Franklin felt very confident in expressing to an English friend what he believed to be an accepted European opinion on how five British generals—Gage, Howe, Clinton, Cornwallis, and Carleton—had all fallen victim to Washington:

> An American planter was chosen by us to command our troops and continued during the whole war. This man sent home to you, one after another, five of your best generals, baffled, their heads bare of laurels, disgraced even in the opinion of their employers. (See Ron Chernow, *George Washington*, 458.)

Franklin knew that his opinion was accepted European opinion and that his English friend would not disagree with him.

CHAPTER FIVE: DAY FIVE, FRIDAY—FINAL PREPARATIONS

LADY WASHINGTON'S POPULARITY WITH THE TROOPS, PAGES 134, 135

Lady Washington's popularity with the troops, which Josiah comments on, is a subject usually ignored. Just as generals did not always lead from the front as Washington did, wives of generals did not always share the suffering of those under their husband's commands. This was certainly true of British generals' wives ensconced back in London. Yet by all accounts, this five-foot-tall, plump but attractive lady who loved the good life of a Virginia plantation not only was adept at putting people from all backgrounds at ease but she shared in and tried to alleviate the soldiers' suffering.

One observer gave this account of Lady Washington, once described as "a one-woman relief agency," at Valley Forge:

> I never in my life knew a woman so busy from early morning until late at night as was Lady Washington, providing comforts for the sick soldiers. Every day, excepting Sunday, the wives of the officers in camp, and sometimes other women, were invited to Mr. Potts' [house] to assist her in knitting socks, patching garments and making shirts for the poor soldiers when material could be procured. Every few days she might be seen, with basket in hand, and with a single attendant, going among the huts seeking the keenest and most needy sufferers, and giving all the comforts to them in her power. (See Helen Bryan, *Martha Washington*, 226, 227.)

For the officers' wives and neighboring ladies, Lady Washington used a log cabin as a sewing center during the day and a pretend drawing room with candles at night. There she conducted singing sessions over meals of potatoes and pieces of salt fish. No wonder regiments competed for her praise and troops greeted her arrival with "God bless Lady Washington."

When men were later clothed with French aid, Martha loved to listen to fifes and drums parading. Like veterans and their wives of many eras, Lady Washington later looked back with nostalgia on army camp life. (See Helen Bryant, *Martha Washington*, 222.)

George Washington and Religion, pages 136-37

There seems to be an industry devoted to proving George Washington's religiosity, or lack thereof. The most thoughtful effort is the book by theologians Michael and Jana Novak, *Washington's God*. Washington was a very private person and did not write of his personal beliefs.

If we mean by "Christian" a twenty-first-century evangelical who writes or speaks of Jesus or Jesus Christ, Washington does not qualify as a religious Christian, for his voluminous letters contain no such references. Yet Washington went way beyond the eighteenth-century Deists who believed that God may have created the world but ignored how the world functioned. Washington was quick to attribute Revolutionary War successes to both human initiative and divine intervention. Unlike Jefferson, Washington not only did not disparage Jesus or organized religion but praised the constructive role that the church could play, as shown in the building of the chapel for worship at Newburgh and his encouragement of religious services in the army. As the Novaks conclude, Washington's serving as an Anglican church vestryman, while at the same time expressing irritation at the formality of Anglican services, probably showed a typical eighteenth-century Episcopalian who wanted to perform his religious and civic obligations but did not like to wear his religion on his sleeve.

More important than Washington's personal religious beliefs for the future of his country was his concern about what official attitude the new country should take toward religion and its various organized manifestations. The observation of Josiah and his fellow aides that Washington believed his role as the new country's leader required him to attend many different church services and reach out to different religious groups has been attested to over and over. (See Ron Chernow, *Washington*, 132; Barry Schwartz, *George Washington: The Making of an American Symbol*, 85.)

Today, we look back on this period and, with the benefit of hindsight, assume that slavery was the main obstacle to the stabile growth of the new democracy. Our forefathers, however, may have seen things differently. My own readings convince me that, based on hundreds of years of religious persecution both before and after the new Americans came here, religious fratricide—not slavery or even, after the Revolution, a British reconquest—was seen as the chief threat to the new republic. How Washington conducted himself, including his attendance at various church services, reflected his desire to meet this threat.

In this regard, the oft-quoted Washington letter to the Hebrew congregation at Newport, Rhode Island, is quite instructive. For years, people of different religious beliefs had, if failing to establish their own church, sought toleration from the established church in their colony. Thus the Baptists sought toleration from the established Anglicans in Virginia, the Anglicans sought toleration from the established Puritans in Massachusetts, the Roman Catholics sought toleration from established churches outside of Maryland, the Jews sought toleration from established churches everywhere, etc. That was the European custom where monarchs ran established churches and tolerated this group and denied toleration to another one. While states still had established churches in the early nineteenth century, Washington was very proud that the federal government officially exercised religious toleration toward every group and, in doing so, went further than any European monarch. As you will notice from his letter to the Newport Hebrew congregation below, however, Washington had given considerable thought to the nature of toleration and concluded that religious toleration was not sufficient but that true religious liberty required that America should go much further:

> The citizens of the United States of America have a right
> to applaud themselves for having given to mankind examples of an enlarged and liberal policy: a policy worthy

of imitation. All possess alike liberty of conscience and immunities of citizenship. It is now no more that toleration is spoken of, as if it was by the indulgence of one class of people, that another enjoyed the exercise of their inherent natural rights. For happily the government of the United States, which gives to bigotry no sanction, to persecution no assistance, requires only that they who live under its protection should demean themselves as good citizens, in giving it on all occasions their effectual support.

In this letter, Washington sets out a different standard for religious liberty, i.e., that the Jews (or any other group) deserved more than mere toleration; so long as they behaved as good citizens, they were welcome and deserved protection. This attitude toward religion set Washington apart, even from many of the other Founding Fathers.

GENERAL VARNUM'S LETTER, PAGES 138-39 (QUOTED IN APPENDIX B, PAGES 270-72)

Major General James Varnum referred to the low opinion the American public had of Congress with his statement "We are too young to govern ourselves." In his letter, Varnum advocated for an absolute monarchy or a military state. "The Citizens at large are totally destitute of that Love of Equality which is absolutely requisite to support a democratic Republick: Avarice, Jealousy, & Luxury controul their Feelings, & consequently, absolute Monarchy, or a military State, can alone rescue them from all the Horrors of Subjugation" (Robert F. Haggard, *Proceedings of the American Philosophical Society*, vol. 146, no. 2, June 2002, 162).

In his reply, Washington was much milder than in his reply to Colonel Nicola. He opined that some credit was due to Congress and the states and that he did not "consent" to Varnum's views, but he agreed that "the conduct of the people at large is truly alarming" and hoped that the "destructive passions, which I confess too generally pervade all Ranks, shall give place to that love of Freedom which first animated us in this contest." This mildness of the General's tone in response to Varnum's suggestion of monarchy must have been noticed by Washington's aides (Robert F. Haggard, ibid., 162).

Taverns and Other Signs of Veneration for Washington, page 140

Josiah reports a trip with the General where they saw a sign with King George III's portrait lying on the ground outside a tavern and a sign with the General's portrait raised in its place. This was highly likely as, even before the end of the war, Washington was idolized by many in our country. In 1783, Princeton University commissioned Charles Willson Peale to replace George III's portrait with Washington's. Congress commissioned an equestrian statue of Washington in 1783. Even earlier in the war, Cambridge, Williamsburg, Richmond, and Milton, Connecticut, were celebrating his birthday, and the army celebrated his birthday at Newburgh. Americans celebrated his birthday as early as 1779. (See John Ferling, *The First of Men*, 314, 319.) Counties and towns were named after Washington in four states during the war. A college was named after him in Maryland in 1782. (See Barry Schwartz, *George Washington: The Making of an American Symbol*, 33.)

Nor was the idolization confined to America. In 1781, the French general Rochambeau proclaimed Washington's birthday a holiday for French troops. Other American leaders may have been idolized, but the evidence of the idolization came after their deaths. With Washington, it came while he was alive. A Russian traveler noticed in the early 1800s that almost every American family had a likeness of Washington in its home, and this practice had started while Washington was alive. This veneration of a living person understandably made Josiah and others leery of Washington assuming greater power at Newburgh in 1783.

National University, page 146-47

Today many colleges have intern programs in Washington, DC, for students to learn about their government. Every college in Washington, DC—Georgetown, American, George Washington, and others—has courses where congressmen, senators, and federal officials lecture to students to give them insights into how our government works. Many times when I served in Congress such students came to visit and talk with me. This was all envisioned by Washington—a national university where students from all over would attend congressional debates and learn about their new government. (See Ron Chernow, *Washington*, 705.)

Josiah was correct about Washington's enthusiasm for a national university. Sixteen years later, Washington devoted several pages in his last will and testament to laying out the case for a national university and bequeathing to such a project shares in inland water navigation companies given him by the legislature of Virginia, shares that Washington had previously declined as improper compensation for his services but that he now deemed appropriate if used for a public purpose such as a national university. Washington stated the purpose of such a university to be "to do away with local attachments and State prejudices" and offer an alternative to the great European universities that Washington believed were teaching "principles unfriendly to Republican Governmnt" (*The Writings of George Washington*, 1025–27). This dream of Washington's in its exact form never came to pass, but when students visit our national capital from all over the United States to see their government in action, they do fulfill part of Washington's dream.

Farming, Gardening, and Hospitality, page 147

To say that General Washington was obsessed with farming and gardening would not be an overstatement. As Josiah notes, Washington believed it was his duty to advance American agriculture through experiments that ranged from herring to whiskey to textile mills to grapes to how to plant six different varieties of corn. For his neighbors, Washington tried to invent a grazing grass that would lead to a superior line of sheep and wool, and he also tried to breed a line of super mules with the gift of a Spanish jackass from the king of Spain and some other mules procured in Malta by Lafayette. (See James Thomas Flexner, *George Washington and the New Nation*, 42–50.) Washington's drill plough, which dispensed seed and corn through a twisting barrel as the plough moved forward, was used by neighbors and even later in the Midwest.

Washington, always conscious of appearances, was well aware that Southern hospitality was not a meaningless phrase and that Mount Vernon was becoming the most visited private residence in America. Many Virginia planters could be called "gentleman farmers," but Washington was more. He talked of trees "which my hands have planted," and it was not idle boasting as visitors noted with surprise that he did not just instruct his slaves but often, stripped to the waist, worked alongside his men. Washington could wax rhapsodic about seeing "the work of one's own hands, fostered by care and attention, rising to maturity . . . which, by the combination of nature and taste . . . is always regaling to the eye, at the same time [that], in their seasons, they are . . . grateful to the palate" (James Thomas Flexner, *George Washington and the New Nation*, 43). Strangers so often stopped by for a day or two that Washington advised his mother that Mount Vernon was becoming a "well resorted tavern" (Andrea Wulf, *Founding Gardeners*, 27).

Citizens today may stop by and gaze at presidents' private residences, but we do not stay overnight and have a few meals!

CHAPTER SIX: DAY SIX, FRIDAY—THE SHOWDOWN

The Exchange of Letters with the French Ambassador, page 152-53

The General and the French ambassador shared some common beliefs: the war was approaching its end but was not yet over and could go on another year, and the war should be pursued until both the Americans and the French had achieved the maximum tactical military advantage prior to the final peace treaty. The General knew that the Americans and Congress were weary of war, but he also knew that peace would depend on where the forces stood on the battlefield. The General wanted to make sure that the final peace treaty gave the Americans New York City as well as Charleston, both then occupied by the British. Thus the General wanted the French to join him in an assault on New York. The French ambassador also knew that the Americans and the Congress were weary of war but wanted to make sure the French maintained their advantage in the West Indies. Thus, the ambassador wanted the Americans to join the French in pressuring the British along the coast to keep them from pushing the French out of the West Indies.

The Temple, pages 155-56

For those interested in seeing the Temple where the dramatic events of March 15, 1783, unfolded, you can visit the New Windsor Cantonment State Historic Site, which has been a New York State historical site since the nineteenth century.

The Temple has been reconstructed and mainly appears like the original Temple (only a cupola and a flagpole have been added), which was constructed in three months. It is a 30-by-110-foot building with large sash windows, a small raised platform with four side offices, two of them for court-martials and administration, and other offices for supplies and the quartermaster. The French greatly admired the American troops' craftsmanship with wood.

"Divine services" were held every Sunday during the months after Chaplain Israel Evans's project came to fruition in December 1782. The wooden barracks, each housing eight soldiers, have yet to be reconstructed. The Temple, like Washington's headquarters a few miles away, is open to the public.

Where Do Washington's Speech and the Resolutions and the Letters Quoted in Chapter Six Come from? pages 156 et seq.

They do not come from the author's imagination. Every quotation is real. Washington's speech was transcribed by many in attendance, including the famous reference to his spectacles. (See *The Writings of George Washington*, 496.) Major Shaw's description of the speech to Josiah is a verbatim quotation from a letter written by Shaw. The resolutions drafted by General Knox's committee are quotes from the actual resolutions. (See the Washington Papers at the University of Virginia.) The letters to the president of the Congress and to Congressmen Jones and Hamilton and the thanks conveyed to the army were all written by Washington exactly as they are quoted. The toast by Washington to his officers at Fraunces Tavern and his speech to Congress in Annapolis resigning his commission are also exact quotations. (All these documents can be found in full in the Washington Papers at the University of Virginia. Most can be found in full in John Marshall's *The Life of George Washington*, vol. 4, pages 75–97. And a few, such as Washington's speech to his officers at the Temple, can be found in *The Writings of George Washington*, page 496. Portions or brief excerpts of these letters and speeches can be found in almost every biography of Washington. Even though the full power of these communications could only be experienced by those in attendance, the written versions are still, as the reader has already realized, quite compelling.)

THE GENERAL'S SPECTACLES, PAGES 161-62

Washington, a great, handsome, six-foot-three, 209-pound specimen at the beginning of the war (see earlier note on page 278 about the new lifelike sculpture of Washington at Mount Vernon), developed many physical infirmities during the war, among them a carbuncle on his leg, a paunch around the middle, graying hair, decaying teeth, and declining eyesight. His heavy correspondence led to increasingly blurry vision, which hampered the General's reading ability. We know from a February 16, 1783, letter to a Philadelphia optometrist and leading American astronomer, David Rittenhouse, that the latter had prepared and delivered spectacles that month enabling the General to read smaller handwriting. (See Ron Chernow, *Washington*, 432.)

MAJOR SAMUEL SHAW'S JOURNAL, PAGE 163

There are numerous and varied accounts of eyewitnesses to Washington's speech on Saturday, March 15, 1783. All contain the basic facts outlined here, including the General's use of his new spectacles, but the most well written and gripping is the *Journals of Major Samuel Shaw*, pages 101–5. Some artistic license is taken by the author; Josiah would have had access to his own and other accounts, and may well have received Major Shaw's written account quoted herein, but he probably did not have access to the full Shaw journals since they were not published until 1847 by Shaw's nephews Robert Gould Shaw and Josiah Quincy. Where Major Shaw's account excels over other accounts is in capturing the difficulties the General faced in winning over his audience and the dramatic impact Washington had on his brother officers:

The meeting of the officers was in itself exceedingly respect-able, the matters they were called to deliberate upon were of the most serious nature, and the unexpected attendance of the Commander-in-chief heightened the solemnity of the scene. Every eye was fixed upon the illustrious man, and attention to their beloved General held the assem-bly mute. He opened the meeting by apologizing for his appearance there, which was by no means his intention when he published the order which directed them to assemble. But the diligence used in circulating the anony-mous pieces rendered it necessary that he should give his sentiments to the army on the nature and tendency of them, and determined him to avail himself of the present opportunity; and, in order to do it, with greater perspi-cuity, he had committed his thoughts to writing, which, with the indulgence of his brother officers, he would take the liberty of reading to them. It is needless for me to say anything of this production; *it speaks for itself.* After he had concluded his address, he said, that, as a corroborat-ing testimony of the good disposition in Congress towards the army, he would communicate to them a letter received from a worthy member of that body, and one who on all occasions had ever proved himself their fast friend. This was an exceedingly sensible letter, and, while it pointed out the difficulties and embarrassments of Congress, it held up very forcibly the idea that the army should, at all events, be generously dealt with. One circumstance in reading this letter must not be omitted. His Excellency, after reading the first paragraph, made a short pause, took out his spectacles, and begged the indulgence of his audi-ence while he put them on, observing at the same time, that he had grown gray in their service, and now found himself growing blind. There was something so natural, so unaffected, in this appeal, as rendered it superior to the most studied oratory; it forced its way to the heart, and you might see sensibility moisten every eye. The General, having finished, took leave of the assembly, and the business of the day was conducted in the manner which is related in the account of the proceedings.

I cannot dismiss this subject [the General's speech on Saturday, March 15, 1783] without observing, that it is happy for America that she has a *patriot army*, and equally so that a *Washington* is its leader. I rejoice in the opportunities I have had of seeing this great man in a variety of situations—calm and intrepid where the battle raged, patient and persevering under the pressure of misfortune, moderate and possessing himself of the full career of victory. Great as these qualifications deservedly render him, he never appeared to me more truly so, than at the assembly we have been speaking of. On other occasions he has been supported by the exertions of an army and the countenance of his friends; but in this he stood single and alone. There was no saying where the passions of an army, which were not a little inflamed, might lead; but it was generally allowed that longer forbearance was dangerous, and moderation had ceased to be a virtue. Under these circumstances he appeared, not at the head of his troops, but as it were in opposition to them; and for a dreadful moment the interests of the army and its General seemed to be in competition! He spoke—every doubt was dispelled, and the tide of patriotism rolled again in its wonted course. Illustrious man! What he says of the army may with equal justice be applied to his own character. "Had this day been wanting, the world had never seen the last stage of perfection to which human nature is capable of attaining."

Washington the "Actor" at Annapolis, pages 166, 176

Earlier Josiah commented on how he agreed with John Adams that Washington was an actor. Whether Washington was an "actor" or, as Josiah now reflects, someone trying to mold his character to accentuate positive traits, Washington's love of theater led him to inject theatrical references into his speeches. In resigning his commission to Congress in Annapolis in what Washington deemed his farewell to Congress, Josiah quotes Washington's references to himself as an actor, retiring "from the great theatre of action." Back in April 1783, in his last general order to the army, Washington resorted to similar theatrical rhetoric:

> Nothing now remains but for the actors of this mighty Scene to preserve a perfect unvarying constancy of character through the last act; to close the Drama with applause; and to retire from the Military Theatre with the same approbation as Angells and men which have crowned all their former vertuous Actions. (See *The Writings of George Washington*, 513, 514.)

Adams and Madison's Lauding of Washington after Newburgh, page 170-71

Josiah comments that congressmen such as Adams and Madison had doubts about whether the General would stop the insurrection but rushed to extol him after the fact, knowing that their congressional powers were secure. Josiah's comments are well supported. James Madison, just two days after Washington's speech at the Temple in Newburgh, wrote John Randolph: "The steps taken by the General to avert the gathering storm, and his professions of inflexible adherence to his duty to Congress and to his Country, excited the most affectionate sentiments toward him" ("Letter to John Randolph, March 17, 1783," *The Writings of James Madison*, vol. 1, 407). For Madison, who had originally doubted that Washington would put down the mutiny, this was "an understatement, if there ever was one" (See Barry Schwartz, *George Washington: The Making of an American Symbol*, 136).

> In June 1783, three months after the showdown at Newburgh, John Adams wrote: "The happy turn given to the discontents of the army by the General, is consistent with his character, which, as you observe, is above all praise, as every character, whose rule and object are duty, not interest, nor glory, which I think has been strictly true with the General from the beginning, and I trust will continue to the end." (Barry Schwartz, *George Washington: The Making of an American Symbol*, 136; "Letter to Livingston, June 16, 1783," *Works of John Adams*, vol. 8, 73.)

The events at Newburgh also undoubtedly influenced Thomas Jefferson's comment in 1784 quoted earlier: "The moderation and virtue of a single character has probably prevented this Revolution from being closed, as most others have been, by a subversion of that liberty it was intended to establish" (James Thomas Flexner, *Washington, The Indispensable Man*, 178).

Epilogue

A Further Mutiny, page 173

Josiah talks of a later spring Pennsylvania mutiny involving fifteen hundred troops put down by Washington. Such a mutiny took place, as well as still another mutiny in August 1783, leading Congress to plead with Washington to move his remaining troops to Rocky Hill, New Jersey, in order to protect Congress from soldiers still again asking for more back pay.

LINCOLN'S VENERATION OF WASHINGTON, PAGE 178

Josiah observes that his congressman, Abraham Lincoln, claimed that the gold ring he wore contained a piece of Washington's hair. A later president, William McKinley, claimed that a ring given to him by Lincoln's secretary, John Hay, was embedded with several strands of Washington's hair. Today, this may all seem unlikely or bizarre, but we must remember the hold that Washington had on the American populace in the nineteenth century. (For a description of such practices, including rings containing relics of Washington, see Stanley Weintraub, *General Washington's Christmas Farewell*, 66, 67.)

THE QUOTES FROM KING GEORGE III AND NAPOLEON, PAGES 179

For years, the quote from George III that if Washington turns down the kingship, "he will be the greatest man in the world" has survived and embellished Washington's reputation. (See Ellis, *His Excellency*, 139. Recently the Washington Papers at the University of Virginia explored the background of this quote. It was originally attributed to a conversation between American artist Benjamin West and George III.)

> We now know that the heavily-used conversation between King George III and West gained its foothold in history because Joseph Farington (1747–1821), a second-tier British artist, met West on December 28, 1799, and then wrote in his diary entry for that date West's recollection

of an exchange with the King during the early summer of 1782 . . . Despite the gap of some seventeen years from the time of the actual event and West's recollection, it is plausible to believe its authenticity and veracity . . . Farington definitely knew West very well and was a faithful diarist. If only such a level of confidence could be felt about all anecdotes and stories concerning George Washington in wide circulation! (See the Washington Papers at the University of Virginia Newsletter, no. 12, Spring 2011.)

THE TRIBUTES TO WASHINGTON, PAGES 179-81

In addition to the tributes to Washington from Abraham Lincoln and King George III, the tributes from Fisher Ames, Gerald Vogel, Lord Byron, Philip Freneau, and others are accurately quoted here. It is impossible for us today to appreciate the outpouring of encomiums while he lived and the eulogies after his death. Not even the eulogies for President Kennedy come close in their depth and variety. "Some clergymen wanted to insert his [Washington's] farewell address into the Bible as an epilogue. 'Every American considers it his sacred duty to have a likeness of Washington in his home, just as we have images of God's saints,' observed a European traveler" (Ron Chernow, *Washington*, 813).

DID WASHINGTON CONSIDER LEADING A COUP?, WHOLE NOVEL

This question is, of course, at the heart of this novel. Historians have differed over whether a coup would have succeeded with Washington's leadership or even without it. But I am not aware of many historians who have focused at length on whether Washington considered the possibility and, if so, how seriously. Given the evidence adduced in this novel of actual letters from Nicola, Duché, Varnum, etc., urging

Washington to take power (we do not know how many other letters there were, but we can assume there were many), the constant oral urgings that aides such as Josiah witnessed and we know took place, and the whole climate of the country, how come this question has received so little emphasis from historians?

I believe the answer lies not with historians ignoring the evidence but with the reasonable assumption that since Washington rejected the offer at Newburgh, that since we know him to be so dedicated to setting up a republic, and that since we believe him to be a man of impeccable integrity and character, it is just beyond us to consider possibilities that would substantially reshape the narrative of our nation's founding or our Founding Father. But as I've alluded to in the Afterword and as Josiah observes in the Epilogue, rather than detract from Washington's character or his commitment to our republic, Washington's wrestling with whether to become king or dictator, and then turning away from those outcomes, only enhances both his character and the nation's commitment to civilian supremacy over the military. (See Ellis's *His Excellency*, 140–44.)

And why shouldn't Washington have considered accepting a crown? Would you not consider such a possibility when, everywhere you turn, you read letters from officers suggesting it is your duty to save the nation by becoming king, you hear toasts to yourself instead of George III, and you see signs such as the one outside the tavern the General and Josiah observed? As Josiah says, Washington should be honored (and was honored in the eighteenth century) less for what he did and more for what he did not do. This is something that is outside our twentieth- and twenty-first-century frame of reference. We judge leaders, whether they be generals or presidents, by what they do or promise to do. But can we name one great American leader whom we honor for what he or she did not do? This is what makes Washington the truly unique American leader.

APPENDIX B

Documents Leading Up to and Including the Week of March 9, 1783, at Newburgh, New York

(Some Corrections Are Made to Make the Documents Understandable in Modern English)

Letter from Reverend Jacob Duché of Philadelphia, First Chaplain of First Continental Congress, to General George Washington on October 8, 1777

IF this letter should find you in council, or in the field, before you read another sentence I beg you to take the first opportunity of retiring and weighing it's important contents.—You are perfectly acquainted with the part I formerly took in the present unhappy contest . . .

[Reverend Duché here alludes to his role as the first chaplain of the First Continental Congress and describes his reluctance to join the War for Independence.]

And now, dear Sir, suffer me, in the language of truth and real affection, to address myself to you. All the world must be convinced you are engaged in the service of your country from motives perfectly disinterested. You risked every thing that was dear to you, abandoned the sweets of domestic life, which your affluent fortune can give the uninterrupted enjoyment of . . .

[The reverend, after describing more the risk of pursuing independence, turns to the decline of the Congress, the poor state of the military, and the perilous condition of the country.]

What then can be the consequence of this rash and violent measure and degeneracy of representation, confusion of councils, blunders without number? The most respectable characters have withdrawn themselves, and are succeeded by a great majority of illiberal and violent men. Take an impartial view of the present Congress, and what can you expect from them? Your feelings must be greatly hurt by the representation of your natural province. You have no longer a Randolph, a Bland, or a Braxton, men whose names will ever be revered, whose demands never ran above the first ground on which they set out, and whose truly glorious and virtuous sentiments I have frequently heard with rapture from their own lips.—Oh! my dear Sir, what a sad contrast of characters now present . . . As to those of my own province, some of them are so obscure, that their very names were never in my ears before, and others have only been distinguished for the weakness of their understandings, and the violence of their tempers . . .

After this view of the Congress, turn to the Army.—The whole world knows that its only existence depends upon you; that your death or captivity disperses it in a moment, and that there is not a man on that side of the question in America, capable of succeeding you.—As to the army itself, what have you to expect from them.—Have they not frequently abandoned you yourself, in the hour of extremity? Can you, have you the least confidence in a set of undisciplined men and officers, many of them have been taken from the lowest of the people, without principle, without courage; take away them who surround your person, How very few are there you can ask to sit at your table?—As to your little navy, of that little, what is left? Of the Delaware fleet part are taken, the rest must soon surrender—Of those in the other provinces some are taken, one or two at sea, and others lying unmanned and unrigged in your harbours; and now where are your resources? Oh my dear Sir, How sadly have you been abused by a faction void of truth, and void of tenderness to you and your country! . . . A British army, after having passed unmolested thro a vast extent of country, have possessed themselves of the Capital of America. How unequal the contest! How fruitless the expence of blood? Under so many discouraging circumstances, can Virtue, can Honour, can the Love of your Country, prompt you to proceed? Humanity itself, and sure humanity is no stranger to your breast, calls upon you to desist.—Your army must perish for want of common necessaries, or thousands of innocent families must perish to support them; where-ever they encamp, the country must be impoverished; wherever they march, the troops of Britain will pursue, and must complete the destruction which America herself has began; perhaps it may be said, it is better to die than to be made slaves. This

indeed is a splendid maxim in theory, and perhaps in
some instances may be found experimentally true; but
when there is the least probability of an happy accom-
modations, surely wisdom and humanity call for some
sacrifices to be made, to prevent inevitable destruction. You well know there is but one invincible bar to
such an accommodation, could this be removed, other
obstacles might readily be removed.

[The reverend then proposes what he sees as
the only way out of the country's dilemma: for the
General, as the revered guardian of the country, to
urge upon the Congress rescission of the Declaration
of Independence accompanied by negotiations and, if
this failed, to pursue negotiations as the head of the
army. Such action, writes the reverend, would give the
General a lustrous place in the annals of our history.]

It is to you, and you alone, your bleeding country
looks and calls aloud for this sacrifice, your arm alone
has strength sufficient to remove this bar; may heaven
inspire you with this glorious resolution of exerting
your strength at this crisis, and immortalizing yourself
as friend and guardian to your country; your penetrating eye needs not more explicit language to discern my
meaning; with that prudence and delicacy therefore, of
which I know you possessed, represent to Congress the
indispensible necessity of rescinding the hasty and ill-
advised declaration of Independency—Recommend,
and you have an undoubted right to recommend, an
immediate cessation of hostilities. Let the controversy
be taken up where that declaration left it, and where
Lord Howe certainly expected to find it left. Let men
of clear and impartial characters, in or out of Congress

liberal in their sentiments, heretofore, independent in their fortunes; and some such may be found in America, be appointed to confer with his Majesty's commissioners. Let them, if they please, prepare, some well-digested constitutional plan, to lay before them at the commencement of the negociation; when they have gone this far, I am confident the usual happy consequences will ensue; unanimity will immediately take place through the different provinces; thousands who are now ardently wishing and praying for such a measure, will step forth, and declare themselves the zealous advocates, for constitutional liberty, and millions will bless the hero that left the field of war, to decide this most important contest with the weapons of wisdom and humanity. Oh! Sir, let no false ideas of worldly honour deter you from engaging in so glorious a task, whatever centuries may be thrown out, by mean illiberal minds, your character will rise in the estimation of the virtuous and noble; it will appear with lustre in the annals of history, and form a glorious contrast, to that of those, who have fought to obtain conquest, and gratify their own ambition by the destruction of their species, and the ruin of their country. Be assured, Sir, that I write not this under the eye of any British officer, or person connected with the British army, or ministry. The sentiments I express, are the real sentiments of my own heart, such as I have long held, and which I should have made known to you by letter before, had I not fully expected an opportunity of a private conference . . .

I love my country. I love you; but the love of truth, the love of peace, and the love of God, I hope

I should be enabled, if called upon to the tryal, to sacrifice every other inferior love. If the arguments made use of in this letter should have so much influence as to engage you in the glorious work, which I have warmly recommended, I shall ever deem my success the highest temporal favour that Providence could grant me. Your interposition and advice, I am confident, would meet a favourable reception from the authority under which you act, if it should not, you have an infallible recourse still left, negociate for your country at the head of your army. After all it may appear presumption as an individual to address himself to you on a subject of such magnitude, or to say what measures would best secure the interest and welfare of a whole continent. The friendly and favourable opinion you have always expressed for me, emboldens me to undertake it, and which has greatly added to the weight of this motive; I have been strongly impressed with a sense of duty upon the occasion, which left my conscience uneasy, and my heart afflicted till I fully discharged it. I am no enthusiast; the cause is new and singular to me, but I could not enjoy one moment's peace till this letter was written, with the most ardent prayers for your spiritual, as well as temporal welfare.

Letter from Colonel Lewis Nicola to George Washington on May 22, 1782

The injuries the troops have received in their pecuniary rights have been, & still continue to be too obvious to require a particular detail, or to have escaped your Excellencies notice, tho your exalted station must have deprived you of opportunity of information relative to the severe distresses occasioned thereby . . .

[Colonel Nicola writes at length of the injuries caused to soldiers by the failure of Congress and the states to meet their financial promises. He then moves on to discuss the possible consequences.]

From several conversations I have had with officers, & some I have overheard among soldiers, I believe it is generally intended not to seperate after the peace 'till all grievances are redressed, engagements & promises fulfilled, but how this is to be done I am at a loss, as neither officers nor soldiers can have any confidence in promises. We have no doubt of Congresses intention to act uprightly, but greatly fear that, by the interested voices of others, their abilities will not be equal to the task.

God forbid we should ever think of involving that country we have, under your conduct & auspices, rescued from oppression, into a new scene of blood & confusion; but it cannot be expected we should forego claims on which our future subsistence & that of our families depend.

Another difference there is between our fellow citizens and us is, that we must live under governments in the forming of which we had no hand, nor were consulted either personally nor representatively, being engaged in preventing the enemy from disturbing those bodies which were entrusted with that business, the members of which would have found little mercy had they been captured . . .

[Before offering his solution to this problem, Colonel Nicola writes that he first wishes to discuss

why he does not support the republican form of government. He goes on to discuss the weaknesses of
absolute monarchy while acknowledging the strengths
of the British version of monarchy.]

Dangers foreseen may be removed, alleviated,
or in some cases, turned to benefits, possibly what I
appreciate may be susceptible, of even the latter, by
means I beg leave to propose, but must request your
Excellencies patience if I digress a little before I open
my prospect.

I own I am not that violent admirer of a republican form of government as numbers in this country are; this is not owing to caprice, but reason &
experience. Let us consider the fate of all the modern
republicks of any note without running into antiquity,
which I think would also serve to establish my system.

The republicks of later days, worth our notice,
may be reduced to three, Venice, Genoa & Holland,
tho the two former are rather aristocratical than republican governments, yet they resemble those more than
monarchical.

These have, each in their turns, shone with great
brightness, but their lustre has been of short duration,
and as it were only a blaze. What figure has Holland,
that, in his infancy, successfully opposed the most for-
midable powers of Europe, made for more than half
of the present century, or actually makes at present?
Mistress of nearly half the commerce of the earth, has
she occasioned any considerable diversion of the naval
power of Britain? Six or eight ships of the line have
been able to oppose her, & unable to protect herself
and her extensive commerce, has she not been obliged

to apply for assistance to a neighbouring monarch? Does not the great similarity there is between her form of government & ours give us room to fear our fate will be like hers. Has it not evidently appeared that during the course of this war we have never been able to draw forth all the internal resources we are possessed of, and oppose or attack the enemy with our real vigour?

In contrast to this scene let us consider the principal monarchies of Europe, they have suffered great internal commotions, have worried each other, have had periods of vigour & weakness, yet they still subsist & shine with lustre. It must not be concluded from this that I am a partisan for absolute monarchy, very far from it, I am sensible of all its defects, the only conclusion I would draw from the comparison is, that the energy of the latter is more beneficial to the existence of a nation than the wisdom of the former. A monarch may often be governed by wise & moderate councels, but it is hardly possible for large bodies to plan or execute vigorous ones.

The inference I would deduce from what I have premised is, that each form of government has its defective & valuable parts, therefore, that form which partakes of all, or most of the latter & is purged of the former, must be the most eligible.

In the british Government we have a sketch of this, far, it is true from perfect, but no despicable basis of a good one. The english constitution has been the result of repeated struggles between prince & people, but never received anything of a regular or stable form till the revolution, & yet is still short of perfection.

The principal defects are pointed out by the experience of almost a century, & I believe may be reduced to two, one in the legislative the other in the executive authorities. Were elections annual, & confined to representatives for counties & few large trading cities only, & all contributing to the support of government priviledged to elect, and had the king no command of money beyond what is requisite to the support of his family & court, suitable to the dignity of his station, I believe the constitution would approach much nearer to that degree of perfection to which sublunary things are limited. In a well regulated legislative body I conceive a third branch necessary. Montesquieu observes that a hereditary nobility is requisite in a monarchy but incompatible with a republick, taking this for granted, some degree of nobility may be proper in a mixed government, but limited, suppose not hereditary.

[Before getting to his monarchy proposal, Colonel Nicola outlines the details of a complicated scheme to compensate all soldiers with a mixture of land and notes.]

I shall now proceed to my scheme.

Congress has promised all those that continue in the service certain tracts of land, agreeable to their grades. Some States have done the same, others have not, probably owing to their not having lands to give, but as all the military have equal merits so have they equal claims to such rewards, therefore, they ought all to be put on a footing by the united States.

Besides those who may actually be in service at the peace, I consider all those dismissed, or put to half pay, through schemes of economy, have equal rights, as their being out of the service was not voluntary.

These things premised, I think Congress should take on itself the discharging all such engagements, made, or that ought to be made, for lands & discharge them by procuring a sufficient tract in some of the best of those fruitful & extensive countries to the west of our frontiers, so that each individual should have his due, all unprofitable mountains & swamps, also lakes & rivers within the limits of this tract not to be reckoned as any part of the lots, but thrown in for the benefit of the whole community. This tract to be formed into a distinct State under such mode of government as those military who choose to remove to it may agree on.

Debts due to the army should be adjusted with dispatch & liquidated in the following manner. One third to be paid immediately, to enable the settlers to buy tools for trades & husbandry, & some stock, the other two thirds by four notes payable, with interest, in three months, & the others on the same terms at three months interval between each payment. In order to give such notes a due value, good funds should be appropriated for the discharge of principal & interest, but previous to such first payment & notes given, a sum should be deducted from each non commissioned & private mans debt, sufficient to victual him & family for one year from the first harvest succeeding the arrival of the colony to the granted lands; during the intermediate time those persons to be victualled at the expence of the continent, & also to receive pay & clothing to the time the accounts are all adjusted & the troops ready to march.

Officers being entitled to half pay, such as choose to emigrate, should have provisions be allowed them as above & quarterly notes with interest for three years full pay to commence & be computed from the time they begin their march, in full discharge of all such half pay.

As I have already observed that it may be objected that depreciations and other payments have been made good; but can a just debt be equitably discharged by certificates of very small comparative value or depreciated paper money? Certainly no, consequently the States are still bound to make good the deficiency. To this it will probably be answered that those certificates having generally passed into other hands, who have paid a consideration for them; but what consideration? A tenth or twentieth of the principal value expressed therein, independent of interest; and is it not generally understood in some States, if not in all, that when those certificates are to be paid off they will be estimated at no more than what was given for them? I therefore conceive the following rules should be observed in discharge of these obligations.

Every person in whose favour a certificate has been or shall be given, and who will keep it to the conclusion of the war, to be paid its full value.

To every person paid in depreciated money the depreciation thereof to be made good.

To the original possessors of certificates sold two thirds of the value expressed, the other third to be considered as received when the certificate was sold. This is certainly much beyond what, on an average, has been received for all certificates sold, but as it will be difficult, if at all possible, to ascertain in a reasonable time the money paid, it is requisite to find some rule.

[The colonel finally outlines his recommended form of government for carrying out the compensation: the adoption of a form of monarchy, implying that the leader of the American army, General Washington (without naming him), should lead such a monarchy (although perhaps without the title of king).]

This war must have shown to all, but to military men in particular the weakness of republicks, and the exertions of the army has been able to make by being under a proper head, therefore I little doubt, when the benefits of a mixed government are pointed out and duly considered, but such will be readily adopted; in this case it will, I believe, be uncontroverted that the same abilities which have led us, through difficulties apparently insurmountable by human power, to victory and glory, those qualities that have merited and obtained the universal esteem and veneration of an army, would be most likely to conduct and direct us in the smoother paths of peace.

Some people have so connected the ideas of tyranny and monarchy as to find it very difficult to separate them, it may therefore be requisite to give the head of such a constitution as I propose, some title apparently more moderate, but if all other things were once adjusted I believe strong argument might be produced for admitting the title of king, which I conceive would be attended with some material advantages.

I have hinted that I believe the United States would be benefited by my scheme, this I conceive would be done by having a savage and cruel enemy separated from their borders by a body of veterans, that would be as an advanced guard, securing the main body from danger. There is no doubt but Canada will some time or other be a separate State, and from the genious & habits of the people, that its government will be monarchical. May not casualties produce enmity between this new State and our Union, & may not its force under the direction of an active prince prove too powerful for the efforts of republicks? It may be answered that in a few years we shall acquire such vigour as to baffle all inimical attempts. I grant that our numbers & riches will increase, but will our governments have energy enough to draw them forth? Will those States remote from the danger be zealously anxious to assist those more exposed? Individuals in Holland abound in wealth, yet the government is poor & weak.

Republican bigots will certainly consider my opinions as heterodox, and the maintainer thereof as meriting fire and faggots, I have therefore hitherto kept them within my own breast. By freely communicating them to your Excellency I am persuaded I own no risk, & that, this disapproved of, I need not apprehend their ever being disclosed to my prejudice.

LETTER FROM MAJOR GENERAL JAMES VARNUM TO
GENERAL GEORGE WASHINGTON ON JUNE 23, 1782

Colo. Olney will have the Honor of delivering this to your Excellency: His Attention to the good of the Service, during his late Residence here, has been equal to his former Assiduities, and I am confident will meet your full Approbation.

[General Varnum goes on to discuss the weaknesses of the Articles of Confederation, why the citizens are incapable of supporting a democratic republic, and why absolute monarchy is the only answer.]

I wish to Heaven the same Application could be made to the Legislation of this State, so far as respects their political Measures. They have granted Money; they collect it as rapidly as could be supposed; & they have done well in raising of Recruits; but they have suffered their Glory to be tarnished in Matters of Finance. Such is the dreadful Situation of this Country that it is in the Power of any State to frustrate the Intention of all the others! This Calamity is so Founded in the Articles of Confederation, and will continually increase 'till that baseless Fabric shall yield to some kind of Government, the Principles of which may be correspondent to the Tone of the Passions. The Citizens at large are totally destitute of that Love of Equality which is absolutely requisite to support a democratic Republick: Avarice, Jealousy & Luxury controul their Feelings, & consequently, absolute Monarchy, or a military State, can alone rescue them from all the Horrors of Subjugation. The circulating Cash of the Country is too trifling to raise a Revenue by Taxation for supporting the War, & too many of the People are obstinately averse to those artificial Aids which would supply its Deficiency. In this Situation, every Moment augments our Danger, by fixing the Habits of Licentiousness, and giving Permanency to British Persevearence: And should Dejection in our Ally succeed to Misfortune, the Instability of national Policy may give Place to the Sentiments of the mediating Powers, "that we are too young to govern ourselves." At all Events, this Country hangs upon the Issue of the present Campaign! If a great Exertion could be made, by Militia or otherwise, to repossess ourselves of New York, we may possibly realise the Blessings of Independence, But Time alone will unfold the Decrees of Fate.

[General Varnum then discusses the individual case of a soldier seeking a discharge.]

First Anonymous Letter Sent Monday, March 10, 1783 Announcing Meeting the Following Day

A Meeting of the Genl & Field Officers is requested, at the public building, on Tuesday next [tomorrow] at 11 oclock—A Commissd Officer from each Company is expected, and a delegate from the Medical Staff— the Object of this Convention, is to consider the late Letter from our Representatives in Philadelphia; and what measures (if any) should be adopted, to obtain that redress of Grievances, which they seem to have solicited in vain.

General Washington's Announcement of a Meeting for Saturday on Further Measures to Be Adopted, Tuesday, March 11, 1783

The Commander in Chief having heard that a General meeting of the officers of the Army was proposed to be held this day at the Newbuilding in an anonymous paper which was circulated yesterday by some unknown person conceives (altho he is fully persuaded that the good sense of the officers could induce them to pay very little attention to such an irregular invitation) his duty as well as the reputation and true interest of the Army requires his disapprobation of such disorderly proceedings, at the same time he requests the General and Field officers with one officer from each company and a proper representation of the Staff of the Army will assemble at 12 o'clock on Saturday next at the Newbuilding to hear the report of the Committee of the Army to Congress.

After mature deliberation they will devise what further measures ought to be adopted as most rational and best calculated to attain the just and important object in view. The senior officer in Rank present will be pleased to preside and report the result of the Deliberations to the Commander in Chief.

Congress have been pleased to promote Job Sumner of the 3d Massachusetts Regiment to be a Major in the Army and to take rank from the 1st of October 1782.

The 3d Massachusetts Regiment will march on Thursday next to the relief of the 2d York Regiment on the Lines.

SECOND ANONYMOUS LETTER LAYING OUT GRIEVANCES AND ALTERNATIVE PROPOSED ACTIONS, MONDAY AFTERNOON, MARCH 10, 1783

Gentlemen

A fellow soldier whose interest and affection bind him
strongly to you, whose past sufferings, have been as
great & whose future fortune may be as desperate as
yours, would beg leave to address you.

Age has its claims, and rank is not without its
pretenses to advise—but tho unsupported by both,
he flatters himself that the plain language of sincerity
& Experience will neither be unheard nor unregarded.

Like many of you he loved private life, and left
it with regret—he left it determined to retire from
the field with the necessity that called him to it, and
not till then, Not, 'till the enemies of his Country,
the slaves of pow'r and the hirelings of injustice were
compelled to abandon their schemes, and acknowledge America as terrible in Arms, as she had been
humble in Remonstrance—with this object in view,
he has long shared in your Toils and mingled in your
dangers—he has felt the cold hand of poverty without a murmur, & has seen the insolence of wealth
without a sigh. But, too much under the direction
of his wishes, and sometimes weak enough to mistake desire for opinion, he has till lately, very lately
believed in the Justice of his Country. He hop'd, that,
as the Clouds of adversity scattered, and as the sun-
shine of peace & better fortune broke in upon us,
the coldness and severity of government would relax,
and that more than Justice, that gratitude, would
blaze forth upon those hands, which had upheld her
in the darkest stages of her passage from impending
servitude to Acknowledged Independence. But faith
has its limits as well as Temper—and there are points

beyond which neither can be stretched, without sinking into Cowardice or plunging into credulity. This, my friends, I conceive to be your situation—hurried to the very verge of both—another step would ruin you forever—To be tame and unprovoked while injuries press upon you, is more than weakness, but to look up for kinder usage without one manly Effort of your own—would fix your Character and shew the world how richly you deserve the Chains you broke— To guard against this evil, let us take a review of the ground on which we now stand, and from thence carry our thoughts forward for a moment, into the unexplored field of expedient.

After a pursuit of seven long Years, the object for which we set out, is at length brot within our reach— Yes, my friends, that suffering Courage of yours was active once, it has conducted the United States of America thro' a doubtfull and bloody War—it has placed her in the Chair of Independancy—and peace returns again—to bless—Whom? a country willing to redress your wrongs?—cherrish your worth—and reward your Services? a Country courting your return to private life, with Tears of gratitude and smiles of Admiration—longing to divide with you, that Independency, which your Gallantry has given, and those riches which your wounds have preserved? Is this the case? or is it rather a country that tramples upon your rights, disdains your Cries—& insults your distresses? have you not more than once suggested your wishes and made known your wants to Congress (wants and wishes, which gratitude and policy should have anticipated, rather than evaded)—and have you not lately, in the meek language of entreating Memorials, begged from their Justice, what you would no longer expect from their favor. How have you been answered? let the letter which you are called to consider tomorrow, make reply.

If this then be your treatment while the swords you wear are necessary for the Defence of America, what have you to expect from peace; when your voice shall sink, and your strength dissipate by division—when those very swords, the Instruments and Companions of your Glory, shall be taken from your sides—and no remaining mark of Military distinction left, but your wants, infirmities & Tears—can you then consent to be the only sufferers by this revolution, and, retiring from the field, grow old in poverty, wretchedness, and Contempt; can you consent, to wade thro' the vile mire of dependency, and owe the miserable remnant of that life to Charity, which has hitherto been spent in honor? If you can— Go—and carry with you the jest of Tories, & the Scorn of Whigs—the ridicule—and what is worse—the pity of the world—go—Starve and be forgotten. But if your spirits should revolt at this—if you have sense enough to discover, and spirit enough to oppose Tyranny, under whatever Garb it may assume—whether it be the plain Coat of Republicanism—or the splendid Robe of Royalty; if you have yet learned to discriminate between a people and a Cause—between men and principles— Awake—attend to your Situation & redress yourselves; If the present moment be lost, every future Effort is in vain—and your threats then, will be as empty, as your entreaties now—I would advise you therefore, to come to some final opinion, upon what you can bear—and what you will suffer—If your determination be in any proportion to your wrongs—carry your appeal from the Justice to the Fears of government—Change the Milk & Water stile of your last Memorial—assume a bolder Tone, decent, but lively, spirited and determined—And suspect the man, who would advise to more moderation, and longer forbearance. Let two or three Men, who can feel as well as write, be appointed to draw up your last Remonstrance (for I would no longer give it the soothing, soft, unsuccessful Epithet of Memorial). Let it be represented in language that will neither dishonor you by its Rudeness, nor betray you by its fears—what has been promised by Congress, and what has been performed—how long and how patiently you have suffered—how little you have asked, and how much of that little, have been denied—Tell them that tho' you were the first, and would wish to be the last to encounter Danger—tho' despair itself can never drive you into dishonor, it may drive you from the field—That the wound often irritated and never healed, may at length become incurable—and that the slightest mark of indignity from Congress now, must operate like the Grave, and part you forever—That in any political Event, the Army has its alternative—if peace, that nothing shall separate you from your Arms but Death—If War—that courting the Auspices, and inviting the direction of your Illustrious Leader, you will retire to some unsettled Country, Smile in your Turn, and "mock when their fear cometh on"— But let it represent also, that should they comply with the request of your late Memorial, it would make you more happy; and them more respectable—That while War should continue, you would follow their standard into the field; and When it came to an End, you would withdraw into the shade of private Life—and give the World another subject of Wonder and applause—An Army victorious over its Enemies, Victorious over itself.

I am, &c.,

Third Anonymous Letter Supporting Second Anonymous Letter and Responding to General Washington's Postponement of Meeting, March 12, 1783

Gentlemen,

The Author of a late Address, anxious to deserve, 'tho he should fail to Engage your Esteem, and determined, at every risqué, to unfold your duty, & discharge his own—would beg leave to solicit the further Indulgence of a few moments attention.

Aware of the Coyness with which his last letter would be received, he feels himself neither disappointed; nor displeased with the caution it has met— Ye well knew that it spoke a language, which till now had been heard only in whispers, and that it contained some sentiments, which confidence itself would have breathed with distrust. But, their Lives have been short, and their Observations imperfect indeed, who have yet to learn, that alarms may be false—that the best designs are sometimes obliged to assume the worst Aspect, and that however synonymous Surprise & disaster may be in military phrase—in moral & political meaning, they convey Ideas, as different as they are distinct.

Suspicion, detestable as it is in private Life, is the loveliest trait of political Character. It prompts you to enquiry—bars the Door against Designs, and opens every Avenue to truth. It was the first to oppose a Tyrant here, and still stands sentinel over the Liberties of America—With this Belief, it would ill become me, to stifle the Voice of this honest Guardian—a guardian, who, (authorized by circumstances, digested into proof) has herself given Birth to the Address you have read, and now goes forth among you, with a request to all, that it may be treated fairly—that it may be considered before it can be abused—and condemned, before it be tortured, convinced that in a search after Error, Truth will appear—that apathy itself will grow warm in the pursuit, and tho' it will be the last to adopt her advice, it will be the first to act upon it.

The General Orders of Yesterday which the weak may mistake for disapprobation, and the designing dare to represent as such, wears, in my opinion, a very different complexion, and carries with it a very opposite tendency—Till now, the Commandr in Chief has regarded the Steps you have taken for redress, with good wishes alone, tho' ostensible Silence has authorized your meetings and his private Opinion has sanctified your Claims—Had he disliked the Object in view would not the same sense of Duty which forbad you from meeting on the third Day of this Week, have forbidden you from meeting on the seventh? Is not the same subject held up for your discussion, and has it not passed the seal of office, and taken all the solemnity of an Order—this will give system to your proceedings, and stability to your resolves, will ripen speculation into fact, and while it adds to the unanimity, it cannot possibly lessen the Independency of your sentiments. It may be necessary to add upon this subject, that from the Injunction with which the general Orders close, every man is at liberty to conclude that the Report, to be made to Head Quarters, is intended for Congress—Hence will arise another motive for that Energy, which has been recommended—for can you give the lie to the pathetic descriptions of your representations & the more alarming predictions of our friends?

To such as make Want of signature an objection to opinion, I reply—that it matters very little who is the Author of sentiments which grow out of your feelings, and apply to your Wants—That in this Instance Diffidence suggested what Experience enjoins, and that while I continue to move on the high road of Arguments and Advice, (which is open to all) I shall continue to be the sole Confident of my own secret— But should the Time come, when it shall be necessary to depart from this general line, and hold up any Individual among you, as an Object of the resentment or contempt of the rest, I thus publicly pledge my Honor as a soldier, and veracity as a Man, that I will then assume a visible existence, and give my name to the Army, with as little reserve as I now give my opinions.

I am &c.

PROCEEDINGS OF THE MEETING WITH OFFICERS'

CANTONMENT, NEWBURGH, NEW YORK, MARCH 15, 1783

Agreeable to the Orders of the 11th instant, the Officers of the American Army being convened, His Excellency the Commander in Chief was pleased to open the meeting with the following address to them on the subject of their being called together which with some other papers were left for the consideration of the Assembly. The Honorable Major General Gates being President.

GENERAL WASHINGTON'S ADDRESS TO THE OFFICERS AT THE TEMPLE,

MARCH 15, 1783

[General Washington's aside about his spectacles was not included in his written formal address, but it has been attested to by numerous accounts by those present at the meeting, including Major Samuel Shaw's, and has been accepted by all biographers of Washington. There is disagreement about the exact words and when during the speech the aside came, but I have included it where I believe it most logically fits.]

Gentlemen,

By an anonymous summons, an attempt has been made to convene you together—how inconsistent with the rules of propriety! how unmilitary! And how subversive of all order and discipline—let the good sense of the Army decide.

In the moment of this summons, another anonymous production was sent into circulation; addressed

more to the feelings & passions, than to reason & judgment of the Army. The Author of the piece, is entitled
to much credit for the goodness of his Pen; and I could
wish he had as much rectitude for his Heart—for, as
Men see thro' different Optics, and are induced by the
reflecting faculties of the Mind, to use different means to
attain the same end; the Author of the Address, should
have had more charity, than to mark for Suspicion, the
Man who should recommend Moderation and longer
forbearance—or in other words, who should not think
as he thinks, and act as he advises. But he had another
plan in view, in which candor and liberty of Sentiment,
regard to justice, and love of Country, have no part; and
he was right, to insinuate the darkest suspicion to effect
the blackest designs.

That the Address is drawn with great art, and is
designed to answer the most insidious purposes. That
it is calculated to impress the Mind, with an idea of
premeditated injustice in the Sovereign power of the
United States, and rouse all those resentments which
must unavoidably form such a belief. That the secret
Mover of this Scheme (whoever he may be) intended
to take advantage of the passions, while they were
warmed by the recollection of past distresses, without giving time for cool, deliberative thinking, & that
composure of Mind which is so necessary to give dignity & stability to measures, is rendered too obvious,
by the mode of conducting the business, to need other
proof than a reference to the proceeding.

Thus much, Gentlemen, I have thought it incum-
bent on me to observe to you, to shew upon what principles I opposed the irregular and hasty meeting which

was proposed to have been held on Tuesday last: and not because I wanted a disposition to give you every opportunity, consistent with your own honor, and the dignity of the Army, to make known your grievances. If any conduct heretofore, has not evinced to you, that I have been a faithful friend to the Army; my declaration of it at this time wd be equally unavailing & improper—But as I was among the first who embarked in the cause of our common Country—As I have never left your side one moment, but when called from you, on public duty—As I have been the constant companion & witness of your Distresses, and not among the last to feel, & acknowledge your Merits—As I have ever considered my own Military reputation as inseparably connected with that of the Army—As my Heart has ever expanded with joy, when I have heard its praises—and my indignation has arisen, when the Mouth of detraction has been opened against it—it can scarcely be supposed, at this late stage of the War, that I am indifferent to its interests.

But—how are they to be promoted? The way is plain, says the anonymous Addresser. If War continues, remove into the unsettled Country—there establish yourselves, and leave an ungrateful Country to defend itself—But who are they to defend? Our wives, our Children, our Farms and other property which we leave behind us? Or—in this state of hostile separation, are we to take the two first (the latter cannot be removed) to perish in a Wilderness with hunger cold & nakedness? If Peace takes place, never sheath your Sword, says he until you have obtained full and ample Justice—this dreadful alternative, of either deserting our Country in the extremest hour of her distress, or turning our Army against it, (which is the apparent object, unless Congress can be compelled into an instant compliance) has something so shocking in it, that humanity revolts at the idea. My God! What can this Writer have in view, by recommending such measures? Can he be a friend to the Army? Can he be a friend to this Country? Rather, is he not an insidious Foe? Some Emissary, perhaps from New York, plotting the ruin of both, by sowing the seeds of discord & separation between the Civil & Military powers of the Continent? And what a Compliment does he pay to our understandings, when he recommends measures in either alternative, impracticable in their nature?

But here, Gentlemen, I will drop the curtain, because it wd be as impudent in me to assign my reasons for this opinion, as it would be insulting to your conception, to suppose you stood in need of them. A moments reflection will convince every dispassionate Mind of the physical impossibility of carrying either proposal into execution.

There might, Gentlemen, be an impropriety in my taking notice, in this Address to you, of an anonymous production—but the manner in which that performance has been introduced to the Army, the effect it was intended to have, together with some other circumstances, will amply justify my observations on the tendency of that Writing. With respect to the advice given by the Author—to suspect the Man who shall recommend moderate measures and longer forbearance—I spurn it as every Man who regards that liberty, & reveres that Justice for which we contend, undoubtedly must— for if Men are to be precluded from offering their sentiments on a matter, which may involve the most serious and alarming consequences, that can invite the consideration of Mankind; reason is of no use to us— the freedom of Speech may be taken away—and dumb and silent we may be led, like sheep, to the Slaughter.

I cannot, in justice to my own belief & what I have great reason to conceive is the intention of Congress, conclude this Address, without giving it my decided Opinion; that that Honble Body entertains exalted sentiments of the Services of the Army; and, from a full conviction of its Merits & sufferings, will do it compleat Justice; That their endeavors to discover & establish funds for this purpose, have been unwearied, and will not cease till they have succeeded, I have not a doubt. But like all other large Bodies, where there is a variety of different interests to reconcile, their deliberations are slow. Why then should we distrust them? and in consequence of that distrust, adopt measures which may cast a shade over that glory which has been so justly acquired; and tarnish the reputation of an Army which is celebrated thro' all Europe for its fortitude and Patriotism? and for what is this done? to bring the object we seek for nearer? No! most certainly, in my opinion, it will cast it at a greater distance.

[General draws letter from pocket . . . Long pause . . . General attempts to read a few words from letter but stumbles and again falls silent . . . Mutterings from audience . . . General draws spectacles from pocket.]
Gentlemen, you will forgive me, and permit me to put on these spectacles . . . for I have not only grown gray but almost blind in the service of our country . . .

[Pause . . . Murmurs from audience . . . We're with you, General . . . Tell us what to do . . . Tell us and we will follow you . . .]

For myself (and I take no merit in giving this assurance, being induced to it from principles of gratitude, veracity & justice)—a grateful sense of the confidence you have ever placed in me—a recollection of the Cheerful assistance, & prompt obedience I have experienced from you, under every vicissitude of Fortune, and the sincere affection I feel for an Army, I have so long had the honor to Command, will oblige me to declare, in this public & solemn manner, that, in the attainment of compleat justice for all your toils & dangers, and in the gratification of every wish, so far as may be Done consistently with the great duty I owe my Country, and those powers we are bound to respect, you may freely command my services to the utmost of my abilities. While I give you these assurances, and pledge myself in the most unequivocal manner, to exert whatever ability I am possessed of, in your favor—let me entreat you, Gentlemen, on your part, not to take any measures which, viewed in the calm light of reason, will lessen the dignity, & sully the glory you have hitherto maintained—let me request you to rely on the plighted faith of your Country, and place a full confidence in the purity of the intentions of Congress; that, previous to your dissolution as an Army they will cause all your Accts to be fairly liquidated, as directed in their resolutions which were published to you two days ago—and that they will adopt the most effectual measures in their power, to render ample justice to you for your faithful and meritorious Services. And let me conjure you, in the name of our common Country, as you value your own sacred honor—as you respect the rights of humanity, & as you regard the Military & national character of America, to express your utmost horror & detestation of the Man who wishes, under any specious pretences, to overturn the liberties of our Country, & who wickedly attempts to open the flood Gates of Civil discord, & deluge our rising Empire in Blood. By thus determining & thus acting, you will pursue the plain & direct road to the attainment of your wishes. You will defeat the insidious designs of our Enemies, who are compelled to resort from open force to secret Artifice. You will give one more distinguished proof of unexampled patriotism & patient virtue, rising superior to the pressure of the most complicated sufferings; And you will, by the dignity of your Conduct, afford occasion for Posterity to say, when speaking of the glorious example you have exhibited to mankind, "had this day been wanting, the World had never seen the last stage of perfection to which human nature is capable of attaining."

RESOLUTION ADOPTED UNANIMOUSLY BY OFFICERS AFTER GENERAL WASHINGTON'S ADDRESS, NEWBURGH, NEW YORK, MARCH 15, 1783

His excellency having withdrawn, on a motion, made by General Knox and seconded by General Putnam,

Resolved, That the unanimous thanks of the Officers of the Army be presented to his Excellency the Commander in Chief, for his excellent address, and the communications he has been pleased to make to them, and to assure him the Officers reciprocate his affectionate expressions with the greatest Sincerity of which the human heart is capable.

The address from the Army to Congress, the Report of the Committee from the Army, and the Resolutions of Congress of the 25th January being read.

On a motion by General Putnam, seconded by General Hand, Voted

That a committee be appointed immediately to draw up some Resolutions, expressive of the business before us, and to report in half an hour, that this committee consist of one General, one Field Officer, and one Captain. That General Knox, Colonel Brooks and Captain Howard compose the said Committee.

The Report of the Committee having been brought in and fully Considered Resolved Unanimously That at the commencement of the present War, the Officers of the American Army engaged in the service of their Country from the purest love and attachment to the rights and liberties of human nature, which motives still exist in the highest degree: and that no circumstances of distress or danger shall induce a conduct that may tend to sully the reputation and Glory of which they have acquired at the price of their blood, and eight years faithful services.

Resolved Unanimously That the Army continue to have an unshaken confidence in the justice of Congress and their Country, and are fully convinced that the representatives of America will not disband or disperse the Army, until their Accounts are liquidated, the Balances accurately ascertained, and adequate funds established for Payment; And in this arrangement the Officers expect that the half Pay, or a commutation for it, should be efficaciously comprehended.

Resolved, Unanimously That his excellency the Commander in Chief be requested to write to His Excellency the President of Congress earnestly entreating the most speedy decision of that Honorable body upon the subjects of our late address, that was forwarded by a Committee of the Army, some of whom are waiting upon Congress for the result. In the alternative of Peace or War, this event would be highly satisfactory, and would produce immediate tranquility in the minds of the Army: and prevent any further machinations of designing men to sow discord between the civil and Military powers of the United States.

Resolved Unanimously That the Officers of the American Army view with abhorrence, and reject with disdain, the infamous propositions contained in a late anonymous address to the Officers of the Army, and resent with indignation the secret attempts of some unknown persons to collect the Officers together, in a manner totally subversive of all discipline and good order.

Resolved Unanimously That the thanks of the Officers of the Army be given to the Committee who presented to Congress the late address of the Army, for the wisdom and prudence with which they have conducted that business and that a Copy of the proceedings of this day be transmitted by the President to Major General McDougall, and that he be requested to continue his Solicitations at Congress until the objects of his mission are accomplished.

The Meeting was then desolved.

> Horatio Gates
> Major Genl Presdt

General Washington's Letter to the President of the Congress Informing Congress of the Outcome of the Meeting

Newburgh, 16 March 1783

Sir:

I have the Honor to inform your Excellency, for the satisfaction of Congress, that the Meeting of the Officers, which was mentioned in my last, has been held Yesterday: and, that it has terminated in a manner, which I had reason to expect, from a knowledge of that good Sense and steady Patriotism of the Gentlemen of the Army, which on frequent Occasions, I have discovered. The Report of the meeting, with the other papers, which will be necessary to accompany it, I shall do myself the Honor to transmit to Congress as soon as they can possibly be prepared.

   With the Highest Respect, I have the Honor to be Your Excellency's most Obedt Servt
      George Washington

General Washington's Letter Thanking His Officers for Their Reception to His Speech at the Temple on March 15, 1783

Newburgh, March 18, 1783

The Commander-in-Chief is highly satisfied with the report of the proceedings of the officers assembled on the 15th instant, in obedience to the orders of the 11th. He begs his inability to communicate an adequate idea of the pleasing feelings which have been excited in his breast by the affectionate sentiments expressed toward him on that occasion, and hopes this may be considered as an apology for his silence.

The original papers being too prolix to be inserted in the records of the army, will be lodged at the orderly office, to be perused or copied by any gentleman of the army who may think proper.

General Washington's Follow-up Letter to the President of Congress Enclosing Report on Proceedings at the Meeting and Pleading the Case for the Army, Read to Congress March 22, 1783, and Referred to Samuel Osgood, Theodorick Bland, Alexander Hamilton, Oliver Wolcot, and Richard Peters

Newburgh, 18 March 1783

Sir:

The result of the proceedings of the grand Convention of the Officers, which I have the honor of enclosing to your Excellency for the inspection of Congress, will, I flatter myself, be considered as the last glorious proof of Patriotism which could have been given by Men who aspired to the distinction of a patriot Army; and will not only confirm their claims to justice, but will increase their title to the gratitude of their Country.

Having seen the proceedings on the part of the Army terminate with perfect unanimity, and in a manner entirely consonant to my wishes; being impressed with the liveliest sentiments of affection for those who so long, so patiently and so cheerfully suffered and fought under my immediate direction; having from motives of justice, duty and gratitude, spontaneously offered myself as an advocate of their rights; and having been requested to write to your Excellency earnestly entreating the most speedy decision of Congress upon the subjects of the late Address from the Army to that Honble. Body, it now only remains for me to perform the task I have assumed, and to intercede in their behalf, as I now do, that the Sovereign Power will be pleased to verify the predictions I have pronounced of, and the confidence the Army have reposed in the justice of their Country.

And here, I humbly conceive it is altogether unnecessary, (while I am pleading the cause of an Army which have done and suffered more than any other Army ever did in the defence of the rights and liberties of human nature,) to expatiate on their Claims to the most ample compensation for their meritorious Services, because they are perfectly known to the whole World, and because, (altho' the topics are inexhaustible) enough has already been said on the subject.

To prove these assertions, to evince that my sentiments have ever been uniform, and to shew what my ideas of the rewards in question have always been, I appeal to the Archives of Congress, and call on those sacred deposits to witness for me. And in order that my observations and Arguments in favor of a future adequate for the Officers of the Army may be brought to remembrance again, and considered in a single point of view without giving Congress the trouble of having recourse to their files, I will beg leave to transmit herewith an Extract from a representation made by me to a committee of Congress so long ago as the 29th of January, 1778, and also the Letter to the President of the Congress, dated near Passaic Falls Octr. 11th

1780. That in the critical and perilous moment when the last mentioned communication was made, there was the utmost danger of a dissolution of the Army would have taken place unless measures similar to those recommended had been adopted, will not admit a doubt. That the adoption of the Resolution granting half-pay for life had been attended with all the happy consequences I had foretold, so far as respected the good of the service; let the astonishing contrast between the State of the Army at this instant, and at the former period determine. And that the establishment of funds, and security of the payment of all just demands of the Army will be the most certain means of preserving the National faith and future tranquility of this extensive Continent, is my decided opinion.

By the preceding remarks it will readily be imagined that instead of retracting and reprehending (from farther experience and reflection) the mode of compensation so strenuously urged in the Inclosures, I am more and more confirmed in the Sentiment, and if in the wrong suffer me to please myself with the grateful delusion.

For if, besides the simple payment of their Wages, a farther compensation is not due to the sufferings and sacrifices of the Officers, then have I been mistaken indeed. If the whole Army have not merited whatever a grateful people can bestow, then have I been beguiled by prejudice, and built opinion on the basis of error. If this Country should not in the event perform everything which has been requested in the late Memorial to Congress, then will my belief become vain, and the hope that has been excited void of foundation. And if (as has been suggested for the purpose of inflaming their passions) the Officers of the Army are to be the only sufferers by this revolution; if retiring from the Field, they are to grow old in poverty, wretchedness, and contempt. If they are to wade thro' the vile mire of dependency and owe the miserable remnant of that life to charity, which has hitherto been spent in honor, then shall I have learned what ingratitude is, then shall I have realized a tale, which will imbitter every moment of my future life. But I am under no such apprehensions, a Country rescued by their Arms from impending ruin, will never leave unpaid the debt of gratitude.

Should any intemperate or improper warmth have mingled amongst the foregoing observations, I must entreat your Excellency and Congress it may be attributed to the effusion of an honest zeal in the best of Causes, and that my peculiar situation may be by apology. And I hope I need not, on this momentous occasion make any new protestations of personal disinterestedness, having ever renounced for myself the idea of pecuniary reward. The consciousness of having attempted faithfully to discharge my duty, and the approbation of my Country will be sufficient recompense for my Services. I have the honor, etc.

With the Highest Respect, Your Most Obedient Servant.

George Washington

ABOUT THE AUTHOR

John Ripin Miller has devoted much of his professional life to public service. After serving in the US Army and graduating from Bucknell University and Yale Law School, he became active in both municipal and state governments, holding seats as a Seattle city councilman, a member of the US House of Representatives, and an ambassador-at-large for the US State Department, where he led the fight against modern-day slavery around the world.

Miller's political experiences helped fuel a fascination with the life of George Washington and how the perception of his legacy changed throughout the decades. This inspired years of research and an exhaustive study into the Newburgh Conspiracy of the Revolutionary War, which Miller later turned into the comprehensive historical novel *The Man Who Could Be King*.

Interspersed with his political career, Miller taught English at Northwest Yeshiva High School on Mercer Island, Washington, taught history of slavery at Yale, served as a Senior Fellow at Discovery Institute, and coached Little League Baseball in Seattle. *The Man Who Could Be King* is his first novel.